D0553655

PRIZE STORIES
OF 1947

THE O. HENRY AWARDS

PRIZE STORIES
OF *1947*

THE O. HENRY AWARDS

SELECTED AND EDITED BY

HERSCHEL BRICKELL

DOUBLEDAY & COMPANY, INC.

GARDEN CITY 1947 NEW YORK

813.508
P961
1947

CONTENTS*

INTRODUCTION. *By Herschel Brickell* vii

THE WHITE CIRCLE. *By John Bell Clayton* 1

REST CAMP ON MAUI. *By Eugene L. Burdick* 9

THE NIGHTINGALES SING. *By Elizabeth Parsons* 22

LITTLE VICTOR. *By Robert Lewis* 37

THE ECHO. *By Paul Bowles* 61

HOMECOMING. *By Ray Bradbury* 76

THE SKELETON AND THE EASTER LILY. *By Bessie Breuer* . . . 89

THE HOT DAY. *By Jane Cobb* 98

THE HOLIDAY. *By Mary Deasy* 111

YOU CAN WRECK IT. *By Walter Elder* 124

AN AMERICAN HOME. *By Helen Eustis* 143

MISS WINTERS AND THE WIND. *By Christine Noble Govan* . . 156

THE RECORD. *By David Cornel DeJong* 162

THE ROSEBUSH. *By Susan Kuehn* 169

THE BURDEN. *By John A. Lynch* 181

THE VALIANT WOMAN. *By J. F. Powers* 194

WHAT WE DON'T KNOW HURTS US. *By Mark Schorer* . . . 204

THE GREAT FIRE OF 1945. *By Margaret Shedd* 218

*After the prize stories, the order is alphabetical by author.

Contents

FIGHTER. *By John Caswell Smith, Jr.* 227

THE HOPE CHEST. *By Jean Stafford* 240

OLD BOY—NEW BOY. *By Benedict Thielen* 246

THE WHOLE WORLD KNOWS. *By Eudora Welty* 257

HORACE CHOONEY, M.D. *By Jessamyn West* 276

BIOGRAPHICAL NOTES 286

INTRODUCTION

ESTABLISHED in 1919 by the Society of Arts and Sciences of New York as a memorial to O. Henry (William Sydney Porter, 1862–1910), this is the twenty-ninth annual collection of stories by American authors selected from American magazines and representing a cross section of contemporary short fiction. The period covered in the present volume is from May 1, 1946, to May 1, 1947. There are twenty-three stories this year, fourteen of them the work of writers who have not hitherto made their appearance here. These fourteen include six which present their writers' first bows to the public.

The high proportion of relatively new talent, which is a repetition of the record of several years past—last year, for example, the book contained the work of fourteen writers not represented before, including five newcomers—shows, the editor trusts and believes, an open mind in the constant search for the best available material. It also indicates something else less encouraging: the marked paucity of production in the short-story field of the established writers of the prewar period, whose names are conspicuously absent from present-day lists, while their better-known juniors continue to write far less than might normally be expected. It is also to be noted that since the establishment in 1941 of the special prize for "first" stories, designed to encourage beginners, none of the winners of this award has so far been represented again in the collection, nor has any one of the writers in this group developed into a consistent producer of stories, good or bad. This seems to be much less of a reflection upon the choices of the prize winners than a sign of the times. The expected creative flow is obviously being blocked by the general uneasiness abroad in the world.

The prizes for 1947, following the custom honored throughout the life of the collection, have been awarded on the final responsibility of the editor, who took into the fullest possible account the opinions of the three distinguished judges chosen by him and working in entire independence in making their choices.

The names of this year's judges appear in alphabetical order:

Struthers Burt, short-story writer, novelist, and author of a wide variety of non-fiction books.

Muriel Fuller, publishers' editor, author of juveniles, and, from 1932 through July 1946, assistant to the editors of this collection.

Paul Jordan-Smith, author and literary editor of the *Los Angeles Times*.

THE AWARDS FOR 1947

First prize of $300 for the best story: To John Bell Clayton of San Francisco, California, for "The White Circle," published in *Harper's Magazine*.

Second prize of $200 for the next best story: To Eugene L. Burdick of Palo Alto, California, for "Rest Camp on Maui," published in *Harper's Magazine*.

Third prize of $100 for the next best story: To "The Nightingales Sing" by Elizabeth Parsons of Vinalhaven, Maine, published in *The New Yorker*.

Special prize for the first published story: To Robert Lewis of Baltimore, Maryland, for "Little Victor," published in *The Atlantic Monthly*.

The most notable feature of these awards, which follow closely the pattern set in 1946, when three of the four prizes went to first stories, is that they again pay striking tribute to the work of new writers. Mr. Clayton's story is only his second to be published, his first having appeared in *Esquire*. Mr. Burdick's is a first, and so, of course, is that of Mr. Lewis. Like John Goss, winner of the first prize last year with "Bird Song," a first, Mr. Clayton is in his middle years, while Messrs. Burdick and Lewis are veterans of World War II.

This year the judges differed much more widely in their opinions than usual, and the final decisions had to be reached by the editor, who gave the votes of his jury the fullest consideration possible and then followed his own conscience in casting the final ballots. From

the birth of the collection, various attempts have been made to evolve
systems that would approach perfect justice in their results, but none
has thus far transcended the human limitations that operate in such
matters.

"The White Circle" was the only story to receive two votes in the
scattered balloting, Miss Fuller placing it second and Mr. Jordan-
Smith third. From its first reading, the editor felt it to be one of the
best of the year's offerings because of the skill with which it is done,
with no word wasted, its climax growing quite naturally from character and situation, and the whole carrying its full burden of over-
tones of meaning. It has the sureness of touch that is essential to the
proper handling of the short-story form, and attains memorability
without imposing the slightest strain upon the material. Miss Fuller
wrote of it: "This story puts more effectively than anything I have
ever read, and in a brief compass, the quite real impulse to murder
that each one of us has had as a child. Without an unnecessary stroke,
the author paints an unforgettable picture of the hateful son of a
half-crazy peddler and the boy who is so much better off in every
way yet who feels no noblesse oblige because of the other boy's pure,
cussed, dirt-meanness. This story has a universality to it, for it touches
everyone. Even if we have never attempted murder, or even revenge,
at some time or other the motive was present in us. The story, therefore, touches a hidden spring of memory and, in so doing, evokes
recognition. Anvil, the mean boy, becomes everyone we have ever
hated, and at the instant of revenge, when the instrument misses,
there is an involuntary intake of breath and a spontaneous thankful-
ness that our own childhood plans either went awry or were never
attempted." Mr. Jordan-Smith's vote was cast without comment.

Three other stories were nominated for the first prize: "Little
Victor" by Mr. Jordan-Smith, "Rest Camp on Maui" by Mr. Burt,
and "The Nightingales Sing" by Miss Fuller. Mr. Jordan-Smith
thought his favorite might well be awarded prizes as both the
best story and the best of the firsts, and Mr. Burt went along with
this opinion with respect to his choice, although neither of these
two stories was selected by Miss Fuller as among those deserving
awards. Mr. Jordan-Smith liked Mrs. Govan's "Miss Winters and the
Wind" next to "Little Victor" among the firsts, and Miss Fuller
gave the Govan story top place among the work of the newcomers,

although Mr. Burt did not mention it and liked John A. Lynch's
war story, "The Burden," next to "Rest Camp."

The basis of the award of second prize to Mr. Burdick's story, then,
was Mr. Burt's rating of it as the best in the collection, plus the editor's admiration for its technical excellence, especially the skillful
handling of the smashing climax, when the war correspondent is hit
between the eyes with what combat veterans really think of his
phony attitude toward their sufferings and heroisms. The minor
racial theme is subtly and effectively woven into the narrative. In
suggesting that the story be given two prizes, Mr. Burt added, and
justly, of course, that "war stories have an unfair advantage, since
because of their subject matter they are from their inception filled
with vigor and action. But," he said, " 'Rest Camp on Maui' seems
to me a tiptop story, meeting every requirement." Miss Fuller, who
mentioned the story only in her general comments, wrote of it: "I
think it is well done, but whether it is because the two previous
O. Henrys have had so many stories on the same theme or whether
it does not seem to me quite so well done as some of those given
prizes in recent years, I grew weary of it. Touching as it does on
both war and racial themes, it is effective, but if freshness of idea
counts for anything, and it should, I rate 'Miss Winters and the
Wind' as decidedly more novel."

For the best story, Miss Fuller, as has been said, chose "The Nightingales Sing." She commented: "This is one of the best stories I have
ever read which undertook to capture the lyrical quality of spring,
youth, and the entry of a girl into the adult world. It stirred me deeply
when I read it the first time a year ago, and I found that I could re-
capture the same emotion upon rereading it. It not only stands beside
the best stories in the present O. Henry, it surpasses them. It has an
earthiness about it that is quite compatible with the realistic world
of literature today. This is a timeless story, and it will be as good a
number of years hence as it is now. It reminded me of Struthers Burt's
'The Fawn,' and shares with that story a beauty that will make them
both endure." Mr. Jordan-Smith also placed the story among his
favorites. The editor esteemed it highly from the first reading. It has
already been reprinted in a collection called *An Afternoon,* along
with sixteen others of the author's pieces, among which it is outstanding in quality.

It has already been suggested that there were also difficulties in the awarding of the special prize for the best first story. In placing "Little Victor" at the top of his list, Mr. Jordan-Smith said it "seemed far ahead of the rest in vitality and meaning," qualities that interested him the most, along with good characterization. Mr. Burt gave it no more than third place among the firsts, ranking it below both "Rest Camp" and "The Burden," while Miss Fuller placed it second among the firsts, with this comment: "Strictly speaking, it belongs in the reportage class, although the author has made the transition to fiction. The reader is kept on the edge of his chair wondering what the child is going to do. It is not so much a war story or a racial story as sheer *story*—whether or not the murderer has an out." The real competition for Mr. Lewis's story came from Mrs. Govan's "Miss Winters and the Wind," of which Miss Fuller wrote: "This story shows an expert handling of fiction. Although its author's first short story, she has long been established in the juvenile field, a sure basis for excellence, and her most recent novel, *Jennifer's House,* published in 1944, revealed her as fulfilling the promise of her books for young people. Her story is at the other end of the scale from reportage, so characteristic of war stories. It also has a unity that 'Little Victor' lacks, since the Lewis story is inclined to be jumpy, although this is perhaps inevitable because of the material. Mrs. Govan gives the entire life of Miss Winters and with no excess verbiage shows how the transition, from an idea to a fixation, that kills her takes place. There is high drama when the only creature whom the poor old woman loves and who loves her, the cat, is killed by her enemy, the wind. The short sentences make the deft, sure strokes of a good story by a craftswoman who knows her art."

Mr. Jordan-Smith also liked Mrs. Govan's story, although he placed two other firsts ahead of it: "Little Victor" and Walter Elder's "You Can Wreck It," which he thought ranked second among all the stories. Mr. Elder's somewhat loosely organized but moving story shared the annual *Kenyon Review*-Doubleday prize for short stories. The editor regarded "Miss Winters" as a real discovery from his first reading of it in *Tomorrow,* although he must confess to a serious prejudice against short stories with a suicide ending because of their extreme popularity among beginners in the art of short fiction. The strength of Mrs. Govan's story lies in its style and in the nice choice of detail to carry the tragedy forward to its conclusion, which is logical enough but not wholly convincing. The whole narrative has much of the tight spareness of a poem.

The awards regrettably omit entirely two stories ranked among the best by two judges but which received only one vote each. These are Margaret Shedd's "The Great Fire of 1945," placed second by Mr. Burt "because of the brilliance of the telling and the symbolism of the incident," and "Homecoming" by Ray Bradbury, placed third by Miss Fuller, neither receiving any mention by Mr. Jordan-Smith. The editor, after repeated rereadings, considers both these stories of exceptional merit and ranks them with any in the collection. His wife, Norma Long Brickell, who was his full-time assistant after the resignation of Miss Fuller in August, rated the Shedd story the best of the lot from her first reading of it, and "Homecoming" second. (Among her other favorites were "Old Boy—New Boy," "The Nightingales Sing," and "The Hot Day." She also liked very much "Rest Camp on Maui" because of Mr. Burdick's presentation of the eternal and impenetrable barrier between people who have actually suffered and endured and those who are only onlookers, which she thought made the story unforgettable. Among the firsts she placed "Miss Winters" at the top of the list, with "The Burden" as runner-up. She also liked "Little Victor" very much.)

Last year Miss Shedd won second prize with "The Innocent Bystander," and the editor fully agrees with Miss Fuller's opinion, expressed in her general comment, that "The Great Fire" is more successful. "She achieves," wrote Miss Fuller, "an emotional quality in this one that the other lacked, at least for me. I read this year's story when it was first published, and the impact was greater then, because we were nearer the atomic bomb in 1946 than in 1947, but it is still a powerful story." It is easy enough to see what Miss Fuller means by her mention of our closer proximity to the atomic bomb in 1946 than in 1947, although our exact distance from it at the moment remains the burning question of the hour. Near or far, however, the appeal of Miss Shedd's story lies in its artistry rather than in its physics, and it is done with much skill, accomplishing completely what she set out to accomplish. The story might very well have appeared at the top of the list of prize winners.

In placing "Homecoming" third, Miss Fuller said: "Like Truman Capote's 'Miriam' in the 1946 volume (also, like "Homecoming," from *Mademoiselle,* incidentally), it casts a spell." Mr. Bradbury's striking success with his fantasy is of even greater significance than the excellence of the Shedd story, since he is a younger and less experienced writer. His stories have shown a pleasing variety and have been consistently interesting since he began writing, but a whole exceptional talent clicks in the present piece of work, a feat of the pure imagination, of which Miss Fuller shrewdly wrote: "It is not only the writing, which is excellent; it is the sheer imagination that created such a story, outlandish, ghoulish, horrible. It is a tour de force. 'Miriam' one could believe; modern psychiatry explains it nicely. In 'The Devil and Daniel Webster' Benét at least started with living people. I fully believed this story as I read it, while my mind said of course this never *could* have happened. Both these stories, the Capote and the Benét, merge realism with fantasy. 'Homecoming,' however, starts with creatures no sane person can believe exist— witches, werewolves, ghouls, all the ghastly population of the graveyards—and makes them entirely convincing to the shivering reader, who is sure they will return in 1970 to a black mass and a devil's dance at Salem. I place my money on this story because of the originality of the theme and the brilliant carrying out of the concept."

It is not very often that a contemporary short story harks back to the work of the early American masters and is able to stand unblushing comparison with the classics of the beginning period of the brief narrative in this country. Mr. Bradbury's opuscule invokes the shades of Irving, Poe, and Hawthorne, all of whom would have understood at once what he was up to and would have admired his skill in achieving his purpose. Much may be made of the symbolism of the presence in the story of a being touched with human frailties amid his unearthly crew of relatives: little Timothy who cannot drink blood with enjoyment and satisfaction, who cannot fly, and who is probably cursed with mortality. Is Mr. Bradbury merely telling us a tale, and doing it well enough to cause us to believe what he says, or is he really saying that Timothy, in his curious plight, stands for the human race at the present sad moment? Who'll be at Salem in 1970 if all goes well with the plans for atomizing us in the meanwhile,

excepting the goblins and ghoulies, the witches and warlocks—not
poor Timothy, and not us, either. Again, as in the case of the Shedd
story, which it in no sense resembles except for its artistic excellence
—it will almost certainly linger even longer in the memory than that
admirable piece of work—it is not possible to view the absence of the
Bradbury story from the list of prize winners without a deep sense of
regret.

Of the other stories which the judges liked especially that have not
already been mentioned, Miss Fuller singled out as a runner-up to
her three top choices one of the particular favorites of the editor and
his wife, Jane Cobb's "The Hot Day" from *McCall's,* a story of mari-
tal discord based upon the binding together of two people by the
terrible strength of hatred and in which very effective use is made
of heat and humidity. "Seldom have I read a story in which the heat
presses so closely," wrote Miss Fuller. "The reader is sodden, clammy,
as thoroughly uncomfortable as Miss Cobb's characters. Here is
realism with a sure touch, and a good deal of beauty." Mr. Jordan-
Smith thought very highly of Mark Schorer's "What We Don't
Know Hurts Us," an opinion shared by the editor. Mr. Burt's nom-
ination for third prize was Benedict Thielen's "Old Boy—New Boy,"
of which he wrote: "This is a quiet story, but moving, tender, and
beautifully told. Very subtle, not so much in the thesis, but in the
incidents." Mrs. Brickell also thought the Thielen story well deserving of a prize, and Miss Fuller wrote of it: "This is even better than
Mr. Thielen's 1946 story, 'The Empty Sky.' He has made the transition from war to non-combat (I can't say peace) successfully. The
present story seems to me even better than Mark Schorer's 'What
We Don't Know Hurts Us.' It shows very clearly the chasm between
generations, the *mores* of one becoming merely silly to another."

Last year Eudora Welty's "A Sketching Trip" was nominated for
second prize by James Gray, although ignored by the other two
judges, Hudson Strode and Helen Hull. This year Miss Welty's "The
Whole World Knows," which seems to the editor a far more moving
story than its immediate predecessor, told somehow at too great a
distance to make a very deep impression, was passed over completely
by the judges, except for Miss Fuller's general comment: "I felt let
down by Miss Welty's story. It is undoubtedly a factual portrait of a
small Southern town, but it failed to hold me as did her memorable

story 'The Worn Path,' second prize winner in 1941, or even 'The Wide Net' and 'Livvie is Back,' first prize winners in 1942 and 1943, respectively." The editor would hesitate to rank the present Welty story with her three prize winners, but he found it admirable in its complete realization of setting and atmosphere, and also touching in its portrayal of the pathetic—not tragic—plight of its betrayed husband still in love with his wandering wife. Perhaps it is his utter helplessness in the face of his problem that weakens the appeal of the story—futility again, the theme of the moment—for all the skill with which it is done. It is interesting to note that Miss Welty has published only the two short stories in the past two years.

Of the nine authors whose stories have hitherto appeared in the O. Henry, Miss Fuller thought six of their efforts poorer and three better, the first half dozen, as has been suggested, including Miss Welty's story. The others she liked somewhat less well than previous stories by the same authors were Mary Deasy's "The Holiday," highly esteemed by the editor and his wife; Bessie Breuer's "The Skeleton and the Easter Lily"; David Cornel deJong's "The Record"; J. F. Powers's "The Valiant Woman"; and Jessamyn West's "Horace Chooney, M.D.," another venture into the realm of morbid psychology. Miss West, whose writing from the beginning of her career has been notable for its variety, struck a new path in "Horace Chooney" and even more noticeably so in a *New Yorker* story called "The Sump Hole," which dealt with another psychopathic individual and which actually arouses the reader's sympathy for a moccasin victim of a sadist's brutality, no mean feat in itself, since moccasins are perhaps the least appealing of the snake family. It is not possible to deny Miss West's right to experiment with different types of stories as she chooses, but there was health in her early Quaker stories such as cannot be found in her recent handling of the morbid and the abnormal. Still, her present story in this collection is a good deal better technically than "The Blackboard," with which she was represented here last year.

The stories Miss Fuller liked better than their predecessors were Mark Schorer's "What We Don't Know Hurts Us," which she preferred to "The Blockbuster" in the 1944 volume. Her comments on the other two in this group, Mr. Thielen's "Old Boy—New Boy" and Miss Shedd's "The Great Fire of 1945," have already been quoted.

As is inevitable, a number of stories of undoubted merit were considered to the last and some of them omitted with real regret. Mary Barnard's "Boundaries: The Shadow," from the December *Harper's Bazaar,* was excluded only because it was presented as the first of a series. Other excellent stories included Patricia Highsmith's "The World's Champion" (*Woman's Home Companion,* April), a simple but very appealing story of a small family in its first contact with New York City, by the author of "The Heroine," in last year's O. Henry; May Davies Martenet's "Father Delacroix," from Number 2, Volume III, of *Quarterly Review of Literature,* introducing another new writer of talent; Edita Morris's "A Ball of Yarn," from *The Western Review,* a symbolical story in Miss Morris's accustomed vein, which was one of Mrs. Brickell's favorites; and Shirley Jackson's "Men with Their Big Shoes," from the spring issue of *The Yale Review.*

Mademoiselle printed in its January issue Robert Penn Warren's "The Patented Gate and the Mean Hamburger," the story of a clash between a husband's love of his farm and his wife's passion for hamburgers, which promised much but which was weakened by its author's failure to explain why the wife and the hamburgers won out over the patented gate, and also by a hurried ending. *Harper's Magazine* printed two groups of three stories, each somewhat shorter than average, two of the best of these being Jessamyn West's "Grandpa Was Her Mirror" and Eugene Kincaid's "Ebu and the Two-ton Lift." Sally Benson's sketch of a woman dipsomaniac in the hands of a hard-boiled nurse, "Lady with a Lamp," in the January 18 *New Yorker* was bitter and brutal enough to be hard to forget, although it did not quite attain the dimensions of a story even in Miss Benson's practiced hands.

George Stiles's "A Short Way by Rail," published in *Chimera's* winter edition, the story of a husband escorting his hopelessly ill wife to a hospital for the insane, suffered from being somewhat overwritten, but had pity, terror, and surprise in its favor. Among the *Atlantic's* several excellent "firsts" were such stories as John Kaufman's "The Good Neighbor," Thomas Manar's "Atabrine Tan," Alan R. Marcus's "Ratachusky's Return," and Cairo-born Jacqueline Shohet's "Such Is Rachel," the last-named, especially, ranking very high among the stories barely omitted. Messrs. Kaufman, Manar, and

Marcus are like so many of the *Atlantic's* new crop of writers, all veterans of World War II.

It is set down with regret that the brilliant 1946 debut of young Truman Capote with "Miriam" and "Tree of Night," which attracted widespread attention outside this volume, was not followed up in later months. His only story was "The Headless Hawk," in the November *Harper's Bazaar,* an overwritten tale of unpleasantly abnormal people which did no more than suggest the distinction of the earlier pieces. Mr. Capote was ill a good part of the past year and is working on a novel besides, so that there is still plenty of time for a realization of the promise seen in his early work by the editor of this collection and others.

The Short-Story Scene

As a worn and battered world, where stable peace seemed farther away than ever, continued to search for a way out of its crowding difficulties, which trod upon one another's heels, the American short-story writer reflected in his general confusion and pessimism of outlook the atmosphere in which he lived and worked. While the average quality of the stories in the present collection is at least as high as those of its immediate predecessors, it is necessary to say that striking new talents are rare indeed, and that the touch of the master hand, sure of itself and its material, and promising the production of any very large body of work marked by the exercise of the creative imagination, was conspicuously absent from the picture.

So far as subject matter is concerned, the larger questions of the moment found their way into the short story only infrequently and then not very impressively. (The atomic bomb's potential effects were treated humorously in at least one recent short story!) There was a natural holdover of war stories, most of them based upon actual experiences and coming closer to reportage than to the legitimate short story. In 1945 half the stories in this collection dealt with the war, while in 1946 this figure had dropped to six out of twenty-two. This year another half dozen were more or less related to the conflict or its aftermath, with four showing an intimate connection. Race prejudice, which has ranked next to the war itself as subject matter, dropped off sharply this year in popularity, furnishing the subject for only one story, while last year there were four on the theme, which is wearing threadbare from overuse, although it remains timely enough.

Stories dealing with abnormal mental states of one kind or another continued to engage the attention of many writers, and the psychological approach so marked in the current novel was also popular in the short story, tending to make for overemphasis on weak characters, whose lack of will to struggle against their difficulties, however carefully explained by the rules of Freud, Jung, and Adler, removed from the short story in general the elements of contrast and conflict that have been regarded as essential in fiction from the beginning of the art. The short story based upon the troubles of the non-heroic individual was therefore in grave danger of finding itself up a blind alley, like its big brother, the novel, if indeed they were not both already there.

Two of the judges, Paul Jordan-Smith and Struthers Burt, remarked upon this phase of the situation. Mr. Jordan-Smith, after confessing without a perceptible blush that he was "brought up on Matthew Arnold, and then turned over to Saintsbury, G. Lowes Dickinson, and Charles Whibley, with a postgraduate course in MacNeile Dixon," went on to say that he shrank from Freud "as I do from all the current religions," adding that what depressed him most about the stories under consideration was that practically all the writers chose insignificant people and events for their subjects, with mental pathology as a close runner up. He went on: "I cannot blame writers for a feeling of futility about the state of the world, but it seems odd that they cannot find contrast to emphasize the feeling of *personal* futility. An educated, decent character flitting across the pages would serve to underscore the futility: a character with some significant purpose would also help in showing how these morons look. That is why I felt so deeply about the Negro in Walter Elder's 'You Can Wreck It.' He at least found something to interest him." [And furthermore he did something about it, Mr. Smith might well have added.] "I cannot escape the feeling that too many young writers are following a dogmatic thesis about writing; or perhaps it is a fad, just as in my youth we went out of our way to create unhappy endings on the theory that any state of happiness must indicate stupidity . . . No, I hold no brief for 'happy endings,' but I do believe that *reality* offers contrasts, and that the writer, to set forth what he conceives to be reality in his stories, gains by using that contrast. You wouldn't know a scoundrel unless you had seen a decent man, or at least heard of one."

Mr. Burt's comment upon the technical excellence of the stories is in sharp contrast to what he says about their pessimistic slant. He wrote: "As always, I am struck by the sheer virtuosity of all these stories, but this year, all of them being written during the war or shortly after, I have been equally impressed by their psychological content. Marked as the separation has always been between the deliberately blithe, cynical cheerfulness of the average story in the 'big flats' and the stories of our more thoughtful writers, never have I seen this separation more distinct than in this collection." [This is shrewd and timely comment. One thing wrong with our fiction is that when it entertains it does nothing else and when it preaches it just preaches, while really sound fiction, short or long, both diverts and edifies.]

Mr. Burt continued: "I wish these stories could fall into the hands of our leaders, political, business, clerical, and so on. And I wish these men would read them carefully and ponder them. This collection represents a fairly accurate cross section of what is going on in the minds of the more sensitive Americans. It is not a very happy picture." [Especially when one pauses to consider that these stories were written by citizens of the most fortunate country on the globe and read with a measure of approval by other citizens of the same country.] "Not a single one of these stories presents a ray of hope for things as they are. And this runs from the average American marriage to the country in general. Here is not the age-old revolt of the artist against things as they are, with the underlying implicit belief that they can be better, but a sort of grim acceptance that 'the American Dream,' personally and otherwise, has gone badly askew. This collection is extremely important in many ways, but so far as I am concerned, its greatest importance lies in the fact that there is the most convincing sort of testimony that, and fairly soon, we must find some way out of our present spiritual dilemma. I do not mean that these stories go in for social comment as did the short stories of a few years back." [Mr. Burt is thinking of the period of the proletarian story, which followed the Great Depression of the early thirties and very nearly drowned us all under a wave of the troubles of the downtrodden.] "That they do not is a great step forward artistically. These stories are personal, psychological experiences, as short stories should be. It is the implication from the personal to the larger picture I am talking about." At the risk of appearing boresomely repetitious, the extreme dearth of humorous stories of any merit at all is mentioned once more. Humor may be out of keeping with the spirit of the times, but Americans have not forgotten how to laugh in order to save some of their sanity, and they must be hard put to it for laughing material except for the hundreds of small anecdotes that fill out the pages of the pocket-sized magazines. Frankly, the editor of this collection has not seen a humorous story in so long he might be hard put to it to recognize one if he came across it, but he is more than willing to try.

The standing of the magazines this year shows *Harper's Magazine* furnishing three stories and two prize winners, first and second, while the *New Yorker's* lone offering won a prize. Last year three *Atlantic* firsts won prizes out of four stories selected from the magazine, while this year one of its three took a prize. Last year *Harper's Bazaar,* whose fiction continued to be uniformly excellent, furnished four stories, and this year six, none of them among the prize winners, although Margaret Shedd's "The Great Fire of 1945" might very well have been. Three stories in the present collection are from *Mademoiselle,* including Ray Bradbury's extraordinary "Homecoming." This magazine continued to devote much attention to young talent, and Susan Kuehn, who wrote "The Rosebush" as an undergraduate, won a prize in a college contest. *Tomorrow,* which has shown steady improvement throughout the year, is successfully featuring the work of new writers and has turned up a number of promising talents in addition to Mrs. Govan.

Of the literary quarterlies, which have supplied the collection year after year with many excellent stories, which is natural, since their editors are on the lookout for exactly the same qualities in writing that appeal to the editor of this volume, and others seriously interested in short fiction, *The Yale Review, The Kenyon Review, The New Mexico Quarterly Review,* and *Accent* are each represented by one story this year. *Town and Country* accounts for one more, which winds up the list. *The New Yorker* supplied a prize winner, but its fiction suffered a sharp slump otherwise, after a long and unbroken period of excellence in a type of short story it had made its own.

The annual acknowledgment of the indebtedness of the editor to those who help him carry his burdens must include special mention of the regrettable resignation of Miss Muriel Fuller as assistant editor, a post she filled for fifteen years. She undertook this arduous assignment in 1932, the year Harry Hansen succeeded the late Dr. Blanche Colton Williams as editor and continued until August 1, 1946, when she gave up the work because of the pressure of other duties. Her capable handling of the tremendous amount of routine involved in putting together the collection, which had its special importance during the two years the present editor was perched on a South American mountaintop trying to cope with the uncertain mails of wartime, together with her ability to read and appraise vast quantities of fiction year after year without letting anything really worth while slip through the net, made her contribution to the history of this volume one of first importance. She deserves to be thanked for her consistently faithful, loyal, and efficient help, and the editor would like to add to this his gratitude for her exceptionally fine service as a judge this year.

Miss Fuller, whose long and intimate relationship to the work of putting together this anthology gave her comment peculiar value, felt, as did the editor and his wife, that the present collection is better than that of 1946, "more interesting and varied." Miss Fuller has had much more of an opportunity to become hardened to the generally bilious outlook of most of our serious short-story writers than the other two judges, and so remarked upon something else rather than the philosophical and social significance of the stories. She wrote: "What interested me chiefly about this year's collection was the almost complete break with war atmosphere and the transition to other themes. There is less straight reporting, as much of the war material had to be, and more story. There is also a change from the intense absorption with the state of the human mind. When done, the approach seemed more subtle. The episodic piece of fiction appeared to be giving way to fiction that told a story, but retained the brevity of the conversation piece. In other words, a definite style seemed to be emerging that enabled the writer to handle in smaller compass what it would have taken him twice as long to handle previously. This not only makes for narrative movement, but it prunes stories of excess verbiage, certainly something on the profit side of the ledger. It was also encouraging to find one of the large circulation women's magazines [*McCall's*] represented in 'The Hot Day.' I think this story can stand with the best of the stories here. For some time it has seemed to me that when the women's magazines published a story with some literary quality they felt it had to be thoroughly unpleasant. While this story has that sort of ending, it is entirely logical and right, and does not jar the reader."

Where to Find Stories

As in previous years, the stories of 1947 come from a relatively narrow range of magazines, although the untiring search for something worth reprinting from the popular periodicals, "big flats," and all other kinds, continues unabated. Dozens of these stories are read faithfully and carefully year after year, many of them by the editor, although the bulk of this work falls to his assistant. There is little new to be said on a subject often discussed here, namely the prevalence of formula fiction in magazines of mass circulation, and while the short story inevitably remains the form most readily responsive to what is going on in the world and in men's minds, romance, or "Love Among the Pin-Ups," continued to hold its own in the opening months of the Atomic Age, as it has since the first man saw the first woman, or vice versa.

To his customary thanks for the invaluable help of his wife from the beginning of his association with the collection, the editor now adds his even deeper gratitude for her work as his full-time assistant. She read hundreds of stories and exercised diligence and ingenuity in keeping up the complete coverage of all types of magazines that is the basis of the volume's claim to be performing its function. Both she and the editor have many reasons to be warmly grateful for the generous hospitality of friends, old and new, in Pass Christian, who helped with the work in every way they could.

For the unstinted and unfailing aid of busy magazine editors, of authors, agents, and publishers, the best thanks. Their enthusiastic interest in the making of the collection is another indication of the place it has made for itself in its generation of existence. While O. Henry might be surprised at most of the stories reprinted in his honor, he would undoubtedly be grateful, as are the rest of us concerned with the enterprise, to all who contribute in any way toward this effort at keeping alive and glowing the memory of a great storyteller.

HERSCHEL BRICKELL

Beach Hurst
Pass Christian, Mississippi
May 15, 1947

THE WHITE CIRCLE

by John Bell Clayton

From *Harper's*

———————◆◆◆———————

As soon as I saw Anvil squatting up in the tree like some hateful creature that belonged in trees I knew I had to take a beating and I knew the kind of beating it would be. But still I had to let it be that way because this went beyond any matter of courage or shame.

The tree was *mine*. I want no doubt about that. It was a seedling that grew out of the slaty bank beside the dry creek-mark across the road from the house, and the thirteen small apples it had borne that year were the thirteen most beautiful things on this beautiful earth.

The day I was twelve Father took me up to the barn to look at the colts—Saturn, Jupiter, Devil, and Moonkissed, the whiteface. Father took a cigar out of his vest pocket and put one foot on the bottom plank of the fence and leaned both elbows on the top of the fence and his face looked quiet and pleased and proud and I liked the way he looked because it was as if he had a little joke or surprise that would turn out nice for me.

"Tucker," Father said presently, "I am not unaware of the momentousness of this day. Now there are four of the finest colts in Augusta County; if there are four any finer anywhere in Virginia I don't know where you'd find them unless Arthur Hancock over in Albemarle would have them." Father took one elbow off the fence and looked at me. "Now do you suppose," he asked, in that fine, free, good humor, "that if I were to offer you a little token to commemorate this occasion you could make a choice?"

"Yes sir," I said.

"Which one?" Father asked. "Devil? He's wild."

"No sir," I said. "I would like to have the apple tree below the gate."

Father looked at me for at least a minute. You would have to understand his pride in his colts to understand the way he looked. But at twelve how could I express how *I* felt? My setting such store in having the tree as my own had something to do with the coloring of the apples as they hung among the green leaves; it had something also to do with their ripening, not in autumn when the world was full of apples, but in midsummer when you *wanted* them; but it had more to do with a way of life that had come down through the generations. I would have given one of the apples to Janie. I would have made of it a ceremony. While I would not have said the words, because at twelve you have no such words, I would have handed over the apple with something like this in mind: "Janie, I want to give you this apple. It came from my tree. The tree stands on my father's land. Before my father had the land it belonged to his father, and before that it belonged to my great-grandfather. It's the English family land. It's almost sacred. My possession of this tree forges of me a link in this owning ancestry that must go back clear beyond Moses and all the old Bible folks."

Father looked at me for that slow, peculiar minute in our lives. "All right, sir," he said. "The tree is yours in fee simple to bargain, sell, and convey or to keep and nurture and eventually hand down to your heirs or assigns forever unto eternity. You have a touch of poetry in your soul and that fierce, proud love of the land in your heart; when you grow up I hope you don't drink too much."

I didn't know what he meant by that but the tree was mine and now there perched Anvil, callously munching one of my thirteen apples and stowing the rest inside his ragged shirt until it bulged out in ugly lumps. I knew the apples pressed cold against his hateful belly and to me the coldness was a sickening evil.

I picked a rock up out of the dust of the road and tore across the creek bed and said, "All right, Anvil—climb down!"

Anvil's milky eyes batted at me under the strangely fair eyebrows. There was not much expression on his face. "Yaannh!" he said. "You stuck-up little priss, you hit me with that rock. You just do!"

"Anvil," I said again, "climb down. They're my apples."

Anvil quit munching for a minute and grinned at me. "You want an apple? I'll give you one. Yaannh!" He suddenly cocked back his right arm and cracked me on the temple with the half-eaten apple.

I let go with the rock and it hit a limb with a dull chub sound and Anvil said, "You're fixin' to git it—you're real-ly fixin' to git it."

"I'll shake you down," I said. "I'll shake you clear down."

"Clear down?" Anvil chortled. "Where do you think I'm at? Up on top of Walker Mountain? It wouldn't hurt none if I was to fall out of this runty bush on my head."

I grabbed one of his bare feet and pulled backwards, and down Anvil came amidst a flutter of broken twigs and leaves. We both hit the ground. I hopped up and Anvil arose with a faintly vexed expression.

He hooked a leg in back of my knees and shoved a paw against my chin. I went down in the slate. He got down and pinioned my arms with his knees. I tried to kick him in the back of the head but could only flail my feet helplessly in the air.

"You might as well quit kickin'," he said.

He took one of my apples from his shirt and began eating it, almost absent-mindedly.

"You dirty filthy stinkin' sow," I said.

He snorted. "I couldn't be a sow, but you take that back."

"I wish you were fryin' in the middle of hell right this minute."

"Take back the stinkin' part," Anvil said thoughtfully. "I don't stink."

He pressed his knees down harder, pinching and squeezing the flesh of my arms.

I sobbed, "I take back the stinkin' part."

"That's better," Anvil said.

He ran a finger back into his jaw to dislodge a fragment of apple from his teeth. For a moment he examined the fragment and then wiped it on my cheek.

"I'm goin' to tell Father," I said desperately.

" 'Father,' " Anvil said with falsetto mimicry. " 'Father.' Say 'Old Man.' You think your old man is some stuff on a stick, don't you? You think he don't walk on the ground, don't you? You think you and your whole stuck-up family don't walk on the ground. Say 'Old Man.' "

"Go to hell!"

"Shut up your blubberin'. Say 'Old Man.' "

"Old Man. I wish you were dead."

"Yaannh!" Anvil said. "Stop blubberin'. Now call me 'Uncle Anvil.' Say 'Uncle Sweetie Peetie Tweetie Beg-Your-Pardon Uncle Anvil.' Say it!"

"Uncle Sweetie . . . Uncle Peetie, Tweetie Son-of-a-bitch Anvil."

He caught my hair in his hands and wallowed my head against the ground until I said every bitter word of it. Three times.

Anvil tossed away a spent, maltreated core that had been my apple. He gave my head one final thump upon the ground and said "Yaannh!" again in a satisfied way.

He released me and got up. I lay there with my face muscles twitching in outrage.

Anvil looked down at me. "Stop blubberin'," he commanded.

"I'm not cryin'," I said.

I was lying there with a towering, homicidal detestation, planning to kill Anvil—and the thought of it had a sweetness like summer fruit.

There were times when I had no desire to kill Anvil. I remember the day his father showed up at the school. He was a dirty, half-crazy, itinerant knickknack peddler. He had a club and he told the principal he was going to beat the meanness out of Anvil or beat him to death. Anvil scudded under a desk and lay there trembling and whimpering until the principal finally drove the ragged old man away. I had no hatred for Anvil then.

But another day, just for the sheer filthy meanness of it, he crawled through a classroom window after school hours and befouled the floor. And the number of times he pushed over smaller boys, just to see them hit the packed hard earth of the schoolyard and to watch the fright on their faces as they ran away, was more than I could count.

And still another day he walked up to me as I leaned against the warmth of the schoolhack shed in the sunlight, feeling the nice warmth of the weather-beaten boards.

"They hate me," he said dismally. "They hate me because my old man's crazy."

As I looked at Anvil I felt that in the background I was seeing that

demented, bitter father trudging his lonely, vicious way through
the world.

"They don't hate you," I lied. "Anyway I don't hate you." That
was true. At that moment I didn't hate him. "How about comin'
home and stayin' all night with me?"

So after school Anvil went along with me—and threw rocks at me
all the way home.

Now I had for him no soft feeling of any kind. I planned—
practically—his extinction as he stood there before me commanding
me to cease the blubbering out of my heart.

"Shut up now," Anvil said. "I never hurt you. Stop blubberin'."

"I'm not cryin'," I said.

"You're still mad though." He looked at me appraisingly.

"No, I'm not," I lied. "I'm not even mad. I was a little bit mad,
but not now."

"Well, whattaya look so funny around the mouth and eyes for?"

"I don't know. Let's go up to the barn and play."

"Play whut?" Anvil looked at me truculently. He didn't know
whether to be suspicious or flattered. "I'm gettin' too big to play.
To play much, anyway," he added undecidedly. "I might play a
little bit if it ain't some sissy game."

"We'll play anything," I said eagerly.

"All right," he said. "Race you to the barn. You start."

I started running toward the wire fence and at the third step he
stuck his foot between my legs and I fell forward on my face.

"Yaannh!" he croaked. "That'll learn you."

"Learn me what?" I asked as I got up. "Learn me what?" It
seemed important to know that. Maybe it would make some difference in what I planned to do to Anvil. It seemed very important
to know what it was that Anvil wanted to, and never could, teach
me and the world.

"It'll just learn you," he said doggedly. "Go ahead, I won't trip
you any more."

So we climbed the wire fence and raced across the burned field
the hogs ranged in.

We squeezed through the heavy sliding doors onto the barn floor,
and the first thing that caught Anvil's eye was the irregular circle
that father had painted there. He wanted to know what it was and

I said "Nothing" because I wasn't yet quite ready, and Anvil forgot about it for the moment and wanted to play jumping from the barn floor out to the top of the fresh rick of golden straw.

I said, "No. Who wants to do that, anyway?"

"I do," said Anvil. "Jump, you puke. Go ahead and jump!"

I didn't want to jump. The barn had been built on a hill. In front the ground came up level with the barn floor, but in back the floor was even with the top of the straw rick, with four wide, terrible yawning feet between.

I said, "Nawh, there's nothin' to jumpin'."

"Oh, there ain't, hanh!" said Anvil. "Well, try it——"

He gave me a shove and I went out into terrifying space. He leaped after and upon me and we hit the pillowy side of the straw rick and tumbled to the ground in a smothering slide.

"That's no fun," I said, getting up and brushing the chaff from my face and hair.

Anvil himself had lost interest in it by now and was idly munching another of my apples.

"I know somethin'," I said. "I know a good game. Come on, I'll show you."

Anvil stung me on the leg with the apple as I raced through the door of the cutting room. When we reached the barn floor his eyes again fell on the peculiar white circle. "That's to play prisoner's base with," I said. "That's the base."

"That's a funny-lookin' base," he said suspiciously. "I never saw any base that looked like that."

I could feel my muscles tensing, but I wasn't particularly excited. I didn't trust myself to look up toward the roof where the big mechanical hayfork hung suspended from the long metal track that ran back over the steaming mows of alfalfa and red clover. The fork had vicious sharp prongs that had never descended to the floor except on one occasion Anvil knew nothing about.

I think Father had been drinking the day he bought the hayfork in Staunton. It was an unwieldy involved contraption of ropes, triggers, and pulleys which took four men to operate. A man came out to install the fork and for several days he climbed up and down ladders, bolting the track in place and arranging the various gadgets. Finally, when he said it was ready, Father had a load of hay pulled into the barn and called the men in from the fields to watch and assist in the demonstration.

I don't remember the details. I just remember that something went very badly wrong. The fork suddenly plunged down with a peculiar ripping noise and embedded itself in the back of one of the work horses. Father said very little. He simply painted the big white circle on the barn floor, had the fork hauled back up to the top, and fastened the trigger around the rung of a stationary ladder eight feet off the floor, where no one could inadvertently pull it.

Then he said quietly, "I don't ever want anyone ever to touch this trip rope or to have occasion to step inside this circle."

So that was why I didn't now look up toward the fork.

"I don't want to play no sissy prisoner's base," Anvil said. "Let's find a nest of young pigeons."

"All right," I lied. "I know where there's a nest. But one game of prisoner's base first."

"You don't know where there's any pigeon nest," Anvil said. "You wouldn't have the nerve to throw them up against the barn if you did."

"Yes, I would too," I protested. "Now let's play one game of prisoner's base. Get in the circle and shut your eyes and start countin'."

"Oh, all right," Anvil agreed wearily. "Let's get it over with and find the pigeons. Ten, ten, double ten, forty-five——"

"Right in the middle of the circle," I told him. "And count slow. How'm I goin' to hide if you count that way?"

Anvil now counted more slowly. "Five, ten, fifteen——"

I gave Anvil one last vindictive look and sprang up the stationary ladder and swung out on the trip rope of the unpredictable hayfork with all my puny might.

The fork's whizzing descent was accompanied by that peculiar ripping noise. Anvil must have jumped instinctively. The fork missed him by several feet.

For a moment Anvil stood absolutely still. He turned around and saw the fork, still shimmering from its impact with the floor. His face became exactly the pale green of the carbide we burned in our acetylene lighting plant at the house. Then he looked at me, at the expression on my face, and his Adam's apple bobbed queerly up and down, and a little stream of water trickled down his right trouser leg and over his bare foot.

"You tried to kill me," he said thickly.

He did not come toward me. Instead, he sat down. He shook his head sickly. After a few sullen, bewildered moments he reached into his shirt and began hauling out my apples one by one.

"You can have your stinkin' old apples," he said. "You'd do that for a few dried-up little apples. Your old man owns everything in sight. I ain't got nothin'. Go ahead and keep your stinkin' old apples."

He got to his feet and slowly walked out of the door.

Since swinging off the trip rope I had neither moved nor spoken. For a moment more I stood motionless and voiceless and then I ran over and grabbed up the nine apples that were left and called, "Anvil! Anvil!" He continued across the field without even pausing.

I yelled, "Anvil! Wait, I'll give them to you."

Anvil climbed the fence without looking back and set off down the road toward the store. Every few steps he kicked his wet trouser leg.

Three sparrows flew out of the door in a dusty, chattering spiral. Then there was only the image of the hayfork shimmering and terrible in the great and growing and accusing silence and emptiness of the barn.

REST CAMP ON MAUI

by Eugene L. Burdick

From *Harper's*

———————◆◆◆———————

THE REST CAMP was as ugly as a place can be in the Hawaiian Islands, which is saying that it was as ugly as slums in New York, mud flats in Georgia, or drought land in Arkansas. Bulldozers had scraped the foliage and trees off several hills and left them red and naked. The hills had been covered with tents and a few Quonset huts. The only tropical thing about the camp was the sun and the heavy, sweet sugarcane odor which was laced with the sharper odor of flowers when the wind shifted away from the valley.

Lieutenant Terry walked down a row of tents with the correspondent at his side. He stopped in front of a tent and pulled the flap aside to let the correspondent in. Three Marines stood up. A fourth Marine standing in front of a mirror was rubbing Aqua Velva on his face. He rubbed it with short, smooth strokes along his chin and then up his cheeks, splitting his fingers apart to pass on either side of his ears. Terry watched the Marine rub the liquid on his face and said nothing. Then the Marine turned around and clicking his heels together said, "Lieutenant Terry." He said it in a mocking, affected way that meant he liked Terry and felt at ease with him.

Terry started to speak rapidly: "Men, this gentleman here is a correspondent who wants to talk to you for a while. Give him whatever information he wants and we'll check it later for security. Mr. Black, this is Sergeant Fellows, Corporal Young, Private Selfensky, and Private Shannon."

By the end of the introduction the Marines all seemed relaxed and their faces went a little blank. They shook hands with the cor-

respondent, squinting over his shoulder as they grasped his hand.

Fellows was round and red, like a beery friar.

"Glad to meet you, Mr. Black. Glad to help you any way we can," he said.

His voice was so flat that the cordiality of the words seemed to be squeezed thin and reluctant. He went back to the mirror and sprinkled some more Aqua Velva in his hands and started to rub his face.

The correspondent picked up his knapsack and opening it slipped out a bottle of whisky and put it on the table, saying, "Something to help pass the afternoon."

The four Marines all heard the bottle come down on the table and turned to stare hard at it. The bottle looked big and new and shiny. Their faces were eager and individual now. Their eyes glistened and Fellows licked a corner of his mouth several times quickly, without looking away from the bottle. They turned and looked at Terry. It was against regulations to drink in camp and they watched to see what Terry would say. Terry looked at Fellows and winked and said, "I'll be back for you in two hours, Mr. Black." He turned and walked out the flap.

Fellows laid out four heavy, metal mess cups and a chipped glass. He picked up the bottle, ripped the cellophane cover off the top, and unscrewed it. He poured out the whisky until the whole bottle was neatly divided into five equal parts.

"I'm not drinking today. Go ahead and use mine," the correspondent said.

Fellows looked up from the bottle and smiled at the correspondent. He picked up the chipped glass and split the whisky in it equally among the four metal cups. The whisky had a heady, rich odor that quickly filled the tent. Selfensky laughed and picking up a cup said, "*Skol.*" They rinsed their mouths with the liquor and the heavy fumes flooded up their noses and tickled beautifully. The strength of the whisky brought tears to their eyes and they swallowed it quickly. They all smiled at the correspondent and when he started to talk again the conversation was more relaxed.

The correspondent took off his cap and laid it on the table. It was crumpled like the caps that Army pilots wear. It was cleverly bent and the wire stretcher had been removed from it.

"Men, I'm trying to get the personal angle on some of these shows you've been in," he said.

They felt good now and they grinned when he said "show." Correspondents always said "show," "bloody do," or "rat race," especially in the books they wrote.

"I want to get your attitude on politics and women and how you feel about things back in the States. There weren't any women on Tarawa or Iwo, but how about the women in Sydney and the Hawaiian girls?"

Fellows started to talk loudly about the Australian chicks. The correspondent kept grinning and saying he couldn't print that, but you could see he wanted to hear more of it. Fellows talked about the Sydney girls out at King's Cross and down at Woolamooloo Dock and how at first they would always shack up with a girl apiece, but later when they got broke a half dozen of them would all shack up with one girl to save money. The Marines hardly listened to Fellows' talk. They sipped at the whisky and smoked cigarettes.

Lord, Young thought, it's wonderful how good cigarettes taste when you suck in the smoke through the whisky breath of your throat.

Usually Young liked to listen to the older fellows' talk about women. He was only nineteen, the youngest man in his platoon. He'd joined the Corps when he was seventeen and never had a chance to hang around girls much. He had never had a girl, but he picked up the salty talk quickly and felt pretty sure that he sounded like any other Marine talking about women. Today he felt good and mellow, and leaning back in his chair he thought about the time on Okinawa.

He and Fellows had been on a patrol on the northern end of the island and they had come to another one of those little villages that were almost deserted. As they walked past the little houses they saw a few stunted people disappearing around corners or sitting in front of the tiny houses. Even the dogs looked runty and little. In front of one house a woman and her husband were seated on the ground. The husband was puffing on a small clay pipe and looking straight ahead. He looked as if he had been carved and lacquered, and he had a smooth, oily, little potbelly that gleamed out of a hole in his shirt. The woman was seated with her back to the wall and she had dark, long hair. It was so black that it looked steel-blue. She must have been forty years old and her skin had an exquisite pattern of wrinkles over it, but somehow it looked soft and well cared for. Perhaps she had powder on her skin. It looked as if it might have a nice odor to it.

Fellows laughed and said, "Look," as he tossed her a small, wax-covered package of K ration. It landed on her lap and she picked it up and examined it slowly and then looked up at the sergeant. A gift from a man in uniform could mean only one thing to her. She slid down until her shoulders were on the ground, but her head was still angled up against the house. She unfolded her kimono and drew it carefully back from her body until she was naked from the waist down. Young looked at her husband and he was still puffing his pipe slowly and looking straight ahead. The woman looked at the sergeant again and turned her head until the side of her face was flat against the rough material of the house. She closed her eyes. Young thought for a moment it was an odd movement of coquetry, but knew instantly it wasn't. It was artless and completely uninspired, the movement of a tired animal. Lying in the sun on her kimono in the peculiar posture she should have seemed disgusting, but to Young she seemed very lascivious, although she made not the slightest movement and lay inert on the ground.

Young said hoarsely, "Come on, Sarg, let's get going."

"Yeh, yeh," said Fellows, looking at the woman. "She's probably got a lot of screwy Jap diseases we never heard of."

Fellows was no longer smiling and as they went on through the village he said, "You know, kid, they always lay still like that. They're screwy people. I had Asiatic duty once. I know the screwy bastards."

Young stopped in the middle of the street and suddenly vomited. He felt greatly relieved and laughed loudly as Fellows hit him on the shoulder and said, "Take it easy, kid, take it easy."

Later Young had thought of the woman when they'd start to talk about their girls and wives and what they'd do when they got back to the States.

Fellows was still talking about the Aussie women and the correspondent was writing occasionally in a black notebook. Young moved behind him and read what he had written. *"Marines like Aussie girls, but first love still clean-cut American girls."*

The correspondent's pen moved across the notebook again. *"Jews in the Corps. Personal, human angle?"* He looked up.

"How have the Jews in the Corps made out? I'd like to give them a good write-up in my book," he said.

Fellows nodded at Selfensky and said, "Ask Selfensky, he's a Jew." Selfensky looked straight at the correspondent for a moment and the Marines knew he wanted to talk about Lieutenant Cohen. Usually Selfensky clammed up when someone made a mistake and talked about Jews in front of him, but today he felt loose and oily inside and talking seemed easy. He chewed at his lip, trying to form words, and then the correspondent said, "Yeah, Selfensky, you probably know more about this than anyone here. You know, some of my best friends are Jews. Damn fine fellows, I really like them."

Selfensky's face went a little hard and he stopped chewing his lip and said, "Ask Fellows. I don't know hardly anyone outside my company."

"Yeah, yeah, I know just about everyone in this damn division," Fellows said. He started telling the correspondent about Horowitz, a pfc in the quartermaster, who organized an all-Marine show.

Selfensky took a sip of the whisky and he felt a little tight and beautifully lightheaded. He hadn't thought about Lieutenant Cohen for a long time. Selfensky remembered how proud he had felt when he got the word that his company was getting a Jewish officer for a platoon leader replacement. There were only a few Jewish enlisted men and no Jewish officers in his company. He had been disappointed when he first saw Cohen. He was of medium height and had dark eyes and long and very white graceful hands. Selfensky had hoped he would be a big rugged Jewish football player like Sid Luckman or a huge, fast, powerful boxer. Cohen was very quiet and kept to himself, but he was marvelous on weapons. Instead of field-stripping his platoon's weapons on a clean, canvas-covered table he made them take them out in the sand in a foxhole. They had to strip them with their eyes bandaged and put the parts in their pockets to keep them from getting sandy or losing them. Cohen could beat anyone by a minute or so. He was always asking questions about new gear and equipment and remembered most of it. Once he took a two-day pass and went to visit a tank outfit. When he came back he could drive a tank. The men started to like him.

One day a big Polack had called Cohen a kike. Loud and clear so that Cohen could hear it, and then looked at Cohen so that he couldn't ignore it. Cohen told him to report to the back of the rifle range and about twenty men drifted along to see what would happen.

Cohen took his shirt off and said, "Corporal, take off your shirt."

The Pole was a little nervous, but he laughed when he saw that Cohen was actually going to fight him with no rank or rate showing. He outweighed Cohen by forty pounds.

Cohen stood very straight and white and said, "Corporal, I can't possibly beat you in an ordinary fist fight. This is going to be a no-holds-barred fight. Do you agree?"

"Yeah, Jew-boy, that's OK with me," the Pole said.

Selfensky felt sick and wondered if he should try and stop the fight, but the Pole had already started after Cohen. The Pole hit Cohen twice—hard blows on the chest. Then Cohen seemed to be all over the Pole, like a mongoose after a dog. He kicked the Pole hard in the shins and as the Pole straightened up Cohen had his finger inside the Pole's lip and ripped it back from the corner of his mouth. The Pole kept hitting Cohen hard, but he was a little scared now. Cohen went after his hands next and when they separated he had broken the little finger of the Pole's right hand. It hung back from his hand at such an impossible angle that it hurt you to look at it.

Cohen drove his knee into the Pole's groin a couple of times and Selfensky could see panic in the Pole's eyes. The Pole tried to kick and knee too and that ended it quickly. Cohen stood back and smashed him time after time in the face. The Pole got weaker and soon his knees buckled and he put his face in his hands and sank to the ground. The broken little finger stuck straight out from the other fingers curled around his face.

The Pole turned into sick bay and said he'd been in a fight with some civilians. Cohen visited him in the hospital and when the Pole got out he transferred to Cohen's platoon. Cohen still worked his men hard and by the time they were ready to stage for Iwo his platoon was the toughest in the company. The men were lean and hard and they all looked tougher than Cohen, whose hands were still white and graceful looking.

Their company went into Iwo on D plus 2. Selfensky remembered how much like practice it all had seemed as they went down the nets into the LCVPs and circled around waiting for the rest of their wave. They joked and kidded a bit and a BAR man pretended he was seasick over the side. It didn't seem too bad even when they got up close to the beach and could hear the mortars crumping and could see the

F6Fs suddenly leave their 500-pound bombs hanging still in the air and then the bombs would start to speed up and go so fast you could hardly see them as they hit into the big mounds of sand and exploded blackly.

As soon as the platoon hit the beach, however, and started to muck through the black volcanic sand, things didn't look so good. The first thing they saw was an aid station that had been hit. There were broken plasma bottles hanging from rifles and a long stream of bandage unrolled neat and white across the black sand. Cots and crates and blankets were all smashed together and big, tarry clots of blood and flesh were plastered over everything. The corpsmen had already set up a few yards down the beach, but you could tell that they didn't expect to stay there long. Funny how corpsmen always looked like kids. Even the middle-aged men looked like kids when they wore the big helmets with red crosses on them and brassards on their arms. Like kids playing soldier.

They moved off the beach fast and alongside the air strip, avoiding the little flags that indicated mines. The mortar fire started to pick up. They hit the line very soon and found the outfit they were supposed to flank. There were a lot of dead Marines around, but no one was bothering about them and Selfensky wondered where the Japs were. He hadn't seen a Jap body or a Jap position yet, although the machine-gun fire was heavy now and occasionally there was some artillery fire. Then a company runner arrived and gave Cohen a field dispatch and he moved the platoon to the right and into a big shell hole.

"We're going to clean out that pillbox on the hill," he said. "We'll have tank support and everyone except the BAR men keep close to the tank. BAR men keep the pillbox under fire all the time. A couple of grenades ought to do it, but don't pitch one until you're sure you can hit the slit."

Selfensky looked up the low hill and finally saw the long, camouflaged slit. It looked like a crevice between two rocks, but occasionally there would be a stream of smoke-puff from it.

They had to wait a half hour for the tank so they broke open their K rations. Selfensky didn't like the candy in the ration and traded it to another man for the little can of cheese.

The tank came early, lumbering down the side of the air strip, with

dust thick and black all over it. Wherever there was grease on the
tank the dust bulged out in huge mounds, like soft, black cancers
growing out of the steel. The tank didn't stop when it came to their
shell hole, but the turret swung toward them as if in question and
then turned back toward the pillbox. The gun barrel pointed at the
pillbox like a long, commanding finger. They threw the paper and
tins into the bottom of the hole and started out behind the tank. At
once the fire started to increase and mortar shells began to plop
around the tank. The pillbox was firing fast now and the smoke
puffed steadily out of it. The BAR men lagged a little behind and
suddenly they started to fire into the pillbox. You could see the hot,
angry tracers powdering the stone around the pillbox and smoke
stopped coming out of it.

They were only a hundred yards from the pillbox when they all
heard the first screaming ricochet of an anti-tank shell. Mortar projectiles don't ricochet, they just plop into the ground and explode,
but high-velocity anti-tank projectiles will ricochet off almost anything. The turret of the tank spun around frantically, trying to locate the anti-tank gun. All you could see was dust and mortar shells
exploding and ugly little hills held together by dust and great chunks
of concrete that you couldn't see. There were two more snarling
ricochets and then the fourth round shattered into the tank. It made
a terrible ringing sound and Selfensky's ears stopped hearing for a
minute and he felt a sharp, cold pain at the base of each tooth. The
hatch of the tank was blown off and the tank captain came out behind it. The hatch and the tank captain turned slowly over in the air,
the tank captain's clothing shredding away from him in the air.
When he hit the ground he lay there white and broken and naked.

The tank was smoking, but the motor was running smoothly. The
dust had been shaken from the tank and the green and brown cam-
ouflage paint looked smooth and new. Selfensky felt fear grip his
stomach and suddenly felt very exposed against the sand. He wished
he had had a bowel movement back in the shell hole. He heard his
name called and looking up saw Cohen lowering himself into the
hatch of the tank and motioning to him to follow.

Inside, the tank was hot and dusty and the sweat started to stand
out on Selfensky's face. He felt secure inside the thick steel walls de-
spite the hole in the side of the tank and the two men who had died,

looking over their shoulders into the turret. Cohen boosted the gunner up to him and Selfensky pushed him out the hatch and let him slide to the ground. The driver was harder to get out and Selfensky was sweating hard. He was feeling better all the time, however, and he was amazed at how safe and snug a tank was. He looked at the hole in the side of the tank and saw that the steel was several fingers thick. Damn it, this was all right! Cohen looked up from the driver's seat and said, "Tell the Pole to take over the platoon and we'll try to get up to the pillbox."

The tank started slowly up the slope and through the periscope the pillbox slit got larger and suddenly smoke started to puff out of it again. Selfensky could feel the bullets hitting the side and bouncing off and he grinned down at Cohen.

Cohen's greens were dark with sweat now and his large white hands were moving over the controls rapidly. They were about fifty feet from the pillbox when a scrawny little Jap started to slide sideways out of the slit and Selfensky saw he had a satchel charge in his right hand. The Jap came hopping bowlegged down the hill, his face all contorted and probably yelling. He had covered about half the distance to the tank when he started to stagger. It looked as if someone were hitting him with an invisible sledge hammer. His forehead dissolved in a red splash and his legs snapped back from under him as the BAR slugs tore into them. Sudden red decorations started to spread over his shirt. He smacked backward into the ground and the satchel charge slipped from his hand. Cohen stopped the tank and crawled over into the gunner's position. He didn't know how to work the sight, but at this range he could fire by eye and not miss. He fired five rounds into the slit and when the pillbox looked like a smoking black eye in the hill he stopped.

Cohen grinned up at Selfensky and started the tank back down the hill. They were about halfway down when they hit one of the 500-pound aerial bombs the Japs had mined the island with. Later, Selfensky was told that the tank flopped over on its back and lay there like a great, helpless turtle. Selfensky only remembered coming to and knowing he didn't hurt anywhere, and almost immediately he knew where he was. Cohen was hanging face down from the driver's compartment and the explosion had clamped the compartment around his legs. He hung from his knees down into the turret. Selfensky was puzzled at Cohen's position for a few minutes and then he started to crawl toward him. At once he heard a rasping sound and a great pain inched up his leg. The bone was sticking almost straight out from his leg and when he moved he had pulled it across the rough surface of the tank. He looked again at Cohen and hoped he was dead because he was sure to lose both his legs.

Cohen's voice sounded low and clear in the hot turret. "Take it easy, Selfensky. Stay where you are and they'll get you out of here."

Cohen's eyes looked big and soft and Selfensky felt embarrassed looking at them upside down. He tried to turn his head so he could see straight into Cohen's face, but Cohen said, "No, no, Ski. Take it easy, boy." Selfensky's whole body ached to have Cohen die or faint before he looked up and saw his legs.

"Two little Jew-boys gone astray, eh, Lieutenant," Selfensky said and wondered if it sounded funny.

Cohen closed his eyes as blood started to bubble out of his nose down into them and Selfensky reached over and wiped them out. The eyes opened and were big and soft again.

Cohen started to sing and Selfensky couldn't place the words for a while. Then he remembered the song. He'd learned it long ago at the synagogue and forgotten it. He started to sing softly with Cohen. Cohen sang beautifully, like a cantor. The words sounded big and glorious in the tank. It sounded like many voices singing. Selfensky felt that his voice was huge and powerful and a queer exultation seized him. He didn't know how long they sang, but gradually Cohen's voice became softer and then it stopped. Selfensky hated to look up because he knew that if Cohen's eyes were open and big and soft he'd go crazy. Finally he looked up and Cohen's eyelids were closed and there was a stream of blood from each nostril that ran out his nose, across the eyelids, and into the dark hair. Selfensky reached out and took Cohen's cold hand and started to say the old Jewish prayer for death: ". . . O, may death be an atonement for all the sins, iniquities, and transgressions of which I have been guilty before thee. . . ."

He was holding Cohen's hand and sitting in the same position when they came and cut the tank open with a welder's torch.

Fellows had just finished telling the correspondent about the show

Horowitz had put on. How he'd dressed up a bunch of big Marines like women and brought them out as a chorus line.

"It was really a laugh," Fellows said. "Horowitz had cut coconuts in two and they wore them under brassières. They did an awful dance and one big gook fell on his butt twice. Then one of them dropped a coconut out of his brassière and it bounced on the deck and that really brought down the house. So they all started dropping them out on purpose and pretty soon the whole deck was covered with them. Horowitz was mad about that, but it sure made a good laugh."

Fellows was red-faced now; sweating a little. He had just enough whisky left in his cup to twirl around and he was waiting before he drank that. He kept thinking he wouldn't see any more for a long time. Fellows wished suddenly that he had a whole quart to start in on. He could drink forever and not get sick or sleepy; he'd just keep feeling better and better. The correspondent had an indifferent look on his face and they all knew this wasn't the kind of stuff he wanted to hear, but they didn't care.

The correspondent started to write in his notebook again and Fellows could see the words: *"Jewish boys in the Marines, famed for their entertainment on Broadway and in Hollywood, arrange musicals, shows, and other laugh-fests to keep America's finest fighting men relaxed between battles."*

"Where does this Horowitz come from in the States?" the correspondent asked. "People like to read about where the boys come from."

"Oh, he came from Nebraska. His old man had a peanut farm or something out there," Selfensky answered.

"Not so good, Ski." The correspondent winked at Selfensky. "Jewish boys should come from Brooklyn or Chicago. Gives them more human interest."

The correspondent looked at the empty bottle and Selfensky could see that he was measuring the dope he had got against the whisky and feeling cheated.

"Any of you boys pick up any medals in these shows?" the correspondent asked, changing the subject rapidly. The Marines looked at one another for a second and then, because they were feeling good, they all started to laugh.

"Sure, we all got the Purple Heart," Fellows said.

The correspondent shook his head patiently. "No good. People expect Marines to have Purple Hearts. Any other medals aside from that?" His voice hung somewhere between irritation and patience.

"Yeah, Shannon there has a Silver Star and a Navy Cross. He's got so many medals that they had him go on a bond tour back in the States."

Shannon held back the good, loose feeling in his head and chest and grinned at the correspondent.

"That must have been a pretty fast life after being out here for a couple years. I'll bet you were anxious to get back to your outfit after all those cocktail parties and speeches by politicians," the correspondent said.

"No, I liked it. They sent me back right after Iwo and it was swell. Lots of good food; I gained twenty pounds the first month back. They always fixed me up with a date and I hadn't been out with a girl for three years. Some of the girls still write me. It was a hell of a lot of fun. Everyone was swell to me and the workers at the plants would come up and ask questions about their kids in the Corps and take me out to their homes for dinner. I hated like hell to come back out." Shannon's grin had faded to a serious smile and the other Marines were looking at him oddly.

"I don't know, Shannon," the correspondent said. "What would you say if I wrote you up as being more scared by the speeches and the good-looking girls than you ever were on Iwo? I'll put your name in it and it ought to make a good story. People like that human-interest angle. What do you say?"

The correspondent was mildly excited about the new angle. He didn't notice that the Marines were all quiet and they were watching Shannon.

Shannon was not smiling now and he was trying to understand what the correspondent meant. His mind telescoped the long hot months of training; the nights in combat he had urinated into his pants rather than look for the pit; the grease-packed K rations; the sleep that was not sleep, but unconsciousness; the pfc who threw himself on a grenade that had been dropped by accident and whose body jumped two feet into the air and fell back a crumpled sack of khaki; the warm canteen water that turned the dust in his throat into mud. All these his mind telescoped into one experience. He laid it next to the memories of the laughing girls and iced lemonade and the keen exhilaration of three beers and the fragrant pork roasts and blue water in country streams and the yellowing corn.

Shannon smiled uncertainly over his shoulder at Fellows. He felt a sudden relief, for he could tell that Fellows knew what the correspondent meant.

Fellows finished off his whisky and looked in the bottom of the cup and put it on the table. He stood up and walked over in front of the correspondent.

"Get out of here, you son-of-a-bitch," he said.

His voice sounded a little tired, but the words came like cold drops of metal out of his mouth. The correspondent looked up, startled, and started to say something.

"Get out, you lousy bastard," Fellows said again.

His face wasn't red any more and there was even a little white around the nose. He wasn't the slightest bit drunk.

"Look, old man, you don't understand . . ." the correspondent started to say.

"Come on, bum, move on," Fellows said, and walked back to his chair.

Five minutes later the correspondent went into Lieutenant Terry's tent and said he was ready to go back to town. Terry looked at him and started to whistle.

"How did you make out?" he asked.

"So-so; they didn't have a hell of a lot to say. A little too primadonnaish," the correspondent answered.

They went back down the road that overlooks the beautiful valley of Maui. As the sea came into view, sparkling and blue, Terry started to sing:

> *"There'll be no promotions,*
> *This side of the ocean,*
> *So cheer up my lads,*
> *Bless 'em all.*
> *Bless 'em all, bless 'em all,*
> *The long and the short and the tall . . ."*

THE NIGHTINGALES SING

by Elizabeth Parsons

From *The New Yorker*

———————◆—●—◆———————

THROUGH THE FOG the car went up the hill, whining in second gear, up the sandy road that ran between the highest and broadest stone walls that Joanna had ever seen. There were no trees at all, only the bright green, cattle-cropped pastures sometimes visible above the walls, and sweet fern and juniper bushes, all dim in the opaque air and the wan light of a May evening. Phil, driving the creaking station wagon with dexterous recklessness, said to her, "I hope it's the right road. Nothing looks familiar in this fog and I've only been here once before."

"It was nice of him to ask us—me, especially," said Joanna, who was young and shy and grateful for favors.

"Oh, he loves company," Phil said. "I wish we could have got away sooner, to be here to help him unload the horses, though. Still, Chris will be there."

"Is Chris the girl who got thrown today?" Joanna asked, remembering the slight figure in the black coat going down in a spectacular fall with a big bay horse. Phil nodded and brought the car so smartly around a bend that the two tack boxes in the back of it skidded across the floor. Then he stopped, at last on the level, at a five-barred gate that suddenly appeared out of the mist.

"I'll do the gate," Joanna said, and jumped out. It opened easily and she swung it back against the fence and held it while Phil drove through; then the engine stalled, and in the silence she stood for a moment, her head raised, sniffing the damp, clean air. There was

From "An Afternoon," by Elizabeth Parsons. Originally published in *The New Yorker*, May 11, 1946. Copyright, 1946, by Elizabeth Parsons Warner; reprinted by permission of the Viking Press, Inc., New York.

no sound—not the sound of a bird, or a lamb, or the running of water over stones, or wind in leaves; there was only a great stillness, and a sense of height and strangeness, and the smell of grass and dried dung. This was the top of the world, this lost hillside, green and bare, ruled across by enormous old walls—the work, so it seemed, of giants. In the air there was a faint movement as of a great wind far away, breathing through the fog. Joanna pulled the gate shut and got in again with Phil, and they drove on along the smooth crest of the hill, the windshield wipers swinging slowly to and fro and Phil's sharp, redheaded profile drawn clearly against the gray background. She was grateful to him for taking her to the horse show that afternoon, but she was timid about the invitation to supper that it had led to. Still, there was no getting out of it now. Phil was the elder brother of a school friend of hers, Carol Watson; he was so old he might as well have been of another generation, and there was about him, still incredibly unmarried at the age of thirty-one, the mysterious aura that bachelor elder brothers always possess. Carol was supposed to have come with them, but she had developed chicken pox the day before. However, Phil had kindly offered to take Joanna just the same, since he had had to ride, and he had kept a fatherly eye on her whenever he could. Then a friend of his named Sandy Sheldon, a breeder of polo ponies, had asked him to stop at his farm for supper on the way home. Phil had asked Joanna if she wanted to go, and she had said yes, knowing that he wanted to.

Being a good child, she had telephoned her family to tell them she would not be home until late, because she was going to Sandy Sheldon's place with Phil.

"*Whose* place?" her mother's faraway voice had asked, doubtfully. "Well, don't be too late, will you, dear. And call me up when you're leaving, won't you. It's a miserable night to be driving."

"I can't call you," Joanna had said. "There's no telephone."

"Couldn't you call up from somewhere after you've left?" the faint voice had said. "You know how Father worries, and Phil's such a fast driver."

"I'll try to." Exasperation had made Joanna's voice stiff. What earthly good was *telephoning*? She hung up the receiver with a bang, showing a temper she would not have dared display in the presence of her parents.

Now suddenly out of the fog great buildings loomed close, and they drove through an open gate into a farmyard with gray wooden barns on two sides of it and stone walls on the other two sides.

A few white hens rushed away across the dusty ground, and a gray cat sitting on the pole of a blue dumpcart stared coldly at the car as Phil stopped it beside a battered horse van. The instant he stopped, a springer ran barking out of one of the barn doors and a man appeared behind him and came quickly out to them, up to Joanna's side of the car, where he put both hands on the door and bent his head a little to look in at them.

"Sandy, this is Joanna Gibbs," Phil said.

Sandy looked at her without smiling but not at all with unfriendliness, only with calm consideration. "Hello, Joanna," he said, and opened the door for her.

"Hello," she said, and forgot to be shy, for, instead of uttering the kind of asinine, polite remark she was accustomed to hearing from strangers, he did not treat her as a stranger at all, but said immediately, "You're just in time to help put the horses away. Chris keeled over the minute we got here and I had to send her to bed, and Jake's gone after one of the cows that's strayed off." He spoke in a light, slow, Western voice. He was a small man about Phil's age, with a flat, freckled face, light brown, intelligent eyes, and faded brown hair cut short all over his round head. He looked very sturdy and stocky, walking toward the van beside Phil's thin, New England elegance, and he had a self-confidence that seemed to spring simply from his own good nature.

"Quite a fog you greet us with," Phil said, taking off his coat and hanging it on the latch of the open door of the van. Inside, in the gloom, four long, shining heads were turned toward them, and one of the horses gave a gentle, anxious whinny.

"Yes, we get them once in a while," said Sandy. "I like 'em."

"So do I," Joanna said.

He turned to her and said, "Look, there's really no need in your staying out here. Run in the house, where it's warm, and see if the invalid's all right. You go through that gate." He pointed to a small, sagging gate in one wall.

"All right, I will," she answered, and she started off across the yard toward the end gable of a house she could see rising dimly above some apple trees, the spaniel with her.

"Joanna!" Sandy called after her, just as she reached the gate.

"Yes?" She turned back. The two men were standing by the runway of the van. They both looked at her, seeing a tall young girl in a blue dress and sweater, with her hair drawn straight back over her head and tied at the back of her neck in a chignon with a black bow, and made more beautiful and airy than she actually was by the watery air.

"Put some wood on the kitchen fire as you go in, will you?" Sandy shouted to her. "The woodbox is right by the stove."

"All right," she answered again, and she and the spaniel went through the little gate in the wall. A path led from the gate under the apple trees, where the grass was cut short and neat, to a door in the ell of the house. The house itself was big and old and plain, almost square, with a great chimney settled firmly across the ridgepole, and presumably it faced down the hill toward the sea. It was conventional and unimposing, with white-painted trim and covered with gray old shingles. There was a lilac bush by the front door and a bed of unbudded red lilies around one of the apple trees, but except for these there was neither shrubbery nor flowers. It looked austere and pleasing to Joanna, and she went in through the door in the ell and saw the woodbox beside the black stove. As she poked some pieces of birchwood down into the snapping fire, a girl's voice called from upstairs, "Sandy?"

Joanna put the lid on the stove and went through a tiny hallway into a living room. An enclosed staircase went up out of one corner, and she went to it and called up it, "Sandy's in the barn. Are you all right?"

"Oh, I'm fine," the voice answered, hard and clear. "Just a little shaky when I move around. Come on up."

Immediately at the top of the stairs was a big, square bedroom, papered in a beautiful, faded paper with scrolls and wheat sheaves. On a four-posted bed lay a girl not many years older than Joanna, covered to the chin with a dark patchwork quilt. Her short black hair stood out against the pillow, and her face was colorless and expressionless and at the same time likable and amusing. She did not sit up when Joanna came in; she clasped her hands behind her head and looked at her with blue eyes under lowered black lashes.

"You came with Phil, didn't you?" she asked.

"Yes," Joanna said, moving hesitantly up to the bed and leaning against one of the footposts. "They're putting the horses away and they thought I'd better come in and see how you were."

"Oh, I'm fine," Chris said again. "I'll be O.K. in a few minutes. I lit on my head, I guess, by the way it feels, but I don't remember a thing."

Joanna remembered. It had not seemed possible that that black figure could emerge, apparently from directly underneath the bay horse, and, after sitting a minute on the grass with hanging head, get up and walk grimly away, ignoring the animal that had made such a clumsy error and was being led out by an attendant in a long tan coat.

Joanna also remembered that when people were ill or in pain you brought them weak tea and aspirin and hot-water bottles, and that they were usually in bed, wishing to suffer behind partly lowered shades, not just lying under a quilt with the fog pressing against darkening windows. But there was something here that did not belong in the land of tea and hot-water bottles—a land that, indeed, now seemed on another planet. Joanna made no suggestions but just stood there, looking with shy politeness around the room. It was a cold, sparsely furnished place, and it looked very bare to Joanna, most of whose life so far had been spent in comfortable, chintz-warmed interiors, with carpets that went from wall to wall. In this room, so obviously untouched for the past hundred years or more, was only the bed, a tall chest of drawers, a washstand with a gold-and-white bowl and pitcher, two plain, painted chairs, and a threadbare, oval, braided rug beside the bed. There were no curtains or shades at the four windows, and practically no paint left on the uneven old floor. There was dust over everything. The fireplace was black and damp-smelling and filled with ashes and charred paper that rose high about the feet of the andirons. Joanna could not make out whether it was a guest room or whose room it was; here and there were scattered possessions that might have been male or female—a bootjack, some framed snapshots, a comb, a dirty towel, some socks, a magazine on the floor. Chris's black coat was lying on a chair, and her bowler stood on the bureau. It was a blank room, bleak in the failing light.

Chris watched her from under her half-closed lids, waiting for her to speak, and presently Joanna said, "That was really an awful spill you had."

Chris moved her head on the pillow and said, "He's a brute of a horse. He'll never be fit to ride. I've schooled him for Mrs. Whittaker for a year now and ridden him in three shows and I thought he was pretty well over his troubles." She shrugged and wrapped herself tighter in the quilt. "She's sunk so much money in him it's a crime, but he's just a brute and I don't think I can do anything more with him. Of course, if she wants to go on paying me to ride him, O.K., and her other horses are tops, so I haven't any kick, really. You can't have them all perfect."

"What does she bother with him for?" Joanna asked.

"Well, she's cracked, like most horse-show people," Chris said. "They can't resist being spectacular—exhibitionists, or whatever they call it. Got to have something startling, and then more startling, and so on. And I must say this horse is something to see. He's beautiful." Her somewhat bored little voice died away.

Joanna contemplated all this seriously. It seemed to her an arduous yet dramatic way of earning one's living; she did not notice that there was nothing in the least dramatic about the girl on the bed beside her. Chris, for her part, was speculating more directly about Joanna, watching her, appreciating her looks, wondering what she was doing with Phil. Then, because she was not unkind and sensed that Joanna was at loose ends in the strange house, she said to her, suddenly leaving the world of horses for the domestic scene where women cozily collaborate over the comforts of their men, "Is there a fire in the living room? I was too queasy to notice when I came in. If there isn't one, why don't you light it, so it'll be warm when they come in?"

"I'll look," said Joanna. "I didn't notice, either. Can I get you anything?"

"No, I'll be down pretty soon," Chris said. "I've got to start supper."

Joanna went back down the little stairs. There was no fire in the living room, but a broken basket beside the fireplace was half full of logs, and she carefully laid these on the andirons and stuffed in some twigs and old comics and lit them. In a few minutes the tall flames sprang up into the black chimney, shiny with creosote. Joanna sat on the floor and looked around the room. It was the same size as the bedroom above it, but it was comfortable and snug, with plain gray walls and white woodwork. A fat sofa, covered with dirty, flowered linen, stood in front of the fire. There were some big wicker chairs and four little carved Victorian chairs and a round table with big, bowed legs, covered with a red tablecloth. A high, handsome secretary stood against the long wall opposite the fire; its veneer was peeling, and it was filled with tarnished silver cups and ribbon rosettes. A guitar lay on a chair. There were dog hairs on the sofa, and the floor was dirty, and outside the windows there was nothingness. Joanna got up to look at the kitchen fire, put more wood on it, and returned to the living room. Overhead she heard Chris moving around quietly, and she pictured her walking about the barren, dusty bedroom, combing her short black hair, tying her necktie, folding up the quilt, looking in the gloom for a lipstick; and suddenly a dreadful, lonely sadness and longing came over her. The living room was growing dark, too, and she would have lit the big nickel lamp standing on the table but she did not know how to, so she sat there dreaming in the hot, golden firelight. Presently she heard the men's voices outside, and they came into the kitchen and stopped there to talk. Joanna heard the stove lids being rattled. Sandy came to the door and, seeing her, said, "Is Chris all right?"

"Yes, I think so," Joanna said. "She said she was, anyway."

"Guess I'll just see," he said, and went running up the stairs. The spaniel came in from the kitchen to be near the fire. Joanna stroked his back. His wavy coat was damp with fog, and he smelled very strongly of dog; he sat down on the hearth facing the fire, raised his muzzle, and closed his eyes and gave a great sigh of comfort. Then all of a sudden he trotted away and went leaping up the stairs to the bedroom, and Joanna could hear his feet overhead.

Phil came in next, his hair sticking to his forehead. He hung his coat on a chair back and said to Joanna, "How do you like it here?"

"It's wonderful," she said earnestly.

"It seems to me a queer place," he said, lifting the white, fluted china shade off the lamp and striking a match. "Very queer—so far off. We're marooned. I don't feel there's any other place anywhere, do you?"

Joanna shook her head and watched him touch the match to the wick and stoop to settle the chimney on its base. When he put on the shade, the soft yellow light caught becomingly on his red head and his narrow face, with the sharp cheekbones and the small, deep-set blue eyes. Joanna had known him for years, but she realized, looking at him in the yellow light, that she knew almost nothing about him. Before this, he had been Carol's elder brother, but here, in the unfamiliar surroundings, he was somebody real. She looked away from his lighted face, surprised and wondering. He took his pipe out of his coat pocket and came to the sofa and sat down with a sigh of comfort exactly like the dog's, sticking his long, thin, booted feet out to the fire, banishing the dark, making the fog retreat.

Sandy came down the stairs and went toward the kitchen, and Phil called after him, "Chris O.K.?"

"Yes," Sandy said, going out.

"She's a little crazy," Phil said. "Too much courage and no sense. But she's young. She'll settle down, maybe."

"Are she and Sandy engaged?" Joanna asked.

"Well, no," said Phil. "Sandy's got a wife. She stays in Texas." He paused to light his pipe, and then he said, "That's where he raises his horses, you know; this place is only sort of a salesroom. But he and Chris know each other pretty well."

This seemed obvious to Joanna, who said, "Yes, I know." Phil smoked in silence.

"Doesn't his wife *ever* come here?" Joanna asked after a moment.

"I don't think so," Phil answered.

They could hear Sandy in the kitchen, whistling, and occasionally rattling pans. They heard the pump squeak as he worked the handle, and the water splashed down into the black iron sink. Then he, too, came in to the fire and said to Joanna, smiling down at her, "Are you comfy, and all?"

"Oh *yes*," she said, and flushed with pleasure. "I love your house," she managed to say.

"I'm glad you do. It's kind of a barn of a place, but fine for the little I'm in it." He walked away, pulled the flowered curtains across the windows, and came back to stand before the fire. He looked very solid, small, and cheerful, with his shirtsleeves rolled up, his collar unbuttoned, and his gay, printed tie loosened. He seemed so snug and kind to Joanna, so somehow sympathetic, that she could have leaned forward and hugged him around the knees. But at the idea of doing any such thing she blushed again, and bent to pat the dog.

Sandy took up the guitar and tuned it. He began playing absent-mindedly, his stubby fingers straying across the strings as he stared into the fire. Chris came down the stairs. Instead of her long black boots she had on a pair of dilapidated Indian moccasins with a few beads remaining on the toes, and between these and the ends of her breeches' legs were gay blue socks. The breeches were fawn-colored, and she had on a fresh white shirt with the sleeves rolled up. Her curly hair, cropped nearly as short as a boy's, was brushed and shining, and her hard, sallow little face was carefully made up and completely blank. Whether she was happy or disturbed, well or ill, Joanna could see no stranger would be able to tell.

"What about supper?" she asked Sandy.

"Calm yourself," he said. "I'm cook tonight. It's all started." He took her hand to draw her down on the sofa, but she moved away and pulled a cushion off a chair and lay down on the floor, her feet toward the fire and her hands folded, like a child's, on her stomach. Phil had gone into the kitchen, and now he came back carrying a lighted lamp; it dipped wildly in his hand as he set it on the round table beside the other one. The room shone in the low, beneficent light. Sandy, leaning his head against the high, carved back of the sofa, humming and strumming, now sang aloud in a light, sweet voice:

> *"For I'd rather hear your fiddle*
> *And the tone of one string,*
> *Than watch the waters a-gliding,*
> *Hear the nightingales sing."*

The soft strumming went on, and the soft voice, accompanied by Chris's gentle crooning. The fire snapped. Phil handed around some glasses and then went around with a bottle of whisky he found in the kitchen. He paused at Joanna's glass, smiled at her, and poured her a very small portion.

> *"If I ever return,*
> *It will be in the spring*
> *To watch the waters a-gliding,*
> *Hear the nightingales sing."*

The old air died on a trailing chord.

"That's a lovely song," Joanna said, and then shrank at her sentimentality.

Sandy said, "Yes, it's nice. My mother used to sing it. She knew an awful lot of old songs." He picked out the last bars again on the guitar. Joanna, sitting beside him on the floor, was swept with warmth and comfort.

"My God, the peas!" Sandy said suddenly, in horror, as a loud sound of hissing came from the kitchen. Throwing the guitar down on the sofa, he rushed to rescue the supper.

Joanna and Chris picked their way toward the privy that adjoined the end of the barn nearer the house. They moved in a little circle of light from the kerosene lantern that Chris carried, the batteries of Sandy's big flashlight having turned out to be dead. They were both very full of food, and sleepy, and just a little tipsy. Chris had taken off her socks and moccasins and Joanna her leather sandals, and the soaking grass was cold to their feet, which had so lately been stretched out to the fire. Joanna had never been in a privy in her life, and when Chris opened the door she was astonished at the four neatly covered holes, two large and—on a lower level—two small. Everything was whitewashed; there were pegs to hang things on, and a very strong smell of disinfectant. A few flies woke up and buzzed. Chris set the lantern down on the path and partly closed the door behind them.

There was something cozy about the privy, and they were in no particular hurry to go back to the house. Chris lit a cigarette, and they sat there comfortably in the semidarkness, and Chris talked. She told Joanna about her two years in college, to which she had been made to go by her family. But Chris's love was horses, not gaining an education, and finally she had left and begun to support herself as a professional rider.

"I'd known Sandy ever since I was little," she said. "I used to hang around him when I was a kid, and he let me ride his horses and everything, and when I left college he got me jobs and sort of looked after me."

"He's a darling, isn't he?" Joanna said dreamily, watching the dim slice of light from the open door, and the mist that drifted past it.

"Well, sometimes he is," Chris said. "And sometimes I wish I'd never seen him."

"Oh, *no!*" cried Joanna. "Why?"

"Because he's got so he takes charge too much of the time—you know?" Chris said. "At first I was so crazy about him I didn't care, but now it's gone on so long I'm beginning to see I'm handicapped, in a way. Or that's what I think, anyway. Everybody just assumes I'm his girl. And he's got a wife, you know, and he won't leave her, ever. And then he's not here a lot of the time. But the worst of all is that he's spoiled me; everybody else seems kind of tame and young. So you see it's a mixed pleasure."

Joanna pondered, a little fuzzily. She was not at all sure what it was that Chris was telling her, but she felt she was being talked to as by one worldly soul to another. Now Chris was saying, "He said that would happen, and I didn't care then. He said, 'I'm too *old* for you, Chris, even if I was single, and this way it's hopeless for you.' But I didn't care. I didn't want anybody or anything else and I just plain chased him. And now I don't want anything else, either. So it *is* hopeless. . . . I hope you don't ever love anybody more than he loves you."

"I've never really been in love," Joanna said bravely.

"Well, you will be," Chris said, lighting a second cigarette. The little white interior and their two young, drowsy faces shone for a second in the flash of the match. "First I thought you were coming here because you were Phil's girl, but I soon saw you weren't."

"Oh, *no!*" cried Joanna again. "He's just the brother of a friend of mine, that's all."

"Yes," said Chris. "He always picks racier types than you."

Racy, thought Joanna. I wish *I* was racy, but I'm too scared.

"I've seen some of his girls, and not one of them was as good-looking as you are," Chris went on. "But they were all very dizzy. He has to have that, I guess—he's so sort of restrained himself, with that family and all. I went to a cocktail party at his house once, and it was terrible. Jeepers!" She began to laugh.

Vulgarity is what he likes, then, said Joanna to herself. Perhaps I like it myself, though I don't know that I know what it is. Perhaps my mother would say Chris and Sandy were vulgar, but they don't seem vulgar to me, though I'm glad Mother isn't here to hear their language and some of Sandy's songs.

She gave it up as Chris said, with a yawn, "We'd better go back."

As they went toward the house, it loomed up above them, twice its size, the kitchen windows throwing low beams of light out into the fog. Still there was no wind. In the heavy night air nothing was real, not even Chris and the lantern and the corner of the great wall near the house. Joanna was disembodied, moving through a dream on her bare, numb feet to a house of no substance.

"Let's walk around to the front," she said. "I love the fog."

"O.K.," said Chris, and they went around the corner and stopped by the lilac bushes to listen to the stillness.

But suddenly the dampness reached their bones, and they shivered and screeched and ran back to the back door, with the bobbing lantern smoking and smelling in Chris's hand.

When they came in, Phil looked at them fondly. "Dear little Joanna," he said. "She's all dripping and watery and vaporous, like Undine. What in God's name have you girls been doing?"

"Oh, talking," said Chris.

"Pull up to the fire," Sandy said. "What did you talk about? Us?"

"Yes, dear," said Chris. "We talked about you every single second."

"Joanna's very subdued," remarked Phil. "Did you talk her into a stupor, or what?"

"Joanna doesn't have to talk if she doesn't want to," said Sandy. "I like a quiet woman, myself."

"Do you, now?" said Phil, laughing at Chris, who made a face at him and sat down beside Sandy and gave him a violent hug.

Joanna, blinking, sat on the floor with her wet feet tucked under her, and listened vaguely to the talk that ran to and fro above her. Her head was swimming, and she felt sleepy and wise in the warm lamplight and with the sound of the banter in which she did not have to join unless she wanted to. Suddenly she heard Phil saying, "You know, Joanna, we've got to start along. It seems to me you made a rash promise to your family that you wouldn't be too late getting home, and it's nearly ten now and we've got thirty miles to go." He yawned, stretched, and bent to knock out his pipe on the side of the fireplace.

"I don't want to go," Joanna said.

"Then stay," said Sandy. "There's plenty of room."

But Phil said, getting up, "No, we've got to go. They'd have the police out if we didn't come soon. Joanna's very carefully raised, you know."

"I *love* Joanna," said Chris, hugging Sandy again until he grunted. "I don't care how carefully she was raised, I love her."

"We all love her," Sandy said. "You haven't got a monopoly on her. Come again and stay longer, will you, Joanna? We love you, and you look so nice here in this horrible old house."

They really do like me, Joanna thought, pulling on her sandals. But not as much as I like them. They have a lot of fun all the time, so it doesn't mean as much to them to find somebody they like. But I'll remember this evening as long as I live.

Sadly she went out with them to the station wagon, following the lantern, and climbed in and sat on the clammy leather seat beside Phil. Calling back, and being called to, they drove away, bumping slowly over the little road, and in a second Chris and Sandy and the lantern were gone in the fog.

Joanna let herself in the front door and turned to wave to Phil, who waved back and drove off down the leafy street, misty in the midnight silence. Inland, the fog was not so bad as it had been near the sea, but the trees dripped with the wetness and the sidewalk shone under the street light. She listened to the faraway, sucking sound of Phil's tires die away; then she sighed and closed the door and moved sleepily into the still house, dropping her key into the brass bowl on the hall table. The house was cool, and dark downstairs except for the hall light, and it smelled of the earth in her mother's little conservatory.

Joanna started up the stairs, slowly unfastening the belt of the old trench coat she had borrowed from Phil. The drive back had been a meaningless interval swinging in the night, with nothing to remember but the glow of the headlights so blanketed by the fog that they had had to creep around the curves and down the hills, peering out until their eyes ached. Soon after they had left the farm, they had stopped in a small town while Joanna telephoned her family. Through the open door of the phone booth she had watched Phil sitting on a spindly stool at the little marble counter next to the shelves full of

Westerns, drinking a coke. She had a coke herself and she sipped it as the telephone rang far away in her parents' house, while back of the counter a radio played dance music. And twice after that Phil had pulled off the road, once to light his pipe, and once for Joanna to put on his coat. But now, moving up the shallow, carpeted stairs, she was back in the great, cold, dusty house with the sound of Sandy's guitar and the smell of the oil lamps, and the night, the real night, wide and black and empty, only a step away outside.

Upstairs, there was a light in her own room and one in her mother's dressing room. It was a family custom that when she came in late she should put out her mother's light, so now she went into the small, bright room. With her hand on the light chain, she looked around her, at the chintz-covered chaise longue, the chintz-skirted dressing table with family snapshots, both old and recent, arranged under its glass top, the polished furniture, the long mirror, the agreeable clutter of many years of satisfactory married life. On the walls were more family pictures, covering quite a long period of time—enlargements of picnic photographs, of boats, of a few pets. There was Joanna at the age of twelve on a cow pony in Wyoming; her father and uncle in snow goggles and climbing boots on the lower slopes of Mont Blanc, heaven knows how long ago; her sister and brother-in-law looking very young and carefree with their bicycles outside Salisbury Cathedral sometime in the early thirties, judging by her sister's clothes. In all of them the sun shone, and everyone was happy in the world of the pictures, which was as fresh and good and simple as a May morning. She stared at the familiar little scenes on the walls with love—and with a sympathy for them she had never felt before—and then she put out the light and went back along the hall.

In her own room she kicked off her sandals and dropped Phil's coat on a chair. A drawn window shade moved inward and fell back again in the night breeze that rustled the thick, wet trees close outside. Her pajamas lay on the turned-down bed with its tall, fluted posts. Joanna did not stop to brush her teeth or braid her hair; she was in bed in less than two minutes.

In the darkness she heard the wind rising around Sandy's house, breathing over the open hill, whistling softly in the wet, rusted window screens, stirring in the apple trees. She heard the last burning log in the fireplace tumble apart, and a horse kick at his stall out in the barn. If I'd stayed all night, she thought, in the morning when the fog burned off I'd have known how far you could see from the top of the hill.

For in the morning the hot sun would shine from a mild blue sky, the roofs would steam, the horses would gallop and squeal in the pastures between the great walls, and all the nightingales would rise singing out of the short, tough grass.

LITTLE VICTOR
by Robert Lewis
From *The Atlantic*

THE MAJOR was out when the phone rang, so Captain Huggins answered it. Captain Huggins was a British officer who looked like a Hollywood version of a British officer, and enjoyed acting the part in a certain ironic vein, as if smiling at himself. That is why he lifted the receiver and said tersely, "Huggins." Any American officer would have said "Captain Huggins," or "Lieutenant Huggins," or "General Huggins."

Smith, Spiegel, and I bent over our typewriters to hide our smiles. There was a long silence. Captain Huggins listened in his bored, polite manner, said, "Yes," once, listened some more, said, "Very well," and hung up. He came over to me and said, "I'm afraid they want you for another case, Lewis. It's that Golbey affair. What are you working on now?"

I made a face. "I was afraid of that," I said.

"Nasty?" said Captain Huggins, with that humorous quizzical look I admired so much.

"Quite juicy," I answered in the same vein. I never sirred Huggins. Neither of us liked it. "Nice little murder. Negro driver shot a white sergeant in the home of a Frenchwoman. The only witnesses were the woman and her seven-year-old son. The woman's husband is in a German prison camp. I was hoping they'd get another interpreter for it."

"It's very complimentary on their part," said Huggins.

"No, just laziness. They can't be bothered finding someone else. Well, I guess Göring can wait a while."

"What is it?" said Huggins with vast interest, which we both knew was simulated. "The art treasure affair? Spiegel can take over."

"Sure," I said, "except that he gets upset over it."

Spiegel had of course heard the conversation, being only two yards away. He interrupted to say, "That's all right. I didn't come here for a pleasure trip."

As I left the office, Captain Huggins was very earnestly telling Spiegel that one must be hard, damned hard, mustn't one? One must let the iron enter one's soul. Both he and Spiegel were smiling.

It was quite true that I did not like the Golbey affair. A week before, Lieutenant Tenick from the Judge Advocate General's office had taken me to Golbey to interview the Frenchwoman, Mme. Ernestine Cayrou, and her son, Victor. Mme. Cayrou was about thirty-five, not unattractive, with a clear pale complexion and very dark eyes. Lieutenant Tenick, who had been selected to prosecute the Negro driver at the forthcoming court-martial, had got the story from her.

It appeared that both the white sergeant and the Negro driver had been in the habit of visiting Mme. Cayrou frequently. The sergeant was stationed in Golbey; the driver's unit was camped only a few miles away and the driver often passed through Golbey on his trips to the front, his Army truck loaded with ammunition or gasoline. Previous to the evening of the murder, the two had never met, but that night the Negro was there when the white man, whom they called "Jim," came in. The two men were hostile from the first. Mme. Cayrou was unable to speak or understand English, but felt their hostility from their tone. There were words, they glared at each other across the table; the woman succeeded in pacifying them and asked the Negro to go home. The Negro went to the door, turned around, pulled out a pistol, and shot the sergeant.

Mme. Cayrou kneeled over the sergeant, saw that he was dead, and lost her head completely. Since the Negro, the pistol still in his hand, was between her and the door, she rushed to her bedroom and climbed out the window, forgetting about her son, who had hidden behind the large tile wood stove in the living room and had seen everything. She ran to the house of her neighbor, a doctor. By coincidence both the mayor of Golbey and the head of the district police station were there. When they learned that the Negro was still in the house, they showed a natural reluctance to rush in. By the time Mme.

Cayrou had prevailed upon them to do their duty, the Negro was gone and Jim's body had disappeared.

The little boy told them that the Negro had dragged the body out the front door. They found heel tracks in the snow and, following them, discovered the body lying on the sidewalk beside a telephone pole, thirty yards away. The street was deserted.

The doctor verified that the sergeant was dead, and the mayor notified the orderly room of the American unit stationed in the town.

Within an hour the CID had found the Negro driver. There was only one Negro truck company in the neighborhood. Every man in the company was lined up, and with no hesitation Mme. Cayrou picked out the man. Her little boy also identified him and called the man "Georgia," which the company commander verified as being the nickname by which the Negro was known to his friends.

It was an open-and-shut case, but it was a nasty case, complicated by race, sex, and the fact that the only two witnesses were the woman, who had clearly been having an affair with the murdered sergeant, and the seven-year-old boy.

Lieutenant Tenick was waiting for me in the hall outside the courtroom. He briefed me quickly. "The court took a ten-minute break. We've been grilling the man for an hour and a half. The woman and the boy are here, in the witness room. Colonel Withers is in charge of the court-martial."

"Who's the law member?" I asked. That was important in a case like this, where admissibility of evidence was in question.

"Lieutenant Colonel Burton. But actually Colonel Withers is a lawyer too."

"Well!" I said. "How did that happen?"

Tenick flushed a little, but he took it nicely. He knew that I was referring to the seemingly haphazard method of selecting Army officers to conduct courts-martial. The last case I was on with Tenick had been conducted by a former Oklahoma rancher who was all for stringing up the varmint in time for chow, and was surprised and annoyed at the insistence of the law member of the court that some little formalities, such as evidence, had to be gone through first.

"Colonel Withers is a good man, Sergeant," said Lieutenant Tenick, "and I'm glad of it. There's no doubt in my mind that the nigger is guilty, but I'm not trying to railroad him. I want him to get every break there is, and the colonel will give it to him."

Like hell you do, I thought. I asked, "Is the kid going to give evidence, Lieutenant?"

Tenick hesitated. "I'm going to ask the court to accept his testimony," he said finally. "I'm afraid to rely exclusively on the woman. You know as well as I do she was sleeping with the sergeant. Lieutenant Bedell is defense counsel—he'll worm that out of her in no time. That'll color everything she says."

"I know, Lieutenant," I said, "but to make a man's life depend on a statement from a seven-year-old boy!"

"Age doesn't make any legal difference. It's up to the court to decide how much weight they will give his testimony. And the kid makes sense. He's a smart little boy."

"Oh, sure, Lieutenant," I said, "but I'll bet that's one wise child who doesn't know his own father."

"We're not trying Mme. Cayrou," Tenick said gloomily, "although I'd like to. Anyway, it's not up to me. I'm going to request that the boy's testimony be admitted as evidence. You'd better talk to Mme. Cayrou and the boy. The woman is nervous. Better explain some of the details—the oath, where she is to sit, and so on. Calm her down. I'll call you when we're ready."

The witness room was full of Negro soldiers standing about in groups, smoking and talking somewhat loudly. At first I did not see the woman and the boy; then I saw them in a corner of the room. Mme. Cayrou was sitting stiff and motionless on a backless bench, and Victor was leaning on her knee and whispering something to her. She was shaking her head vigorously as I approached.

"Bonjour, madame," I said, *"est-ce que tout va bien?"*

"Ça va, monsieur," she replied, standing up. There was no denying that she was shapely, or that she knew how to dress. A great deal of study had gone into the tailoring of her dress about her waist and hips. It clung to her without a wrinkle. Except for a touch of lipstick, she was not wearing make-up. She was pale. The effect was just right; she was well-groomed and demure.

"Et toi, Victor," I said, turning to the boy, *"comment ça va?"*

"Assez bien, monsieur," said Victor with dignity. "But you know, these American soldiers of color are making Mama nervous."

"Victor!" said Mme. Cayrou warningly. She sat down again abruptly.

I glanced around the room. The Negro soldiers had stopped talking and were watching us, not with hostility but with interest. I noticed a first sergeant among them. *"Pardon, madame,"* I said, and walked over to him. He was sitting down, a big black man, somewhat stout, with a good-natured face.

"Say, Sarge," he said to me lazily, "do you parley-voo this stuff?"

"Yes, Sergeant," I said. "I'm the interpreter for the French witnesses. Are these men all testifying?"

"That's right. Most of 'em have been in already."

"Maybe there's more to this than I know about. I thought the woman and the boy were the only witnesses."

"Oh, sure," said the first sergeant, "but there's other stuff that has to be proved. Now, for instance, I got the dispatcher's records to prove that Georgia was out on a run at the time the white boy was shot. They'd have a hell of a time proving Georgia done it if I swore he was in camp the whole time." He nodded toward a tall Negro standing by the window. "Johnny over there was Georgia's assistant driver. He testified that he was with him up to the time that Georgia went into her house. He saw him go in. Mike over there seen the pistol."

"What kind of pistol?"

"Mike!" called the first sergeant. "Come over here a minute." A stocky Negro sauntered over, a cigarette drooping from his lip. "Tell the sergeant what kind a pistol Georgia was carrying."

Mike regarded me briefly. "I never seen one like it before, Sarge. Georgia told me it was a Spanish pistol. It was kind of old-fashioned, with pearl handles. It took a regular .45 cartridge. Georgia told me he took it off'n a German prisoner."

"Georgia a friend of yours?" I asked.

"Used to be. Not no more. A guy that shoots down an unarmed man, white or brown, ain't no friend of mine. The white boy wasn't carrying nothing. Georgia didn't have no call to shoot him. The woman told him to go home, didn't she?"

"Sure," I said. I thanked Mike and the first sergeant and returned to Mme. Cayrou.

"These soldiers are not hostile to you," I told her. "They are here to testify against Georgia. You need not be nervous in their presence."

"I am not nervous, *monsieur*," said Mme. Cayrou, but she seemed relieved. "What is it, Victor?" The boy had come up and stood beside her.

"Mama, I wish to talk to the soldiers of color."

"You must not annoy them, Victor."

"Oh no, Mama," said Victor. "If I see that they have ennui, I shall return."

"Very well, then." We watched Victor walk over to the soldiers. They seemed embarrassed, until he said to the group at large, very clearly and politely, *"Bonjour, messieurs";* then they grinned and gathered around him. In a moment they were laughing; it was clear that Victor was not annoying them.

"Mme. Cayrou," I said, "Lieutenant Tenick requested me to inform you about the procedure you are to follow. Do you know what you have to do?"

"I shall tell the truth, *monsieur.*"

"Of course. But there are a few details. Let me explain them to you. I will enter the court first; you must wait outside, near the door. I shall call you a moment later. I shall ask you to raise your right hand and swear to tell the truth. Then you will sit down in the chair I shall point out to you. The two lieutenants will take turns asking you questions. Sometimes the judges will ask you questions. They will be in English, of course, but I shall repeat them exactly in French. Do not talk to me, but to the officer who asks the question. Talk in a normal voice and slowly. Stop after each sentence, until I have repeated it in English. Do you understand?"

"You are very kind," said Mme. Cayrou, but she was not listening to me. She was watching Victor, who was earnestly telling the delighted Negro soldiers something they almost certainly did not understand. She sighed and looked at me with tears in her eyes. "It is very hard, *monsieur,* that such a young boy should be exposed to such a disgrace."

"He is young," I said. "He will soon forget."

She smiled pathetically. Damn it, I thought, quit acting.

"Victor is a strange boy," she said. "He has a very vivid imagination. I sometimes have difficulty persuading him that his fantasies never happened. And he never forgets anything. He will never forget this horrible affair."

"Madame, that is not the worst thing about this affair. Can you imagine the grief of Jim's parents to learn of his death? I can only hope that they will be informed that he died in action."

Mme. Cayrou flushed and bit her lip. Her color receded and left her pale. She stammered, "I have thought of that. I am not so heartless as you think."

"Madame——"

"Oh, I know what you are thinking," she flared. "A vulgar squabble over a woman! An American soldier killed! But it was not I who killed him, after all."

"No one holds you accountable for his death. Both Jim and Georgia were old enough to know what they were doing. Please do not cry."

She fished in her purse for a handkerchief and dried her eyes. "I am a fool," she said. "Please forgive me." She succeeded in smiling wanly. "There will be a great deal of explaining to do when my husband returns."

Yes, that would be worth seeing, I thought.

Victor was back. "You are crying again, Mama," he said reprovingly.

"Victor," I said, "I must talk to you." I drew him to a bench on one side of the room. He sat down and looked at me. He may have talked like a grownup, but he certainly had the face of a child. His eyes were large and had long lashes, like a girl's. His face was oval and delicate.

"Victor, in a little while you will go with me into that other room and we shall have a chat with some American *messieurs.* They are very nice men. They are interested in finding out how Jim was shot and they will ask you to tell them what you saw. Georgia will be there too. He has already told them what he knows about the matter. First your mother will go in and talk to them, and then you. Do you understand?"

"Oh yes, *monsieur.*"

"These men are Americans like Jim and Georgia, Victor. They do not speak French. You will not be able to understand what they say. But I shall be there too, and I shall tell you what they say. In that way we shall all be able to have a chat together."

"I shall be glad to speak to them, *monsieur,*" said Victor politely. "Will Georgia be punished severely?"

"I do not know, Victor. You must not think of that."

"I should not want Georgia punished too severely," he said earnestly. "Georgia is very kind. He used to bring me chocolate and tell me stories. I could not understand them, but I laughed to be polite, and Georgia laughed too and then I ate the chocolate."

I gazed at his thin, undernourished body. I thought, This is war, this slow starvation of children. Seven years old, and he looks a scrawny five.

"Do you like chocolate, Victor?"

"Oh yes, *monsieur,*" he breathed, his eyes glowing.

"Well, Victor, if you are a good boy today, and tell these *messieurs* exactly what happened, I shall give you some chocolate. But remember, you must not say anything that is not true. I shall know if you do, and then I shall not give you any chocolate."

"I understand," he said with dignity. He put his hand into mine and looked up into my eyes. "Will they put Georgia into prison, *monsieur?*"

I said in wonder, "What do you know of prison, Victor?"

"We have a prison in Golbey and I went there once to see Papa. Mama says I must not talk of this, but I do not think she would mind if I told you. She says you are very *gentil*. One night Papa became very angry at Mama and went to the café, where he struck a man with his fist. The gendarmes took him to the prefect of police, and Papa spent three days in prison. The prefect was very angry. Fortunately Papa was drunk at the time."

"Fortunately, Victor?"

"Yes, *monsieur,* because a man does not know what he is doing when he is drunk, and so the prefect was very lenient. I visited Papa on the second day, and had the honor of making the acquaintance of the prefect. He was very kind to me."

Of course the prefect was kind. I could not imagine anyone not being kind to this fragile, exquisitely mannered child. Victor added, "Of course, *monsieur,* I must ask you not to mention this matter to anyone, because it is not nice to be in prison. Papa was ashamed and promised Mama never to become drunk again."

I was promising Victor not to tell a soul when Lieutenant Tenick came out of the courtroom and beckoned to me.

Seven American officers were sitting behind seven Army field tables set up end to end in a row. Colonel Withers sat at the center table; on his left sat Lieutenant Colonel Burton. I did not know any of the other judges—three majors, a captain, and a first lieutenant. The Army was doing this in style.

To the right and in front of this row of tables there were two more set up at right angles to it. Behind one sat a Negro soldier, evidently Georgia; Lieutenant Bedell sat behind the other. In the middle of the floor an empty chair faced the judges. To the right of this sat the court stenographer at another field table.

As Lieutenant Tenick took his place to the left of the judges, opposite Lieutenant Bedell, I walked to the center of the floor behind the empty chair, came to attention, and saluted Colonel Withers.

"Sergeant Lewis reporting to Colonel Withers as interpreter, sir," I said.

Colonel Withers returned the salute. "At ease, Sergeant," he said. "Lieutenant Tenick, swear the interpreter."

Tenick said, "Sergeant Lewis, raise your right hand. Do you swear to interpret faithfully and to the best of your ability all statements which you are called upon to interpret?"

"I do, sir."

"Very well," said Colonel Withers. "Call Mme. Cayrou."

Mme. Cayrou entered and stood beside the witness chair in the middle of the floor. After she was sworn, I motioned to her to sit down. She stated that her name was Ernestine Aubert Cayrou, that she was married and a resident of Golbey, France.

Lieutenant Tenick said, "Mme. Cayrou, please tell the court what happened at your home on the evening of January 12 of this year."

"Mme. Cayrou," I repeated, *"vous êtes priée de dire à la cour ce que s'est passé chez vous le soir du 12 janvier de l'année courante."*

Mme. Cayrou sighed and settled back into her chair. A great calm had descended upon her. All traces of nervousness had vanished. She spoke slowly in a clear voice:

"On the evening of January 12 I was at home with my son Victor. I gave him dinner around six-thirty. About an hour later some friends came to visit me, Mme. Sénan and her daughter-in-law, Marie. They stayed until about eight-thirty and then went home.

"At nine o'clock Georgia came in. He had just returned from a trip with his truck and he was cold. He would often come in to warm himself after such a trip, before he returned to his camp. He was always quiet and well-behaved, and was kind to Victor. He always brought him a gift, some candy or a toy. Victor was fond of him.

"That night Georgia had a pistol with him. He always carried one in his truck and he used to wear it when he came to visit us. Firearms have always made me nervous and once I asked him not to bring them into my house. He stopped doing so, but that night he brought in the pistol to show it to me, because it was an odd pistol he had taken from a German prisoner. It had a mother-of-pearl handle and was very ornate. He said it was of Spanish manufacture. When he saw that I did not like it, he put it in his pocket and sat down near the stove.

"About fifteen minutes later Jim came in. He did not know Georgia and asked me who he was. I explained to him; he seemed very annoyed."

Colonel Withers interrupted to ask if Jim spoke French.

"Yes, *monsieur,* but very badly. However, it was not difficult to understand him. Georgia does not speak French, other than a few simple words. Georgia could not have understood what we said to each other, but Jim made no effort to hide his displeasure, and Georgia became sullen.

"Jim sat down across the room from Georgia, and I sat down also and began to knit. I tried to make conversation, but Jim answered only 'Yes' or 'No,' and at about a quarter to ten I rose and put Victor to bed. While I was in the bedroom I heard Jim and Georgia speaking to each other."

One of the majors wanted to know where the bedroom was situated in regard to the living room. Mme. Cayrou explained that she lived on the first floor of a two-story house. Her apartment consisted of three rooms and bath. One entered by a little hall; to the right of this hall was the kitchen; to the left, the living room. The bedroom lay at the back of the house. One had to cross the living room to enter it.

"When I came out of the bedroom a few minutes later, the two men were glaring at each other across the room. Jim turned to me and told me to tell Georgia to go home. I did not wish to be unkind to Georgia, but I realized that his staying would only provoke a quarrel, and so I asked him to leave. But he only became more sullen.

"When Jim saw that he would not leave, he addressed several remarks to him in an angry voice. Georgia answered in the same way. They both stood up and shouted at each other across the table. Then I noticed that Victor was standing behind the stove in his nightgown. I do not know how long he had been there.

"I succeeded in calming the two, and they resumed their seats, more sullen than ever. I began to knit again; I did not know what else to do. I knitted for about fifteen minutes before I began to cry. I then asked Georgia again to go home, and Victor, who was still behind the stove, did so too.

"Georgia stood up, and Jim said something to him that made him very angry. He seized the edge of the table and shouted at Jim in a very loud voice. Jim pushed the table hard and Georgia staggered back. I stood up and cried, 'Jim!' and he stopped. For a moment he and Georgia stared at each other across the table. Then Georgia turned abruptly and walked toward the door. As he did so, Jim said a word that sounded like *nègre,* and Georgia whirled around, pulled out the pistol, and shot him."

For the first time Mme. Cayrou showed emotion. Her voice broke on the last word. She lifted a handkerchief to her eyes and glanced sideways at the Negro prisoner. His face was expressionless.

Colonel Withers tactfully gave her a moment's respite by saying "Harrumph," and asked Lieutenant Tenick what state Jim was from. Tenick thumbed through his papers and answered, "North Carolina." The officers glanced at each other. The captain nodded to no one in particular.

Mme. Cayrou had regained her poise. "I kneeled down beside Jim, who had fallen to the floor. His chest was bleeding. He was either dead or unconscious. Georgia was still by the door with the pistol in his hand. I cried, 'What have you done? You have killed Jim!' Then I lost my head and ran to the bedroom door. I climbed out of the bedroom window and ran next door to the house of Dr. Bénoit. Mayor Caën and the subprefect of police were there. I told them what had happened and begged them to come immediately. Perhaps Jim was not yet dead. They questioned me at such great length that I became hysterical. I think they were afraid to go into the house because of the pistol. I must have been in there ten or fifteen minutes before they came with me. When we entered the front door, Georgia and Jim were gone. Victor was there in his nightgown. He told us that Georgia had dragged the body outside."

Lieutenant Bedell objected when this last statement was interpreted, on the grounds that this was hearsay evidence. It was sheer quibbling. Lieutenant Tenick said nothing, probably because the implication that Victor had some information to add to that of his mother would bolster his argument that the boy should be allowed to testify. Colonel Withers ordered the court stenographer to strike the last sentence from the record.

Mme. Cayrou went on. "We left the house and in the snow saw signs that something heavy had been dragged up the street. About twenty-five or thirty meters away we found Jim's body lying on the sidewalk near the gutter——"

Lieutenant Tenick said, "I will interrupt here, as the court has already heard adequate testimony, in the form of affidavits from Dr. Bénoit, Mayor Caën, and Prefect Gaulois, as to the manner of discovery of the body and its condition when discovered. The court has also been apprised of the steps leading to the arrest of Clarence Scott, known as 'Georgia,' and of information linking him to the murder of James William Buchanan, known as 'Jim.' I shall now ask the interpreter to put this question to Mme. Cayrou: Do you see in this court the person you have called 'Georgia'?"

"Yes," said Mme. Cayrou. "He is sitting over there." She nodded toward the Negro prisoner.

"That's all," said Lieutenant Tenick, and sat down.

Lieutenant Bedell stood up. He was a short, heavy-set man, with a face marked by smallpox. I knew him from previous cases as a heckler, a bullier of witnesses. His face wore a constant look of disbelief, so that witnesses became unnecessarily emphatic in their most commonplace statements.

Bedell began, as usual, with deceptive smoothness. He desired Mme. Cayrou to inform him just when her acquaintance with James William Buchanan, known as "Jim," began. She answered that she had met Jim about three months previous to the night of the murder. And Georgia? About a month later.

How frequently did they visit her? That was difficult to say, since their visits were irregular. Perhaps once or twice a week.

"Did they ever spend the night at your home?" Bedell asked.

A spot of color came into Mme. Cayrou's cheeks, but she looked steadily at Bedell as she said clearly, "Not Georgia."

"Then the other man, Jim, did sometimes spend the night at your home?"

"Yes," said Mme. Cayrou, "he sometimes did."

Bedell leaned forward a little as he said quietly, "Madame, where is your husband?"

As I repeated the question in French, Mme. Cayrou looked at me and did not remove her gaze to reply, "He is a prisoner of the Germans."

I made the statement in English, and bent forward to whisper, *"Répondez au lieutenant, madame."*

Bedell straightened up abruptly and said to Colonel Withers in a poisonous tone, "If the court please, I should like to know exactly what the interpreter said to the witness over and above the question I addressed to her."

Colonel Withers frowned. "What was that remark, Sergeant?"

"Sir," I replied, "I requested the witness to address her statements to the defense counsel and not to me."

The colonel's face cleared. "I do not believe, Lieutenant," he said dryly, "that the interpreter has exceeded the limits of his duty. You may proceed."

"Very well, sir," said Bedell. "Madame, you would have the court believe that Georgia never spent the night at your home?"

"I have already informed the court," said Mme. Cayrou, "that I allowed the Negro soldier to sit in my living room and warm himself at my fire. I did so because he was kind to my son. Our relationship was never more intimate." Her tone was calm and dangerous.

Bedell did not seem to notice it at all. "May I ask," he said with mock politeness, "whether any man, other than your husband and Jim, was in the habit of spending the night at your home?"

Lieutenant Tenick, who had been becoming more and more restive, stood up and objected to the question as irrelevant and because it was an attempt to blacken the character of the witness.

"May it please the court," said Bedell, "it is precisely because the character of the witness is of the utmost importance to this inquiry that I have asked the question. I wish to point out to the court that this is a very unusual case, in that the only responsible witness of the crime is one whose relationship with the victim was such that she would have every reason to bear a personal grudge against the prisoner, and one whose morals would not prevent her from gratifying that grudge."

Neat. Very neat. Especially the marked emphasis on the word "responsible."

Tenick said, "Would defense counsel have the court believe that a lonely woman who has found consolation in the arms of a lonely man is incapable of telling the truth?"

"Just a moment, gentlemen," said Colonel Withers. He leaned over and whispered to Lieutenant Colonel Burton. Burton pursed his lips and nodded. Withers said slowly, "The court realizes that this is indeed an unusual case, the conditions of which may excuse questions possibly improper under other circumstances. The character of the witness is important here. Objection denied."

Tenick sank back into his chair. Bedell said to me triumphantly, "Please interpret the question."

"Would you repeat it, sir?" I said.

Bedell flushed but kept his temper, and repeated the question. As I restated it in French to Mme. Cayrou, she gazed at me for a moment in incomprehension. Then fury leaped into her eyes. At that moment she was beautiful. She turned to look at the seven officers one by one, striving to control herself. She said slowly and distinctly, "I have never loved more than one man at a time."

It was brazen, it was magnificent; it deflated Bedell completely. The officers shifted uneasily on their chairs. Tenick smiled. Bedell was now a brute, Mme. Cayrou an erring but unrepentant woman who would not stoop to lie. Bedell had lost all possibility of insinuating that Georgia had lost his head through jealousy.

Bedell had a chastened look as he asked, "At any time during the evening did either of the two men strike the other?"

"No," said Mme. Cayrou tersely.

"When Jim pushed the table against Georgia, did Georgia fall to the floor?"

"No, he staggered back."

"Was the table overturned?"

"No, *monsieur*," said Mme. Cayrou. "Georgia's position on the other side of it prevented it from toppling."

"Would you explain to the court the exact positions of you, Jim, Georgia, and Victor when the shot was fired?"

"Very well, *monsieur*. Georgia was about a meter in front of the door leading to the hall. He was facing the living room. Directly in front of him was the living-room table and just behind it was Jim. They were about four meters apart. I was on Jim's right, about a meter from him. Victor was out of the way in the corner behind the stove."

"You have already stated, madame," said Bedell, "that Jim showed displeasure at Georgia's presence. Did you share his attitude?"

"No," said Mme. Cayrou calmly. "Georgia was welcome at my house."

At this point the Negro prisoner, who had sat unmoving the whole time, leaned forward and rested his forehead on his hands, palms down on the table. The entire court, including the perspiring stenographer, turned to look at him. There was an uncomfortable pause.

Colonel Withers coughed and said, "Please proceed, Lieutenant."

Bedell said, "Did you think his attitude unreasonable?"

"Yes."

"Then you had never seen him act that way before?"

Mme. Cayrou regarded Bedell steadily. There were daggers in the air, but when she spoke, her voice was mild. "After all," she said, "the occasion had never risen before."

Bedell said quickly, "What I am driving at, madame, is that his unusual conduct may have been the result of intoxication. Do you believe that he was intoxicated?"

"No. He merely seemed to be in a bad humor."

"Was Georgia intoxicated?" Bedell was casual.

"No. Until Jim came in, Georgia behaved as usual, except for showing me the pistol. It frightened me, and he put it away immediately. He sat near the stove and was very quiet. I have no reason to believe that he was intoxicated."

Bedell seemed disappointed. "Have you ever seen Georgia intoxicated?" he asked.

"I have seen him drink, *monsieur,* but I have never seen him affected by it."

"Did you ever give him liquor to drink?"

"No," said Mme. Cayrou. "But sometimes he brought a bottle of liquor with him." She turned to the judges. *"Messieurs,"* she said earnestly, "I wish to impress upon you that Georgia always acted like a perfect gentleman. He was always quiet and well-behaved. When he brought a bottle to the house, he never drank more than a *petit verre* or two. Even now, although I saw it with my own eyes, I find it hard to believe he did this thing."

Bedell shook his head impatiently. He wished to make the point that Georgia was drunk, or might have been drunk, or had at least had a drink. This, like the jealousy angle, was a bid for leniency from the court.

"Madame," he said, "on the night in question did Georgia have a bottle with him?"

"I saw no bottle, *monsieur.* But it was a cold night and he was wearing an overcoat when he entered. I cannot vouch for what was in the pockets."

"Did you offer him a drink?"

"No, *monsieur,*" said Mme. Cayrou wearily, "I did not. I do not keep liquor in my house."

Bedell frowned. "Did you leave the room at any time while the two men were there?"

The implication was that the moment Mme. Cayrou had left the room Georgia had produced a bottle of liquor and guzzled it down; thereupon, crazed by liquor and irresponsible for his actions, he had shot down an unarmed man. Tenick's eyebrows showed he thought the question silly.

"I put Victor to bed. Otherwise I was with them the entire time. Oh yes, I had forgotten; after they had had their first quarrel and Victor had re-entered the living room, I left for a few minutes."

"Where did you go?" A gleam of hope lighted Bedell's eye.

"To the bathroom, *monsieur,*" said Mme. Cayrou dryly.

Bedell threw up his hands and said, "That's all."

Colonel Withers said, "The interpreter will conduct the witness to the witness room and remain in readiness to be called again, if necessary."

"C'est tout, madame," I said. *"Venez avec moi, s'il vous plaît."* I saluted, turned, and walked out, followed by Mme. Cayrou. As we left, Lieutenant Tenick was saying, "May it please the court, the prosecution at this time wishes to present as a witness Victor Cayrou,

son of——" The door, closing behind us, cut off the disclosure of Victor's parentage.

The Negro soldiers watched us return. They made no comment. Mme. Cayrou sat down on the bench she had formerly occupied. Victor was waiting for her.

"Were the *messieurs* nice, Mama?" he asked.

"Quite nice, Victor," Mme. Cayrou replied. She looked at me with the beginnings of a smile. "Was it all right?" she asked.

"You were an excellent witness, madame," I said.

"I am sure the officers thought I was very bold," she said. Her eyes fluttered once and then looked down demurely. There goes her act again, I thought.

I said, "Sometimes boldness is a good defense."

She said softly, "Did *you* think I was bold, *monsieur?*"

I had a good answer for that one, but the courtroom door opened before I could use it. Lieutenant Tenick leaned out and told me to conduct Victor Cayrou before the court. He looked triumphant.

When we entered, Lieutenant Bedell was sitting down nursing a disgruntled look.

"Sergeant," said Colonel Withers, "the court has decided to examine this child in order to discover whether he is mature enough to remember what he saw and whether he has enough understanding to tell the truth. Bring him here."

I placed Victor directly in front of the colonel's table. All the officers leaned forward and gazed down at the boy. Most of them were smiling.

"What is your name, my boy?" Colonel Withers said gently.

Victor looked at me. I repeated the question in French.

"My name is Victor Cayrou, *monsieur*," he said politely.

"How old are you, Victor?"

"I am seven, *monsieur*."

"Do you go to Sunday school?"

"Yes, *monsieur,* and to day school too; I can already read and write and I am making progress with numbers."

Lieutenant Colonel Burton asked, "What do you learn in Sunday school?"

The boy took a deep breath. His tiny hand crept into mine. "Oh, I learn about *le bon Dieu* and our Saviour, and the angels and the saints, and they tell me stories about Heaven and that other place."

Colonel Withers asked, "Did you learn about what happens to bad little boys?"

"Oh yes, *monsieur,* they are damned and go to Hell."

"Victor, is it bad to tell a lie?"

"One must never tell lies, *monsieur.*"

"Then you understand that if you tell lies, you will not go to Heaven, but to Hell?"

The boy gazed up at the colonel. "You need not fear, *monsieur,*" he said with dignity. "I shall reply truthfully to anything you ask me."

Colonel Withers straightened up with a grunt and glanced at the other officers. "It seems to me," he said, "that the boy is quite intelligent and honest, and understands the difference between right and wrong. While I should ordinarily hesitate to place reliance on the uncorroborated testimony of anyone so young in a case as serious as this, it should be borne in mind that the boy can say very little that cannot be compared with the information furnished by his mother. I shall ask you for a vote. Is there any man opposed to accepting the testimony of this child?" No one stirred. "Very well, then, we shall proceed. Tell us, Victor, are you acquainted with anyone in this room?"

Victor glanced around. "I know this *monsieur,*" he said, pointing to me, "and this *monsieur.*" He pointed to Tenick. The light from the window behind the prisoner prevented him from getting a good look at Georgia's face. He walked over to the prisoner's table, peering up over its edge. "And this is Georgia. *Bonjour,* Georgia," he added politely. The prisoner nodded with a forced smile.

"Very well, Victor," said the colonel. "Do you remember what happened the last time Georgia visited your home?"

"Oh yes, *monsieur,*" he breathed, his eyes shining with intelligence. "Georgia shot Jim with a pistol."

"Did you see this, Victor?"

"Yes, *monsieur,* I was behind the stove."

Colonel Withers put on a big frown. "How can that be, Victor? Your mother informed us that you were in bed."

The boy hastened to put him straight. He pointed out that it was quite true that his mother had put him to bed, but that he had heard

the quarrel and had returned to the living room. There he had seen
the whole thing. "So you see," he said gently, "my mother must have
been mistaken."

"Well, perhaps she was," admitted the colonel. "What did you see
from behind the stove?"

"Both Jim and Georgia were angry, *monsieur*. They sat without
talking. Mama was knitting. I was very sorry to see them so angry,
and so when Mama came back——"

"Came back from where, Victor?"

"From the bathroom, *monsieur*. When she came back, I asked
Georgia to go home."

The colonel pretended not to understand. "I suppose you liked
Jim better than Georgia, since you asked Georgia to leave."

"Oh no, *monsieur*." The child was emphatic. "I liked Georgia
much better than Jim. Jim came to see Mama, but Georgia came
to see me. But Mama wanted Jim to stay, so I asked Georgia to
leave. Georgia and Jim shouted at each other, and Jim pushed the
table. Then Georgia started to go, and Jim called him a name and
Georgia shot him with the pistol."

"What happened then, Victor?"

"Mama became excited and climbed out of the bedroom window.
The noise had frightened me, but I went up to Georgia and took
the pistol from his hand."

The entire court was staring at the boy in amazement as Colonel
Withers said, "Why did you do that?"

"I knew the gendarmes would come to take Georgia away. All the
gendarmes in Golbey are my friends, and I did not wish Georgia
to shoot any of them with the pistol."

Lieutenant Bedell said, "Good God!" The two colonels looked at
each other. Tenick's mouth was open. Colonel Withers recovered
himself first and said gently, "What did you do with the pistol,
Victor?"

"I put it on the table, *monsieur*. Then Georgia dragged Jim out the
door. I sat down to wait for Mama. A few minutes later Georgia returned and took the pistol from the table. I thought he would shoot
me too, but he put it in his pocket, finished the bottle, and threw it
out the window into the snow. Then he went away."

There was a moment of silence as this statement sank in. Then I saw Bedell's head lift with a question in his eyes. Georgia, who had been staring stonily at his hands on the table before him, looked up at the boy. Tenick stood up. The same question was in everybody's mind as Lieutenant Colonel Burton asked, "What bottle?"

"The bottle of cognac, *monsieur,*" said Victor respectfully.

Bedell, Tenick, and one of the majors all started to say something at the same time.

"Just a minute, gentlemen," said Colonel Withers, spreading out his hands. He looked down at the boy standing before him. "Victor, I wish to remind you that you promised to tell the truth. You must be very careful what you say. I want you to tell us all about this bottle of cognac."

"Yes, *monsieur.* When Papa went away to fight the Boches, he left a bottle of cognac hidden in the house. It was hidden because he was afraid Mama would destroy it. Mama did not wish him to drink cognac, only wine. Mama did not know that he had left it, but I knew. That night I showed Georgia the bottle and he took three drinks very quickly."

Bedell was staring at the boy as at an angel. He leaned toward the prisoner and whispered in his ear. The Negro shrugged his shoulders.

Colonel Withers said, "Now, just a moment." His voice was sharp. "Victor, your mother told us that Georgia had nothing to drink at your home. Are you sure you are telling us the truth?"

"Oh, *monsieur!*" Victor was reproachful. "Mama did not see Georgia drink the cognac. She was in the bathroom. I hid the bottle again afterward, before she came out."

Colonel Withers looked at Burton and then at the other officers. The captain was clearing his throat to say something when Tenick said, "If the court please, I should like to ask the boy some questions." His face was stern.

"Very well."

"Victor," said Tenick, "where was this cognac hidden?"

"In the china closet," said Victor tranquilly. "The bottle was in the large earthenware teapot that Mama never uses."

"What did you do with the glass he drank from?"

"He drank from the bottle, *monsieur.*"

Tenick stared at the boy. The boy's eyes were clear and honest; he waited courteously for the next question. Tenick looked over

Victor's head to Bedell, who was smiling. Bedell's eyes said, "This is your witness. This is the boy you insisted on hearing, because it would hang the nigger. And here he is, giving me a perfect bid for clemency. My boy was drunk. He didn't know what he was doing."

Tenick went to work on the boy. He had him tell the whole story of the evening all over again. He made him repeat each detail about the cognac twice. What kind of bottle opener was used? Could Victor reach the earthenware teapot without assistance? Did he offer Jim a drink? Tenick's attitude had changed. He seemed anxious to disprove the boy's story. He tried to trip him up on details. The court listened patiently. To all these questions Victor replied clearly and to the point. He did not repeat himself word for word, but his facts were substantially the same.

Tenick stopped harping on the cognac and tried another tack. He asked, "Which one of the two men overturned the table?"

The boy was surprised. "Oh, the table was not overturned, *monsieur*. Jim pushed it against Georgia, but it did not fall."

"Where was your mother standing when the shot was fired?"

Victor stepped backward and surveyed the room. Putting his hand on the stenographer's table, he said, "This is the table." He pointed to Lieutenant Tenick, who had moved forward in front of it. "This is Jim." He pointed to me. "This is Georgia." He walked to Tenick's right side, about a yard from him. "I am Mama." The tableau he had arranged was exactly that described by his mother.

All seven officers leaned back in their chairs and looked at each other. Tenick said, "That's all," and sat down. He looked sick.

Colonel Withers's eyes asked a question of Lieutenant Bedell, who shrugged his shoulders, still smiling.

"Very well," said the colonel. "Sergeant, you will conduct Victor Cayrou to the witness room. While the court is hearing the summing up of the two counsels, you will make arrangements with the mess to have supper brought on trays to the witness room for yourself and the two witnesses. I am sorry to have to keep them here, but it may be necessary to ask them additional questions."

I saluted and left the courtroom with Victor.

At seven Mme. Cayrou, Victor, and I had our supper on trays. We were alone in the witness room. The Negro witnesses had left long ago. At seven-thirty Spiegel, who had been waiting for me in the witness room when Victor and I came out and whom I had asked to scout around to find some chocolate, brought me half a dozen bars wrapped in a sheet of paper.

Victor fell asleep shortly afterward, and at eight-thirty Mme. Cayrou and I were still waiting for some sign of life from beyond the courtroom doors. I was on my third pipeful and Mme. Cayrou had made a big dent in my pack of cigarettes when Tenick came out and told me to bring her into the court. There Tenick asked her what was kept in the large earthenware teapot in her china closet.

Mme. Cayrou was surprised, but answered that she kept a large bottle of cough syrup in the teapot. When Victor was five he had had bronchitis, which had left him with an irritating cough. She had dosed him through one bottle and had just started the second bottle, containing half a liter, or about a pint, when Victor got rid of the cough. Since that time she had kept the bottle in the teapot. No, it was not a bottle of the type used for cognac, it was a large medicine bottle which she had purchased from the town apothecary.

The last time she had seen the bottle? The night of the murder. She had used the teapot that very evening, since she had made a cup of tea for her guests, the Mesdames Sénan. She remembered positively removing the bottle in order to scald the pot.

Was the bottle still in her home? No. After the Mesdames Sénan had left her home, she had rinsed and dried the teapot and replaced the cough syrup. She had not used the teapot again since that time. But only two days ago she had looked for the syrup bottle, as Victor had started coughing again, and it was not there. Had she asked Victor if he knew where it was? Yes, but he had said something silly about Georgia having taken it. Really, it was unlike Victor to say such a foolish thing.

No, she had never tasted the syrup herself, nor for well over a year had Victor. Was she sure it was cough syrup? Well, of course. What else would it be?

At this Colonel Withers looked grim and told me to conduct Mme. Cayrou to the witness room and to bring Victor in. This time there was no smiling as the American officers looked down at the little boy. Victor felt the difference in their attitude, and his little-girl face was grave and his eyes watchful.

"Victor," said Colonel Withers, "you have told us that there was a bottle of cognac hidden in the earthenware teapot in the china closet. Your mother has told us it was not cognac, but something else."

"Mama thought it was cough syrup," said Victor.

"Oh, for God's sake!" said Lieutenant Tenick.

"Just a moment; Lieutenant," said Withers sharply. "What do you mean, Victor?"

"When I was little, *monsieur,* I was ill with a cough and Mama gave me cough syrup. When I was better, Papa poured out the cough syrup and put cognac in the bottle. In this way he was able to keep some in the house without Mama finding it. Mama did not see him do it, but I did."

The expression on Tenick's face said, I'll just bet you did. All the officers but Colonel Withers began to smile, and he looked as if he wanted to, but controlled himself.

"Now, Victor, do you mean to say that your father went away with the Army and left the cognac behind?"

Victor glanced up at the colonel quickly, then looked away. He seemed confused; his face was delicately pink.

"No, *monsieur,*" he said miserably. "Papa meant to take it with him. He put the bottle in his pack, but I took it out when he went into the kitchen to kiss Mama good-by, because I knew Mama did not want him to drink cognac. I put it back in the teapot for when he would come home."

That finished little Victor's testimony. I led him away by the hand.

There is not much more to tell. Clarence Scott, known as Georgia, was given ten years by the general court-martial, which took into consideration the fact that he was intoxicated at the time of the murder and acted under provocation of insult. It would have been from twenty years to life if, as Tenick put it, "that damned kid hadn't gummed up the works with that cognac deal." Tenick thought the whole business an invention, but had to concede that the boy's story was corroborated at every other point by his mother's testimony, and that the uncorroborated part *could* have been true.

I asked him what Georgia had said about the cognac. Tenick growled in disgust, "Until the kid mentioned it, Georgia never said a word. But Bedell made sure his memory was refreshed. Sure he remembered having drunk the cognac. Why shouldn't he?"

There is one point that has always puzzled me. When the trial was over and little Victor was being bundled up for the cold jeep ride back to Golbey, I handed him the chocolate wrapped in paper.

"What is this, *monsieur?*" he asked.

"Your chocolate, Victor. I promised you some if you were a good boy and told the truth. Here it is."

He looked unhappy; there was a wistful look in his eyes, but his delicate jaw was firm as he handed it back to me.

"Forgive me, *monsieur,*" he whispered. "I cannot."

And I couldn't make him take it. As he climbed beside his mother in the back of the jeep, he kept repeating, *"Je ne le peux pas, je ne le peux pas*—I cannot."

Of course I gave the chocolate to his mother. Mme. Cayrou could not imagine what had got into Victor. "He loves sweets so, poor darling," she said. "He is undernourished, like all the children in France. I shall make him take it when we get home. Perhaps someday you will visit us and bring Victor some sweets?"

I was standing beside the jeep. The driver had started the motor. For no reason at all, I seemed to hear again little Victor's girl-like voice saying, "Jim came to see Mama, but Georgia came to see me." Mme. Cayrou was leaning toward me slightly. Her eyes were an open invitation. Her lips were parted. Her whole face seemed transformed. I thought, What, me next? It was just as well that the driver started off then without warning. After all, how do you say, "Not on your life, sister!" in French?

THE ECHO

by Paul Bowles

From *Harper's Bazaar*

—————◆◆◆—————

AILEEN pulled out her mirror, which the vibration of the plane shook so rapidly that she was unable to see whether her nose needed powder or not. There were only two other passengers and they were asleep. It was noon; the tropical sun shone violently down upon the wide silver wings and cast sharp reflections on the ceiling. Far below, the uniform green carpet of the jungle moved slowly by. She was sleepy, but she was also excited to be going to a new home. From her handbag she pulled a folded letter which she read again intently, as if to decipher a meaning that did not lie in the sequence of the words. It was in her mother's script:

AILEEN, SWEET—

I must begin (and finish) this before supper. Prue has just gone out for her shower, and that means that by the time she has Luz (the cook) heat the water and can find José (the gardener) to carry it up on the roof to the tank, it will be about an hour. Add to that the time it takes her to do her actual bathing and to dress, and you can see I'll have just about time for a nice chat.

Perhaps I should begin by saying that Prue and I are sublimely happy here. It is absolute heaven after Washington, as you can pretty well imagine. Prue, of course, never could stand the States, and I felt, after the trouble with your father, that I couldn't face anyone for a while. You know how much importance I have always attached to relaxation. And this is the ideal spot for that.

Of course I did feel a little guilty about running off down here without seeing you. But I think the trip to Northampton would have sealed my doom. I honestly don't believe I could have stood it. And Prue was nervous about the State Department's passing some new law that would prevent citizens from leaving the U. S. because of the disturbed conditions, and so on. I also felt that the sooner we got down here to Jamonocal the more of a home we could make out of the old place, for you to spend your vacation in. And it *is* going to be beautiful. I won't drag out my reasons for not letting you know beforehand or it will sound apologetic, and I know I never have to apologize to you for anything. So I'll leave that and get on. I'm sure anyway that the eight months passed very quickly up there for you.

We have had swarms of men working on the house ever since last October. Mr. Forbes happened to be in Barranquilla for a new American project in the interior, and I wanted to be sure of having him supervise the construction of the cantilever in the foundation. That man is really a prince. They don't come much finer. He was up again and again, and gave orders down to the last detail. I felt guilty about making him work so hard, but I honestly think he enjoyed himself with us girls. In any case it seemed silly, when one of the best architects in the U. S. was right here in Colombia and happened to be an old friend, not to use him when I needed him. Anyway, the old house is now the old wing and the new part, which is so exciting I can't wait for you to see it, is built right out over the gorge. I think there's not likely to be another house like it in the world, if I do say it myself. The terrace makes me think of an old cartoon in the *New Yorker* showing two men looking over the edge of the Grand Canyon, and one is saying to the other: "Did you ever want to spit a mile, Bill? Now's your chance."

We are all installed. The weather has been wonderful, and if Luz could only learn a little more about what white people like to eat and how they like it served, the setup would really be perfect. I know you will enjoy being here with Prue. She and you have many things in common, even if you do claim to "remember not liking her much." That was in Washington and you were, to put it mildly, at a difficult age. Now, as an adult (because you really are one by now), you'll be more understanding, I'm sure. She loves books, especially on philosophy and psychology and other things your poor mother just doesn't try to follow her in. She has rigged up a kiln and studio in the old guest house which you probably don't remember. She works at her ceramics out there all day, and I have all I can do keeping the house tidy and seeing that the marketing is done. We have a system by which Luz takes the list to her brother every afternoon, and he brings the things from town the following day. It just about keeps him fully busy getting up and down the mountain on his horse. The horse is a lazy old nag that has done nothing but plod back and forth between house and the valley all its life, so it doesn't know the meaning of the word speed. But after all, why hurry down here?

I think you will find everything to your liking, and I'm sure you won't require more than five minutes to see that Prue is a dear, and not at all "peculiar," as you wrote in your letter. Wire me as soon as you receive this, and let me know just what week you'll be finishing classes. Prue and I will meet you in Barranquilla. I have a list of things I want you to get me in New York. Will wire it to you as soon as I hear. Prue's bath finished. Must close. Love,

MOTHER.

Aileen put the letter away, smiling a little, and watched the wings diving in and out of the small thick clouds that lay in the plane's way. There was a slight shock each time they hit one, and the world outside became a blinding whiteness. She fancied jumping out and walking on such solid softness, like a character in an animated cartoon.

Her mother's letter had put her in mind of a much earlier period in her life: the winter she had been taken to visit Jamonocal. All she could recall in the way of incidents was that she had been placed on a mule by one of the natives, and had felt a painful horror that the animal would walk in the wrong direction, away from the house toward the edge of the gorge. She had no memory of the gorge. Probably she had never seen it, although it was only a few paces from the house, through a short but thick stretch of canebrake. However, she had a clear memory of its presence, of the sensation of enormous void beyond and below that side of the house. And she recalled the distant, hollow sound of water falling from a great height, a constant, soft backdrop of sound that slipped into every moment of the day—between the conversations at mealtimes, in the intervals of play in the garden, and at night between dreams. She wondered if really it were possible to remember all that from the time when she had been only five.

In Panama there was a plane change to be made. It was a clear green twilight, and she took a short walk beyond the airport. Parakeets were fighting in the upper branches of the trees; suddenly they became quiet. She turned back and went inside, where she sat reading until it was time to go aboard.

There was no one there to meet her when she arrived at Barranquilla in the early hours of the morning. She decided to go into town and take a room in the hotel. With her two valises she stepped outside and looked about for a cab. They had all gone into town with passengers, but a man sitting on a packing case informed her that they would soon be coming back. Then suddenly he said, "You want two ladies?"

"What? No. What do you mean?"

"You want two ladies look for you this night?"

"Where are they?" said Aileen, understanding.

"They want a drink," he answered with an intimate grin.

"Where? Barranquilla?"

"No. Here." He pointed down the dark road.

"Where? Can I walk?"

"Sure. I go you."

"No! No, thanks. You stay here. Thank you. I can go all right. Where is it? How far?"

"O. K."

"What is it? A bar? What's the name?"

"They got music. La Gloria. You go. You hear music. You look for two ladies. They drinking."

She went inside again and checked the bags with an airline employee who insisted on accompanying her. They strode in silence along the back road. The walls of vegetation on each side sheltered insects that made an occasional violent, dry noise like a wooden ratchet being whirled. Soon there was the sound of drums and trumpets playing Cuban dance music.

"La Gloria," said her escort triumphantly.

La Gloria was a brilliantly lighted mud hut with a thatch-covered veranda giving onto the road. The juke box was outside, where a few drunken Negroes sprawled.

"Are they here?" she said out loud, but to herself.

"La Gloria," he answered, pointing.

As they came opposite the front of the building, she caught a glimpse of a woman in blue jeans, and although instantaneously she knew it was Prue, her mind for some reason failed to accept the fact, and she continued to ask herself, "Are they here or not?"

She turned to go toward the veranda. The record had finished playing. The ditch lay in the dark between the road and the porch. She fell forward into it and heard herself cry out. The man behind her said, *"Cuidado!"* She lay there panting with fury and pain, and said, "Oh! My ankle!" There was an exclamation inside the bar. Her mother's voice cried, "That's Aileen!" Then the juke box began to scratch and roar again. The Negroes remained stationary. Someone helped her up. She was inside the bar in the raw electric glare.

"I'm all right," she said, when she had been eased into a chair.

"But, darling, where've you been? We've been waiting for you since eight, and we'd just about given up. Poor Prue's ill."

"Nonsense, I'll recover," said Prue, still seated at the bar. "Been having a touch of the trots, that's all."

"But, darling, are you all right? This is absurd, landing here this way."

She looked down at Aileen's ankle.

"Is it all right?"

Prue came over from the bar to shake her hand.

"A dramatic entrance, gal," she said.

Aileen sat there and smiled. She had a curious mental habit. As a child she had convinced herself that her head was transparent, that the thoughts there could be perceived immediately by others. Accordingly, when she found herself in uncomfortable situations, rather than risk the danger of being suspected of harboring uncomplimentary or rebellious thoughts, she had developed a system of refraining from thinking at all. For a while during her childhood this fear of having no mental privacy had been extended to anyone; even persons existing at a distance could have access to her mind. Now she felt open only to those present. And so it was that, finding herself face to face with Prue, she was conscious of no particular emotion save the familiar vague sense of boredom. There was not a thought in her head, and her face made the fact apparent.

Mornings were hard to believe. The primeval freshness, spilled down out of the jungle above the house, was held close to the earth by the mist. Outside and in, it was damp and smelled like a florist's shop, but the dampness was dispelled each day when the stinging sun burned through the thin cape of moisture that clung to the mountain's back. Living there was like living sideways, with the land stretching up on one side and down on the other at the same angle. Only the gorge gave a feeling of perpendicularity; the vertical walls of rock on the opposite side of the great amphitheater were a reminder that the center of gravity lay below and not obliquely to one side. Constant vapor rose from the invisible pool at the bottom, and the distant, indeterminate calling of water was like the sound of sleep itself.

For a few days Aileen lay in bed listening to the water and the birds, and to the nearby, unfamiliar, domestic sounds. Her mother and Prue both had breakfast in bed, and generally appeared just before the midday meal for a few minutes of conversation until Concha brought the invalid's lunch tray. In the afternoons she thumbed through old magazines and read at murder mysteries. Usually it began to rain about three; the sound at first would be like an augmentation of the waterfall in the distance, and then as its violence increased it came unmistakably nearer—a great roar all around the house that covered every other sound. The black clouds would close in tightly around the mountain, so that it seemed that night would soon arrive. She would ring a small bell for Concha to come and light the oil lamp on the table by the bed. Lying there looking at the wet banana leaves outside the window, with the rain's din everywhere, she felt completely comfortable for the precarious moment. There was no necessity to question the feeling, no need to think—only the subsiding of the rain, the triumphant emergence of the sun into the steaming twilight and an early dinner to look forward to. Each evening after dinner her mother came for a lengthy chat, usually about the servants. The first three nights Prue had come too, carrying a highball, but after that her mother came alone.

Aileen had asked to be put into the old part of the house, rather than into a more comfortable room in the new wing. Her window looked onto the garden, which was a small square of lawn with young banana trees on either side. At the far end was a fountain; behind it was the disordered terrain of the mountainside with its recently cut underbrush and charred stumps, and still further beyond was the high jungle whose frontier had been sliced in a straight line across the slopes many years ago to make the plantation. Here in her room she felt at least that the earth was somewhere beneath her.

When her ankle ceased to pain her, she began going downstairs for lunch, which was served out on the terrace on a table with a beach umbrella stuck in its center. Prue was regularly late in coming from her studio, and she arrived in her blue jeans, which were caked with clay, with smears of dirt across her face. Because Aileen could not bring herself to think what she really felt, which was that Prue was ungracious, ugly, and something of an interloper, she remained emotionally unconscious of Prue's presence, which is to say that she was polite but bored, scarcely present in the mealtime conversations. Then, too, Aileen was definitely uncomfortable on the terrace. The emptiness was too near and the balustrade seemed altogether too low for safety. She liked the meals to be as brief as possible, with no unnecessary time spent sipping coffee afterward, but it never would have occurred to her to divulge her reasons. With Prue around she felt constrained to behave with the utmost decorum. Fortunately her ankle provided her with a convenient excuse to get back upstairs to her room.

She soon discovered a tiny patio next to the kitchen where heavy vines with sweet-smelling flowers grew up an arbor that had been placed at one side. The air was full of the humming of hundreds of bees that clung heavily to the petals and moved slowly about in the air. After lunch she would pull a deck chair into the arbor's shade and read until the rain began. It was a stifling, airless spot, but the sound of the bees covered that of the waterfall. One afternoon Prue followed her there and stood with her hands in her hip pockets looking at her.

"How can you take this heat?" she asked Aileen.

"Oh, I love it."

"You do?" She paused. "Tell me, do you really like it here, or do you think it's a bloody bore?"

"Why, I think it's absolutely wonderful."

"Mm. It is."

"Don't you like it?"

Prue yawned. "Oh, I'm all for it. But I keep busy. Wherever I can work, I get on, you know."

"Yes, I suppose so," said Aileen. Then she added, "Are you planning on staying long?"

"What the hell do you mean?" said Prue, leaning backward against the house, her hands still behind her. "I live here."

Aileen laughed shortly. To anyone but Prue it would have sounded like a merry, tinkling laugh, but Prue narrowed her eyes and thrust her jaw forward a bit.

"What's so funny?" she demanded.

"I think you're funny. You're so tied up in knots. You get upset so easily. Perhaps you work too hard out there in your little house."

Prue was looking at her with astonishment.

"God Almighty," she said finally, "your I.Q.'s showing, gal."

"Thank you," said Aileen with great seriousness. "Anyway, I think it's fine that you're happy here, and I hope you go on being happy."

"That's what I came to say to you."

"Then everything's fine."

"I can't make you out," said Prue, frowning.

"I don't know what you're talking about," replied Aileen, fingering the pages of her book impatiently. "It's the most pointless conversation I've ever had."

"That I *don't* think," Prue said, going into the kitchen.

The same evening, when her mother came for her usual after-dinner chat, she looked a little unhappy.

"You don't seem to be getting on very well with Prue," she said reproachfully, as she sat down at the foot of the bed.

"Why, we get on perfectly well. Oh. You're talking about this afternoon, probably."

"Yes, I am, probably. Really, Aileen. You simply can't be rude to a woman her age. She's my guest, and you're my guest, and you've got to be civil to each other. But she's always civil and I have a feeling you're not."

Aileen caught her breath and said, "I'm your guest . . ."

"I invited you here for your vacation and I want things pleasant, and I don't see the slightest reason why they shouldn't be."

Suddenly Aileen cried, "She's a maniac!"

Her mother rose and quickly left the room.

In the quiet days that followed, the incident was not mentioned by any of them. Aileen continued to haunt the little patio after lunch.

There came a morning sweeter than the rest, when the untouched early mist hung inside her bedroom, and the confusion of shrill bird cries came down with perfect clarity from the uncut forest. She dressed quickly and went out. There was a white radiance in the air that she had never seen before. She walked along the path that led by the native huts. There was life stirring within; babies were crying and captive parrots and songbirds laughed and sang. The path swung into a stretch of low trees that had been planted to shield the coffee bushes. It was still almost nocturnal in here; the air was streaked with chill, and the vegetable odors were like invisible festoons drooping from the branches as she walked through. A huge bright spider walked slowly across the path at her feet. She stood still and watched it until it had disappeared in the leaves at one side. She put her hand over her heart to feel how insistently it was beating. And she listened to its sound in her head for a moment, not wanting to break into its rhythm by starting to walk again. Then she began to walk ahead fast, following the path upward toward the lightest part of the sky. When it came out suddenly onto an eminence directly above the plantation, she could barely discern the cluster of roofs through the mist. But here the sound of the waterfall was stronger; she supposed she was near the gorge, although there was no sign of it. The path turned here and went along rough open ground upward. She climbed at a steady gait, breathing slowly and deeply, for perhaps half an hour, and was surprised to find that the jungle had been cut away on all sides in this portion of the mountainside. For a time she thought the sky was growing brighter, and that the sun was about to break through, but as the path leveled out and she was able to see for some distance ahead, she saw that the mist was even thicker up here than down below.

At certain points there was a steep declivity on each side of the path. It was impossible to see how deeply the land fell away. There were a few nearby plants and rocks, the highest fronds of a tree fern a little beyond, and white emptiness after that. It was like going along the top of a wall high in the air. Then the path would make a wide turn and go sharply upward and she would see a solitary tree above her at one side.

Suddenly she came up against a row of huts. They were less well made than those down at the plantation, and smaller. The mist was full of woodsmoke; there was the smell of pigs. She stood still. A man was singing. Two small naked children came out of the door of one hut, looked at her a moment in terror, and ran quickly back inside. She walked ahead. The singing came from behind the last hut. When she came opposite the hut, she saw that it was enclosed by a tangled but effective fence of barbed wire which left a runway about six feet wide all the way around. A young man appeared from the farther side of the closed-in space. His shirt and pants were tattered; the brown skin showed in many places. He was singing as he walked toward her, and he continued to sing, looking straight into her face with bright, questioning eyes. She smiled and said, *"Buenos días."* He make a signaling gesture, rather too dramatically. She stopped walking and stood still, looking hesitantly back at the other huts. The young man signaled again and then stepped inside the hut. A moment later he came out, and still staring fascinatedly at her, made more summoning motions. Aileen stood perfectly quiet, not taking her eyes from his face. He walked slowly over to the fence and grasped the wire with both hands, his eyes growing wider as he pressed the barbs into his palms. Then he leaned across, thrusting his head toward her, his eyes fixing hers with incredible intensity. For several seconds they watched each other; then she stepped a little nearer, peering into his face and frowning. At that point with a cry he emptied his mouth of the water he had been holding in it, aiming with force at Aileen's face. Some of it struck her cheek, and the rest the front of her dress. His fingers unclenched themselves from around the wire, and straightening himself, he backed slowly into the hut, watching her face closely all the while.

She stood still an instant, her hand to her cheek. Then she bent down, and picking up a large stone from the path, she flung it with all her strength through the door. A terrible cry came from within; it was like nothing she had ever heard. Or yes, she thought as she began to run back past the other huts, it had the indignation and outraged innocence of a small baby, but it was also a grown man's cry. No one appeared as she passed the huts. Soon she was back in the silence of the empty mountainside, but she kept running, and she was astonished to find that she was sobbing as well. She sat down on a rock and calmed herself by watching some ants demolish a bush as they cut away squares of leaf and carried them away in their mouths. The sky was growing brighter now; the sun would soon be through. She went on. By the time she got back to the high spot above the plantation the mist had turned into long clouds that were rolling away down the mountainside into the ravines. She was horrified to see how near she stood to the ugly black edge of the gorge. And the house looked insane down there, leaning out over as if it were trying to see the bottom. Far below the house the vapor rose up from the pool. She followed the sheer sides of the opposite cliff upward with her eye, all the way to the top, a little above the spot where she stood. It made her feel ill, and she stumbled back down to the house with her hand to her forehead, paying no attention to the natives who greeted her from their doorways.

As she ran past the garden a voice called to her. She turned and saw Prue washing her hands in the fountain's basin. She stood still.

"You're up early. You must feel better," said Prue, drying her hands on her hair. "Your mother's been having a fit. Go in and see her."

Aileen stared at Prue a moment before she said, "I was going in. You don't have to tell me."

"Oh, I thought I did."

"You don't have to tell me anything. I think I can manage all right without your help."

"Help isn't exactly what I'd like to give you," said Prue, putting her hands into her pockets. "A swift kick in the teeth would be more like it. How do you think I like to see your mother worrying about you? First you're sick in bed, then you just disappear into the goddam jungle. D'you think I like to have to keep talking about you, reassuring her every ten minutes? What the hell d'you think life is, one long coming-out party?"

Aileen stared harder, now with unmasked hatred. "I think," she said slowly, "that life is pretty awful. Here especially. And I think you should look once in the mirror and then jump off the terrace. And I think Mother should have her mind examined."

"I see," said Prue, with dire inflection. She lit a cigarette and strode off to her studio. Aileen went into the house and up to her room.

Less than an hour later, her mother knocked at her door. As she came into the room, Aileen could see she had been crying only a moment before.

"Aileen darling, I've got something to say to you," she began apologetically, "and it just breaks my heart to say it. But I've got to."

She stopped, as though waiting for encouragement.

"Mother, what is it?"

"I think you probably know."

"About Prue, I suppose. No?"

"It certainly is. I don't know how I can ever make it right with her. She told me what you said to her, and I must say I found it hard to believe. How could you?"

"You mean just now in the garden?"

"I don't know where you said it, but I do know this can't go on. So I'm just forced to say this. . . . You'll have to go. I can't be stirred up this way, and I can tell just how it'll be if you stay on."

"I'm not surprised at all," said Aileen, making a show of calm. "When do you want me to leave?"

"This is terribly painful——"

"Oh, stop! It's all right. I've had a vacation and I can get a lot of work done before the term starts. Today? Tomorrow?"

"I think the first of the week. I'll go to Barranquilla with you."

"Would you think I was silly if I had all my meals up here?"

"I think it's a perfect idea, darling, and we can have nice visits together, you and I, between meals."

Now, when the tension should have been over, somehow it was not. During the four nights before she was to leave, Aileen had endless excruciating dreams. She would wake up in the darkness too agonized even to move her hand. It was not fear; she could not recall the dreams. It was rather as if some newly discovered, innermost part of her being were in acute pain. Breathing quickly, she would lie transfixed for long periods listening to the eternal sound of the waterfall, punctuated at great intervals by some slight, nearby nocturnal noise in the trees. Finally, when she had summoned sufficient energy to move, she would change her position in the bed, sigh profoundly, and relax enough to fall back into the ominous world of sleep.

When the final day came, there was a light tapping on her door just after dawn. She got up and unbolted it. Her mother was there, smiling thinly.

"May I come in?"

"Oh. Good morning. Of course. It's early, isn't it?"

Her mother walked across to the window and stood looking down at the misty garden.

"I'm not so well today," she said. "I'm afraid I can't take you to Barranquilla. I'm not up to getting onto a horse today. It's just too much, that three-hour trip to Jamonocal, and then the train and the boat all night. You'll just have to forgive me. I couldn't stand all three. But it won't matter, will it?" she went on, looking up at last. "We'll say good-by here."

"But, Mother, how can I go alone?"

"Oh, José'll go all the way to Barranquilla with you and be back by Wednesday night. You don't think I'd let you go off by yourself?"

She began to laugh intensely, then stopped suddenly and looked pensive.

"I rather hate to be here two nights without him, but I don't see any other way to get you down there by tomorrow. You can go shipside to Panama. There's usually a seat somewhere. Now, breakfast, breakfast. . . ."

Patting Aileen's cheek, she hurried out and downstairs to the kitchen.

The birds' morning song was coming down from the forest; the mist lay ragged in the tops of the great trees up there. Aileen shifted her gaze to the garden at her feet. Suddenly she felt she could not leave; in a sense it was as if she were leaving love behind. She sat down on the bed. "But what is it?" she asked herself desperately. "Not Mother. Not the house. Not the jungle." Automatically she dressed and packed the remaining toilet articles in her overnight case. But the feeling was there, imperious and enveloping in its completeness.

She went downstairs. There was the sound of voices and the clatter of china in the kitchen. Concha and Luz were preparing her breakfast tray. She went out and watched them until everything was ready.

"*Ya se va la señorita?*" said Concha sadly.

She did not answer, but took the tray from her and carried it through the house, out onto the terrace, where she set it on the table. Everything on the terrace was wet with dew and moisture from the gorge. She turned the chair cushion over and sat down to eat. The sound of the waterfall took her appetite away, but she thought, "This is the last time." She felt choked with emotions, but they were too disparate and confused for her to be able to identify any one of them as outstanding. As she sat there eating intently, she was suddenly aware that someone was watching her. She started up and saw Prue standing in the doorway. She was wearing pajamas and a bathrobe, and in her hand she held a glass of water. She looked very sleepy.

"How are you?" she said, sipping her water.

Aileen stood up.

"We're all up bright and early this morning," Prue went on cheerily.

"I'm—leaving. I've got to go. Excuse me, it's late," mumbled Aileen, glancing about furtively.

"Oh, take your time, gal. You haven't said good-by to your mother yet. And José is still saddling the nags. You've got a lot of grips with you."

"Excuse me," said Aileen, trying to slip past her through the doorway.

"Well, shake," Prue said, reaching for Aileen's hand.

"Get away!" cried Aileen, struggling to keep clear of her. "Don't touch me!" But Prue had succeeded in grasping one frantic arm. She held it fast.

"A dramatic entrance is enough. We don't have to have the same sort of exit. Say good-by to me like a human being." She twisted the arm a bit, in spite of herself. Aileen leaned against the door and turned very white.

"Feel faint?" said Prue. She let go of her arm, and holding up her glass of water, flicked some of it into Aileen's face with her fingers.

The reaction was instantaneous. Aileen jumped at her with vicious suddenness, kicking, ripping, and pounding all at once. The glass fell to the stone floor; Prue was caught off her guard. Mechanically, with rapid, birdlike fury, the girl hammered at the woman's face and head, as she slowly impelled her away from the doorway and across the terrace.

From Prue's lips came several times the word "God." At first she did very little to defend herself; she seemed half asleep as she moved toward the outer edge beneath the onslaught. Then suddenly she threw herself to the floor. Aileen continued to kick her where she lay doubled over, trying to protect her face.

"Nobody! Nobody! Nobody! Nobody can do that to me!" she cried rhythmically as she kicked.

Her voice rose in pitch and volume; she stopped for an instant, and then, raising her head, she uttered the greatest scream of her life. It came back immediately from the black wall of rock across the gorge, straight through the noise of water. The sound of her own voice ended the episode for her, and she began to walk across the terrace.

Concha and Luz stood frightened in the doorway; it was as if they had come to watch a terrible storm pass over the countryside. They stepped aside as Aileen walked through.

Outside the stable, José was whistling as he finished saddling the horses. The valises were already strapped on the burro.

Still in the midst of her deep dream, Aileen turned her head toward the house as they rode past. For a brief second, between the leaves, she saw the two figures of her mother and Prue standing side by side on the terrace, the wall of the gorge looming behind. Then the horses turned and began to descend the trail.

HOMECOMING
by Ray Bradbury
From *Mademoiselle*

"Here they come," said Cecy, lying there flat in her bed. "Where are they?" cried Timothy from the doorway. "Some of them are over Europe, some over Asia, some of them over the Islands, some over South America!" said Cecy, her eyes closed, the lashes long, brown, and quivering.

Timothy came forward upon the bare plankings of the upstairs room. "Who are they?"

"Uncle Einar and Uncle Fry, and there's Cousin William, and I see Frulda and Helgar and Aunt Morgiana and Cousin Vivian, and I see Uncle Johann! They're all coming fast!"

"Are they up in the sky?" cried Timothy, his little gray eyes flashing. Standing by the bed, he looked no more than his fourteen years. The wind blew outside; the house was dark and lit only by starlight.

"They're coming through the air and traveling along the ground, in many forms," said Cecy, in her sleeping. She did not move on the bed; she thought inward on herself and told what she saw. "I see a wolflike thing coming over a dark river—at the shallows—just above a waterfall, the starlight shining up his pelt. I see a brown oak leaf blowing far up in the sky. I see a small bat flying. I see many other things, running through the forest trees and slipping through the highest branches; and they're *all* coming this way!"

"Will they be here by tomorrow night?" Timothy clutched the bedclothes. The spider on his lapel swung like a black pendulum, excitedly dancing. He leaned over his sister. "Will they all be here in time for the Homecoming?"

"Yes, yes, Timothy, yes," sighed Cecy. She stiffened. "Ask no more of me. Go away now. Let me travel in the places I like best."

"Thanks, Cecy," he said. Out in the hall, he ran to his room. He hurriedly made his bed. He had just awakened a few minutes ago, at sunset, and as the first stars had risen, he had gone to let his excitement about the party run with Cecy. Now she slept so quietly there was not a sound. The spider hung on a silvery lasso about Timothy's slender neck as he washed his face. "Just think, Spid, tomorrow night is Allhallows Eve!"

He lifted his face and looked into the mirror. His was the only mirror allowed in the house. It was his mother's concession to his illness. Oh, if only he were not so afflicted! He opened his mouth, surveyed the poor, inadequate teeth nature had given him. No more than so many corn kernels—round, soft and pale in his jaws. Some of the high spirit died in him.

It was now totally dark and he lit a candle to see by. He felt exhausted. This past week the whole family had lived in the fashion of the old country. Sleeping by day, rousing at sunset to move about. There were blue hollows under his eyes. "Spid, I'm no good," he said, quietly, to the little creature. "I can't even get used to sleeping days like the others."

He took up the candleholder. Oh, to have strong teeth, with incisors like steel spikes. Or strong hands, even, or a strong mind. Even to have the power to send one's mind out, free, as Cecy did. But no, he was the imperfect one, the sick one. He was even—he shivered and drew the candle flame closer—afraid of the dark. His brothers snorted at him. Bion and Leonard and Sam. They laughed at him because he slept in a bed. With Cecy it was different; her bed was part of her comfort for the composure necessary to send her mind abroad to hunt. But Timothy, did he sleep in the wonderful polished boxes like the others? He did not! Mother let him have his own bed, his own room, his own mirror. No wonder the family skirted him like a holy man's crucifix. If only the wings would sprout from his shoulder blades. He bared his back, stared at it. He sighed again. No chance. Never.

Downstairs were exciting and mysterious sounds. The slithering sound of black crape going up in all the halls and on the ceilings and doors. The smell of burning black tapers crept up the banistered stair well. Mother's voice, high and firm. Father's voice, echoing from the damp cellar. Bion walking from outside the old country house lugging vast two-gallon jugs.

"I've just got to go to the party, Spid," said Timothy. The spider whirled at the end of its silk, and Timothy felt alone. He would polish cases, fetch toadstools and spiders, hang crape, but when the party started he'd be ignored. The less seen or said of the imperfect son the better.

All through the house below, Laura ran.

"The Homecoming!" she shouted gaily. "The Homecoming!" Her footsteps everywhere at once.

Timothy passed Cecy's room again, and she was sleeping quietly. Once a month she went belowstairs. Always she stayed in bed. Lovely Cecy. He felt like asking her, "Where are you now, Cecy? And *in* who? And what's happening? Are you beyond the hills? And what goes on there?" But he went on to Ellen's room instead.

Ellen sat at her desk, sorting out many kinds of blond, red and black hair and little scimitars of fingernail gathered from her manicurist job at the Mellin Village beauty parlor fifteen miles over. A sturdy mahogany case lay in one corner with her name on it.

"Go away," she said, not even looking at him. "I can't work with you gawking."

"Allhallows Eve, Ellen; just think!" he said, trying to be friendly.

"Hunh!" She put some fingernail clippings in a small white sack, labeled them. "What can it mean to you? What do you know of it? It'll scare the hell out of you. Go back to bed."

His cheeks burned. "I'm needed to polish and work and help serve."

"If you don't go, you'll find a dozen raw oysters in your bed tomorrow," said Ellen, matter-of-factly. "Good-by, Timothy."

In his anger, rushing downstairs, he bumped into Laura.

"Watch where you're going!" she shrieked from clenched teeth.

She swept away. He ran to the open cellar door, smelled the channel of moist earthy air rising from below. "Father?"

"It's about time," Father shouted up the steps. "Hurry down, or they'll be here before we're ready!"

Timothy hesitated only long enough to hear the million other sounds in the house. Brothers came and went like trains in a station, talking and arguing. If you stood in one spot long enough the entire household passed with their pale hands full of things. Leonard with his little black medical case, Samuel with his large, dusty ebon-bound book under his arm, bearing more black crape, and Bion excursioning to the car outside and bringing in many more gallons of liquid.

Father stopped polishing to give Timothy a rag and a scowl. He thumped the huge mahogany box. "Come on, shine this up, so we can start on another. Sleep your life away."

While waxing the surface, Timothy looked inside.

"Uncle Einar's a big man, isn't he, Papa?"

"Unh."

"How big is he?"

"The size of the box'll tell you."

"I was only asking. Seven feet tall?"

"You talk a lot."

About nine o'clock Timothy went out into the October weather. For two hours in the now-warm, now-cold wind he walked the meadows collecting toadstools and spiders. His heart began to beat with anticipation again. How many relatives had Mother said would come? Seventy? One hundred? He passed a farmhouse. If only you knew what was happening at our house, he said to the glowing windows. He climbed a hill and looked at the town, miles away, settling into sleep, the town hall clock high and round white in the distance. The town did not know, either. He brought home many jars of toadstools and spiders.

In the little chapel belowstairs a brief ceremony was celebrated. It was like all the other rituals over the years, with Father chanting the dark lines, Mother's beautiful white ivory hands moving in the reverse blessings, and all the children gathered except Cecy, who lay upstairs in bed. But Cecy was present. You saw her peering, now from Bion's eyes, now Samuel's, now Mother's, and you felt a movement and now she was in you, fleetingly, and gone.

Timothy prayed to the Dark One with a tightened stomach. "Please, please, help me grow up, help me be like my sisters and brothers. Don't let me be different. If only I could put the hair in the plastic images as Ellen does, or make people fall in love with me as

Laura does with people, or read strange books as Sam does, or work in a respected job like Leonard and Bion do. Or even raise a family one day, as Mother and Father have done. . . ."

At midnight a storm hammered the house. Lightning struck outside in amazing, snow-white bolts. There was a sound of an approaching, probing, sucking tornado, funneling and nuzzling the moist night earth. Then the front door, blasted half off its hinges, hung stiff and discarded, and in trooped Grandmama and Grandpapa, all the way from the old country!

From then on people arrived each hour. There was a flutter at the side window, a rap on the front porch, a knock at the back. There were fey noises from the cellar; autumn wind piped down the chimney throat, chanting. Mother filled the large crystal punch bowl with a scarlet fluid poured from the jugs Bion had carried home. Father swept from room to room lighting more tapers. Laura and Ellen hammered up more wolfsbane. And Timothy stood amidst this wild excitement, no expression to his face, his hands trembling at his sides, gazing now here, now there. Banging of doors, laughter, the sound of liquid pouring, darkness, sound of wind, the webbed thunder of wings, the padding of feet, the welcoming bursts of talk at the entrances, the transparent rattlings of casements, the shadows passing, coming, going, wavering.

"Well, well, and *this* must be Timothy!"

"What?"

A chilly hand took his hand. A long hairy face leaned down over him. "A good lad, a fine lad," said the stranger.

"Timothy," said his mother. "This is Uncle Jason."

"Hello, Uncle Jason."

"And over here——" Mother drifted Uncle Jason away. Uncle Jason peered back at Timothy over his caped shoulder, and winked.

Timothy stood alone.

From off a thousand miles in the candled darkness, he heard a high fluting voice; that was Ellen. "And my brothers, they *are* clever. Can you guess their occupations, Aunt Morgiana?"

"I have no idea."

"They operate the undertaking establishment in town."

"What!" A gasp.

"Yes!" Shrill laughter. "Isn't that priceless!"

Timothy stood very still.

A pause in the laughter. "They bring home sustenance for Mama, Papa and all of us," said Laura. "Except, of course, Timothy. . . ."

An uneasy silence. Uncle Jason's voice demanded, "Well? Come now. What about Timothy?"

"Oh, Laura, your tongue," said Mother.

Laura went on with it. Timothy shut his eyes. "Timothy doesn't—well—doesn't *like* blood. He's delicate."

"He'll learn," said Mother. "He'll learn," she said very firmly. "He's my son, and he'll learn. He's only fourteen."

"But I was raised on the stuff," said Uncle Jason, his voice passing from one room on into another. The wind played the trees outside like harps. A little rain spatted on the windows—"raised on the stuff" passing away into faintness.

Timothy bit his lips and opened his eyes.

"Well, it was all my fault." Mother was showing them into the kitchen now. "I tried forcing him. You can't force children, you only make them sick, and then they never get a taste for things. Look at Bion, now, he was thirteen before he . . ."

"I understand," murmured Uncle Jason. "Timothy will come around."

"I'm sure he will," said Mother, defiantly.

Candle flames quivered as shadows crossed and recrossed the dozen musty rooms. Timothy was cold. He smelled the hot tallow in his nostrils and instinctively he grabbed at a candle and walked with it around and about the house, pretending to straighten the crape.

"Timothy," someone whispered behind a patterned wall, hissing and sizzling and sighing the words, *"Timothy is afraid of the dark."*

Leonard's voice. Hateful Leonard!

"I like the candle, that's all," said Timothy in a reproachful whisper.

More noise, more laughter, and thunder. Cascades of roaring laughter. Bangings and clickings and shouts and rustles of clothing. Clammy fog swept through the front door. Out of the fog, settling his wings, stalked a tall man.

"Uncle Einar!"

Timothy propelled himself on his thin legs, straight through the fog, under the green webbing shadows. He threw himself across Einar's arm. Einar lifted him.

"You've wings, Timothy!" He tossed the boy light as thistles. "Wings, Timothy; fly!" Faces wheeled under. Darkness rotated. The house blew away. Timothy felt breezelike. He flapped his arms. Einar's fingers caught and threw him once more to the ceiling. The ceiling rushed down like a charred wall. "Fly, Timothy!" shouted Einar, loud and deep. "Fly with wings! Wings!"

He felt an exquisite ecstasy in his shoulder blades, as if roots grew, burst to explode and blossom into new, moist membrane. He babbled wild stuff; again Einar hurled him high.

The autumn wind broke in a tide on the house, rain crashed down, shaking the beams, causing chandeliers to tilt their enraged candle lights. And the one hundred relatives peered out from every black, enchanted room, circling inward, all shapes and sizes, to where Einar balanced the child like a baton in the roaring spaces.

"Enough!" shouted Einar, at last.

Timothy, deposited on the floor timbers, exaltedly, exhaustedly fell against Uncle Einar, sobbing happily. "Uncle, uncle, uncle!"

"Was it good, flying? Eh, Timothy?" said Uncle Einar, bending down, patting Timothy's head. "Good, good."

It was coming toward dawn. Most had arrived and were ready to bed down for the daylight, sleep motionlessly with no sound until the following sunset, when they would shout out of their mahogany boxes for the revelry.

Uncle Einar, followed by dozens of others, moved toward the cellar. Mother directed them downward to the crowded row on row of highly polished boxes. Einar, his wings like sea-green tarpaulins tented behind him, moved with a curious whistling and through the passageway; where his wings touched they made a sound of drumheads gently beaten.

Upstairs, Timothy lay wearily thinking, trying to like the darkness. There was so much you could do in darkness that people couldn't criticize you for, because they never saw you. He *did* like the night, but it was a qualified liking; sometimes there was so much night he cried out in rebellion.

In the cellar, mahogany doors sealed downward, drawn in by pale hands. In corners, certain relatives circled three times to lie down, heads on paws, eyelids shut. The sun rose. There was a sleeping.

Sunset. The revel exploded like a bat nest struck full, shrieking out, fluttering, spreading. Box doors banged wide. Steps rushed up from cellar damp. More late guests, kicking on front and back portals, were admitted.

It rained, and sodden visitors laid their capes, their water-pelleted hats, their sprinkled veils upon Timothy who bore them to a closet. The rooms were crowd-packed. The laughter of one cousin, shot from one room, angled off the wall of another, ricocheted, banked and returned to Timothy's ears from a fourth room, accurate and cynical.

A mouse ran across the floor.

"I know you, Niece Leibersrouter!" exclaimed Father.

The mouse spiraled three women's feet and vanished into a corner. Moments later a beautiful woman rose up out of nothing and stood in the corner, smiling her white smile at them all.

Something huddled against the flooded pane of the kitchen window. It sighed and wept and tapped continually, pressed against the glass, but Timothy could make nothing of it, he saw nothing. In imagination he was outside staring in. The rain was on him, the wind at him, and the taper-dotted darkness inside was inviting. Waltzes were being danced; tall thin figures pirouetted to outlandish music. Stars of light flickered off lifted bottles; small clods of earth crumbled from casques, and a spider fell and went silently legging over the floor.

Timothy shivered. He was inside the house again. Mother was calling him to run here, run there, help, serve, out to the kitchen now, fetch this, fetch that, bring the plates, heap the food—on and on—the party happened around him but not to him. The dozens of towering people pressed in against him, elbowed him, ignored him.

Finally, he turned and slipped away up the stairs.

He called softly, "Cecy. Where are you now, Cecy?"

She waited a long while before answering. "In the Imperial Valley," she murmured faintly. "Beside the Salton Sea, near the mud pots and the steam and the quiet. I'm inside a farmer's wife. I'm sitting on a front porch. I can make her move if I want, or do anything or think anything. The sun's going down."

"What's it like, Cecy?"

"You can hear the mud pots hissing," she said, slowly, as if speaking in a church. "Little gray heads of steam push up the mud like bald men rising in the thick syrup, head first, out in the broiling channels. The gray heads rip like rubber fabric, collapse with noises like wet lips moving. And feathery plumes of steam escape from the ripped tissue. And there is a smell of deep sulphurous burning and old time. The dinosaur has been abroiling here ten million years."

"Is he done yet, Cecy?"

"Yes, he's done. Quite done." Cecy's calm sleeper's lips turned up. The languid words fell slowly from her shaping mouth. "Inside this woman's skull I am, looking out, watching the sea that does not move, and is so quiet it makes you afraid. I sit on the porch and wait for my husband to come home. Occasionally, a fish leaps, falls back, starlight edging it. The valley, the sea, the few cars, the wooden porch, my rocking chair, myself, the silence."

"What now, Cecy?"

"I'm getting up from my rocking chair," she said.

"Yes?"

"I'm walking off the porch, toward the mud pots. Planes fly over, like primordial birds. Then it is quiet, so quiet."

"How long will you stay inside her, Cecy?"

"Until I've listened and looked and felt enough; until I've changed her life some way. I'm walking off the porch and along the wooden boards. My feet knock on the planks, tiredly, slowly."

"And now?"

"Now the sulphur fumes are all around me. I stare at the bubbles as they break and smooth. A bird darts by my temple, shrieking. Suddenly I am in the bird and fly away! And as I fly, inside my new small glass-bead eyes I see a woman below me, on a boardwalk, take one two three steps forward into the mud pots. I hear a sound as of a boulder plunged into molten depths. I keep flying, circle back. I see a white hand, like a spider, wriggle and disappear into the gray lava pool. The lava seals over. Now I'm flying home, swift, swift, swift!"

Something clapped hard against the window. Timothy started.

Cecy flicked her eyes wide, bright, full, happy, exhilarated.

"Now I'm *home!*" she said.

After a pause, Timothy ventured, "The Homecoming's on. And everybody's here."

"Then why are you upstairs?" She took his hand. "Well, ask me." She smiled slyly. "Ask me what you came to ask."

"I didn't come to ask anything," he said. "Well, almost nothing. Well, oh, Cecy!" It came from him in one long rapid flow. "I want to do something at the party to make them look at me, something to make me good as them, something to make me belong, but there's nothing I can do and I feel funny and, well, I thought you might . . ."

"I might," she said, closing her eyes, smiling inwardly. "Stand up straight. Stand very still." He obeyed. "Now, shut your eyes and blank out your thoughts."

He stood very straight and thought of nothing, or at least thought of thinking nothing.

She sighed. "Shall we go downstairs now, Timothy?" Like a hand into a glove, Cecy was within him.

"Look, everybody!" Timothy held the glass of warm red liquid. He held up the glass so that the whole house turned to watch him. Aunts, uncles, cousins, brothers, sisters!

He drank it straight down.

He jerked a hand at his sister Laura. He held her gaze, whispering to her in a subtle voice that kept her silent, frozen. He felt tall as the trees as he walked to her. The party now slowed. It waited on all sides of him, watching. From all the room doors the faces peered. They were not laughing. Mother's face was astonished. Dad looked bewildered, but pleased and getting prouder every instant.

He nipped her, gently, over the neck vein. The candle flames swayed drunkenly. The wind climbed around on the roof outside. The relatives stared from all the doors. He popped toadstools into his mouth, swallowed, then beat his arms against his flanks and circled. "Look, Uncle Einar! I can fly, at last!" Beat went his hands. Up and down pumped his feet. The faces flashed past him.

At the top of the stairs before knowing it, flapping, Timothy heard his mother cry, "Stop, Timothy!" far below. "Hey!" shouted Timothy, and leaped off the top of the well, thrashing.

Halfway down, the wings he thought he owned dissolved. He screamed. Uncle Einar caught him.

Timothy flailed whitely in the receiving arms. A voice burst out of his lips, unbidden. "This is Cecy! This is Cecy!" it announced, shrilly. "Cecy! Come see me, all of you, upstairs, first room on the left!" Followed by a long trill of high laughter. Timothy tried to cut it off with his tongue, his lips.

Everybody was laughing. Einar set him down. Running through the crowding blackness as the relatives flowed upstairs toward Cecy's room to congratulate her, Timothy banged the front door open. Mother called out behind him, anxiously.

"Cecy, I hate you, I hate you!"

By the sycamore tree, in deep shadow, Timothy spewed out his dinner, sobbed bitterly and threshed in a pile of autumn leaves. Then he lay still. From his blouse pocket, from the protection of the matchbox he used for his retreat, the spider crawled forth. Spid walked along Timothy's arm. Spid explored up his neck to his ear and climbed in the ear to tickle it. Timothy shook his head. "Don't, Spid. Don't."

The feathery touch of a tentative feeler probing his eardrum set Timothy shivering. "Don't, Spid!" He sobbed somewhat less.

The spider traveled down his cheek, took a station under the boy's nose, looked up into the nostrils as if to seek the brain, and then clambered softly up over the rim of the nose to sit, to squat there peering at Timothy with green gem eyes until Timothy filled with ridiculous laughter. "Go away, Spid!"

Timothy sat up, rustling the leaves. The land was very bright with the moon. In the house he could hear the faint ribaldry as Mirror, Mirror was played. Celebrants shouted, dimly muffled, as they tried to identify those of themselves whose reflections did not, had not ever appeared in a glass.

"Timothy." Uncle Einar's wings spread and twitched and came in with a sound like kettledrums. Timothy felt himself plucked up like a thimble and set upon Einar's shoulder. "Don't feel badly, Nephew Timothy. Each to his own, each in his own way. How much better things are for you. How rich. The world's dead for us. We've seen so much of it, believe me. Life's best to those who live the least of it. It's worth more per ounce, Timothy, remember that."

The rest of the black morning, from midnight on, Uncle Einar led him about the house, from room to room, weaving and singing. A horde of late arrivals set the entire hilarity off afresh. Great-great-great-great and a thousand more great-greats Grandmother was there, wrapped in Egyptian cerements. She said not a word, but lay straight as a burnt ironing board against the wall, her eye hollows cupping a distant, wise, silent glimmering. At the breakfast, at four in the morning, one-thousand-odd-greats Grandmama was stiffly seated at the head of the longest table.

The numerous young cousins caroused at the crystal punch bowl. Their shiny olive- pit eyes, their conical, devilish faces and curly bronze hair hovered over the drinking table, their hard-soft, half-girl half-boy bodies wrestling against each other as they got unpleasantly, sullenly drunk. The wind got higher, the stars burned with fiery intensity, the noises redoubled, the dances quickened, the drinking became more positive. To Timothy there were thousands of things to hear and watch. The many darknesses roiled, bubbled, the many faces passed and repassed. . . .

"Listen!"

The party held its breath. Far away the town clock struck its chimes, saying six o'clock. The party was ending. As if at a cue, in time to the rhythm of the clock striking, their one hundred voices began to sing songs that were four hundred years old, songs Timothy could not know. They twined their arms around one another, circling slowly, and sang, and somewhere in the cold distance of morning the town clock finished out its chimes and quieted.

Good-bys were said, there was a great rustling. Mother and Father and the brothers and sisters lined up at the door to shake hands and kiss each departing relative in turn. The sky beyond the open door colored and shone in the east. A cold wind entered.

The shouting and the laughing bit by bit faded and went away. Dawn grew more apparent. Everybody was embracing and crying and thinking how the world was becoming less a place for them. There had been a time when they had met every year, but now decades passed with no reconciliation. "Don't forget, we meet in Salem in 1970!" someone cried.

Salem. Timothy's numbed mind turned the word over. Salem, 1970. And there would be Uncle Fry and Grandma and Grandfather and a thousand-times-great Grandmother in her withered cerements. And

Mother and Father and Ellen and Laura and Cecy and Leonard and Bion and Sam and all the rest. But would he be there? Would he be alive that long? Could he be certain of living until then?

With one last withering wind blast, away they all went, so many scarves, so many fluttery mammals, so many sere leaves, so many wolves loping, so many whinings and clustering noises, so many midnights and ideas and insanities.

Mother shut the door. Laura picked up a broom.

"No," said Mother, "we'll clean up tonight. We need sleep first."

Father walked down into the cellar, followed by Laura and Bion and Sam. Ellen walked upstairs, as did Leonard.

Timothy walked across the crape-littered hall. His head was down, and in passing a party mirror he saw himself, the pale mortality of his face. He was cold and trembling.

"Timothy," said Mother.

He stopped at the stair well. She came to him, laid a hand on his face. "Son," she said. "We love you. Remember that. We all love you. No matter how different you are, no matter if you leave us one day," she said. She kissed his cheek. "And if and when you die, your bones will lie undisturbed, we'll see to that. You'll lie at ease forever, and I'll come see you every Allhallows Eve and tuck you in the more secure."

The house was silent. Far away the wind went over a hill with its last cargo of small dark bats, echoing, chittering.

He walked up the steps, one by one, crying to himself all the way.

THE SKELETON AND THE EASTER LILY

by Bessie Breuer

From *Harper's Bazaar*

IN THE BEGINNING their hands lazily repeated motions they had made since childhood summers on other beaches. Then as the castle grew into splendid height, with ramparts, moats, drawbridges, and a garden improvised of palm and pine and sea grape and flowering Spanish bayonet, their hands worked with purpose and pride, and the forts and outbuildings spread over an area of sand so wide that the behatted old women with skirts tucked up would slosh into the water or detour to the upper sands, or stand still to oh and ah, and the girl and boy would politely smile their thanks, and go on with their work. And the spectators they would politely go on with their endless work of preying for shells from the sea's recurring discard.

And they worked on, sand-gritty and very happy, until along came another trespasser, and she also said, How lovely, and they smiled, and then he felt the tide's lacy foam tickling at his toes, and at the selfsame moment a rampart fell, invaded by the sea, and they furiously began patching and rebuilding, racing against time and tide.

Quickly their hands flew, and the woman dropped to her knees and helped, scrabbling at the chunks of wet sand, and soon the ramparts stood high and twice as thick and solid. They sank back, but the woman did not go on. Her gray eyes wandered all over his face and body, and she said, "You look like my son. Exactly."

"That's just what that nurse at the hospital said about her son," the bride cried. "Remember?" The bridegroom frowned. He did not want to remember. (*Old Hatchet Face with her blasted cooing cheer.*

And how are we *this morning, Lieutenant? Let's try. . . . Just once,* Lieutenant. Pulease.)

"Hospital?" The woman's eyes stared and her hands dropped. "Oh," her voice came lighter, higher. "Look at those wonderful coquinas!" A froth of rainbow-hued coquinas bubbled in the foamy tide around her feet, gasping for survival. She scooped up a handful and patted them into a sand rampart. "Let's make it coquina all over —like a mosaic, shall we? Coquina Castle!" She looked up with eyes too keen, voice too feverish, hands that robbed them of their possession.

The boy arose abruptly. "I'm tired. I'm going home." His bride smiled placatingly at the woman, but followed, and caught up with him at the door of their palm-shaded and very modern cottage. "What on earth?"

"It's that woman, butting in." She was gone, the girl told him. But by the time they came back their castle had become a lump of high formless sand, its sharp fine towers dribbled, its garden a bit of sea drift.

"Drat her," he muttered.

"It's your blue eyes and yellow hair."

"My bones. Some skinny runt that kid of hers must be."

"My Skeleton Bridegroom," said the girl softly. They sat on their rug, facing each other, each with a knee updrawn, like a sculptured frieze, self-contained. She looked at her bridegroom, his back hunched in a great arc, his belly accordion-ridged. His shoulder bones under the pitiful thin flesh were wide as the top frame of a harp. The sun was striking on each shoulder, tender-knobbed as a young goat's, and every rib gleamed against its concavity in shadow. The sun-gleaming lozenges of smooth muscle, the lean strings of tendon plainly pinned to the huge buckle of knee. Oh Beautiful is My Love, the Tender Knobs of his shoulders, his Ribs, his Sinews so strongly corded.

"You're all ridges," she observed. "Long ridge, short ridge, round ridge, bumps and bones." She looked carefully away from his sun-splattered head. "If ever you fill out like these creamy-smooth boys loping along the beach, I think"—she paused—"I *think* I'll hate it, Mr. Gandhi."

Bliss. Oh love, love, love, the single words floated weakly awash. The world all love, the tender-stilted birds all love. Bliss and love and a world all love. . . .

"It's time for our dip," she said, and then sat on, like him. "You know what the doctor said. . . . It's the water that counts."

And still they sat without moving. She looked at him, her dark eyes indrawn. The Lyre of thy Shoulders tender-knobbed all love the white light glancing Golden-Shafted on every rib all love, the Hair of thy Head slabs of butter-pale light all love. . . . My Beloved, my Lyre on Stilts of legs all love. . . .

Maybe his wife, he thought. But more like a tiny-waisted tulip, or a stilted violin. And then that was dropped, for the flower on long and delicate legs rose up, and held out a hand. "It's no use dodging. . . . In we go."

Into the liquid ice. And quickly out. Burning with cold, they ran up the beach, and warming, slowed into a walk. The pin-small dots far up the beach grew into people as they passed. His bride's hand tightened on his—and it was the woman who had spoiled their fun. But any greeting died unsaid. She stared straight ahead and beyond them.

"She's mad at us. You were rude. A nasty, rude man," repeated his bride, and they smiled in easy content.

And very necessary, this amputation, since, on their return from the walk, there the woman was, sitting on the sand near the path that led to their cottage. She might be a new vacationer living in any of the cottages that ran along under the palms and Australian pines. He'd had a gullet full of talk—endless years it seemed in the ward-room. Now this, a silence that was a song, and the sweet words of continuous assent a song, no tensions, no sharp debate, no minds, no wills in clash.

They dropped on their rug again facing each other. They would sit in this jackknife attitude for hours—the hand lax on the book, the magazine pages whipping unnoticed, dozing, sun-dazed, his sun-gleaming head toward hers, a camellia or hibiscus or oleander like a star in her dark hair. Together they were one—the most complete and delicate organism ever devised. More wonderful than planets and stars, more perfect than a Thunderbolt fighter, more mysterious and subtle than any power of science, and all this metaphysic contained in bodies so fragile. (How many many he'd seen vanish in the sky in balls of flame.)

Yes, he was rude. And he would be rude again. For until that woman had knelt on the sand with them, claiming intimacy, no one had really disturbed their deep and dreamy indolence. Day after day, as it grew warmer, they lay torpid under the sun, or swam, nailheads of sunlight sparkling up from the rippled blue water around them. Or, straddling a blown-up inner tube, they would rock between sea and sky, tide foams sousing them with sheets of silver bubbles instantly obliterated.

It wasn't that they disliked people. They were languidly aware of neighbors passing outside the periphery of their trance, and the bride turned them into images of her fancy. The long-bosomed woman in white bathing suit, on her stately airing, she named The White Heron; a sun-black little man with long straight nose outflung was The Ant Eater. There was Owl and glance-darting Fox, and Mournful Cow munching gossip to another woman. Boss Lion with pallid lumps of powerful flesh and gold-graying mane, who growled his shy Good Morning. And Prancer, a red-flushed Englishman, hip-rolling and stiff-kneed, and Dancer, her little feet stepping delicately high, and many another.

But none of them tried to reach in. They were as remote from them as the cries of the lolloping babies plumping prodigiously along, or the oversweet cooing of the grannies, the flat grieving voices of middle age, or the cawing man voices so powerless and sad. An echo like the muffled thud of boys' feet racing on the tidal sand.

But when that woman passed them on her walks it was the stone rigidity of her self-conscious body, the single dart of her devouring eyes that stabbed through the haze of his well-being. It was the intensity that clutched at him that corded his lean belly in revulsion. He never wanted to feel for people again. The marrow was dried out of his bones by the agony of those who had come too close. Even the suspicion of the most tenuous sort of attachment disturbed him. He wanted the past scooped out of him and the empty shell filled with his present happy state, and forever. No strange woman would knead him into the shape of her loneliness. Let everything stay outside—be an echo. Nothing of heavier substance than these cloud shadows to weigh on body or mind. Only his Bride, the dark seraph, floating in light and joy, and forever.

And that seemed the end of the matter. Although on this single strip of beach and in the little huddle of shops she was to be met with everywhere, her eyes were always averted or she stared blankly ahead.

But sometimes their encounters seemed stronger than chance, more organized by fate. If he appeared at the top end of the single stretch of sidewalk, she rounded the corner at the bottom and they would advance toward each other like two locomotives on a single track, head on. If he went into the post office by one door, she would be entering at the other. If they landed at the pier from a day's fishing there she'd be, sitting on the sea wall, looking straight down at him. Your Shadow, said the Bride, for like a shadow she avoided direct encounter, stepping out of the mail line at the post office, or getting up from the sea wall or crossing the street.

Early in the morning when they alone inhabited the pale, pure ball of world, the land still shadow, the feeding shore birds suspended above their shadows in the mirror swish of sea before the tide drew breath, and the air like a pineapple fresh cut—out of the vast distance a dark spot would move larger and larger, finally resolve into dark shorts and sweater and that unmistakable carriage of head. And just when they were stiffening for the unavoidable encounter she swerved up a path through the grass, her head inclined in silent greeting. A faint smile played around her lips, as if in apology for her presence in their private world. Following the print of her bare feet on the wet sand, her delicate avoidance preyed on them and they carried her dark, slender image in their mind.

"Her son can't be very old," said he. And his Bride answered, "About nineteen, I should imagine." The sun struck gold above the trees and the sea slipped up the beach in rosy lavender sheen. And feet swishing along in the water, he stopped suddenly and exclaimed, "Where in Sam Hill is he?" And the Bride answered, "In prep school or maybe college." "Or drafted," said he.

"Probably," said the Bride. And then they took their dip, and raced out, hungry for their breakfast.

Sometimes, walking far up the beach, they would come upon her solitary figure lying inert, and something about her stillness made them quickly look away. She would be standing right behind them, sprung up from nowhere. Or, when the boy stood reluctant before his swim, the waves roiling sand, and shells grinding at his lean shanks, down along the beach a figure would cut into the water, in, in, swerving and thrown back by the breakers, but doggedly advancing. Was it design or the strong tide that brought her always nearer, a woman alone in all that heavy sea, jumping or diving through the onrushing head foams, half turned toward him as though she were coaxing him on. . . . Come come, my boy. Bitterly he'd run back and burrow in the warm rug, and when he'd heave and turn she had vanished from sea and beach.

He felt as if she were the monitor of all his actions. It got so he first looked up and down the beach, and somewhere, always around, the turn of her head, the essence of her, amorphous but unmistakable. She became to him a presence, like an eye in a nightmare, huge and inscrutable, that loomed, bodiless, faceless, in the vast sea world, anxious, hovering over, spinning nearer and nearer in glittering vortex, until, at last, the person, the eye, focused precisely down upon him. For, one day, as they came up to their rug from their swim, there she was on the sand near them, the hungry watching eye fastened on him before it closed in seeming sleep. Supine, quiet, like a gull circled softly down to her homing nest, she lay. And day after day, there she remained.

Every day they would find her there—near enough so that no one perched between them, far enough away so that he could not clearly see her features in the brief instant that she turned their way. Always she sat with her back turned to them, a beach hat or towel covering her face when she lay prone in a sun bath.

She has tracked you down, said the Bride. "The Hunter. And the Hunted. The Barnacle, the Limpet." And then she was ashamed. For the woman never trespassed, never set foot on the sand between her and them. And it was this scrupulous care for their privacy, as if she were guarding them, that irritated the boy the most.

With all her stillness she was like a ghost set down in their living room. He had an obscure feeling that she was a shadow of something that might menace his profound well-being. He would look out at her white-capped head, swimming, floating, arms flashing, treading water, and coming up on the beach far below, so that she never passed near. She never presumed. She never sat on the charred bole of coconut tree where he liked to sit until the water dripped off his body. And when his Bride and he lay in the hot and blinding sand so long that they seemed all burning glowing light, existing on a shelf below the green-glittering transparent walls of water racing toward them, he would heave and turn, suddenly across the sand he would catch her eyes, profound and grave and burning, holding his like a thick rope spinning, before, with an almost visible jerk, her eyes would disengage, her body turn ostentatiously away.

Now there were times when the Bride did not come down to the beach. For a little while she must be very careful, the doctor said. And while she took a nap the boy would take his book and go down to the sand. And always the woman was there.

Once when for a day or more the woman's place was empty, and nowhere did they come across her, on the beach or in the village, he finally spoke of it. His Bride said that the season was coming to the end, and like Owl and Prancer and Dancer, and the rest, she had probably disappeared forever.

"I'm glad," said the Bride. "Sometimes she stared at the empty sand between us as if it were the Promised Land itself."

What nonsense of his Bride's poetic imagining. The whole thing was a figment, ridiculous, fantastic. Yet time after time that day he looked toward *her* sand, as if a shape could be stared into being, wondering where she was, what had happened. He would go back to his book, his sense of loss a puzzle to him.

And then, between the turning of one page and another, there she was, quiet, settled as a dove, her head, her body turned away from them as always.

A strange sensation overwhelmed him. He got up and plunged into the waves, and dry sobs shook his body. Why? he asked himself. What is it? And did not come out of the water until he was calmed out of this strange emotion.

Now only nine more days were left of their honeymoon. They would leave early Monday after Easter. Her Skeleton Bridegroom was disappearing. His great chest was smooth now, his belly and his arms like doeskin. But still he was not, she observed, a fatty. The outlines of his body remained pure and fine, all honey-brown, his hair paler than taffy.

"She'll miss you," said the Bride. "But then maybe she'll disappear before us, the way people do . . . go back to that son of hers."

Easter Sunday morning he found his uniform laid out, from the gray tunic with the gold wings and every medal ribbon carefully pinned on, down to the black socks and his black shoes polished.

Gently he shook his head, and went to the closet and took out his new civilian suit. He would consent to go to the tiny community church, since she wanted it so badly, but the other was over, forever.

Inside the shingled building that stood out of the sand on stilts, the white glare, the suffocating blend of oak varnish, altar flowers and women's perfumes in the hot and restive air. The reluctant, shy mumbling of the responses, the smooth-flowing modulation of the rector. This my Body My Blood . . . Broken for Thee . . .

Broken for Thee. In what communion? thought the boy. Surely not in love. How could these devout ones know, thought the boy, how empty the symbol . . . how monstrous the unreason? His nerves began to race in bitterness. Through the weary gravity of the minister intoning he saw again the dark heaving water, heard the splash of the canvas bags, the chaplain's words blown thinly in the breeze. His Bride's hand touched his. His arm trembled under the shock. Closer to the bone than she . . . the bone itself, and flesh of his flesh; every lumpy canvas bag himself, every plane disintegrating in the mocking nothingness of air, himself. If I forget thee Oh Israel . . . What a fool he had been to think it could ever be forgotten, that this fairy tale of the last two months was life, and forever. He was dead dead dead. For him as for them there would be no resurrection.

The lady violinist scraped away, and the high pure voices of the four little girls primped in a row quavered on the Hallelujah.

They arose for the final blessing. After it the sudden stir and scrape of chairs, the burst of happy voices as people turned toward each other. They stood waiting while families ahead of them surged into the one aisle, met and clotted in greeting with others. Why were they here, the sly and the cynical, the unfortunate and the hopelessly lost? What did they hope for? Whom did they propitiate by their coming? He searched their faces, and for the moment all were open and pure, and turned in kindness to one another, the weak and the old, the resigned and the evil and hard and proud, the girls and boys, expectant and glowing . . . and his bitterness melted into pity. He could tell them. There would be no transfigurations today, the poor things. But if any fables could give them comfort, they were more than welcome.

They reached the aisle. At first he did not recognize her, the sundark woman all in white moving toward them from the opposite row of chairs.

"Good morning." She spoke to them without constraint. Her face, her eyes were warm and smiling, and her hands went out to them, and then she shepherded them before her as if they were her cherished possession as slowly they moved up toward the door.

After the rector's handclasp they turned and she stood with them, her face as glad as if she had always known them. "I'm so glad you came." She patted the Bride's hand. "Thank you for coming," and she looked from one to the other and back again. It was love, radiant and grave, that poured out of her large eyes, that trembled on her lips. And then she turned and swiftly walked away to the rack of religious tracts that stood outside the door in the sunshine.

Down on the street the Bride asked quietly, "Did you see it?"

"Yes." His voice was so cold she thought he could not have understood.

"Inside her coat I mean . . . when it flapped open. The gold star over the wings?"

"Yes." His profile was stony, rigid.

"Oh," his wife breathed softly. "I know now—I have the perfect name for her . . . The Easter Lily."

He did not answer.

"Well, then, The Madonna, the Resurrection Lily? Yes?" His Bride was smiling up at him, asking his approval.

A nameless desolation choked him. For one terrible moment he stared down into the sweet face turned up to his, and her gay brightness seemed stupid, unfeeling and cruel. Hate filled him.

"Come." His fingers closed down on her hand, crushing it, his voice harsh. "Let's get out of this. Quick."

"Oh . . . please." She pulled away from him. A shadow came into her wildly innocent eyes, staring up at him. The first wound, dark, and apprehensive.

He remembered, and now he recognized. The burning eye of the woman had spun and completed the coil of pain and connection. Terror and pity for this gay young girl overcame him. He felt like crying.

His arm went around her.

Carefully he subdued his stride to the measure of her slender feet walking.

THE HOT DAY

by Jane Cobb

From *McCall's*

———————◆◆◆———————

THEY had quarreled before, so cruelly and so continually that it was finally as though there were no separate quarrels but only an endless, rank-growing banyan tree of dissent, in which every grievance, every resentment in their life together rooted itself and sent up fresh shoots. There was no longer any escaping from it; it was the last reality they shared—evil, life-sucking, all-consuming.

She awoke into the quarrel as she awoke into the sick, sticky dawn. Hostility tore at her lungs and stomach, and she was aware of it in the same physical sense that she felt the slippery sweat roll down her body, or the little clammy line where her damp hair lay against her neck. She lay face down and stiffly still, listening to him curse thickly at the alarm clock. She did not stir nor open her eyes as he swung heavily from his bed, though her awareness of him twisted her stomach from the mattress and her spine ached against the small of her back. Not until the bathroom door clicked safely behind him was it possible to slide out of bed, pull on her clothes and slip noiselessly down to the kitchen.

It was a big kitchen, ponderous with the yellow-brown varnish of the early nineteen-hundreds, expensive and ugly. The cupboards were too high and too big, the sink resisted all cleansing powders and remained defiantly dingy, the ancient kerosene stove smoked greasily. The first summer they had spent at his parents' "cottage" —he always spoke of it in direct quotes—she had been amused at this museum piece designed for four servants and a butler who rakishly discarded his tails in deference to the simple life. Later the manifold inconveniences had annoyed her. Now she scarcely noticed the kitchen at all, so great was her preoccupation with mortal strife.

She brought his food into the breakfast room, a sunny octagon with french windows looking over the garden. They were both silent. They had quarreled nearly all night, stimulated by whisky, by coffee, by resentment. Now she served his eggs and toasted his bread with no comment, and he accepted them with a nod. Her throat closed against food and she was sick with bitterness against him, but she could not remember how the quarrel had begun, nor into what strange irrelevancies it had taken them.

Regarding him now, across the table, her anger seemed a little grotesque. It was absurd to feel so intense a dislike of this man, this normal, average-looking man in the neat palm-beach suit, whose immediate plans were to finish his coffee, drive to the station and blend, indistinguishably, with the rest of the commuters. You could hate a man who had done you a great wrong—you might even forgive him—but Arthur? She had nothing to forgive him for, and, in any case, he would dislike being forgiven.

"Well," he said, rising, "good-by."

"Good-by."

"Try to be a little less sullen when I get home, will you?"

"I might try," she said, smiling the even-tempered smile that most annoyed him, "if you'd ever give me any reason for it."

He hesitated only a moment and then slammed out of the house. He had, as he frequently pointed out, a business to attend to.

She sat staring out of the french windows, listening to the familiar sound of the engine roaring, subsiding, roaring again and then fading away.

Did he *have* to say that? she asked herself dramatically. Did he *have* to? And all the time she knew that of course he had to, just as she had to smile maddeningly and make the reply she had made. Between them they formed an irresistible machine, gears turning against each other to drive them both deeper into suffering.

She left the dishes untidily on the table and climbed through the french window out into the garden. The early sun was pale in a sky the color of skimmed milk, and the garden was filled with mist. Silver tendrils curled among the red peonies, and she waded knee-deep in white sheets of fog hanging over the wet lawn. Absently she realized that this was a familiar sight, that it had been seen before:

> *. . . that turquoise dawn*
> *When we stood on our mist-hung velvet lawn.*

That was one of the things Arthur disliked in her, the helpless associativeness of her mind, as reflex as knee jerks.

"For God's sake, do you have to be a walking book of Bartlett's *Familiar Quotations?*" he demanded. "Always an appropriate poem for every occasion?"

Well, *The Chinese Nightingale* was no poem for this occasion. A little something by Edgar Allan Poe, she thought. Or perhaps:

> *Mephis:* Where are you damned?
> *Faustus:* In hell.
> *Mephis:* Why this is hell, nor am I out of it.

She was wryly pleased. You can move over, Mephis, old boy. I'm right there with you. Funny thing about the peonies. Though I suppose hell is just the place for big red peonies.

This burst of fantasy, she realized at once, was a mistake. For months now, the slightest contemplation of any object destroyed its wholesomeness for her. She could regard it without intentness, or even interest, and somehow, through no volition on her part, it became riddled with evil. Now the viable horror in the back of her mind suggested slyly, in a way not altogether to be disbelieved, that the peonies suffered, that they dripped blood, that they were evil souls in a poison-scarlet pain.

She wrenched her mind away from them. Just full of pretty notions this morning, aren't we? Here comes the milkman, walking straight into hell, with two quarts of Grade B. Bet you didn't know you were in hell, milkman. Or maybe you do. Maybe you carry your own around with you and spread it over whatever landscape is handy. Like other people I could mention.

She wandered aimlessly about the lawn, kicking off her moccasins so that shreds of wet grass stuck to her feet. Arthur's parents had gone in heavily for rhododendron, mock orange, laurel and spruce. There were brief periods of clotted bloom, but after early summer the place was a jungle of blackish green. In previous years she had tried to lighten it with zinnias and marigolds, but now the quarrel had taken all her vitality, and her hands fell limp at her sides at the thought of planting seeds.

She heard the clink of glass behind her. The milkman was returning.

"Good morning," she said.

The milkman smiled. Wryly? Out of his own private horror?

"Good morning, Mrs. Parton. Hot enough for you?"

"It is awfully hot."

"Be worse before it's better," said the milkman cheerily. "Going to be a regular scorcher."

"I think you're right."

The milkman resumed his clinking way to his truck, and she looked again at the spruces. She disliked them particularly at this time of year, when they looked to her like pyramids of many-fingered hands with dangling green fingertips. But briefly the milkman's words changed them. Her cozy, one-family hell was invaded suddenly by the smell of hot sun on pine.

A scorcher, she thought, a hot day. That had been an event when she was a child, when the hot-pine smell had permeated her summer days. She remembered the picnic baskets, the shiny stuffed eggs, the festive, early morning swims, the iced lemonades, the aspics that sparkled through the cool meals.

"It's going to be a scorcher," everyone had said. "Let's make ice cream, let's eat at the beach, let's spend the day in the water."

Now, she reflected, it meant simply physical discomfort piled on the mental. That was the trouble with hell-building. You destroyed everything else.

The sun was growing stronger now, and the mists were burning off, but she knew it would never become a day of glittering light and dark shadows. That was not the way of scorchers. They patterned themselves blurrily, pale yellow and pale green almost fusing in the shimmer of pale blue heat.

Already the house would be cooler than the out-of-doors, but she disliked the house; disliked its forty-year-old aura of white duck and canvas shoes, wicker furniture and heavy-handed informality. She started toward it, turned away and, without bothering to close the french windows, made her way to the gate.

The street was heavily shaded and lined with summer cottages, big, brown-shingled, frequently cupolaed. Few retained their former grandeur. Some were empty, with boarded windows and knee-high grass growing shaggily from the doorstep to the gate. Most of them, however, were boardinghouses filled with noisy, two-week vacationists. Arthur hated these people, resented their intrusion on the select Elysium of his youth.

"God!" he would say. "Half the Bronx is sprawling and squalling over the Hollanders' lawn."

"It isn't the Hollanders' lawn," she would remind him sweetly. "It belongs to a Mrs. Shrumberger. And I have no doubt that the people of the Bronx need sunlight quite as much as the Hollanders."

Actually, she supposed, she didn't care for noise and crowds any more than he. Her reply was made simply, in inevitable obeisance to their mutual damnation.

Damnation was, in a way, a better word than hell. Hell was, after all, warm and busy—the red flames leaping. Damnation was colder, lonelier, more suggestive of life blighted, doomed and decaying.

The lake lay flat and slippery as glass under the colorless sky. Only the deep-water cove had color; pine-green and paint-white, in exact imitation of the trees and cottages that edged it. Each little boat lying at anchor had another of its kind hung from its water line, upside down and motionless in the still harbor. On the beaches outside the cove the water lay still and clear upon the sand.

She put on her bathing suit in the old splintery bathhouse Arthur had rented for the summer. It was a point of pride with Arthur to prefer these to the newer, airier cement houses. Usually the dank cell filled her with choking resentment, but today she was too hot to think of anything but reaching the water quickly.

The white sand burned her feet, and the water near the shore was warm as soup. She disliked the lake. To anyone accustomed to the strong, salt tides of the Atlantic, fresh, land-bound water was insipid, the little chopping waves as annoyingly unadventurous as the slapping of kittens' paws. She mentioned this to Arthur whenever he praised the water, whenever he returned from a swim refreshed.

Nevertheless, driven by the heat, she swam far out, and the rhythm of swimming drugged her. Coolness embraced her gradually, with no shock, and she began to take pleasure in the air-clear water —its light feel, the sweet taste on her lips, the pale green of the under-surface light. When she emerged, dripping on the beach, she had a positive sense of physical well-being, a delighted realization of hot sun on cool skin, of blood refreshed and cleansed, of sluggishness rinsed away.

In pure pleasure at this reprieve, however temporary, she smiled, and her smile was returned by a girl sitting on the beach.

"Hi!" said the girl. "How beautifully you swim."

"Thanks," Nan said. "I'm awfully out of practice."

It was a senseless remark, and not even true, but the girl had startled her and she wanted time to look. There was little enough to see.

The girl was young and rosy-cheeked, and she wore her brown hair pinned up untidily, indicating that this was an emergency measure in deference to the hot day. Her smile was easy. Beside her, in a white basket under the striped umbrella, sat a propped-up baby, stout, bald-headed and pompous.

"What a darling baby," Nan Parton said inanely, apprehensively, dreading the moment when the hell-blight would creep over the two, waiting to see the girl grow doughy and stupid and fretful, waiting for the baby to become sticky and smelly and unbeloved before her eyes.

"I'm glad you think he's darling," the girl said, grinning. "Personally, I think he's a riot. He's a cartoonist's dream of a capitalist. I get simply hysterical watching him, and that makes *him* laugh, and then he looks like an Irish politician and that's even worse."

"Like the mayor?" Nan suggested.

The girl was delighted. "*Just* like the mayor! The lifeguard calls the baby Shaughnessy." She looked up the beach. "Where *is* that lifeguard, anyway? I'm dying of heat stroke, and I can't swim till he comes back to keep an eye on Joe."

It was silly to offer. It was the last thing she wanted to do. But because the girl and her baby still remained immune from the involuntary malignance of her vision Nan said: "I'll watch him for you."

The girl accepted without too many dramatic protestations. The baby wouldn't really need any attention, she said, and the lifeguard was coming down the beach now.

Nan sat beside the baby even after the lifeguard arrived. She watched him count and recount his fingers. Once he opened his mouth and said, "A-a-a-a-ah," and she thought he was going to cry, but he was only exploring the possibilities of his vocal cords. His preoccupation with his own development excluded her completely and she found him restful.

"He's been very good," she reported to his mother.

The girl glowed with the simple, animal pleasure of a cat displaying its kitten. "He *is* good," she said, and then, unable to drop the subject, "he's really no trouble at all. On a hot day like this I'd expect him to fuss terribly, but he doesn't at all. I wouldn't blame him if he did. I've been in a foul humor all morning."

"So have I," Nan said and regarded her with awe.

She was invulnerable. In the withering shadow of Nan's contemplation she remained untouched by it, no sharer of damnation, no hell-caster in her own right, a brown girl in a white bathing suit toweling her hair. If her face was round, if her eyes were clear and shallow, if she spoke with the exaggerated cadences of a schoolgirl, it was not to her discredit.

Nan sat beside the girl, soaking herself into the scene. This picture from a picture book—pale-gold sand, pearl-blue water, slices of green and scarlet screaming on a quarter globe of canvas, and two girls (both of them pretty, mind you, both of them slim and golden) sitting beside the shell-pink baby—surely it was proof against the seeking fingers of damnation.

The girl's name was Marion, and her talk was as light and easy as her name. Problems of housekeeping and baby-tending absorbed her, not in the hypnotized manner of a cow chewing its cud, but as new and fascinating problems, part of her growing up. Listening to her was like listening to the baby's experiments with his vocal cords.

"I'm in a sort of jam now," Marion said, "because I forgot to ask his doctor about his cod-liver oil before we came up here. I mean, with all this sun he's surely getting enough vitamin D. Doesn't something awful happen if they get too much?"

"You cut down his cod-liver oil in the summer," Nan said. "But don't stop it entirely. Just give him enough to keep him used to the taste so he'll take it in the fall."

Her mind was filled—cluttered, Arthur said in irritation—with odd bits of quite accurate and entirely unrelated information. She seemed hopelessly unable to forget anything, and for years had remained inexorably familiar with the manner of the formation of Roxbury puddingstone, with the plots of Disraeli's novels, and with the type of cactus used by the Papago Indians in the brewing of fermented beverages. She was humbly grateful when one of her scraps of knowledge worked its way into a useful niche.

"That's marvelous," Marion said. "I haven't given him any today, but I will as soon as we get home. Which reminds me——" She rummaged in the baby's basket and produced a watch on a leather fob. "Darn!" said Marion. "It's time for his dinner right now. Every time I turn around it's time for that child to eat."

"I expect I ought to get some lunch too," Nan said. "I didn't eat any breakfast." The sickness of the early morning reappeared, thickening about her, dark and choking.

She was startled at the matter-of-factness of Marion's voice. "I didn't eat much either," Marion said. "It was so hot and everything's so hectic in the mornings. Look—why don't you come along with me? I can feed Joe and we'll fix some iced tea and stuff. We won't even bother to get out of our bathing suits."

She was smiling, clear-eyed and companionable. She was innocent in the best sense of the word—empowered to walk in light through darkness.

"I'd love to," Nan said.

Their exodus was complicated, involving the folding of beach pads, struggles with the umbrella and a change of pants for the baby. Ordinarily Nan liked to come and go easily, without clutter, but today she shared Marion's tranquillity which put all minor mishaps beyond the possibility of irritation.

Marion's house was one of the new ones, less than a block from the lake, and it was impossible to tell what it was like since its entire atmosphere was absorbed by the baby. His crib and bathinette were prominently displayed, and his bottles and sterilizer took up half the kitchen. Big squares of diapers and little squares of shirts hung in complicated tiers on the furniture, and the front room was almost invisible beneath the pink and white and pale blue of his toys, rattles and discarded garments. The effect, however, was less squalid than wind-blown, and good-humoredly rowdy.

Marion made no apologies, and as she fed Joe she laughed continually at the green spread of spinach across his face, at the spurts of regurgitated milk, at his howls for faster service. Nan was astonished at the active pleasure she took in watching. She was astonished, too, to find that she enjoyed the lunch they prepared, that tomatoes and mayonnaise were fresh and sharp, that iced tea was fragrant. For a long time food had been tasteless, not worth the bother of chewing and swallowing.

They sat lazily on the screened porch, their feet propped up, grateful for the dampness of their bathing suits. Outside, the little garden lay drowned in heat, blue and red petunias limp on their stalks, the shadows motionless on the short, yellowing grass.

Again they talked of the things that interested Marion, babies and grocers and men's colleges. Nan did not ask her questions about herself. She felt, superstitiously, that Marion had a secret, but that she must tell it without being asked. In all fairy stories the secret must reveal itself. To question means to be dismissed from the palace, denied marriage with the prince, returned in rags to the wood chopper's cottage.

"I'll bet it's terrible in town today," Marion said.

"Foul."

"I feel sorry for Bill. Heat always infuriates him."

"It does my husband too."

"Honestly," Marion said, beginning the quick rush of words in which she told stories, "you should have been here this morning. It was already hot, and we were out of coffee and Joe was howling, and Bill couldn't find a shirt. I thought he was going to tear the house apart, and me too. You'd have thought I'd deliberately taken that shirt and buried it, in the dark of the moon."

"There's a demon especially assigned to hide commuter's clothes," Nan said. "It begins to operate about fifteen minutes before train time."

"Well, it's taking its life in its hands around here," Marion said. "Bill was simply appalling. And he couldn't find the demon so he took it out on me. I have never been so sore at anybody in my life.

I could have killed him. Literally. I remember standing in the kitchen and saying out loud, 'I could kill him. I'd really like to kill him.' And then, of course, I got absolutely hysterical, because of course you *can't* want to kill a man just because he's lost a shirt."

Nan drew her breath in sharply. This was it. This was how you lived in the real world; not one so distorted and diseased that the shapes of familiar things were frightening, and horror blew like the desert wind. You cannot wish to kill a man for mislaying his shirt. Neither can you want to kill a man for regretting an ancestral income, and enjoying heavy furniture, any more than a man can kill a woman for forgetting to call the cleaners and remembering too much poetry.

Belatedly she laughed at Marion's story and said something appropriate, but excitement was turbulent within her and in a little while she said she really must be going.

"It's been a wonderful day!" she said, with so much fervor that Marion looked startled.

As well she may, poor lamb. How can she know that I've found the special secret, the magic phrase, the talisman that will save me?

The light was rose-yellow now, like the flesh of a peach, but still not brilliant, still dulled and vaporous. It would be hot when Arthur got home, and perhaps he would like to swim before dinner. She would swim with him through the colorless water, so clear it would be like swimming in the twilight itself. Surely if they did enough things like that together, pleasant, happy things, they would be healed.

She could have what Marion had—a man, a baby, a life lived on the surface of the earth among sunlight and people, not swamped and alone in the underworld. She felt pity for Arthur and great tenderness. *He* was still there. But she would help him out. She could not hate him. He could not hate her. That was the thing to remember.

Hurriedly, she turned to her belated housekeeping, straightening the rooms, ordering the lake bass he enjoyed, clipping peonies from the garden and arranging them in big bowls. She put on her smartest slacks and combed her hair high in the elaborate smoothness that he admired.

Surely there was nothing she had overlooked. They would have cocktails before dinner and a liqueur afterward and he should *feel* that they were celebrating, even if he didn't know what for. It might take a little time, but she was strong and happy and it could be done.

"Hello," Arthur said, opening the door.

"Hello, darling." Nan stood awkwardly while he put down his briefcase and newspaper. It was hard, just at this moment, to choose the right phrases.

"I'm sorry I was rotten last night," she said.

"Oh, you weren't rotten. I guess I was pretty bad myself."

The gesture, classic for this moment, would be to fling herself into his arms and proclaim that they would never, never quarrel again. The thought of behavior so foreign to her, no less than the prospect of his astonishment, daunted her.

He looked about him. "Hey!" he said. "How come you've cut off all the peonies?"

"Well, we didn't have any flowers in the house," she said, "and I thought they'd look nice."

"They look all right," he said. "Only, if you pick them off for the house you never have anything to look at in the garden."

Well, she could hardly have expected him to fling himself into *her* arms and say that all misunderstandings were over now that she had made a home for him.

"Would you like a swim before dinner?"

He shook his head. "It's pretty late. I took a late train. I called you but you weren't in."

"I'm sorry."

"I guess I'll go have a shower. It was hotter than the hinges in town."

"Poor Arthur!"

When he came down she had made cocktails, and he was pleased.

"These are good," he said. "If there's anything I hate it's this quick-snort habit we've gotten into."

They sat companionably in beach chairs on the lawn, watching the pines turn black. A breeze blew in from the lake smelling of reeds and water.

He poured another cocktail. "Say," he said, "where *were* you all day? I called about ten times."

"I was at the lake."

"All that time?"

"I picked up a nice girl and her baby. We had lunch together."

Arthur grew portentous. "Frankly," he said, "I wish you wouldn't do that sort of thing. Remember, this place isn't what it used to be. There's a lot of riffraff hanging around."

"Arthur!" It was impossible to keep the outrage from her voice. "Arthur, for God's sake, don't you think I have any sense? I know a nice girl when I see one, and we had a lot of fun together."

It was Marion, and she saved my soul and she'll save yours—and you call her riffraff.

She tried to stop her next words, but they came in spite of her. "Must you *always* be such a stuffed shirt?" she said.

"If requesting my wife not to have lunch with people she picks up on the beach is stuffy, then I intend to stay that way," Arthur said. "You're sure it *was* a girl, by the way?"

"You can say the most insulting——" she began, and then, with great effort, stopped, trembling a little. "Yes, of course it was a girl, Arthur. Do relax, darling, and drink your drink."

"Nevertheless," Arthur insisted, "after you've said at every opportunity for the past three years that you don't like fresh water, it certainly seems funny that you should spend the whole day at the lake talking to a strange woman. And don't tell me you didn't spend the day there, because I called you every half hour."

"Why don't you hire a detective?" she said. "You'd cut down on your phone bill. What do you mean by spying on me?"

"I wasn't spying on you. I was trying, for God's sake, to tell you I'd be late to dinner, and I find you haven't been home all day. A man has a right to ask his wife where she's been. There surely shouldn't be anything offensive in that."

"No," she said, smiling her controlled, maddening smile. "There shouldn't be anything offensive in that. It's just, Arthur dear, that everything you do and everything you think puts mere swinishness on a very high level of behavior." Her voice grew shrill. "I'll tell you where I was today. I'll tell you all about it and everything that happened and it will serve you right!"

They were there waiting for her, the yawning pit, the hagridden darkness, the undying torment. They were all waiting for her but she did not think of them nor see them, nor remember that this was her last chance to be free of them. She thought only of Arthur, and of giving pain, and she prepared to take her secret, her hot day, her talisman—and smash them against his face.

THE HOLIDAY

by Mary Deasy

From *The Yale Review*

———◆———

By five o'clock they were all up and dressed, the children—Liza, Clay, and Albie—coming downstairs to find their mother and father already in the kitchen eating breakfast.

The light of the early September dawn showed each the commonplace room and the faces of the others in cool aqueous shadow.

Liza went to the door, which stood open in spite of the early morning chill outside, and looked up at the sky.

"Is it going to be a *good* day today?" she said to her father.

"Liza," said Mrs. Froom, "come and eat your breakfast now. Clay—Albie——"

The boys scuffled to their seats.

"A fine day," Matt Froom said to Liza. He was looking at a map which he had spread out on the table before him; his stout shoulders, in a clean white-and-blue shirt, were slightly rounded as he leaned on his elbows, bending his fresh jowled face serenely to the study. "A little fog in the morning at this time of year's a sure sign."

"Maybe we'll get as far as Frankfort," said Clay.

He ate quickly, shoveling his rolled oats into his mouth with eager haste, his eyes lighted in his dark solemn face.

"I shouldn't wonder," said his father. "Might get even farther if we make an early start and the old bus holds out."

"We're goin' on a trip," Clay said to Albie. "You never been on a trip before, Albie."

"I'm goin' now," said Albie stolidly. "I'm goin' clear to Frankfort."

Liza said to Clay: "You don't remember when you were on a

trip either." She was standing behind her father's chair, leaning over his left shoulder while she looked at the map spread out before him. "I'm the only one of us three who remembers that."

"I do too remember," Clay said. "I remember ridin' on the train, and Aunt Bess's house——"

"You were only six months old," said Liza. "You couldn't remember. You only think you do because you've heard us talking about it." She stood up straight, flinging her arms up and catching her hands together behind her head. "Do you know what?" she said. "Sometimes I feel like I remember the big farm Pop's grandfather had over in England. It's like I was really there once, a long time ago; I close my eyes and it seems like I can just see it, the river, and the house, and the hills, and all."

"Liza, come and eat your breakfast now," said Mrs. Froom. She had finished her own, and she got up, clearing a place on the table before her where she could begin to make the sandwiches for their lunch. She stood beside the table, her deft thin fingers moving almost automatically as she talked.

"I've been hearin' about that farm ever since I married your father," she said. "I don't see what good it does to talk about a place you've never even seen. A person might just as well go around braggin' because his folks once lived in the Garden of Eden."

"Pop wasn't bragging," Liza said. "He was just telling us. Weren't you, Pop?"

She ate her rolled oats absently, sitting next to her father and leaning her head sideways so that she could look at the map.

"The Frooms are an unlucky family; I heard that before I ever married your father," said Mrs. Froom. She worked swiftly, her thin mobile ingenuous face, which resembled Liza's, visibly reflecting the trend of her thoughts. "It wasn't only his grandfather losin' his farm and all his money over there in England," she said. "There was his father, he had a nice little place down in Kentucky when he was a young man, and his uncle Lance that had the blacksmith shop in Covington; they both lost every cent they owned, and I wouldn't doubt a bit that if your father'd had anything to lose he'd have lost it too, long before this. It's the way the luck runs in a family sometimes; my grandmother used to say some families had a hex on them."

"We haven't got a hex on our family," Liza said.

"No," said Clay. "We haven't got a hex on our family. We've got an automobile now. I guess we wouldn't have an automobile if we had any old hex on our family."

Mrs. Froom went on making the sandwiches; she wrapped the thick double slices of bread in waxed paper and packed them neatly in a shoe box.

"Maybe we can stop some place and buy a couple of cokes when it's time to eat," she said. "There's no use taking coffee along without a thermos bottle."

"I think we ought to buy a thermos bottle," Liza said. "We'll be going on lots of trips, now that we've got an automobile. We'll be going way out in the country where there isn't even any place to buy a coke."

She finished her rolled oats and got up from her chair again to look out of the door.

"It's getting lighter," she said. "Can't we start pretty soon? The fog's clearing away."

Matt Froom went outside to get the automobile out of the Ferrises' driveway next door, and Clay and Albie went along. Liza helped her mother finish packing the lunch and then ran outside to join the others.

The automobile was standing in front of the house: a black battered touring car, twelve years old. Clay and Albie were sitting in the front seat, pretending to drive, and her father was polishing the windshield with a rag. The street was empty except for the little group before the house. In the foggy gray-violet dawn the close rows of shabby frame houses looked deserted and strange.

In a quarter of an hour they were ready to start. Liza sat in the front seat beside her father; her thin figure, which was just beginning to show the outlines of adolescence beneath the homemade yellow print dress and cotton sweater that she wore, was shaken now and then with a chill of nervous excitement. The whole family felt that there was something splendid and incredible in their riding down the narrow street, past the awakening houses, on their holiday. They spoke in rapid fragments of sentences, as meaningless as the happy morning chirping of birds, turning their eyes eagerly from one side to the other as they watched the familiar houses roll by.

"There's Mr. Howett," Clay said; and Matt Froom sounded the horn while the whole family waved a proud greeting to a neighbor passing, carrying his dinner pail to work.

Matt Froom stopped at a gas station a few blocks away to have the tank filled for the trip. The proprietor, a sandy-haired middle-aged man with sharp-boned red cheeks, said to him as he counted out his change:

"That's some jalopy you've got there all right."

His sly disparaging look set them all more erect in their seats; a sudden chill of dignity descended upon them.

"He just wishes he had an automobile this good himself," Clay said loyally as they chugged away.

Matt Froom sat up straight behind the wheel, smiling a little as he looked through the windshield at the quiet morning streets steadily unrolling before him. Beside him, Liza had already spread the map open upon her knees, though they had not yet left the city behind. Then they crossed the bridge over the broad gray river, where the mist still hung damp and rank-smelling and cool, and in a little while the houses thinned, the sidewalks ended, and quickly, as the red sun climbed in the sky on their left, the morning fields and hills of the country appeared.

There was little traffic; now and then a truck passed, headed towards the city, or a car whirled past them with a smooth rush of sound. The boys, one on each side of their mother, sat on the edge of the seat—staring out of the sides of the car. They pointed, shouting to each other.

"Looky! A horse!"

"Cows! Lots of them! Hey, Albie, look!"

Between them Mrs. Froom sat erect, her eyes, alive with interest in her thin mobile face, moving quickly from one side of the road to the other. She talked to her husband.

"Matt, look at that old house. I'll bet it's more'n a hundred years old."

Or: "I remember my grandpa drivin' me and Bess and Hazel down this way the summer we stayed out at the Kincaids' when Ma was so sick."

Liza sat close to her father; the map, disregarded, fluttered on her knees.

"Look," she said, "when the mist fades off, it's like it was the first day of the world and everything was sparkling new, just waiting for somebody to come and look at it, and smell it, and live in it. It's like it's been waiting here, all wrapped up in the mist, for a long time, maybe just waiting for *us*."

"Maybe it has been," Matt Froom said. "Maybe it has been just waiting for us."

He began to sing:

"What kind of shoes do the angels wear
When they walk around the heavens and through the air?"

He had a nice tenor voice. The others kept time, tapping their feet and nodding their heads.

Everything went smoothly until, a little before nine o'clock, the automobile began driving unevenly and swerving to one side of the road. Matt Froom stopped the car and got out, and when he looked at the tires he found that the left front one was flat.

They all had to get out then and stand at the side of the road while he took off the left front tire and put the spare in its place. The spare was not very good, and he said that they would have to stop at the next gas station and have the flat fixed, because they could not go far on the spare. The mist had fully disappeared by now, and the sun was beginning to be hot. There were no trees around the place where the automobile had stopped, only a field with a billboard in it advertising a brand of shaving cream. Liza and Mrs. Froom stood on the shady side of the automobile while the tire was being changed, and Clay and Albie looked through the fence into the field and tried to catch a grasshopper that they found beside the road.

When the tire was changed they got into the car again, and Matt drove along briskly till they came to the next little town. He drew up at a gas station, and they all got out again and stood around waiting till the left front tire had been fixed. It took nearly two hours to get the tire fixed and put back on the automobile.

The gas station stood on the main street of the little town. They saw the people of the town walking past, going about their day's business in this unfamiliar street that was, however, familiar to them. Another car drove into the gas station, and the proprietor addressed the driver by his first name and spoke to him about some-body called Joe.

"Tell Joe I'll see him tonight," the proprietor said.

When the other car had gone, the proprietor began talking to Matt Froom about the tire.

"I can fix it for you, but I won't guarantee it'll last you very long," he said. "It's in bad shape; all of your tires are pretty bad. My advice to you is to get a whole new set as soon as you possibly can or you'll be having trouble like this all the time."

Mrs. Froom had heard what the gas station man said, and an anxious look settled on her thin ingenuous face.

"Matt, I told you this automobile would get to be too much ex-pense for us to keep up," she said to her husband in a worried voice, speaking low so that the man could not hear her.

She began looking about with a sharp shrewd hard look on her face, the look that always came when she was worried about money.

"Maybe he's only tryin' to sell us something. Don't you buy any-thing off him," she warned Matt in a whisper.

The two boys began to grow noisy and quarrelsome after a while because they were tired of waiting. They teased their mother to let them have the coke she had intended to buy for their lunch till at last she gave them a dime and sent them across the street to a grocery store to buy it there. They came back with the cold dark bottle, and for a little while they were quiet and satisfied; but when the coke was gone they began to get restless and noisy again. The gas station man told them once in a surly voice to keep out of his way, and after that Mrs. Froom spoke to them sharply and made them get into the car and sit beside her. When they had climbed in, however, she did not look at them sharply; instead she gave a defiant ambiguous glance in the man's direction, and then she bent down and straightened Clay's tie and smoothed Albie's hair back out of his eyes.

Even after they had left the gas station and were driving along in the country again the hard shrewd worried look did not go out of Mrs. Froom's face. She sat between the two boys, looking straight ahead instead of at the hills and fields and houses that they were passing.

"Matt, how much did that fellow charge you to fix that tire?" she said.

"Now never mind about that, Sally," Matt Froom said. "We're not going to worry about money on a holiday."

"Was it more'n fifty cents?" Mrs. Froom persisted.

"Well, maybe it was a little more."

"Not more'n a dollar, Matt?"

"Now, Sally, there's no use *worrying* about it," Matt Froom said.

Liza glanced sidewise at him and saw that there was a worried look on his face too. But he noticed that she was looking at him and brightened up at once.

"A trip's not a trip without a little accident," he said. "Now we've had ours we can settle down and enjoy ourselves."

It was close to eleven o'clock when they left the gas station; they had lost almost two hours because of the flat tire. They began to get hungry soon because they had had such an early breakfast, and after they had driven a little while Mrs. Froom told Matt to keep his eye out for a good place to eat their lunch. She thought they might find a roadside park or picnic ground, but they did not find any, and at twelve o'clock they decided to turn off the main road to a side road and park the car. They found a shady spot under some trees and stopped there. It was a quiet pretty place; only every once in a while another car would pass and the people inside would stare at them sitting around outside the automobile and eating their lunch.

Mrs. Froom sat on the running board of the automobile with the shoe box beside her from which she distributed the sandwiches, and the rest of them sat on the grass beside the road. The sandwiches tasted dry without anything to drink with them, but Mrs. Froom said that they could not afford any more cokes, and the water that they had brought along in a half-gallon canning jar was hot and had a queer rubbery taste.

When they had finished eating their sandwiches they sat around for a while looking at the trees and the fields and the dusty road with self-conscious and uncertain expressions on their faces. When another automobile passed by they averted their eyes and pretended to be looking at something in another direction. They were afraid that someone would tell them that they had no right to be there. Every time a passing automobile disappeared down the road they felt a sense of relief.

The midday sun was hot. The leaves of the trees hung down and swayed gently in the hot breeze, and the long grass beside the road bent and lifted silently. When there were no automobiles passing they could not hear anything but the hum of insects and the rustle of the trees and the occasional twitter of a bird. They were not used to such a large, pervading, living silence. They spoke instinctively in low voices, and their voices sounded strange and small to them in the large living silence.

Inside the fence beside which they sat was an empty field with a cluster of trees at the far end. Liza stood up and looked over the fence. There was no one in sight.

"Maybe we could go inside a little while," she said to her father.

"Sure," he said. "We won't do any harm."

He got up and began to climb over the fence.

"Matt, maybe you'd better not," said Mrs. Froom.

She shaded her eyes with her hand and looked up the road to see if anyone was coming.

"We won't do any harm," said Matt.

He helped Liza over the fence. She stood looking about her.

"Maybe your grandfather's farm looked like this," she said after a while.

"I wouldn't be surprised," he said.

They walked on a little farther into the field.

"Matt, don't go too far," Mrs. Froom called to him from the other side of the fence.

"Sure. We won't," said Matt.

"Listen to the bees," said Liza. "Listen to how quiet it is. Couldn't you just stay here all day long?"

"It's mighty pretty," said her father.

"And at night," said Liza, "I'll bet it's nice. I'll bet it's cool and smells good and you can't see anything but the trees and the stars. I'll bet it's pretty at night."

She sat down on the grass.

"Liza," called Mrs. Froom.

"I'm not doing any harm," Liza said.

She looked over at the trees, and there was a man coming towards them. She got up in a hurry.

"We'd better go; there's somebody coming," she said to Matt.

She took his hand and tried to pull him away, but he walked

slowly, looking back over his shoulder at the man coming out from behind the trees.

"We weren't doing any harm," he said stubbornly.

The man called out to them: "Hey—you there!"

"Come on, Pop; come on, Pop," Liza said in an urgent frightened voice. "We'd better go."

"Can't you see this is private property?" the man said in a loud voice, walking towards them across the field. "What do you think that fence is for?"

"We weren't doing any harm," Matt Froom muttered defiantly.

He pulled his hand out of Liza's and walked slowly towards the fence, assuming an air of dignity. When he came to the fence, however, he had to climb it, and it was not easy to look dignified climbing a fence. Liza had already scrambled over to the other side. She and Mrs. Froom and the two boys got into the automobile and watched anxiously while Matt climbed the fence and came over to join them.

The man in the field followed them all the way over to the fence and stood leaning on it and looking at them for a few moments while Matt Froom was trying to start the automobile.

"Damn' nervy hillbillies," he said in an audible voice, so that they all could hear.

He turned back into the field, not waiting for them to drive away. They all sat silently in the automobile as it plunged crazily forward up the road. Liza stole a look at her father's face; it was covered with a heavy red flush.

"He's nothin' but a damn' hillbilly himself," Clay blurted out after a while.

Mrs. Froom turned on him with nervous vehemence.

"Clay Froom," she said, "don't you ever let me catch you usin' language like that again! Do you understand me, young man? I'm not goin' to have you boys pickin' up words like that."

"I didn't say anything," Albie said.

"Well, you better not let me catch you," Mrs. Froom said sharply.

She sat tensely erect, folding her hands in her lap and looking straight before her. After they had driven a little while she said: "Matt, don't you think we'd better be startin' back soon?"

"No," he said.

"We want to get back by suppertime," she said.

"No," said Matt.

He kept right on driving. It was full afternoon by that time. They drove on past the trees and the fields and the houses, none of them saying much. A hot wind blew into the car, and they all got thirsty.

About three o'clock the water in the radiator began to boil. Steam and rusty-looking water came spurting out, some of it spattering back on the windshield. Matt Froom got out and took off the radiator cap, unscrewing it with his handkerchief so that he would not burn his hand. The water gurgled and churned up and then subsided. He said he thought that most of the water had either boiled away or leaked away, and that he would have to get some more before they went on.

There was a farmhouse about five hundred yards down the road, and he said that he would try to get some water there. The others sat waiting for him in the automobile. It was hot and dusty. They looked at the other automobiles passing them on the road with silent envy.

"I wisht we had an automobile like that," Albie said, after a big blue one had passed.

"Hush up, Albie," Clay said angrily. "This is a good automobile."

It was almost half an hour before Matt Froom came back carrying a bucket full of water. The bucket was heavy, and he had to carry it carefully so that the water would not spill. He said that he had had a hard time finding anybody on the farm to give him the water.

After he had brought the bucket back to the farmhouse he told them that they would have to turn around and start for home because the radiator seemed to have a leak in it. Nobody said anything against that but Albie.

"This ain't Frankfort," Albie said. "You said we were goin' clear to Frankfort."

"We'll go to Frankfort some other day," Clay said. "We been far enough. We never said we'd get to Frankfort today."

To make Albie feel better they let him sit up in the front seat with his father. There was half a sandwich left from lunch, and Mrs. Froom gave it to him to eat.

The sun began to get low. They drove slowly so that the water in the radiator would not heat up again, but the leak seemed to be getting worse and they had to stop every few miles for more water. They stopped at gas stations, and when the attendants came out Matt Froom said that he only wanted some water. He bought some gas at one station finally because he felt ashamed of always driving in and just asking for water.

At seven o'clock they were still almost twenty miles from home. Albie was so tired that he kept slipping down in the seat till his whole body was slumped against his father's shoulder, and when Matt Froom glanced around he saw the eyes of the other three shining silently in the dusk out of their white dusty faces. They were all hungry. Albie began to cry because he was so hungry. The tears washed little clean channels on his dirty face.

"The next town we come to," Matt Froom said, "we're going to get us something to eat."

He stopped the automobile in front of a place that had a neon sign in the window saying—EAT. They all got out and Mrs. Froom and Liza tried to straighten their crumpled dresses. The children had never been inside a restaurant before, and Mrs. Froom and Matt had not been inside one for more than a dozen years.

There were only a few people inside when they went in. They sat down at the first empty table. The dishes used by the people who had eaten there before them were still on the table: a cup of coffee three-quarters empty, a glass coated inside with a whitish film of milk, plates covered with pastry crumbs and smeared with dark stains of blackberries, crumpled napkins, half-full glasses of water.

A stout blonde waitress in a white dress and a green apron came up and gave them two menus and began to clear the dishes away. Liza read one menu with her father, and Clay read the other over his mother's shoulder.

"We'll just get a sandwich and a cup of coffee," Mrs. Froom said in a voice loud enough for the waitress to hear. "I can fix us a real nice supper when we get home."

The waitress went away with the dirty dishes.

Clay whispered, pointing to the menu over his mother's shoulder: "Mom, they got pie; look at all the different kinds of pie they got. Peach, apple, blackberry, coconut cream, butterscotch——"

"That goes with the dinner," Mrs. Froom said. The hard shrewd worried look was on her face again. "Likely you can't get pie unless you buy the whole dinner. Here's some sandwiches now."

She ran her finger slowly down the list.

"They cost fifteen cents," Clay whispered to her. "They got some that cost twenty-five cents. That's dear, ain't it, Mom?"

He glanced up and saw the waitress standing beside him, listening. He flushed dark scarlet, screwing nervously in his chair.

"I can't say I'm very hungry," Mrs. Froom said, speaking in a bright determined voice. There was a thin red flush on her cheeks too. "Matt, supposin' you and me just have a cup of coffee," she said, "and the children can each have a peanut-butter sandwich."

The waitress took the order and went away again. They sat waiting. A constrained silence fell heavily upon them. They stole glances at the other people eating around them.

Presently the waitress came back again with their order. She set the two cups of coffee down carelessly, and the coffee slopped over into the saucers. The children looked at their peanut-butter sandwiches.

"They ain't very big for fifteen cents," Mrs. Froom said when the waitress had gone again. She began to count: "Three fifteens is forty-five, and ten, that's fifty-five, fifty-five cents for this little dab of food that you can hardly see."

She looked worried. The children ate their sandwiches silently, and she and Matt quickly drank their scalding coffee. Then they all got up. Albie's chair made a loud scraping noise on the floor when he pushed it back, and some of the other people sitting at the tables looked at them. They stood clustered nervously together, waiting for Matt to get out the money to pay the bill.

It was dark when they went outside again. They got into the automobile without saying anything. When they had been driving for about fifteen minutes Clay and Albie began quarreling, and Mrs. Froom had to speak sharply to them. They were all tired, and they were still hungry. In the front seat Liza sat beside her father and silently watched the dark road before them which was faintly lit by the advancing shaft of light from the car. Since the sun had gone down it had turned much cooler, and she shivered a little in her thin cotton sweater.

When they finally reached home it was almost ten o'clock. Matt

Froom put the automobile away in the Ferrises' driveway, and the others went on into the house. They turned on the lights. There was something unfamiliar to them about the familiar rooms. The rooms seemed smaller and darker after the long day outdoors, after the space of the fields and the endless unwinding patterns of the roads. They looked around.

Mrs. Froom went back into the kitchen and fried up some bacon and some boiled potatoes that had been left from supper the day before. The children ate; Albie fell asleep at the table. Mrs. Froom carried him upstairs, and Clay straggled after them. Their footsteps creaked on the flimsy stairs.

Liza and Matt Froom were still sitting at the kitchen table. They were not eating. Liza sat with her cheek propped on her left hand. Her eyes looked big in her thin mobile face.

"Pop——" she said.

"I guess we'd better go to bed," he said.

He pushed back his chair and got up. His ruddy face looked old and flaccid. Liza did not get up. She spoke in a flat voice.

"It seems like we was meant to stay right here," she said. "It seems like this is the only place where we belong."

YOU CAN WRECK IT

by Walter Elder

From *The Kenyon Review*

———◆◆◆———

GEORGE THOMAS LINCOLN and young Paul were friends and partners this summer. George had been working on Paul's father's farm since his return from the Clayton hospital, and now that school was out, Paul could spend every day all day working with George. He carried a hoe and replanted corn with George, two rows to George's four; he cut away the small branches of the locust trees which George cut to make fence posts; he placed tiles along the ditch which George was digging to drain the lower field. Paul's father thought that it was fine for the boy to help on the farm and that George was fit company for any growing boy; Paul's mother wanted him to play with some of the neighbor children, but he was allowed to stay away only two hours at a time. Although they knew plenty of regular games, Paul enjoyed being with George much more than playing with other kids.

The only game which Paul and George played was one in which they tried to outdo each other in the recitation of delicious desserts. There were no rules; one of them, usually George, would start saying "chocolate sundae" or "strawberry parfait," and the other would have to counter with a more complicated, thus more delectable-sounding, confection. George always won, and the prize would go, for instance, to a "pistachio-creamed, melted-honey, burnt-butterscotch, cherry-marshmallow, almond-striped, soda-cream, pineapple upside-down cake." When these games began or concluded where Mrs. Tuttle could hear, she would frown; she told Paul that George was just hinting for some food from her because he spent all his money on that silly Marmon roadster. Even though the game was so

much fun, George and Paul liked talking about the Marmon roadster more than anything else.

George had bought the roadster after Owen Shipley had wrecked
it trying to pass John Cortland one Saturday night on the Forks
River bridge. He had loved the Marmon since Owen had driven it
to Johnson's blacksmith shop the day he had bought it. It was red,
long, and low; the muffler was open, Owen said, "because the exhaust
couldn't handle the engine's power"; the tires had white sidewalls
and the sides of the hood carried six chrome exhaust ports; it had
ninety as the top number on the speedometer, and because it was
slung so low, Owen said, "you can wreck it, but you can't turn it
over." George had shown his love for the Marmon by patting it, by
putting his head under the opened hood and saying, "um-huh," and
by riding several times with Owen on speed runs out and back the
Charleston pike. He laughed and smiled, saying, "yes SIR," as he
watched the speedometer needle and listened to the unmuffled engine.

The Sunday morning after Owen had wrecked the Marmon,
George went out to the bridge with the Cortland garage man and
Johnson, the blacksmith. The car was lying upside down half in
the water of the river, and Owen was standing on the bridge with
his head and left arm bandaged. He told them that the car wouldn't
have turned over if it hadn't rolled down the bank by the bridge
abutment. They clambered down to look at the car, and the garage
man said that it was fit for nothing but junk. He offered to buy it
for twenty-five dollars, and Owen was nodding his head when
George said,

"I'll give you thirty dollars for it."

They looked at George who was staring at the Marmon with tears
in his eyes. They shrugged their shoulders at each other, and George
said,

"Thirty-five dollars, Mr. Shipley."

Johnson turned a wheel with his finger along his temple, and Owen
said,

"You can have it for twenty-five, George, but when do I get my
money?"

Everyone in Cortland knew that George had no money, and that
even though he came from one of the best colored families in the
town, he couldn't borrow from anyone. George had quit school when

he was sixteen and still in the fifth grade. Since then he had worked for Johnson, the blacksmith, for three dollars a week and the use of the shanty next to the blacksmith shop. The shanty had ground enough for a garden plot, but George bought all his groceries. He had sown the yard and garden space with mixed flower seed as if he were sowing timothy, and there was barely a path from the house to the street. Several years ago he had painted the shanty mauve where the vines and the flowers hadn't covered the walls. All the other houses on Freedom Street, where George lived, were neat, white cottages, and his shanty was one of the few dwellings in town which did not have a whitewashed maple tree in the front yard or flower beds bordered with whitewashed limestone slabs.

His sister, who had married Mr. Sloan, proprietor of the local grain and feed store, was always the first to call him shiftless and no-good. She was president of the Women's Society of the colored Baptist Church, and she had given up even his soul after he had splattered the back of her Ford with a Thanksgiving basket of food which the church ladies had been distributing to the colored poor people. She had brought a basket to George's shanty, and instead of leaving it on the porch without knocking, as she had been doing at other places, she put it beside the front door, knocked, and when George came to the door, she began talking about his soul. George saw the basket and shut the door. But as Mrs. Sloan was starting away in her car, George ran out, grabbed the basket of food and slung it at the car, strewing the food all over the back of the Ford. Mrs. Sloan and her children used hair-straightener, and they always wore shoes, even in the summer. Her children played with white children at their houses, except at mealtimes, and they joined all the Cortland children in forbidden explorations of George's flower jungle.

George was not loved nor feared by the children of Cortland; nor were there any complaints against him by the adults except that he did not go to church and that his house was not kept neatly. (No one had ever been in George's house, and he had not entered a Cortland home since he had left school to live in the Johnson shanty.) He collected discarded newspapers and magazines from the barbershop, the pool hall, and the lodge rooms, and since they never appeared again, it was rumored that he had several rooms full of paper, a fire menace in the house. He annoyed the grocer by ordering black caviar, assorted exotic fruits and desserts, but he bought and lived on beans, molasses, and white bread. He worked faithfully for Johnson, but he never seemed to learn anything about blacksmithing except for a few simple, isolated operations. He would take a horseshoe off the forge, cool it after it had been beaten, but then he would have to be told to turn the bellows to heat the iron again.

Shipley, Johnson, and the garage man had never seen George evince strong interest in anything, yet there he stood by the wrecked Marmon with tears in his eyes. They knew that he had enjoyed being around the car and riding in it, but he had seemed just as happy when he had painted his house. They stood by the wreck a while, and they told him that it could never be fixed; that it would cost at least five dollars to haul it out of the river and back to Cortland; that it would be worth about ten dollars for the spare parts which could be stripped from it. Shipley wanted to know how and when George could pay him twenty-five dollars, and Johnson said that he wouldn't lend George a penny. The garage man said that he wouldn't touch the pile of junk unless he got five dollars towing charge cash in advance.

"Please let me buy your car, Mr. Shipley."

The tears rolled down George's cheeks, and Shipley agreed to sell him the Marmon. He kicked one of the crumpled fenders in disgust, and George began to cry and told Shipley,

"You leave my car alone."

George dug out two dollar bills, and the garage man agreed to haul the Marmon to his shanty as soon as he saw the other three dollars. Shipley agreed to take two dollars a week until the twenty-five was paid if George would sign a note to the effect that if he missed more than two weeks in succession he would lose the car. As they climbed up the bank, the garage man and Shipley agreed that their original bargain still held good. George rode back to Cortland with Johnson, and he was smiling and humming as they rode.

The next morning a truck from the junk yard hauled three loads of wastepaper from George's house, and George took three dollars to the garage man. While he waited for his car to be delivered, he cleared the front yard with a scythe and sickle whenever Johnson left him a free minute. The Marmon arrived, still upside down, on the back of a hay wagon towed by the garage wrecker, and the whole street came out to watch the unloading. There was no particular colored section in Cortland, and there were colored and white neighbors present to agree that the Marmon would be another eyesore to the town and that George must be crazy to buy that pile of junk. To unload the car, the wrecker pulled it over the side of the wagon, and it landed right side up, blowing the front and rear tires on the left side as it fell into the new stubble of George's neat front yard. George smiled and told his neighbors,

"See? You can wreck it, but you can't turn it over."

George built a canopy of old pieces of canvas, chicken wire, and scraps of his dilapidated garden fence over the Marmon, and he began to work on it. Since he worked for Johnson all day, he did almost all his banging on the wreck at night and on Sundays. He began by removing all the fenders, the doors, the convertible top, and the hood. These he distributed about the house and yard under the shelter of the back porch, the front porch, and a smaller tent of canvas and fence lumber. These operations involved enough noise to irritate and to interest the neighbors, and since they talked not only among themselves, George became known throughout the town as a harborer of a nuisance, or as a nuisance. The large bangings diminished into more delicate sounds of metal against metal as George turned his attention to the engine. He stopped buying groceries, and with the dollar left after he had paid Owen Shipley each week he combed the Cortland junk yards buying Marmon engine parts.

There was some speculation, principally among the grocer and his customers, about the sources of George's food, but the discussions were never conclusive and more often than not they ended with a jest about God looking after fools and drunkards. With his sober cash customers this was the grocer's favorite joke. He told George's sister that after all, it was only three dollars a week and not worth worrying about. Still he did not find out what George was eating until the same night that the midnight calm of Freedom Street was broken by the roar of a Marmon engine. The noise persisted, and those who went to investigate and to protest found George bending over the hoodless Marmon engine adjusting the carburetor. By the light of two coal-oil lanterns they could see him grinning as he depressed the throttle by hand and released it. The engine roared and idled and backfired and finally died. There was a leak in the gas tank.

That same night George had been seen by a group of children picking through the garbage can behind the Elite Café, and they reported that he had carried away something in a newspaper-wrapped bundle. The adults concluded rightly that George was eating from garbage cans and that this sort of behavior was not to be allowed in Cortland. The garage man said that their reputation as a wholesome community was as important, if not more so, than their sleep, and that something must be done about poor George. He told George's sister that he was amazed that George had made the Marmon engine run, but that something must be done to save him from this obsession which made him stoop to eating what other people had thrown away. The residents of Freedom Street began to mutter more about having their sleep interrupted as George began straightening a bent place in the body frame. The blacksmith said that George was borrowing his tools after work, and he thought that there was a rasp file missing from the shop. Owen Shipley said that George was paying his two dollars a week all right, but he felt as if he were partly responsible for this business of eating out of people's garbage cans. He stopped around to look at the Marmon when George had finished with the wheel rims and was preparing to patch the tires and tubes. George would talk with Owen and with anyone who stopped by only about the Marmon and how he was going to fix it.

Only the young men at Haberkorn's Pool Room said that a colored man ought to know his place, and if he bothered the town, he ought to be shown his place. They did not say this outside their own circle very much. There was no color line in Cortland, and Paul's father reported this conversation as a sign of bad blood. The population of the town was about equally divided between white and colored, and all the children went to the same school. They played on the athletic teams together, had parts in the school plays together, and in Paul's class the boys who ran the gangs were both colored. He remembered once when a new boy had come in from the South, and, basking in the newness of his unprovable stories and his wonderful way of speaking, the white boys had organized. This left the colored boys in a group, and when they approached the white boys had shouted as planned,

"It's going to rain. Here come a bunch of black clouds."

The colored boys looked puzzled as the white boys fled shouting, "black cloud, black cloud," and the groups remained black and white for two days. The third day, as the white boys rounded the corner of the school building, they came on the gang of colored boys who greeted them,

"It's going to snow. Look at all the white clouds."

The colored boys did not flee, and the groups re-formed with much shouting into mixed gangs, including the Southern boy who became a follower, and that was the end of the black and white clouds.

The adults in Cortland maintained more distinctions, but it was said that the white people and the colored people were equal when it came to the ceremonies of birth, marriage, and death. Mixed crowds attended christenings, weddings, and funerals, but the two groups had their own churches and their own doctors; Sunday callers and table guests were always of the same color. Both races traded and worked in the stores; both were elected to municipal offices; both used a handshake for greeting and parting. Paul's father said in his campaign speeches that a man's worth had nothing to do with the color of his skin, and the Republican committeemen were counting on him to carry the big colored seventh ward in the county seat when he ran for re-election to the county commission. Paul remembered how his father had laughed when Paul had come home crying because an older boy had chalked his name and that of Rebecca Kitchen, a colored girl, on the gym wall where he couldn't reach it. His father had asked him if he were thinking of getting married, and Paul had cried all the harder because Rebecca was a girl. There had been no mixed marriages in the memory of anyone in Cortland.

George kept on with his daytime working at the blacksmith shop, his nighttime working on the Marmon, and the payments to Owen Shipley, and he continued to probe garbage cans. The people of Cortland became more and more interested in his welfare, especially since he did not see the necessity of replying to all their questions nor of following all their advices. The grocer, the garage man, and Mrs. Sloan neglected their affairs more and more to worry about George. His sister talked with her lawyer, with her church society, with the people on Freedom Street, and with the justice of the peace. She learned that George was not capable of legal responsibility; that he was on the road to ruin by working on Sundays and not attending church; that he was a nuisance; and that as his nearest of kin she could take certain steps to save the poor boy from starving to death or from bringing shame to the Lincoln family and Cortland.

George took the Marmon, without a hood, doors, top, or fenders, for a trial run on a Sunday morning. The colored Baptist and the white Methodist church services were interrupted three times by the roaring of an unmuffled engine out and back on the Charleston pike. Members of the congregations were told by people who were not at church that George should not be allowed to drive and they mentioned that the car had no license plates and that George had no driver's license. George had learned to drive by watching, but his first actual manipulation of the Marmon was complicated by the fact that brakes on the left side didn't work, and he traced an erratic course. He didn't hit anything and he returned the Marmon to his yard humming because the car ran and because he still had much care to lavish on it. He worked the rest of that Sunday and far into the night, but he was no busier than his sister.

At nine o'clock Monday morning a deputy sheriff called at Johnson's smithy and asked for George Thomas Lincoln. Johnson had just been berating George for his wild, illegal driving of the morning before, and when he saw the deputy's badge, he told George,

"Well, they've come to arrest you now, boy. I told you you was crazy to get that junk pile."

When the deputy asked if he were George Thomas Lincoln, George nodded. When the deputy told him that he had an order to take him to the county courthouse, George looked puzzled. The deputy told him that since he might have to stay a few days, he had better get some clothes and things to take along.

Johnson asked the deputy, "Why can't the Cortland justice of the peace try a traffic case? He always does."

"This appears to be more than a traffic case," said the deputy. "Lincoln's sister has got herself appointed legal guardian of George, and she must have sworn out some sort of complaint. She and her lawyer have been with the judge all morning."

"Can they take my car?" George asked.

The deputy shrugged, "Depends upon what the court decides."

"I live right next door. I'll get my stuff and be right back."

George left the shop, and Johnson and the deputy were talking when they heard a clatter from the yard of George's shanty. They ran over and found George stripping parts from the Marmon and throwing them into the tangle of his uncleared back yard. He stopped when they called to him, went into his house, and came out shortly with a bundle wrapped in a newspaper. He got into the deputy's car and rode to the county courthouse, not saying a word but watching intently all the motions which the deputy made driving.

The meeting in the judge's chambers was brief, and the judge was very kind and gentle to George. He explained to George that his sister was now his legal guardian because she had been worried about him, and that she was willing to take the responsibility of his actions to see that he didn't get into any more trouble. He explained to George how he had broken the law by driving the Marmon without legal permits, and he said that they were going to overlook it this time if he would do something for the judge and Mrs. Sloan. The favor was a slight one. George was to go to Clayton for a few days to talk to some doctors about what he had been doing and what he wanted to do. George agreed and asked a question.

"Who'll take care of my Marmon?"

"No one will bother your car, George. Your sister will be responsible for it while you're gone."

"Do I get it back when I get back?"

"Certainly. Everything is yours when you get back, George, as long as you behave yourself."

George smiled, the judge smiled, Mrs. Sloan and her lawyer smiled, and the judge brought out some papers to sign. After they had all signed their names, George left the judge's chambers with the deputy who had brought him from Cortland. The deputy drove George to Clayton and delivered him and some papers to the office guard at the State Hospital for the Mentally Ill. George watched the deputy drive, and several times he urged him to drive faster.

After George went to Clayton, Johnson found another man to help him in the shop, and the Marmon engine was silent. Mrs. Sloan, Owen Shipley, and the garage man came to look at the car, and after looking at the engine and talking with Johnson, they began kicking around the edge of the back-yard tangle looking for parts. They hired a man to scythe the back yard, and although they found some of the pieces which George had thrown away, the engine still lacked much of the wiring, the carburetor, and the distributor. Mrs. Sloan made an agreement with Shipley to keep up the weekly payments for George, and they agreed further that if the car could be repaired to run the price should rise to one hundred dollars. The garage man was to repair the Marmon. Marmons were scarce around Cortland, and two weeks passed without their being able to locate the necessary parts. They were standing around the car debating how to settle their obligations if the garage man bought the car for junk when a sheriff's car pulled up in front of the shanty, and George got out.

George came back with "a clean bill of health" from the State Hospital. According to the report which the doctors had sent to the judge, and which the judge had called to Paul's father's attention, they had found him "cheerful, co-operative, somewhat childish in his likes, perhaps mentally retarded, but in no way menacing or dangerous." They recommended that the guardianship be continued.

At the hospital George had helped on the laundry truck, finally doing some driving, and he came back to Cortland with a set of license plates for the Marmon, a driver's license for himself, a job on Paul's father's farm, and the same newspaper-wrapped bundle with which he had left. Paul's father had advanced George enough money to buy the legal permits and to pay Shipley the back payments, the loan to be deducted from his wages. He rented his shanty from Johnson for two dollars a week. From the bundle he brought out a mass of engine wiring, a distributor, and a carburetor. Before dark Freedom Street heard the roar of a Marmon engine again.

Paul's father had to spend three mornings a week in his office at the county seat, and he needed a man to help on the farm. He told Paul that there was nothing wrong with George that a little kindness wouldn't cure. George couldn't fit a series of events together, so his work on the farm was a series of repetitive exercises, such as cutting locust trees, replanting corn, and digging ditches. Mr. Tuttle paid him fifteen cents an hour, which was below the standard wage for farm work, but then George couldn't do the feeding, the milking, and the planting. Working ten hours a day six days a week earned him nine dollars a week. He paid Mr. Tuttle two dollars a week on the loan; Shipley two dollars a week for the car; Johnson two dollars a week for the shanty; and he had three dollars a week for the Marmon and groceries. Johnson wouldn't lend him any smithy tools because as he told George,

"I'll have no part in helping you bust your damn-fool neck in that junk pile if and when it runs again."

The garage man said that he couldn't spare any of his tools, so George began to comb the junk yards for wrenches, hammers, a small anvil, and Marmon parts. He found parts where the garage man had found none, and his grocery budget shrank to less than a dollar a week. After George had paid Mr. Tuttle, his payments to Shipley rose to four, sometimes five dollars toward the new price of one hundred dollars.

George was driving the Marmon to and from the Tuttle farm, and even though he wangled some desserts from Mrs. Tuttle, the Cortland children saw him in the garbage cans again. The grocer began to speculate with his customers, and he became more and more annoyed with George's requests for anchovy filets and pistachio nuts. Mrs. Sloan conferred with her lawyer and with her church society, and they agreed that they felt sorry for Mrs. Sloan because her hands were tied. The Marmon appeared with a windshield, red and white checked seat covers, and one day with the left rear fender.

Paul was invited to ride in the Marmon, but Mrs. Tuttle would not hear of it. Paul's father said that the wheels were out of line, that the frame was bent, and God only knew what else George had done to it. Paul liked the Marmon, and he began to share George's love for it through hearing nothing else.

"That'll be the best car in these parts time I get her all fixed up. Her back wheels are a little out of line, but that's the way a dog runs, with his back legs off center, ready to go any direction. She uses some oil; there's a leak in the radiator and one in the gas tank, but I don't buy no more than a dime's worth of gas at a time. She's long and low, and the muffler can't even handle the engine power. She's safe, too. If she hadn't rolled down the bank when Shipley hurt her, she'd never have turned over. You can wreck it, but you can't turn it over."

Paul nodded to this speech many times as the grocer nodded when he confirmed a customer's opinion on the weather or on politics. George nodded when Paul told him what to do on the farm. Paul was the boss, but George always won the "game," and Paul liked to hear about the Marmon. Each seemed to know the other's superiority, and they exchanged grave nods and smiles when Mr. Tuttle gave George nine dollars and Paul seventy-five cents each Saturday.

Paul had a desk, which he called his office, and here he made plans for his allowance. He worked in his office with stacks of discarded stationery pencil stubs, several sporting-goods catalogues, and his newest addition an old copy of *Motoring*. George had given it to him, and it contained a long article with pictures of the Marmon car when it had first appeared on the market. The double-page middle picture was a color drawing of a red roadster with all the trimmings. Paul's computations were concerned now more with the cost of air horns and special mudguards than with catcher's mitts and baseball spikes. This indecision had bolstered his saving to three dollars, and he was ready to buy the first half of a set of air horns to be attached to the outside of the Marmon hood. George knew nothing of this, and Paul fooled him by chanting,

"I know a secret."

George usually thought that it was another dessert from Mrs. Tuttle, and when she sometimes gave him a piece of chocolate cake, he would say,

"Now I know your secret, don't I?"

Paul smiled. This made his secret better.

The day that Paul filled out the mail-order blank for the air horn, the Marmon had a hood with six rather battered, rusty, chrome exhaust ports, three fenders, but no top. Mr. Tuttle decided suddenly to go to the opening of the racing season instead of to the office, so George and Paul were left with few instructions and plenty of time to talk about the car. Paul didn't mail the order, but that seemed to add something to talking about the car.

Paul's father returned about dusk laughing and joking because he had won money betting on the races. He gave Paul a two-dollar bill for his week's allowance, and he gave George a two-dollar bill besides his regular nine dollars. It was almost enough for the other horn, and it was more than enough for something exotic from the grocery.

George drove home, parked the Marmon under the shelter in his front yard, paid Johnson two dollars, paid Shipley seven dollars, and went to the grocery with the two-dollar bill. The store was crowded and the grocer ignored George as long as he could. George kept asking for lemon-meringue pies, broiled lobster, and burnt-almond toffee until the grocer gave up trying to wait on his other customers.

"Damn it, George, I haven't got any of those things, and you don't want any of them. I'll get you your bread and beans in just a minute."

"I don't want bread and beans. I want something scrumptious. I've got a big bill."

He waved the two-dollar bill for the grocer to see. The grocer raised his eyebrows to the other customers. They smiled to the grocer, and he waited on George. George searched the whole store and bought a thirty-five-cent angel's-food cake, a quart of tutti-frutti ice cream for thirty cents, and thirty-five cents' worth of assorted cupcakes. He gave the grocer the two-dollar bill, and the grocer put it in the large bill drawer and gave George four ones in change. George picked up the bills and his packages, and the grocer went back to his customers who were still smiling patiently at the grocer's patient smile. The pool hall crowd was on the front steps of the store, and they asked George how his Marmon was getting along.

"She'll be the best car in these parts time I get her all fixed up. Mr. Shipley wrecked it, but he couldn't turn it over. It was the rolling——"

"Come back here, you thievin' nigger."

"Yes sir, yes sir. I didn't notice I was wrong. I was thinking about my ice cream."

The grocer charged through the front door and grabbed George by the arm. The pool hall crowd stopped laughing at George's eulogy; women in the store stopped poking vegetables; men on the street stopped and moved toward the store; George resisted the pull on his arm. "Nigger" was a very strong word in Cortland, and its use demanded extraordinary circumstances.

"You gave me a two-dollar bill and tried to pass it off as a five. Give me back that three dollars."

Shipley was in the pool hall crowd.

"Where did he get a two-dollar bill? He paid me seven and Johnson two. He don't make but nine a week."

"A two-dollar bill is race-track money. If he didn't steal, it still ain't decent money."

"He's been stealing something besides garbage."

"Come on. Give me my three dollars."

"Yes sir, yes sir. I didn't notice I was wrong. I was thinking about my ice cream."

The grocer shook George's arm, and George dropped a package. The cupcakes rolled in the dust. George watched them and tried to think about the money. He had known only that it was not a one-dollar bill, and no one had ever called him "nigger" before. He had spent a dollar, and now he had four, but that wasn't stealing. There was a trick about this somewhere. He tensed, thinking about the money and about the grocer, till he was crushing his precious ice cream and cake. Shipley was asking him where he got the two-dollar bill. Shipley wanted the Marmon. He grumbled every week when George paid him. He had wrecked the Marmon; he had hurt it; now he wanted it back.

George dropped the rest of his packages and pulled his left arm free to get his pocketbook from his overalls.

"Here's your three dollars. Mr. Tuttle gave me that bill. I didn't know what it was."

The grocer took the money and said to the crowd around the store, to Shipley, and to George,

"All right. Now don't try that again."

No one stirred. The grocer started toward the front door, and George began picking up his cupcakes. Everyone was still and watching, so the grocer kicked one of the cakes toward George and said,

"Here. Feed one of these to your damn Marmon. It looks sick enough to need some dessert."

Someone snickered; the pool hall crowd laughed; then the customers and Shipley laughed. The grocer picked his lips with his thumb and forefinger to show how modestly he received the appreciation of his jest. He had his money; he had called George a "nigger" and had gotten away with it; he had made a joke about George's Marmon, and that was a sure-fire joke.

Some one of the pool hall crowd filled the first lull after the laughter by asking George,

"Hey, how's that Marmon coming along?"

George bent up from gathering his cupcakes, and with the beginnings of a smile on his face, he was ready to tell them about his Marmon; but he was met by loud laughing. He had no chance to say a word. The people around the store, and especially the pool hall gang, continued to joke George while he finished collecting his groceries from the ground.

"Rub the ice cream on the engine, George. It'll take the hoarseness out."

"You can use that cake for a tire. The left rear looks pretty weak."

"Take care of that car, George. I'd hate to see anything happen to it."

Everyone laughed heartily, and George looked from face to face as the jokes were made. His eyes fell on Shipley at the last remark. Shipley had made that joke; he wanted the Marmon.

George ran home and sat panting in the front seat of the Marmon, eating what was not too dirty of his treasures from the store. Tomorrow, he planned, he would give Shipley two more dollars, and he would build a stronger shelter for his car. Tonight he would put the fourth fender on, and maybe he could patch the top.

The men from the pool hall, with the billiards parlor closed for repairs, could not let the only piece of excitement of the day lie unused. They hatched a joke to make their Saturday evening less dull. They would put on white sheets and go around to George's shanty about midnight acting as if they were ghosts coming to put the Marmon back into its rightful grave from which George had stolen it. They tried the story of their planned joke on everyone who came to the store, and everyone agreed that not only was it funny, but also that it might have some merit in it. Mrs. Sloan thought that it might scare the poor boy into his right senses for a change. Shipley thought that if they were loud enough the Marmon would fall to pieces, and then he could sell it to the garage man for junk. The grocer said that he would like to go along, but that he was a little too old for that sort of stuff.

George put the last fender on the car that night, and after he had looked it over, he went to bed. He was awakened by moanings and groanings outside the house. He looked out the front window and saw that the road was filled with white-sheeted figures waving their arms, moaning and crying in deep voices,

"Back to the grave, O Marmon. Give up the corpse, George Thomas Lincoln. Give us our car, O George."

There were smothered giggles and laughs, too, and George sat and stared at his car and at the white sheets. The figures came into his front yard, and one of them kicked at the fender which George had just fastened on.

It fell off with a crash, and the men began to laugh. There was the sound of a shot from the house, a sound of breaking glass, and screaming men ran in all directions, with and without sheets. One of them tripped into a ditch, and he lay screaming,

"I'm shot. I'm shot."

George listened and laughed. Lights went on in houses, but no one came back. He examined the car, put the fender against the wheel, and went back to bed. He looked at his gun on the floor and laughed,

"I'm shot. I'm shot."

He was awakened about an hour later by the screaming of sirens, and three sheriff's cars skidded to a stop in front of his house and trained their spotlights on his bedroom window. Men with guns piled out of the cars and went running around both sides of the house. Someone cried,

"There he is at the window. Watch out. He's armed."

George could hear the sounds of many voices behind the lights, and he heard the sheriff call,

"Come on out with your hands up, you crazy nigger. We've got you covered."

As George came out the front door, two deputies grabbed him under the arms and carried him to the nearest car. They searched him, handcuffed him, and threw him into the back seat. A man sat on each side of him with a drawn revolver, and they rode to the county jail with sirens screaming and spotlights sweeping back and forth across the road. George watched the man driving, but there was no need to ask him to go faster.

Paul's father had been called after someone had called the sheriff, and Paul heard all about poor George at the Sunday breakfast table. Poor George had become dangerous, and he would have to be sent away. He had gotten so wrapped up in that old car that he hadn't paid any attention to the everyday things of decent living. Luckily he hadn't hit anyone when he fired. The man in the ditch had just scratched his knee on some loose gravel.

Friends of Mrs. Sloan made a special effort at church to tell her that she had done all that she could and that the Marmon had finally gotten the best of poor George. Colored Baptists mentioned that both the grocer and the sheriff had called George a nigger, but they agreed that in this case he had acted like one. White Methodists used the word nigger rather freely, and they talked about respective places for black and white people. Friends of Owen Shipley commiserated his lacerated knee and told him that he was lucky that he hadn't been shot actually.

The hearing was scheduled for Monday morning, and so many Cortland people called about it that the judge held it in the courtroom. The sheriff wanted George put away quick to teach a lesson to the west-end "nigras" who had been acting up lately. Mrs. Sloan and her lawyer were there to act as George's counsel, but he ignored their consultations. He laughed at Shipley's testimony about the shooting, and a deputy pulled him back by the shoulder and said,

"Shut up, nigger."

This created such a stirring among the Cortland people in the courtroom that the judge had to threaten to clear the court to restore quiet. Paul's father rose and asked permission to address the court. It was granted.

He addressed the court, facing the spectators.

"Friends, nigger is a nasty word, and I believe that it has no place in this court or in any court in this fair state of ours. A man is being tried here for having committed a dangerous criminal act, but his race had nothing to do with it. A man's worth has nothing to do with the color of his skin. I respectfully request the court to ask its guardians of the law, brave though they may be, to refrain from using what many of us taxpayers believe to be indecent language."

He bowed to the spectators, who applauded him, and to the judge, who reprimanded the deputy. He sat down beside Paul and squeezed his hand. Paul whispered a question,

"Remember when old Mr. Conklin shot at us when we were halloweening? He got off, didn't he?"

"That was different, Paul. You might have damaged some of his property, and besides, he just shot into the air. He's a responsible member of the community."

"Well, the Marmon was George's property; he didn't hit anyone, and isn't he a good member of the community?"

"He's been in the State Hospital, Paul."

"They let him out."

"Hush."

The judge asked George if he had shot at anyone in particular last Saturday night.

"No sir. I shot away high so I wouldn't hit my car."

"Why did you shoot at them? Why didn't you shout? Why did you get a gun in the first place?"

"Everybody worried so about me having a car. I never knew what would happen. Shipley wanted it; my sister wanted it; the garage man wanted it; everybody else, except Paul, hated it. He and I, we love it."

Shipley denied that he wanted the Marmon. He stood with a cane. Mrs. Sloan conferred with her lawyer, and she denied that she wanted the Marmon. The garage man stood up, but the judge wouldn't hear him. The judge told George that he would have to go back to the hospital at Clayton until such time as the authorities decided that he was well enough to live peaceably in a law-abiding community. George asked a question.

"May Paul keep my car until I get back?"

"Your legal guardian will look after your property until you get back."

"She'll wreck my car. I want Paul to have it."

George began to cry, and the judge told the deputies to take him away. They dragged him out, and Paul asked his father to take him to Mrs. Sloan. She was in the judge's chambers, and Paul went up to her.

"Mrs. Sloan, I have five dollars. Will you sell the Marmon to me?"

"Whatever would you do with it, Paul?"

"I'll keep it until George gets back."

"That may be a long, long time. Besides, I'm going to sell it to Mr. Shipley for the rest of the payments if it will run."

"He'll wreck it. He did it once."

The judge smiled at Mr. Tuttle, and Paul's father took him by the arm and said,

"Come on, Paul, we're going home."

"What about the car?"

"It is Mrs. Sloan's worry. Personally I don't want to hear another word about it."

Paul and his father left the judge's chambers, and they stopped by the county agent's office to inquire about someone to help on the farm. Mr. Tuttle said that he wanted a good colored man, but that he couldn't afford to pay too much. The agent said that he thought that Mr. Tuttle had had enough trouble with niggers. Mr. Tuttle glared at the agent, said that he didn't like the word nigger, and he and Paul left without saying anything more.

They got into the car and started home. Neither Paul nor his father had anything to say until Paul remembered that he still had the five dollars for the set of air horns. When they were almost home Paul asked his father,

"May I start a savings in the bank with my five dollars?"

"That sounds like a fine idea, Paul. Then you can add to it every week until——"

"I might add a dollar, but that's all."

Mr. Tuttle said no more, and as soon as they were home, Paul went directly to his office, put the five dollars and the order blank for the air horns in an envelope and took them to his father. Mr. Tuttle opened the envelope, took out the five dollars, and read the mail-order blank. He frowned and said to Paul,

"I'll keep this in my strongbox. They won't want it at the bank."

"All right, but please don't lose it."

The Marmon didn't run, and it shrank into the weeds of the yard as the summer went by. Another fender fell off, and the paint began to rust. Paul watched when he went to Cortland, and when it was still in front of the shanty, he knew that it would be there when George got back.

AN AMERICAN HOME

by Helen Eustis

From *Harper's Bazaar*

———————◆———————

Now THIS is how it was: there was Mrs. Harrington, there was Rose, and there was Pearl. They lived together in a pretty apartment in the East Sixties on Mrs. Harrington's alimony and a small income left to her by her father. Out of these moneys Mrs. Harrington paid a maid's wages to Pearl and supplied the material necessities of an upper-middle-class five-year-old girl to Rose. She also bought herself very nice clothes in good shops, had a decorator do the apartment, and sometimes gave cocktail parties. Everything always cost a little more than she had expected.

Rose was Mrs. Harrington's daughter. She was large for her age, with a determined chin, stringy brown hair which was the despair of her mother, and eyes like blue flowers.

Pearl was a young woman with dark brown skin. She had a small pretty face, but she was obese to the point of deformity, and her features were nearly lost in the largeness of her cheeks and chins, just as her personality was nearly lost in the neuroses of her size and race. When she walked she looked like a balloon in Macy's Thanksgiving parade, seeming to balance for an age on one foot before floating gently onto the other.

Every morning except Saturday and Sunday, Pearl would take Rose to nursery school, then do the marketing. In some shops she would be prim and ladylike, giving her order softly in her little bell of a voice. In others she would be loud and strident, rude in an attempt to be funny, saying things she never wanted to say at all. How she was depended on the clerks, whether they were matter-of-fact or kidding. When they were serious and she spoke softly, she felt smaller, lighter, more like other people. When they teased her and she responded noisily, she felt enormous and ashamed afterward, as when the kids in school had called her "Fatso."

When Pearl came home from shopping, she would prepare Mrs. Harrington's breakfast, laying it daintily on a tray, the coffee in a thermos jug. Soon the clip-clop of Mrs. Harrington's mules would sound in the hall, stop at the bathroom, come to the kitchen.

"Ah-ah!" Mrs. Harrington would yawn intimately, stretching in the kitchen doorway. "Good morning, Pearl. Is it a nice day?"

"It's all right," Pearl would answer, not wanting to give in too easily.

Mrs. Harrington was dainty and pink, a divorcée. She wore negligees with lace and mules with high heels. Her face was small and mischievous and pointed; you noticed how straight she sat and stood. She was very helpless, and it was a wonder she had no man to look after her, but you felt this was a temporary state. Meantime, she had Pearl. With Mrs. Harrington, Pearl felt very large, but in a useful way, as a protective wall or bulwark sheltering Mrs. Harrington. And at the same time, in a dim, mixed-up way, Pearl felt that inside her, underneath her layers of flesh and her dark skin, there lived a Mrs. Harrington too, loving luxury, waiting to be born and to enjoy the world, beautiful, slim, desirable, and even white. When friends called Mrs. Harrington and Pearl answered the phone, they would often say, "Eva?" taking Pearl's voice for hers. Pearl had picked up a lot of her expressions, too—"gay," "dashing," "tight as a mink." "What would I do without you, Pearl?" Mrs. Harrington often said, meaning that she hoped Pearl would not leave during the maid shortage, but Pearl never replied, "Mrs. Harrington, what would I do without *you?*" Pearl was only Mrs. Harrington's maid, but Mrs. Harrington was Pearl's dream—habit-forming, indispensable.

Although Mrs. Harrington was Rose's mother, she gave everyone the impression that this was a mistake. In the first place, Rose was too big for her. It gave you a shock to realize by what biological process these two were related. Mrs. Harrington was a small-boned woman who wore tiny high-heeled shoes with platform soles to increase her height. Rose was a big lolloping five-year-old, like a Saint Bernard puppy, forever falling down or charging into things. In her mother's presence she usually behaved abominably, whining, interrupting, having temper tantrums and rolling on the floor while Mrs. Harrington stood over her, small, lovely, and helpless, saying, "Now, Rose——" until Pearl came and dragged Rose away. Then it almost seemed that Rose had the better of her mother, but Mrs. Harrington evened the score when friends came to call and she made funny remarks about Rose not quite out of Rose's hearing—clever, helpless remarks which her friends, especially those who had children themselves, would quote a good deal. "Children!" she would cry gaily as Pearl dragged Rose howling to her bedroom. "Huxley was so right when he had 'mother' be a dirty word in *Brave New World!* Sometimes I just feel all mothered up." Rose did not quite know what these remarks meant that made her mother's friends laugh so, but she knew what they were about, and was working out her defenses against them. For one thing, out of no influence at all, she had become a prude. "Oh, Mommy," she would say, "why do you *smoke* so much?" Or "Is that a *highball?*" in the voice of a horrified teetotaler. Or, most often, when her mother and her friends would laugh their private laughter, Rose would run into the room hitting at her mother, crying savagely, "Don't be so *silly!*"

Mrs. Harrington was out a good deal, so that Rose and Pearl were together a good deal, but this did not preclude each of them having a world of her own. Rose, indeed, was in love—with a boy at nursery school named George Melchior. George was five and a half with straight black hair and black eyes and the reputation for being the worst boy in the group. On the whole, George paid very little mind to Rose—he was not in love with her, and her attentions bored him; indeed, there was a demand implicit in their nature which strongly irritated him. Once George came to Rose's house to play, but that afternoon, Janie, who lived upstairs, came visiting too, and all afternoon George and Janie kept saying to Rose, "Go away, you're not our friend," while they played with her toys. She tried telling them that they were not fair, that she would tell her mother, that they couldn't come to her house any more, but she could not think of any threat big enough to move them, and nothing she could do pleased them. It was as if they had something she wanted very much, but she had nothing that they wanted to trade for it. Everything she did was wrong to them. "Rose, Rose, hold your nose!" they chanted until she screamed, "Shut up! Shut up!" hopelessly. Nor was Pearl any help, calling to her from the kitchen, "Now, Rose, is that any way to act when you're the hostess?" She did manage to get George alone in the bathroom once (her best moments with George seemed to come in bathrooms) and asked him, "If I kiss you, will you be my friend?" but George, decently outraged by this useless offer, said, "Who wants to kiss stinky old you?" They went home at last, and Rose was glad to echo Pearl, who grumbled that she didn't want such rough children around no more—*look* at how they tore the house up!

And Pearl had a social life, too. On her days out she went to the movies and shopping—mostly alone for these activities—but in the evening she would go up to Harlem and drop in to see Amalie Jackson, a married friend from her home town. The Jacksons were used to having Pearl drop in—they didn't treat her like company when she came, or even bother to stay home. But the family was big enough so that someone was always around—if Amalie and her husband, Joe, were out, Amalie's mother, Mrs. Kennedy, would be there with Amalie's kids, or Amalie's good-looking sister, Lula, might be entertaining some boy friend. Pearl behaved in her different ways depending on who was home. If it was just Mrs. Kennedy, whom she called Mom, she was soft and gentle, letting her pretty voice flute innocently from her big throat. They would sit in the kitchen together, doing some mending or other quiet work, and they would gossip about old times in New Jersey: who still lived at home, and who had had a baby, and who had died. If Amalie was there, Pearl was sometimes loud and sometimes soft, depending. If Amalie was complaining over her duties as a wife and mother, Pearl would be loud and scornful, saying how *she* was too smart ever to get *herself* tied down with no man, *she* was going to be independent, a free agent, not looking for handouts from no husband. Might as well be on relief. But sometimes it was with Amalie just as it was with Mrs. Kennedy—only soft and half-homesick recollections of old times. " 'Member the time we hid in Tuckers' cellar and——" "Sure, and how your mother hollered when——" When Joe was there, Pearl was neither loud nor soft; she was silent. This was partly because one hot afternoon she had found the door unlatched, and walked in, without ringing, to confront Joe, sitting stark naked on the parlor sofa, reading the *Daily News*. After this, she could never put out of her mind that under his clothing lurked his beautiful, horrifying, caramel-colored body. She died of shame each time she saw him because she could not keep from thinking it, and always imagined Joe read her mind, was laughing at her.

She knew the facts of life and accepted the commonplace that all women are not virtuous; she often determined to indulge herself in a little sin like anybody else and find out what it was like. What prevented her were her enormous tiers and balconies of flesh, her fear of ridicule, her dreams and hopeless ideals. If she could have conceived of herself as a joke, a fat mamma, she might have let go and developed some hilarious allure appropriate to her figure. But this was outside the scope of her personality: How could she declare herself a ludicrous fancy woman while inside her lived the dainty, light-skinned Mrs. Harrington who craved—and even *deserved*— romantic love and honorable marriage? Was she to give herself to some clown who thought of her only as a joke, who had no inkling, nor cared to have, that inside her were truth, dignity, pride—and even beauty? Once Mrs. Kennedy's younger brother was visiting at Jacksons' and invited her to take in a movie. Her heart leapt, for he was an older man, somewhat solemn and religious-minded, unlike the rest. But as she passed into the bedroom to adjust her hat, she overheard Joe exploding, "Man, man, you are a small driver to han'le such a large truck!" and it was spoiled. All evening she was loud and scornful of everything, ungrateful to Mrs. Kennedy's brother, who actually was not in the least disrespectful, only rather unimaginative. In the end she got a little drunk and shouting, drinking rum colas in the Jacksons' kitchen; she went to bed on a too-small studio couch, weeping into her pillow and thinking it was terrible to be so large and so unwelcome in the world—it meant there was more of you to be unwelcome—but then weeping worse to think that if you were unwelcome in the world, no matter how small you were, you were too large.

It went without saying that Mrs. Harrington had a wide and varied social life outside her home. She was *toujours gaie,* like Mehitabel, and wherever she was there was a lot of laughing and drinking and people exerting themselves at having a good time. What she most prided herself on was that she could laugh at anything, which, in point of fact, she could—even the world news. But her laughter and her humor were never bitter or unkind or consciously callous; they were only gay and agreeable, lending to everything a golden glamor, like that of a Turner painting—a beautiful distortion of reality. The only things and people she could not abide were things and people at which or with whom she could not laugh; people who insisted that she be serious, things which could not be laughed away. When she was a girl, she would run up piles of bills which she would carry, rueful and laughing, to her father, who would groan, laugh, and pay them. But when she was a married woman, Tony Harrington would not laugh, but say, "God, Eva, how'll we make out this month?" as if *she* should know. On the whole, Tony had been something of a darling, amused and affable through parties and hangovers alike, but he too had wanted to be a child, a baby, and how could he be with no mother or father in the house? They had maintained the gloss of gaiety until the very last moment, when the battle to shift responsibility had transferred its ground from the bedroom to the lawyer's office, and its weapons from the economy of the household to that of the separation settlement. There was little laughter during this business. Professional people, Eva Harrington observed, were not heavily endowed with humor—neither obstetricians nor lawyers—and even the best of husbands will go sour over alimony arrangements, her divorced friends assured her. But the only times when Eva Harrington was *absolutely* cut off from laughter were in her dreams, for, as she told her more Freudian friends laughingly, she had the saddest dreams of anyone she ever heard of. Over and over she dreamed she was on a festive liner, sailing away. The music was playing, the passengers wore leis, and obviously this was to be a pleasure cruise. But Eva Harrington wept and wept at the boat rail, for she did not want to go away, and the boat was taking her to some strange land where she did not want to go.

When Rose was born (product of carelessness after an evening at the Ruban Bleu, and thus known to her parents as the blue ribbon baby) Eva had been able to laugh away nine months of pregnancy and her ridiculous figure, but not birth, even with nembutal, and not Rose. Because of the comfortable modern custom of confessing one's hostilities, she could admit easily and humorously that her life would have been a great deal simpler and more comfortable without

Rose. It was Rose who put her in the worst danger of becoming serious, or even earnest. Talking to nursery-school teachers—which, mercifully, she had to do only twice a year—was one of the worst things. They made one feel such a *mother*—worse than taking Rose to the park, when women sitting on benches spoke to you as if you were one of them. "The truth is," she would say, speaking the truth so charmingly that you scarcely recognized it, "Rose confronts me so hideously with the fact that I'm grown up." Otherwise (now that she was rid of Tony) she need never have known. Pearl, her friends, her lovers, all treated her as a particularly gay, golden, and adorable child. Gay, golden, and adorable as no child in this world ever was, in fact. If it had not been for Rose, she might have maintained this view of herself, and of childhood, almost without a crack.

But Rose was always before her when she was at home, a large child, attracting much dirt. Sometimes when she was dressed up, and smiled, she had a kind of light in her face. But in her mother's presence she seldom smiled; she was too earnestly engaged in solemn bungling attempts to make her mother love her, whether by force or strategy, which only succeeded in making her mother feel uncomfortable, as she always did with earnest people. Thus Mrs. Harrington stayed out a good deal, leaving Rose with Pearl.

But after Pearl's unsuccessful date with Mrs. Kennedy's brother, when it seemed to Pearl that the Jackson family was rather cool to her because of the way she had acted, Pearl began to draw even closer to Mrs. Harrington and Rose than she was already. She mistook entirely the nature of her relation with them, and in a complicated way began to feel that Rose was her little girl, and Mrs. Harrington was her little girl, yet she was also Mrs. Harrington's little girl, and maybe this was how life was to be, and maybe here was really where to look for love. So she settled down to fixing her room, cleaning the apartment especially clean, planning fancy meals, and taking Rose on excursions, to the Bronx Zoo and to Fort Tryon Park, with the result that the household went into a good period, as households periodically do—everything went better and everybody liked each other better: Pearl would read to Rose when she was in bed at night; Mrs. Harrington had an idea that a permanent might improve Rose's hair (though this never came to anything), and Rose wasn't so earnest with her mother, but told quite funny stories about her dolls, which Mrs. Harrington repeated to her friends. Rose grew very vain and particular about her appearance; she begged an old lipstick from her mother with which she played making up her face; she told her mother she was worried because her legs were so fat (her mother was worried about this, too) and she only cried when she was hungry or tired or when her mother was going out. She would put her arms around her mother, saying, "My mommy, my little mommy, I'm going to keep care of you!" and this her mother found infinitely touching, since it was just the relationship for them she would have chosen herself had it been feasible. Then Mrs. Harrington would go and sit on a kitchen stool, sometimes, chatting companionably with Pearl about different things . . . about what Rose had said, or how hard it was to get meat, or how they might fix over the dining room, or what a gay party Mrs. Harrington had been on last night—*God,* she was dead! And Pearl would seize this opportunity of telling various things she had been thinking, whether they fitted into the conversation exactly or not, and Rose, lying in bed delighting in the peaceful sound of voices, would be able to bear her happiness in silence no longer, and would call out, "*Whatcha* talking about, Mommy?"

It was one of those spans of equilibrium which are limited by the very nature of life; they exist for a moment to delight, like a kaleidoscope pattern, and then disperse, cannot be reproduced.

One morning Mrs. Harrington woke from her sad dream about the ship to find notices in the mail that her charge accounts were frozen in three department stores. She went downtown to lunch with a friend, and in the same restaurant, unaware that she observed him, sat Tony, holding the hand of a statuesque blonde quite the way he used to hold hers—in full view on the tablecloth. Eva Harrington and her friend had a good laugh over that, but when after lunch Eva wanted the two of them to shop together, none of her persuasion could bring her friend to accompany her. At last she had to make a funny little *moue* and go alone before her pleas became boring. In Bonwit's she tried on some killing hats but the salesgirl refused to laugh with her, especially when there was no sale. The shoe department at Saks was jammed with women and hustling salesmen carrying stacks of boxes; she waited and waited for one of them to take notice of her until suddenly she found she had waited too long; she began to see everything too clearly: the hard, painted faces of the women, the hard, smooth surfaces of their hair, the salesmen looking hatred at the nylon-covered feet on which they thrust expensive shoes, the fact that her income did not cover her expenses. It was, she thought, the sad dream come back in wakefulness, the pleasure ship carrying her to a strange land where she did not want to go. Very frightened, she hurried to the ladies' room and closed herself in a toilet booth to weep. Somehow, it seemed—oh, all too clearly!—she had blundered into the wrong life; not the gay and familiar one she had dreamed in boarding school, where the handsome knight carried you off to a colonial house on Long Island and all the bills were paid, and a nurse for the children, and love went on without responsibility. Where was that life? She had waited and waited, looked and looked for it, yet how could she give up her faith in it when it was all the wisdom she had, handed down by her mother and her father, by her books and schoolmates, by a world which believed in it so tacitly, so matter-of-coursely, that it *could* not be a fiction! Oh, thought Eva Harrington, I must get away! I must break the spell, make it change; if only I could—or if I could—and, not for the first time, it came to her that the one thing she meant was: If I could get rid of Rose. Without that nothing could change.

That afternoon Pearl and Rose were at the movies.

"Pearl, Pearl, who is that man?" Rose hissed.

"Sh! He's a German," Pearl whispered back.

"Has he got a *gun?*"

"Yes."

"What's he gonna *do?*"

"I don't know."

"Is he gonna *shoot* the lady?"

"Sh-sh-sh!"

When they came out the long day was beginning to soften; they took the bus toward home.

"What're we having for supper, Pearl?"

"Meat loaf and string beans."

"What for dessert?"

"Applesauce, I guess."

"Will you buy me a Good Humor, Pearl?"

"No, it's too near suppertime."

"George Melchior has a Good Humor twelve times a day. He told me."

"George Melchior is a storyteller."

"He's *rough*," said Rose contentedly, and they got off the bus.

The apartment did not catch much light; it was filled now with cool gloom. Pearl turned the light on in the kitchen but Rose left the living room mysterious and played German until it got too dark and she scared herself.

"Pearl, Pearl!"

"What's the matter?"

"I'm scared."

"What're you scared of?"

"It's dark!"

"Go wash your hands; your supper's ready."

When Mrs. Harrington came home it was later than dinnertime and Rose was in bed.

"Mommy, Mommy!" she cried when she heard her mother's key in the latch.

"Just a *minute,* Rose, let me get my hat off!"

But Rose was out of bed, charging into her mother's room, throwing her arms around her mother's waist, half knocking her down.

"Goodness, Rose, are you planning to play tackle for Yale?"

But, "Mommy, Mommy!" Rose crooned, unheeding.

"Let go of me, darling, it's far too hot. Let go and I'll tell you a surprise."

"A surprise, a surprise!" cried Rose fatuously, letting go of her mother and clapping her hands like a character out of *The Five Little Peppers,* a work which had negatively formed Eva Harrington's tastes.

"How would you like to go to the country and visit your aunty Sue?"

Mrs. Harrington presented the notion in glowing tones, but a veil of suspicion immediately slipped over Rose's features. "You too?" she said.

"No, just you yourself!" her mother cried gaily. "And you'll have Billy and Polly and the dogs to play with——"

"Will Pearl go?"

"No, we'll let Pearl have a little vacation."

"Will my daddy be there?"

"Now, Rose, why on earth should your daddy be there? You know he——"

"I want you or Pearl or my daddy to be there," said Rose, the barometer of her face dropping fast. "I don't *wanna* go to Aunt Sue's!"

"But listen, darling, you can sprinkle with the hose, and go on picnics——"

The tears broke and slipped down Rose's scarlet face of woe. "I want my mommy!" she wept, looking straight at her mother, but pleading as if for something far away and unattainable.

"Oh, Rose——" said Mrs. Harrington, helplessly gazing down at Rose, who presently cast herself to the floor in her passion and kicked and screamed. At last Pearl's slow rescuing tread was heard in the hall; Pearl came and picked Rose up, bore her away howling. Mrs. Harrington sighed, then shook out her hair, went to the kitchen and mixed a drink. She sat on a kitchen stool, sipping, listening to Pearl talking, Rose weeping, until at last both were quiet. She drifted into an old soft dream about a terribly attractive man with a wonderful sense of humor, quite a lot of money, and a marvelous capacity for *handling* things who would fall in love with her this summer, ask her to marry him, take care of them all. . . . It was about the same dream that Tony had slipped into and then out of not so very long ago. It was a good dream, comforting and hopeful as a cool drink on a hot evening. Maybe . . . and maybe . . . Pearl came in. Rose had cried herself to sleep.

"She's asleep," said Pearl. "Do you want your supper now?"

"I ate," said Mrs. Harrington. "Pearl."

"Yes'm?"

"I think I'm going to send Rose to my sister's this summer. I suddenly got this idea and called her today. She'll be much better off in the country, don't you think?"

"Yes'm."

"So then I thought I'd sublet the apartment, because there are several people who want me to visit. Pearl, do you think you could go home for the summer, Pearl?"

"Well," said Pearl, "I guess so."

"Because I'd *die* if you went off and got another job, Pearl, I don't know what I'd *do,* but actually I'm so broke and that's why I want to rent the place all summer and have Rose away. I can live so much more *cheaply.* I mean, there'd be your two weeks with pay, of course, Pearl," Mrs. Harrington pleaded guiltily.

And Pearl, her face an enormous mahogany mask, said, "Yes'm." Inside her head she began doing quick arithmetic about how much money she had in the bank; having quick glimpses of her family's overcrowded shack in the mosquito-ridden New Jersey town where she always seemed fatter because there was so little space, and of how her family would jeer at her for not quitting and getting another job, but what she said was, "Yes'm, I guess so," until Mrs. Harrington's pretty face was smiling with guilty relief, and mercifully the telephone rang to end it all.

Then Pearl began slowly washing up the dishes from her and Rose's supper; she mopped the kitchen floor, she cleaned the sink, she set the garbage out for collection. Many things were moving about inside her, things she could not decipher, things which revealed themselves only in a kind of wheeze in her breathing, like the beginning of a sob. But Mrs. Harrington—a voice in her head kept saying, and then could not go on. But Mrs. Harrington what? Before she could begin to think, Mrs. Harrington fled by in a new hat with a pink rose, calling, "I'm going out, Pearl!" slamming the door after her so that it woke Rose, who began crying, "Mommy! Mommy!" and weeping bitterly. I'm the maid, I quit, the voice finished inside Pearl's head. But that was not it, that was not what she meant to say at all. Slowly, heavily, Pearl began to go in to Rose, the feeling of comfort rising a little in her. After all, Rose was like her own little girl, in lots of ways, and nobody could stop that.

Rose was crying, "I want my mom-my!" faster and faster, working up to hysteria; Pearl took her up in her arms, sat down on the bed with her, cradled Rose in her billows of flesh, as in her very flesh she yearned to have someone do to her, to fat impossible Pearl. But Rose was of a different mind; she did not lie passive and accept grief or substitutes for love; she kicked and struggled and hit out with her fists, hurting Pearl.

"I want my mommy!" she yelled. "You go away!"

"Your mommy's gone out, Rose," said Pearl. "Be quiet and I'll sing to you."

"You go away! I want my mommy, you old Pearl!"

"Sh-sh! Your mommy's not home; it's time to be asleep now, Rose."

"I want my mom-mee!"

"Be quiet now, Rose. You'll see your mommy in the morning."

"I hate you, I hate you, I hate you!" screamed Rose.

"Sh-sh-sh!"

"You're too fat and you're *colored!*" shrieked Rose. "I hate fat old colored people!"

And this was too much for Pearl; this was simply too much. She dumped Rose on the bed and heaved herself up. "You!" she hissed down at Rose. "You're such a mean kid your own mother don't love you!"

And Rose screamed, "I don't care, I don't care; you're fat and you're colored and I hate you! I want my mom-mee!" until someone across the court called, "Shut that child up!" and Pearl slapped Rose, because she did not know what else to do.

MISS WINTERS AND THE WIND
by Christine Noble Govan
From *Tomorrow*

———

MISS WINTERS stood on the corner with her bus transfer in her hand and hated the wind. There had been a feud between Miss Winters and the wind for all the years that she had lived in this flat dreadful city of St. Louis. It seemed to pick her out—a lone, forlorn little figure—to vent its nasty, playful vindicativeness upon. It pulled at her droopy felt hat and whipped her straggly hair about her face, grabbed up her skirt in bawdy mischief, exposing her black cotton stockings.

Once, when she had been coming home from her work, it had snatched the transfer from her hand and blown it under a passing bus. When the bus had gone Miss Winters, peering in the dusk, had searched everywhere but the bit of yellow paper eluded her. People crowding about her had almost pushed her under a truck and had sworn at her impatiently. It had been the day before payday and she had only fare back to work in the morning. She had had to walk the rest of the way home—three miles and all against the wind.

When she had lived in the South as a child the wind had been a lovesome thing. The mountains kept it properly in hand and broke it as one breaks a mettlesome colt. It blew against the mountaintops and was parted into bits by the trees which roiled and hummed with a sound like the sea. Over the fields wild broom swept gently, making them ripple, molten seas of red-gold liquid beauty. In school she read *Hiawatha,* her narrow face lighted momentarily:

> *As in sunshine gleam the ripples*
> *That the cold wind makes in rivers.*

She had not known what a cold wind really was.

But now she knew. It was what seeped in at the ledges and made her feet numb in spite of the fire she so assiduously tended. It got into bed with her at night so that even her striped cat which crept under the covers shivered, getting up all through the cold black hours to turn his aching bones and seek to warm another surface. It blew through her worn coat and crept into the jagged hole in her flannel bloomers, where she had snagged them on the wire clothesline on the roof. It tore at her fingers in their patched gloves until they burned in an agony of freezing.

Her mother had come from this unspeakable section. And after Miss Winters' father had died the old lady had yearned to come home. The wind had been too much for her, Miss Winters remembered with grim satisfaction. Two seasons of it and the old lady had been carried off with pleurisy.

Miss Winters had had a fairly comfortable business then. She did "Fine and Fancy Sewing, Prices Reasonable." A flat-chested spinster whose maidenly longings had burned to a black ash years before, she made babies' frocks with minute embroidered yokes as delicate as frost, bridal gowns, and perky pinafores for chubby little girls.

Her mother's illness and death was an expense. The depression came. She moved to meaner quarters, quarters evidently coveted by the wind since it came in at every opportunity. She was lonely and anxious and sometimes afraid. Fear clutched at her throat like an actual hand, making it difficult to swallow.

Then the WPA gave her sewing to do. She made thick sacks and heavy work garments. Her hands grew stiff and raw at the clumsy work and she thought of the women she had draped in silk and crepe de Chine, of the flounced embroideries of her girlhood.

The worst blow came when the Project was closed. Women wore slacks and worked in factories and bought ready-made things. They had no time to try on Miss Winters' carefully fashioned garments. Her old customers died or went to Florida where the wind was less bitter. Miss Winters' fright crept over her like a slowly rising tide. The hands which had once fashioned sprays of lilies of the valley on batiste and lawn had grown arthritic with the cold and with coarse work. All she could get was mending now and occasional work at an alteration shop.

The bus was crowded and Miss Winters had to stand. On the

street in which she lived the cold had killed even the smell of garlic and cabbage. But the wind was there blowing the papers about, sending smoke and dust into her face and tugging at her hat until her eyes filled with tears of vexation.

She had two flights of stairs to climb before she got to her rooms. The cat was there waiting, curled up in the middle of the bed. He jumped down, stretching his lanky striped body, and called to her— the only creature left who greeted her as a friend. With the cat she could sometimes forget the clutching fear. His confidence in her gave her a meager courage and determination. Yet she feared for him, too; so many people were unkind to cats—especially if they were homeless.

"Wuzzee lonesome, muzzer's booful puwussycat?" she asked through chapped lips. "Muzzer'll build 'ums a fire. Muzzer'll feed him."

The cat, as if in appreciation of such obviously idiotic devotion, writhed against her skirts and purred.

Miss Winters, still gloved, laid the sticks and the precious bits of coal in the ashy grate and set a match to them. The damned wind came down the chimney and blew out the flame, scattering ashes over the hearth and over her desperately polished shoes.

At last she got the fire burning feebly. She set a pan of water on the gas ring for tea. While it heated she sat in the deep-bottomed rocker before the hearth, her legs spread comfortably, her hands folded against her body for warmth. The cat jumped on her lap and nudging her with determined, silken buttings under the chin and she put her arms around him gratefully. He was something alive in the bare room, something to make her forget a little the rising tide of her fright. The rent—it took all she made at the shop—there was thirty-seven cents due the milkman—her shoe soles—the fear was always there. Haunted by it, she had bungled a garment at the alteration shop and had nearly lost her day's work there. Cold that was not from the wind filled her at the memory.

The cat stood on his hind legs purring and sliding his velvety nose against her face, making a winning sound that was both a purr and a mew. In a sudden burst of tenderness she hugged him to her and he stared up at her smugly, his eyes green moons with mysterious golden lights in them.

She jumped up and made the tea, pouring a little milk from a can and some of the hot water into a saucer for the cat. From her purse she took a chop bone she had wheedled from one of her fellow workers. It had a sliver of meat upon it and gave forth an enticing fragrance of pepper and fried flesh. She pulled the meat off, looking about the bare room shamefacedly, and ate it slowly, tears of self-pity welling for a moment in her eyes. Then she stooped and set the bone with its ruffle of cold suet by the cat's saucer. The cat left the milk and began to gnaw fastidiously at the suet, the tip of its tail curling in and out with satisfaction.

Miss Winters took off her hat and made her tea. She sat and sipped it and watched the cat, savoring the beauty of his gaunt grace and the wonder of his green and depthless eyes.

The wind was rising. The room grew colder and colder as the darkness deepened. Miss Winters took off her outer garments and brought her flannel gown and heated it by the fire. She heated more water and filled a fruit jar to slip between the frigid sheets. Then armed with the cat and the jar, and banking the meager coals to hold the heat as long as possible, she crept into bed. The spotted bulb beside her bed gave scarcely enough light to read the sensational love-story magazine with which she escaped into forgetfulness each night.

Hours later she was awakened. The wind, not content to torment her by day, to make every waking hour a misery and a threat, must arouse her by night and bring her back to the grim knowledge from which in her dreams she had a brief escape.

It howled around the chimney, it battered the windows so that they rattled in their frames. The window that Miss Winters had patched with a wide piece of butcher's paper seemed to bulge as if at any moment it would burst and come hurtling across the room.

Something blew down on the roof and continued to rattle and bounce, making it impossible to sleep. The cold seemed a tangible thing, raking her spine, nipping her face, pinching at her feet where the already chilly fruit jar mocked any idea of comfort. She turned on the bulb as though the light might warm her. The cat crawled out and moved nervously about the bed.

There came a particularly vicious gust of wind. It screamed and threw itself at the cracked window. The glass ripped apart and was scattered like shrapnel. The cat leaped from the bed, meeting a spear of the glass in mid-air. He gave a scream and dropped wearily. Over the yellowish matting rug the bright splashes of his blood were blown like the petals of a dark rose.

Miss Winters rose from the intricate wrappings of the bed. She was cold, but with the cold of insensate fury. She went across the broken glass and picked up the limp body. The lovely green eyes were glazing and the blood dripped in warm splotches on her stockinged feet.

She stood there for a long, long time. At last she laid the cat down and said absently, "This has gone far enough."

She knew at last what she must do, and consequently felt calm. Going to the bed, she ripped off the covers, the coat she wore in the daytime, the quilt that was made of all the velvets and silks of her happier days. She got the sheet, a huge, patched affair, and she shook it out, looking at it thoughtfully.

It was so clear, so simple, that she wondered she had not thought of it before. She must catch the wind and tie it firmly in something so that never again could it get away frightening and harassing poor old women, keeping them awake to the knowledge of their misery, killing their cats. She put on her shoes and, without giving the cat another look, opened the door and began to walk resolutely down the stairs.

"Who has seen the wind?" she sang in the treble of her childhood as the wind tore at her long flannel gown and tried to take the sheet away from her.

"Ha-ha!" she chuckled, holding the sheet closer to her. "Not this time, my fine friend! Not this time!

"Who has seen the wind? Where does the wind go—up high-up high, high in the sky!"

She looked up at the church steeple. It was the highest thing in sight. It gleamed there even on this dark night, a dull, gleaming spear. A spear had killed the cat—the wind had a spear, she would kill the wind.

"Q.E.D.," she chuckled, from some forgotten pigeonhole.

You got at the tower of the church through a little door in the rear. As she had expected, it was not locked, and without hesitation she began her purposeful ascent. Up and up, around and around, tripping over the sheet, stepping on the hem of her gown, stumbling, laughing, and going on again. There was no wind inside the tower, but she was not deceived. It was waiting for her at the top—*and she was waiting for it!*

At last she reached the little room where the chimes were, a square room with open Gothic arches and a balcony off to one side. The wind was there, as she had expected, ramping and growling about like a lion. But she was no longer afraid of it.

"We shall see!" she crooned happily. "We shall see!"

She shook out the sheet. Of course the wind tried to take it, but she caught the four corners together skillfully and stepped out on the little ledge. The lights in the town glimmered and twinkled far below. She looked at them placidly as if to say, "Just watch me! I'm fixing this devilish fellow once and for all!"

Just then the wind came at her. It gave a swoop and she caught it in the sheet, which billowed like a huge loaf of rising bread. She had to leap to get it, but she had it there! She was so happy, so relieved, she felt as though she were simply walking on air. . . .

THE RECORD

by David Cornel DeJong

From *The New Mexico Quarterly Review*

—————◆—————

"I'LL PLAY IT AGAIN," he said, lifting the phonograph record unnecessarily off the turntable and examining it closely. "It's good to hear it again. I've missed it, that record."

Still holding the record aloft, he looked somewhat defiantly at the girl on the sofa. Slowly she lifted her eyes from contemplating a minute spot on her bare knee, shook her long blond hair from her eyes and forehead, and pouting a little, she said as with an effort at indifference: "Well, do then. It's good, sure. But what'll she, what'll Lorraine do when she finds out that you've taken one more of her possessions away?"

"It was mine. My brother gave it to me two or three years ago. I remember," he answered truculently, still not putting the record back, as if he needed her full approval.

"Go ahead and play it," she said, examining her knee again. "You must have missed it. It's good, of course. Please, darling, don't wait for me to assure you again. I might become hypersensitive."

He put the record on the phonograph then, and when it started playing, he sat down beside her and started stroking her long fair hair. Her eyes lifted to his, almost forgivingly, and then together—oh, simply unanimously, she was wont to call it on brighter days—they listened to the record. A well-nigh masculine female voice thumped out the words in a fashionably raucous way to the accompaniment of the heavier even more suggestive thumping of a piano:

> "*. . . What ho! said the bishop,*
> *I will not budge an inch until*

> *Another gentle breeze has lifted*
> *The skirt of that sweet young thing*
> *Standing there on that gorgeous hill."*

They smiled at each other, properly, expectantly and understandingly, and both now, as they ought to, waited with slightly parted lips and crinkles of appreciation around their eyes for that really wonderful final rendition of the refrain, with its variation and smash ending:

> *". . . The skirt of that gorgeous young thing*
> *Standing there on that goddamn hill."*

Both chuckled indulgently, appreciatively, as he jumped up to shut off the phonograph. "It's swell, isn't it?" he demanded. "Over and over again, it's swell, isn't it?"

"It is, darling. I'm glad now you swiped it. I'm glad you did, except, of course, that it'll put you full of reminiscences again. . . ."

"I told you, I didn't swipe it," he interrupted her.

"I know, darling. I'm just splitting hairs, aren't I?" she murmured with mock contriteness. "You are so sensitive, aren't you, dear? Especially this time of evening. And always just after you've seen your children."

"Cut it out," he said, slamming the lid of the phonograph down. "Or I'll play it again."

"But do," she purred, giving him her best smile with her widely painted full lips.

He didn't; simply because she had given him permission in that smiling way. He knew better. He didn't sit down beside her again, but in the easy chair at the other end of the narrow apartment, and very deliberately he picked up his pipe and started filling it. Stubbornly then—with that inflection in his voice which warned: See here, we'll have none of this now—he started saying, musingly rather than directly to her, "It's funny, that record. We used to test our friends by it. You could always tell the ones with a sense of humor, the ones with a little enlightenment in their bones. When it'd come to that final punch line, they'd applaud or jump up or laugh and demand immediately to hear it again, and . . ." "You see," she interpolated, looking at him accusingly with her dayflower-blue eyes. "You see."

"See what?" he demanded.

"You are reminiscing. I warned you."

He grimaced and shrugged, but he continued: "And some would be simply immune to it, and some shocked, especially by that ending. But it was at least better to be shocked than immune. Some would talk all the way through it, and then when they'd see the others laugh, they'd say: 'What's it all about? Good, wasn't it, but I didn't get it.' Like Arthur Stuart, for instance. Drunk, of course."

"And now you're elaborating," she said with slightly more malicious pique in her voice. "But continue. I love it."

"Damn you," he said, drawing angrily at his pipe, but persisting. "And the Nortons, they loved it, of course, and the Arnolds."

"And what about her?" She hesitated deliberately before she added, "Lorraine, what about her?"

"Well," he answered, immediately warming up to her jealousy, "well, naturally, just because every real person liked it, she pretended to hate it. She said it was phony."

"Darling, it is, of course."

"Is what?" he demanded, at last looking at her directly.

"Phony."

"Cut it out," he said ineptly. "Quit that new tack of yours, of agreeing with her. It's a little late for that."

She sat up properly, her dress drawn demurely over her knees, her hair pushed back behind her ears, and she grinned. "You're so sweet," she mocked, "when you talk like that. So young, too; you'd never guess that you'll be forty next summer. Or is it the next? Tell me about the kids now. What amazing tricks did little David pull off, and what cute things did little Isbel say? What did they say, for instance, when you walked off with their mama's record? Or did you bribe them? It must be wonderful to be a father."

"My record," he said extremely gently, and not too cruelly he continued, "and my children, too, dear. And I'm still allowed to see them once a week. Don't forget."

She smiled generously, displaying too well the lipstick stains on her teeth. She bowed her head a little, as if to prove to him that she felt his rebuke. "You must forgive me for being jealous," she said then in a small girl's voice. "When you shut me out like that and . . ."

"Don't," he said, uncertain whether to take her seriously or not. "Don't be tantalizing."

She chuckled. Then with a wholly forgiving mien, she walked over to his chair and pulled the pipe out of his mouth and took three or four puffs—something he always loved, something which always oddly flattered and consoled him—and then inserted it carefully between his teeth again. "You do miss your old friends, don't you, dear? It does mean a lot to you, doesn't it? You did sacrifice a lot, when you started putting up with me, didn't you?"

She paused to give him a chance to say his pat but fairly genuine: "But it was worth it." He didn't. He merely examined her warily over his pipe.

"And instead of living in a nice house, the papa of two wonderful children, the husband of a domestic jewel of a wife," she continued lovingly, "you're here with me. In a small furnished apartment, just a little better than a hotel room, because you're here a little longer, and because you could salvage a few things from your nice house without breaking the letter of the law, to make this a bit more homelike." She started pointing at them one by one. "Like those three little pictures, that darling little radio, the smoke stand, that green scarf, the Persian print, and, of course, your pipes. And you were so sweet allowing me to add something petit and intimate here and there. Darling, wasn't it a wonderful year, here among our souvenirs?"

Angrily, and in spite of himself, his eyes had followed her finger as it pointed to each one of the objects, but he made no effort to blow his smoke away from her face now. "And just exactly what are you leading up to?" he asked huskily.

She turned her face and smiled deliberately into the cloud of smoke, and tried to pull the pipe from between his clasped teeth. He didn't let go. "Just this, darling. I want to save you a lot of heartache, and a bad dose of ennui and all that. Don't you realize, three more weeks and we can celebrate our first anniversary?"

"Well?" he asked, his voice edged with remorse.

"Well, darling, I was so afraid you'd be planning things. You know, to have your old friends in to celebrate. The way you do stick your darling impractical neck out. Recall all the series of little housewarmings you tried to pull off? Again and again? And how your

dearest friends, like the Nortons and Arnolds, you know those de-
lightful broad-minded people who appreciate that bishop record so
much, how each time they had an excuse, and each time sent flowers
or whisky instead. Or that silly blue vase, that doesn't fit with the
curtains, and . . ."

"Don't," he pleaded.

"Darling, it's just me reminiscing now. And how the Whites finally did call, but only when they were sure that there'd be nobody
else so that there'd be no witnesses. But the Parsons did come, and
they did report to everybody, and especially to Lorraine, what small
and niggardly furnished quarters we lived in. And, of course, Arthur
Stuart, so he could get cheaply drunk. You see, dear, I'm merely trying to save you from another series of headaches."

He had taken his pipe from his mouth, and his face was drawn and
white. With pale, hard lips he asked: "Okay, okay, what do you want
me to say now? Well, what about your own brother, then? And that
dinner party he and Fay gave us, and . . ."

She chuckled delightedly, caressing the hard lines in his face with
her long tapering fingers and crimson fingernails. "Darling, you are
mixed up, aren't you? And do you look forty when you scowl like
that. Don't forget, I'm only a little over twenty, and it isn't fair. . . .
Of course, it wasn't my brother who gave that dinner party. He's an
innocent, just like you. Like most men, bless them."

"Go on," he said sternly.

"You never did guess, did you? You merely thought we were stepping up into a better strata of people. My kind. It was my sister-in-
law, naturally. Fay could use me as the *pièce de résistance* at that
dinner. You know, Fay needs something like that to keep her interest
in life going. And there I was, a sweet young thing just out of college
who had blithely taken a great big man away from his wife and
kiddies and kept him for herself. It was a too-precious something to
let that go begging."

"I'll hit you!" he growled.

"I wish you would," she said gently.

"Why do you say those things?" he asked helplessly.

"But, darling, just to save you. You would, if you'd remembered
the anniversary, you would have tried to get your old friends to
come. Even though you are still smarting because they haven't so far,

no matter how affable they are to you on the street or in your office. Isn't that right?"

He pushed her away from him and got up. "I'm going to play that record again, and I'll pour myself a drink," he threatened.

"Do play the record," she smiled, cuddling deeper in the chair he had vacated. "But no drink yet, you know. No morose, solitary drinking before ten o'clock. Only when there are friends. And it's barely nine-thirty."

"Well, who'll show up yet? You just got through saying, no one, no one ever . . ." he cried testily, stomping back to her chair, coming to a stop in front of her, his fingers fidgeting, his knuckles white.

All the time she kept smiling up at him, her blue eyes full of steadfast candor and defiance.

And then suddenly the bell rang.

Quickened with relief, he hurried to the buzzer and pressed it. When he looked over his shoulder at her, he saw that she had straightened with as much hopeful anticipation as he had. For one unpalatable moment her eagerness hurt him violently. Then, hearing the footsteps coming up the stairs, he hurried to open the door, and seeing who the caller was, he said brightly over his shoulder: "Why, it's Arthur Stuart. And practically sober at that."

The gangly, half-drunk young man blinked at the light of the room, and grimacing foolishly at both of them, he submitted to their taking off his coat and hat, and their shaking his hand, before he could say with considerable difficulty: "What 'o you mean, practically sober? Dead sober. Just had a beer an hour or so ago. But I said to myself, I've neglected my dear old friends, my . . ."

"But you will have a drink?" she demanded. "We were just about to have one. We just felt like celebrating something, oh, anything, you know."

"Well, yes," he said with a most daring show of reluctance, as he dropped himself unceremoniously in the chair they had just vacated, and sprawled his long legs and outsize feet practically across the room. "I can't refuse when you put it that way. No, I can't very well and be a gentleman."

"Darling," she shouted in the direction of the kitchenette where he was already getting out bottles, glasses, and ice cubes. "Darling, did Arthur ever hear this wonderful record? Is it all right to play it for him? He'll love it, won't he?"

"Do play it for Arthur," he shouted jovially from the kitchenette.

She put the record on the phonograph, and then sat down on the sofa, watching Arthur with an expectant smile on her wide mouth. He started emulating that smile when he became aware of it. In fact, he didn't remove his somewhat blurred eyes from her smile until the record came to the first refrain:

> "*. . . What ho! said the bishop,*
> *I will not budge an inch until*
> *Another gentle breeze has lifted*
> *The skirt of that sweet young thing*
> *Standing there on that gorgeous hill.*"

because she then lifted her hand, indicating the record, warning him that he shouldn't miss it. He put a bigger grin on his face and turned his eyes dutifully toward the phonograph. At that same moment, however, his host came out of the kitchenette with the drinks, and once more his interest was diverted. But once more he turned his head obediently toward the music, when he saw that his host, too, drinks in hand, had stopped to listen.

He readily echoed their laughter, when the punch line

> "*. . . The skirt of that gorgeous young thing*
> *Standing there on that goddamn hill.*"

came, and while both of them looked at him with such bright expectancy.

"Gee, that's good, all right. That's okay. That goddamn hill, that's good, all right," he shouted affably, extending his hand toward the drink. "It's good, all right, but what the devil is it all about?"

THE ROSEBUSH

by Susan Kuehn

From *Mademoiselle*

———◆◆◆———

I DROVE BY our old farm the other day, and it sure seemed different. Maybe it's just that I don't get a chance to come by here often, with all the work at the filling station and everything. We're piled up with jobs there nowadays, what with everyone wanting to keep his old car in condition. It was only because Mr. Hunter out on the turn-pike had his battery run out and needed someone to tow him in that I even left the station at all. As I said, I was driving out to Mr. Hunter's when I passed the farm. It looked dilapidated all right. The white paint on the clapboards has peeled around the edges, and the rosebush that Mother always used to sprinkle in the morning, right after breakfast, is nothing but shriveled canes and them long suckers that used to give Mom a fit 'cause they'd turn the whole thing wild if they was allowed to grow. All the time *we* lived there she'd cut off the suckers regular. It was only when I started to reach for my knife I remembered I had on my monkey suit with SUNOCO on the back.

It's a dirty shame that everything had to break up, but I suppose it couldn't be helped. How Mother used to fuss around that farm. Take the curtains, for instance. One night it rained in our window and got the curtains sopping wet. Mom stayed up practically all night, drying them out and ironing the ruffles, just so they'd look good when people drove by to church next morning. Everything had to be just so. It's too bad we didn't try and help her more, but it just seemed so foolish to try and dress up a plain farm.

Mother always said it wasn't just a plain farm, it was our home too, and it could be just as trim as the houses in the village with their ruffled curtains in the windows and flowers in front. That's why she planted the rosebush. She bought it at the Higgersville greenhouse for a dollar, and the way she took care of it made it grow and blossom out so pretty it was really worth that dollar just to look at it. It was right out by the front door, which seemed kind of a funny place, because our front yard faces the highway, and besides we always used the back door. Anyway, she used to water it so carefully and trim it with shears now and then until soon there were real roses on it—not very many, of course—and sort of small. Still when Mother put them in the round glass bowl on the dining-room table, they looked nice.

Not that Mother spent all her time fooling around with a rosebush. She worked real hard, but so quiet you never realized all she did. She would get up at five in the morning with the rest of us, except Ruth, who got to sleep till almost seven, when the school bus came. Mom had eggs all fried and toast and coffee warming on the stove by the time we came in from the barn. After breakfast she would clean up the house, always picking up the sweaters and boots we dropped around, but never exactly bawling us out for dropping them there in the first place. Then she would start the washing or mending or ironing, according to the day of the week, and work on that all morning. In between she would come out to the barn, with an old brown sweater wrapped around her, to wash up after the milk pans and pails and to work the separator.

It went on like that for her all day long, and after we went to bed around eight-thirty or nine, she would stay up while Ruth did her homework. They always sat in the parlor, because that's where we kept our best lamp. Sometimes, if I didn't go to sleep right away, I could see the light reflected in the upstairs hall until late. While she listened to Ruth say her Latin or read over an English theme, Mother did more mending. Often she crocheted a tidy for one of the parlor chairs or worked on her daisy-pattern tablecloth. She had made a whole piecework quilt a couple of winters ago, just sewing it to-gether after we went to bed.

I suppose she was a little disappointed that it was just Ruth down there working on her homework instead of Joseph and me, too. Both of us quit school when we were sixteen. Joseph left three years before me, and I stopped a year ago last spring. Mother tried to make us keep on, saying it was so important to graduate and all, but we didn't see it that way. She was real pleased Ruth liked school, so I hope she didn't mind too much about us. We hated like anything to beat our brains out over some fool geometry when we knew it wouldn't ever help us any. All Joseph wanted to do was work outdoors on the land, and I was plenty glad to stop studying myself, although I can't say I was too crazy about the whole setup of farming. Helping in George Schroeder's filling station appealed to me more.

Dad sure was tickled enough to have us around the farm all the time. He found plenty for us to do, and before long the farm was really coming along fine. It was Mother that gave Dad the idea to buy a new Jersey and put in some spring wheat aside of the corn, but she was sort of quiet that fall. I wondered if she was mad about our quitting school, but I guess it was just that her head was bothering her again.

We tried to be extra careful after that about not leaving our things slung around the house, and cleaning up before dinner. Mother always liked to have us clean up in the basement laundry basin and put on a fresh shirt and necktie before dinner. It meant extra clothes for her to wash, but she never seemed to mind. Anyway she didn't have to worry about that for long, because after a while we stopped changing before dinner. There was so much to do around the place that we didn't have time for things like that.

After Ruth started taking music lessons, everything seemed all right again. One day, when the music teacher at the high school heard Ruth picking out a tune on the gym piano, she offered to give her music lessons after school. They cost fifty cents an hour, and taking them once a week meant two dollars a month. Dad called this a blamed fool idea, but Mother was all for it. She finally decided to stop going to the doctor in town. He was awful expensive, and her headaches were better anyway, she said.

Ruth loved learning piano music, right from the first. It meant walking back alone to the farm from the village, because the school bus only made one trip after school, but that didn't bother her none. On Wednesday nights she would walk into the house just beaming. After we sat down at the table, she would drum on the table as if it was piano keys she was hitting, and she would hum little tunes to herself. I guess she must have worked pretty hard on her practicing, because it wasn't more than six months after she started that she was in a big recital at the high school.

The recital was in June. I can't remember the exact date, but it had been marked down on the calendar since March. Ruth wouldn't tell us what she was going to play, saying it was a surprise and that we would have to come if we wanted to find out. We all kidded about it, calling her the second Paderewski, and Mother made her a new dress, pink silk I think it was, with a row of pearl buttons down the front and a crocheted lace edge on the collar. By the time the week of the recital came, Ruth would stay down in the village every night after school to practice. She got home late for dinner, too, but it didn't matter much, since we were working later than usual that month, straightening the corn rows and watching the Jersey who was calving. When I told George Schroeder all about the excitement at our house over Ruth, he laughed and asked me when she and her piano intended to go on the stage. I joked too, but somehow I was kind of proud of the kid, staying in to practice all the time and walking home those three miles by herself afterwards.

We ate early the night of the recital. Ruth had to get dressed in time to be ready when the music teacher picked her up. Mother and Dad were going in later, but Joseph and I had decided we would just as soon stay home, rather than get all dressed up for some piano music. Mother flew around the kitchen, hurrying up to get dinner out of the way in time. It was when she asked Dad to have another batch of mashed potatoes, before he even finished his first, that Dad said he wasn't going to the recital. He didn't like the looks of the Jersey, he said. Mother was standing at the stove then, and she turned around quick-like when he spoke, and said, "You're not going to stay home, are you? Please, Johann. This is her night." I remember her words, because it seemed funny to hear her call Dad Johann. Mostly she talked about him to other people as "Mr. Cook" and to us as "your father." Dad only said he was sorry, but that she could represent the family for us anyway. Nobody said anything for a while. Ruth finished eating, pushed aside her plate and ran upstairs to get ready. She looked kind of weepy. After she left, Mother looked at Dad and said, "You know this is a big night for her. She wants us all to be there. After all the practicing she has done, I should

think that you could spare one night." Her voice trailed off at the
end as if there wasn't any more to say.

Dad was spreading butter on a slice of oatmeal bread, and he
didn't look up when he answered. "Sorry. But it can't be done."

"All right, Johann." Mother put her fork down and turned to me.
"Richard, would you like to go in with me? Maybe your father might
let us take the car. You could drive."

At that I got all excited, because no one but Dad ever drove our
Chevvy much, and *he* only drove it a couple of times a month, when
he took the vegetables into the Minneapolis market. I knew how to
drive all right, though, because George Schroeder let me use his car
now and then. "Would I! Dad, how about it?"

When Dad said he thought it would be all right and made some
joke about sending the car in place of himself, I was so pleased I
nearly upset the kitchen table. After I swallowed some dessert, I
hustled upstairs and put on a fresh blue shirt and my red striped
tie. When I came downstairs, Mother was all ready too. She had
stacked up the dishes, she said, to do in the morning, so that we
could start on time. I thought Mother looked nice in that black suit
she was wearing, and the pink flowers on her hat gave her face some
color. Usually she was so white. It was from the headaches, I suppose,
but the high-priced doctor she had gone to in Minneapolis said
nothing was wrong with her. Of course, you don't have much way
of knowing if he was really right, but Dad said he seemed to know
his stuff.

It was fine for driving that night, still almost daylight outside.
June always turns out swell in Minnesota, not hot yet like it gets in
July but just warm and quiet and sweet-smelling. The road stretched
out smooth in front of the car, and I hardly paid much attention to
anything but the road and the slick feel of the steering wheel under
my fingers.

"I'm glad you came tonight, Richard. I hoped your father and
Joseph would come too, but there's the farm to think of." Mother
was staring ahead at the road, too, and smiling a little.

I didn't know how to answer, because I knew that Mother worked
just as hard as any of us, and still she wouldn't have dreamed of
staying home from Ruth's program. "Yeah, with the calf and all,
I guess somebody should stay home." Then, because I didn't want

Mother to know that I had come just to drive the car, I said, "I wonder how Ruth will do tonight. That sure was a nice dress you made for her, Mom."

"I hope it looks all right against the dresses the other girls will be wearing. She's worked so hard on her lessons, Richard." Mother sat there quietly, still looking straight ahead.

"Those other girls will look like they're wearing old rags, and Ruth's not so bad-looking either." At high school the boys in my class used to say that Ruth would be a knockout someday.

"Ruth's a good girl. But so are you boys. Richard, I've been wondering about you."

What was coming off now? I couldn't think of anything I ought to feel guilty about. "What is it, Mom?"

"Why do you spend so much time at the filling station? Are you happier working there than on the farm?" For the first time Mother took her eyes from the road and looked straight at me.

Gosh, I didn't think Mother had noticed that. "Oh, I don't know, Mom. I just like talking to the fellows there and fooling around with cars."

"If your father would let you drive into market with the vegetables, would you like that? I don't see why he wouldn't. I want you to be happy on the farm."

That got me all excited before I realized that Dad probably wouldn't let me. He was awful careful about his car. It made me kind of sad, listening to Mother trying to figure out a way. "Sure, Mom. That would be swell. It isn't that I don't like the farm, though. Maybe I'm just not so crazy about it as Dad and Joseph are. That's all." I was glad that we reached the high school just then, because we didn't have time to talk any more.

After I parked the car, we went into the school auditorium and got seats near the back. It was pretty crowded with all the relations and friends of the kids in the recital. Ruth was at the very end, the program said. Now we wouldn't be able to leave early. The entertainment was a little late in getting started, too. Mom and I sat there, not saying much, but listening to the talk and the paper programs crackling around us. Every now and then an important-looking girl in a rustling orange taffeta would come in with a couple of people and find them seats. By this time I was feeling kind of excited. At quarter after eight a little girl in a fancy white dress with a big pink sash came out and played "Turkey in the Straw." She wasn't too bad, but so many people came on after her that I couldn't help yawning. I didn't see how Mother could sit there so straight. She nudged me when Ruth walked on the stage, and I sat up then.

The pink silk didn't seem very dressy aside of all those other ruffled jobs, but Ruth looked pretty. She walked across the stage slowly and waited a minute after she sat down. Then she began to play. On the program it said "Country Gardens" by some guy named Percy. It was quite a piece, with all those big rolling chords and little running notes. The way Ruth played, there was something bouncy about its rhythm. You could tell it was hard, too, because her fingers went flying over the keys fast as anything, reaching for all those notes. I didn't know she could play like that. When Ruth stood up to bow after it was finished, she got the most applause of anybody. I've never heard much piano music, except over the radio a little, so I can't rightly say how good she was, but they sure liked her.

After the applause died down, she played a short piece that wasn't written down on the program. The clapping started again, just as loud as before, and even when it died down, Mother kept on applauding. When Ruth left the stage, that meant the recital was over, and everyone rushed for the door at once. We met Ruth outside by the steps, where lots of people stopped on the way out to tell her how good she was. I've never seen Mother so happy. The pink in her cheeks almost matched the wreath of flowers on her hat.

Ruth and I started to walk down where I said I had parked the car, when Mother said no, that we should celebrate. We went over to the Higgersville drugstore, that was already packed. We would have had to wait a long time for a booth, but the Paulsons, from down the road, gave us theirs, because they said Ruth was the star of the evening. Amelia Paulson, who is a blonde about twenty years old, with a red face and big white teeth, told Ruth she was good enough for the movies. All three of us ordered large chocolate sodas, the twenty-cent kind. The noises of the juke box blaring out a cowboy song and people's voices, all mixed together with tobacco smoke and the clatter of ice-cream spoons, made me feel good. I felt like a cigarette, but I didn't have one, because Mother didn't like my smoking much, and I didn't want to spoil anything. I'll never forget how happy she looked that night.

It's a shame it couldn't stay that way. It did for a while, of course, and then it was all over. Not that I can blame Ruth. I guess Dad and Joseph must have got her down. They just plain weren't interested. She kept up at her music lessons pretty steady, walking in and back by herself, because school was out for the summer and the school bus didn't run. Then one day Ruth quit.

I had come onto the back porch with a pail of milk when I heard them talking. Ruth was sitting at the kitchen table, sorting out rubber canning rings and saying, "I just don't care any more. It isn't worth it."

"Ruth, you can't give up now. It's what you always wanted." Mother's voice sounded tired and strange, but I couldn't see her face from where I was standing.

"I don't any more."

"I can't understand, Ruth."

"It just doesn't seem worth it. All that practice time. Now that the recital's over, there's nothing left to do except practice and practice. Or else quit."

No one said anything for a minute. Then I heard Mother. "You can't stop. Not now. Don't worry about the money. We can manage that all right."

"I'm not worrying about the money, Mother. It's not that. It's the walking into town that I hate. The sun shines down so hot that I can't stand it, and there aren't any shade trees along the road. Even when I get to town, it's just as bad. There isn't any air in the room, and it's full of flies, You can't get rid of them."

"But, Ruth, isn't it worth it when you see your reward? Don't you understand?" Mother tried, but it was no good. I could see. Darn Ruth, I thought, for spoiling everything like this. But what could I say? I wasn't supposed to be listening. I put the milk can beside the door. They must have heard me because they didn't talk after that.

That noon at dinner I knew something would come up. I could tell by the way Mother's hands shook when she put the food on the table that she was still upset. When Ruth went down in the basement for some more Ball canning jars, Mother said, "She wants to stop taking lessons now. How can we make her see that she can't stop?"

Dad reached for the bowl of potatoes. "Well, now, Mary, why can't she? Playing the piano's a luxury costs money."

"Can't we manage this one luxury? It would be so nice if she could play for programs at the high school."

"Don't go reaching for things like that, Mary. Everything was fine before those fool notions started."

"Just this once, Johann. Couldn't we afford a piano so she could practice here?"

"Buy a piano! If that isn't the best yet!" Dad chuckled, like the whole thing was a big joke.

"It's not so silly. A piano would brighten up the whole house. We could put it in the parlor. It would be nice to sit around evenings and listen to Ruth play. We could sing a little, too. You used to sing, Johann." Mother pushed back the hair from her forehead, as if it hurt her.

"I never heard such nonsense. First you give up the doctor for Ruth's lessons. Now you want a piano. Where would we get the money?" Dad squashed down his potatoes and poured gravy over them.

"You said the other day that we had a little left over from last season. We could buy a secondhand piano or even rent one. This year I'll do the harvest cooking myself instead of paying a woman to help. That way we could start saving."

"I said there was a little profit, Mary, but I'm not spending it on foolishness. If you want something useful for yourself or the house, get it. If not, I'm planning on a new plow."

Mother must have known it was no use, but she kept on trying. "Can't you see? If we got a piano, it would be something we could all enjoy together. Just because we live on a farm doesn't mean that we couldn't give our children a few of the nice things. It's not good for them this way."

"It seems all right to me. I don't hear any complaining, Mary." Dad poured himself a cup of coffee from the stove, and that finished it. After that no one mentioned it any more. Wednesday nights were the same as they always had been. Ruth didn't hum or drum tunes on the table any more, because the music lessons were over for good.

That summer she helped Mother around the house quite a lot, especially at first. Besides their regular work, they put up preserves and worked in the garden. The rosebush was beginning to look pretty good by then. As for me, I still hung around George Schroeder's station quite a bit, but not too often, because there was so much to do on the farm. We had improved the place a little, what with Dad buying a new plow and trying out more wheat on the east acre.

The wheat came along pretty well, although we had a spell of dry weather along the end of August. We planned to cut in October, when the farmers from around here brought over the threshing machine. Threshing day always is a big occasion around here. The neighbors all get together and help one farmer with his wheat for a day. Then they move on to another place. Altogether there were about ten men, and every last one of them ate like an elephant. Mother and Ruth did the cooking when the crew came to our house. They worked all day the day before, husking the corn, simmering the pot roasts, and making three of the biggest, juiciest peach pies I ever saw.

The morning the threshing crew came over, we all worked hard from seven in the morning until noon. Dinner sure tasted good after that. All the men kept wanting seconds, and Mother had to rush around between the stove and the table to keep plates filled.

It happened all of a sudden. Mother was bringing in the last pie when she fell down. I ran to help her up, thinking she had tripped over something. But she hadn't tripped. She was unconscious. We took her upstairs and then we called the doctor, but she never opened her eyes again. She died that night.

I remember everything that happened that week in a blur. All the neighbors brought over baskets of food, so we didn't have to bother about cooking. It seemed almost everyone in Higgersville came over those two days, people that had known Mother, some of them when she was younger, and the things they said about her made me proud. George Schroeder closed up the filling station the afternoon of the funeral. It was a funny feeling not to be working for those two days but just sitting there inside, talking to visitors. The neighbors didn't have to fix up the house none either, because Mother had just finished her fall house cleaning. There were fresh tidies on the backs of the parlor chairs and clean starched curtains.

We hardly realized what had happened until the funeral was over. Although Dad didn't say much, he acted sort of foggy, as if he didn't know what had hit him. Joseph looked just plain bewildered, and Ruth went around with a scared expression. As for me, I was all right until I went to the funeral. Every seat in the Higgersville church was filled with people who had known Mother, some of them complete strangers to me. Seeing all those people and knowing why some of them had come and wondering who all the rest were did something to me. I can't explain it. I just sat there, wishing a lot of things, but knowing all the time that wishing wasn't any good now. The smell of all the flowers made the whole place remind me of spring, somehow, and I knew that spring wasn't for a long time yet. The minister, Dr. Cope, didn't speak very long, and yet I don't suppose I ever will forget what he said about Mother being a monument of love.

I don't have everything that happened after that quite straight in my mind, because in about a month we all split up. Dad sold the farm to some people in Byton Junction who I never heard of. I don't know what came over him so sudden, but he just plain didn't seem to care whether or not he got the crops in. He told us, of course, before he signed the deed away. Nobody disagreed with him. It turned out that Joseph had asked Amelia Paulson to marry him, so he would buy his own farm anyway. Dad said that he was going to take a rest, and he went and bought a trailer with some of the money. He and Ruth were going to take it out to California, to visit Dad's married sister Josephine, who lives in Bakersfield, and maybe settle out there. He asked me to come along, but I said no. I thought I could get a job at the filling station with George Schroeder. They left just before Thanksgiving, and they have been out there a year.

It seems like way over a year when I think of it. Everything is so different now. Joseph and Amelia live only about three miles from George Schroeder's, where I'm staying, so I go out to see them about once a week. Except the furniture we sold with the house, they have all the rest. It kind of hurts me to see Mom's things in that house. The chairs got scratched in the moving. Mother would have them polished up by now, but Amelia doesn't get around to things. Maybe I'm just too fussy for my own good. I don't know. I get letters from Ruth about every three weeks, and Dad writes now and then. Ruth got a job working in a big department store in Los Angeles, where she is an errand girl. The funny thing about it is that she never did finish high school after all. She met a guy out there that she's just crazy about, and they are engaged. He's a movie extra for one of the big Hollywood studios, so he makes pretty good money when he works steady. I'd like to meet him before they go ahead and get married, but I guess Ruth can use her own judgment on that. Dad doesn't seem to have anything against it. He isn't working right now, but he held a couple of odd jobs for a while on some of the truck farms around there. They are living at a trailer camp, which isn't very expensive, and Dad writes that he is really getting plenty of rest. He gets up at any time in the morning that he wakes up, instead of five on the dot, and just sits around the rest of the day or goes in for a swim. I was sure surprised to hear how he's changed.

As for me, I have been working steady at George Schroeder's filling station for almost a year. It isn't quite so wonderful as I always thought it would be, but I guess things never do turn out so well as you want them to if you dream about them too much. I really can't complain. I work five and a half days a week, with Sunday afternoon and all day Tuesday free. I sometimes go to the movies then, or ask one of the Higgersville girls to a dance, if I'm not going to visit Joseph and Amelia. I don't lead a bad life at all. In fact, when I look at it, it's really pretty much what I always wanted.

Of course, I suppose Mother'd want me to do something better. And she'd be worried sick about Ruth. But after all, you have to take things the way they are. Still and all maybe I'll cut them suckers off that rosebush. It's gone all wild being left alone like that. All I got to do is remember to take a knife.

THE BURDEN
by John A. Lynch
From *The Atlantic*

———————◆———————

I DO NOT BELIEVE the moon has anything to do with it. The moon affects the tide perhaps, but I do not believe it twists men's lives as some say. I do not believe it makes one man thrash on the ground and babble to his friends, and another man date his letter Monday when it is really Wednesday. Because that was what was being done and there was no moon on the nights that came immediately before or after these things. But there has been a moon since, and sometimes it has shone when one man would walk past his dying friend and offer no help, and another man would get up from his hole and go away in the night, and not be heard from again. But I do not believe the moon has anything to do with these things.

For the men would do these things themselves, and only themselves, and I could not help wondering about them. And sometimes I myself would do these things, and later on, when not doing them, would wonder again about those who did. Because when you are putting on your letter that it is Monday, you believe it is Monday, and even when a friend says it is Wednesday you put Monday. When you know you are right, you are going to do it that way. And when your friend goes on with his letter dated Wednesday, you know he is wrong, and you wonder about him.

Mike said it was because one thing and another add up until the little things have become a big thing. It is like the straws and the camel, he said. It is like the water dribbling through the dike until it is no longer a dribble but a flood. And when the days of the week come as fast as they sometimes do, you are apt to lose one or more of them.

When the days of the week lose themselves one after the other, the men are apt to lose themselves also, and Carl will shoot at a man who is the enemy and give away your position, which is a good one for the time, when what he knew was a man is really a turkey, and there is no likeness in the two. But it causes you to get out of your holes and go across the saddle of the hill to the other side where the cover is not so good, and you have to spend part of the night digging another hole. And Mike says that Carl should be sent back, that he is good no more; but all they do is put you on the post Carl had and the fear grows that you yourself will soon be shooting at a turkey instead of a man who is the enemy. And when you take off the safety every time you hear a rustle in the bushes, you do this a great number of times, and they are little times, little things, and soon you do shoot at the turkey, only this time it is a goat.

If you do this yourself you do not feel ashamed, but you say it *was* a man, and you were doing your duty, which is outpost. But if it is another man doing this, you wonder about him, and say to yourself that he has been tired too long and should be getting a rest, that he is not a good soldier any more, though he could be if he were to get a rest.

But how can there be rest when you begin at four in the morning of Monday or Tuesday or Wednesday to go out on the hillside, then over the crest of the hill and into the small valley which only yesterday was spaced with other men, who heard Carl's shot and your shot when everything else was still, and wondered if it was a signal that an attack was beginning. And if they thought it was a signal, then it is well that you did fire a shot, because they are not around now and maybe you yourself frightened them away. At least you can think that, and they cannot stop you from thinking it.

Nor can they stop you from wanting a home in Connecticut, all on one floor, and two bars in the house, one for ice cream and one for good liquor. Because you are now two days of fighting beyond the hill where Carl shot the turkey and you the goat, and you have not had water for twenty-four hours. Nor do you crave water now, for the thirst has gone beyond that stage and it is such that only ice cream and liquor will do. And there will be four flavors of ice cream, all in deep, cold holds because it is what you would need now to stop the dryness.

Mike said that he and George, who is dead now, once tasted water from a pool in which two of the dead enemy lay, and the water was good and it stopped their thirst. And when I asked him why they did not remove the dead bodies first, he said they were too tired, and anyway it wouldn't have improved the water a bit just to have the bodies laid to the side. And I wondered about that, because Mike and George had been there longer than I, and I wondered about them too. But I don't any more, because I have been thirsty, and if it was ice cream I would eat it with dead enemy flesh running all through it, because it would be ice cream and not the flesh that I would be eating.

The liquor is a different thing, however. That is for the hour after the thirst has been eased, and it must be pure. It is for the hour when the jaws have begun to function again and they can move up and down as if in eating a good steak. It is for the hour after the roof of the mouth has become softened again after so much dryness, and the tongue is again sensitive to taste. Because liquor must be tasted, and it must be poured through the teeth and in and out between the lips and the gums and around and around, so that you can forget the day of twenty-four hours just passed that you held a pebble in your mouth and rolled it and rolled it on your tongue, but there was no freshness left.

I first thought of the Connecticut home the night we stumbled down the rocks of a mountainside, and the word came down the column to "hold it up," and thirsty and tired I fell to the ground, and lying there wished for ice cream and liquor. "Hold it up" was meant for one thing, and to me it was that I should now let myself fall on the ground. I remembered that a coin put in a machine brought forth a bar of candy, or one could get cigarettes that way, and soft drinks, and in other places a compartment for luggage, or a parking place for a car, or a postage stamp, or even a meal in some places.

Just so, the way to get a place of rest is to hear the words "hold it up" come back through the column, and as each man hears the words he gets a place of rest, which is the place where he happens to be at the moment. And ahead you can see the men falling to the ground as each one hears the words, and when it comes your turn you fall too, but only after you have given the words to the man behind, because he is tired also and is looking for a place to rest, and a reason for it. And if you fall so that your back lies across an uncomfortable stone, you do not move it away you are that tired, but only lie there and are glad for what little rest there is. And rest can be had in all positions, except when spliced on a tree limb.

Because that is what happened to Paul when he fell to the ground that night, but kept falling for another twenty feet as he had rolled off the shelf of rock that we were crossing. And he called three times as he fell, but no more, and that was only because he was unconscious, and they found him hung in a low tree with a branch caught up in his crotch. That is rest also, I suppose, of another kind, more complete than most, but I do not prefer it, because though I have had it, I cannot remember what it was all about. Just that the pain of the mind and body becomes so great that all pain leaves, that is, it is no longer felt. Of course it is still there, but it has passed into an unfeeling stage and that is the equivalent of unconsciousness.

And having come down the mountain with only one casualty, who was Paul and had to be carried to the rear because we were making an advance, we stepped out into a valley at dawn.

There was a town farther on that I remember for one or two important things, and some of little import, of which there are always many, such as seeing a man cross the road holding a dripping, bloody chunk of meat, and the first impression that such a sight will make. I was alone, returning from the headquarters of the battalion to the headquarters of the company, which was lodged in a fine house with a large kitchen, with a stove and a table already set with meat and wine, which of course had been left by the men who were retreating before our advance, and which we didn't touch, at least we didn't the meat. The *vino* is something else again.

The sight of the man and the meat was a shock of a sort, probably anything as bloody as that would be, so I had to call and stop the man. He was a farmer, or so he appeared, and holding the chunk of bloody stuff out in his hand he said over and over, *"Cavallo, cavallo,"* keeping an eye on the rifle I held leveled at his body, because you could never afford to take a man's word in that time. Furthermore, his other hand clutched one of our blankets, and this was a shock in itself, seeing the blanket—perhaps once belonging to a friend whose death I did not yet know of, or at least he was or had been one of us—and the meat in such relationship that a man should emerge from a yard carrying only a blanket and a piece of fresh meat.

"*Tedesci?*" I forced at him, prodding the meat with the muzzle of my rifle, forcing him to step backwards till he was against the wall of the house and could move no further. "*Tedesci?*" I asked, hoping he would answer "*Si, si,*" not because I desired to know he had butchered one of the enemy, but because I feared it was one of our own, the blanket being there and all. But he only uttered "*Cavallo*" again, pointing to the yard from which he had just come, and I didn't go any further. There were no stains on the blanket, and I let him go. But the little thing that it was lodged with me, and went with me into the town and beyond.

We were not the first to try to drive the enemy from the town, and the blanket must have belonged to one of those captured the night before or perhaps killed in the yard. At that time we were still a good distance away, and were moving forward to dig in on the hill below the town. Having arrived at that position early in the morning, we learned that the town was still in enemy hands and the first attacking force had suffered many casualties, and now it was our turn. Digging in, we waited for the dawn and the time we should split up our forces, one platoon to the west, one to the east, and the remainder of us to come in from the south. But even before that, another company was to attack in the low hills on the right flank and attempt to force a withdrawal from the town.

It was while we were leaving our holes on the hillside and gathering our equipment, moving silently into our loose formation, that the shells began to fall. There was a scramble, as there always is at such a time, men running to the holes they have just left, or diving into other men's holes, or throwing themselves to the ground, behind a stone or two, no matter how small. But there were men wounded anyway, and above their cries there was Carl's screaming. He was not in a hole, but rolling on the ground, his face tortured, his eyes mad, and there was not a mark on him. He had tried to go forward one extra hour, he had tried to carry one extra straw, and now he no longer felt the pain in his mind. There was no need to say good-by to him, because he could not hear us at all, but we took his carbine and his belt and the two grenades he was carrying inside his shirt.

Louis was lost also, but with him it was different, and perhaps better. He was ahead of me when the shells began to fall again, and I did not see him get hit, nor did I ever see him after that. But I was told, when I went back after our engagement to find his body, that he had been alive as they carried him down the hill below the town, and he had died there at the bottom, a hole as big as a silver dollar in the back of his skull. I asked had he been unconscious all the time and they said he had, and that made it easier for him. It would make it easier also when I had to tell Scotty, who had been Louis's close friend, but was now in the hospital from a wound of the last campaign.

So Carl and Louis were gone before we went into the town, which by this time—and it was midmorning—had been fairly well evacuated by the enemy because of the action on the right flank. There were only a few shots, which hit no one, but we kept ready for anything, and until the men found the *vino* and the kitchen with the fine stove, it had been an orderly affair, no one taking chances, everyone on the alert. But wine is not to be reckoned with. Even in this town three of the men stood drinking in the front room of one house while one of the enemy stood in the well of the stairs, beckoning to them that he wished to surrender, waving a handkerchief, afraid to move forward, yet not even being able to surrender at that time. It was good wine, each house well stocked, so we had our choice of the bottles, and this time it was in real bottles and not in the straw-jacketed *fiasci* that served in the lower towns through which we had already passed, and at every house through the many hills.

One man who had been in the night attack I particularly remember because he lay on the road to the south of the town, and the one on which we marched, in rather orderly fashion, to make contact with the platoons coming in from the west and the east. He was lying with two others, and of the three he had got closest to the town, but he was actually only in the outskirts and only a few feet closer than his comrades. He was an Indian whom we called The Chief, and he was, of the three, the only one yet alive, and already he had lain there a matter of ten hours or so.

We filed by, the platoon of us, each man moving wearily along with his personal burden, and a few of us spoke to him, and one man gave him water from his canteen, and each man left him to the man behind, until they were all gone and I was the last man. Going down on one knee, I pulled a blanket up on his chest, for he had already been partly covered with it, and he asked me what day it was. I answered, stumbling a little with the words, "I don't know, but maybe it is Thursday." He seemed satisfied with that, because he didn't say anything more, but just continued to look at me in a way I didn't understand just then, but which is the way death looks at you when it is in a man who is being dragged relentlessly and helplessly into the grave.

So we had our wine and we found potatoes in a house and these we cut and sliced into a frying pan in the kitchen, and chucking the stove full of wood, soon had a healthy fire and over it our pan of potatoes, which are good most any way, but best fried when you have not had potatoes for a long time. Our lard had a questionable source, specked with flakes of wood and earth as it was, but such a thing is not noticeable when it is in a pan with fried potatoes. No one spoke of Carl or Louis, but we laughed and sang a song or two. Nor did anyone speak of the Indian still lying on the road. For these things you do not speak of, nor hardly think of, when you have wine and potatoes, even if all you have is wine and potatoes, and nothing else, even though they are not a tasty combination, but only what is on hand. And the men were coming in with their souvenirs from time to time to show them around, a dress sword, a scarlet cap, a picture-postcard album, a set of delicately carved goblets unearthed in some corner of a basement, a silver-headed cane, all of which they knew they would have to throw down again when we moved out of the town. All except the silver-headed cane perhaps.

Mike said the captain wanted me, which was Mike's way of saying that the captain wanted a man and I was the man, and that is how I happened to be returning later on from the battalion headquarters to which I had carried the captain's message, and where I learned how Louis had died. The headquarters was for the time in a shallow cave on the hillside below the town, a perfectly safe place, and an ideal one, for it had space enough for a dozen men. It lay halfway down a path that branched from the road that ran across the top of the hill, one end of which lost itself among the hills to the west and the other wound into the town that was now ours. It was the same road we had come in on, where we had passed The Chief, and where the others lay quietly beneath their blankets in the warm sun.

Going back to headquarters then, I passed the Indian for the second time. But this time he did not speak, but only turned his head slowly and looked at me again in that tired, deathly way. Nor did I speak, because I had not found out what day it was, and that was what he had asked me before. So I went on and delivered my message, which was that the town had been secured and outposts were in effect, and we would set up a roadblock before nightfall. The colonel said there was no message in return, except that he would be there himself as soon as matters with the weapons company had been detailed. He asked in which building company headquarters was, and after I had told him that, I started up the path.

Fifteen minutes can be a quarter of an hour, and again it can be hundreds of seconds. It is a quarter of an hour when you are having wine and potatoes and showing souvenirs with a roof over your head, but it is hundreds of seconds when you are waiting in your hole during the shelling, and counting every one that comes in or goes over or plops with a lifeless sound, a dud. It is hundreds of seconds when you are going up a road into something you cannot see. I imagine it is always hundreds of seconds when you are dying.

The Chief had died in the fifteen minutes it took me to go down and back up the hill path. His blanket was still to the point where I had pulled it the first time I came by, but his eyes were staring madly and his mouth was open, showing his stained teeth, and a dozen blue flies were crawling on his tongue. More were buzzing and darting at his face, and I waved my hand to chase them off, then pulled the blanket over his face.

It was only a little further along that stretch of road that I met the farmer with the chunk of meat, and then I was back in the town, had made my report to the captain, and had gone in search of more wine because someone had taken the bottle that was mine behind a bucket in the corner. We started on the roadblock as the evening began, and we dug our holes methodically, but with care because we would stay there all night. Mike and I dug together and he had brought a light machine gun up to the position, which we set up to face down the left fork of the road, another gun being trained to fire on the right fork, and a bazooka ready to fire either way. We camouflaged our work, drank again of what wine we had brought with us, and having been assigned our watches in one-hour shifts, lay down to sleep. The enemy did not try to come back into the town, and it was a good thing. Mike was on first watch and he fell asleep, and tired and drugged with wine we all slept the night through.

I had meant to ask Mike what day it was. There always seemed to be the question of the days in the week and no one could keep track of them. I remembered that once it had been Friday and the word was passed around that Father Whalen was coming up the next day. So he came up and it was Sunday, and what became of Saturday we asked among ourselves. No one could say about Saturday. Even Father Whalen said he didn't know, but he would ask someone when he got back, because it had seemed a short week. So Saturday was gone in that week, and in another week it was Tuesday that was missing, and in another both Tuesday and Wednesday. But the days were not the only things missing.

When you speak to a man who is dying, and you perhaps smile at him and cover his chest with a blanket, then go into a house with a roof on it and there drink wine and eat potatoes, something is also missing. In every man this thing is missing, for stumbling along they have all, nearly a hundred during the day, gone past a man who is alive, and going past have thought no more about it, until he lay on the road long enough to die. Any one of you could have saved the life of The Chief, but not being on the road for that purpose you push on to the town, for the coin has been inserted and the handle turned and what comes out is your getting to the town and making it secure. Nothing else comes out and only a bullet or a shell can break the machine and prevent it from securing the town. If a man dies because you have secured a town and the wine and potatoes that go with it, is it your fault? The coin in the cigarette machine will not also secure a candy bar to be eaten after the cigarette has been smoked.

And for your defense you make this excuse, that with a town to be secured and a house to be occupied and a message to be delivered, you cannot be everywhere at once, cannot be doing everything. You can tell this to yourself and, when you find it gets weaker with each telling, you can bolster yourself by telling it to others. But they will only say, "So what," as if they do not know what you are talking about, because they have been fed on wine and potatoes and have gone beyond the town and are now looking up another hillside.

Lying along the paths and the road, and once in a while in the brush where they had fallen, were the others of the night attack, each one with a blanket drawn over him. And there were yet others, in green uniforms, ones without blankets, and fewer of them also, and they would be buried by our men later with *Karl* or *Ludwig* or *Josef* over them. For them we could not spare blankets, but would rather look into their stiff and sallow faces and curse them because they were who they were. But you do not like to look into the face of a friend who cannot look in return, so you must cover his face, and also his body, and make him comfortable until the burial detail comes with sacks and trucks to carry your friends away. And if they are a few days in coming, you do not want them to find your friends looking ugly and green, with their arms rigid, their lips drawn back over their gums, and their sad eyes gone back into their heads, and covered up they do not look this way. So finding them, the men of the detail will say that here was fought another battle, and here lie the brave men who fought it, resting beneath their blankets.

But let them find the enemy, and if he is staring purple and green all at once, you do not care, for it is only when the stench of him has become unbearable that he is worth covering. And sometimes then it is easier to move to another position, where you cannot see and smell him, but from which you may return to his side and see that he gets greener, and you say it is good for him, the dirty Kraut.

There were three days of hill fighting that followed before we took a holding position below the river. The attack had slowed down all along the front, and we were now to wait until some higher echelon would decide for us what was best to do, and feeling the coin register, we would do it.

Each night we crossed the hilltop and went to our positions of defense, carrying with us two machine guns, and every man his rifle or carbine or pistol, and each morning just before daybreak we left those positions and returned to the holes we had dug on the near slope of the hill. We slept in the daytime, sometimes in the holes and sometimes beside a haystack in the shade, and we had time to write letters again, and it was decided that the first day should be Monday, and the day following be Tuesday, and so on until we had had seven days, and then we would start over again.

A road ran near us where we were in the daytime, and the cooks found us on the second morning, and there were two wheatcakes for each man and one strip of bacon. There was always water, and not far to go for it, and the wine had been found in the usual places because there were a few simple hillside houses near by. It was beginning to be more of living, and as the body began to get its rest and the old ways came back to it, the mind also freshened, and we talked of Louis for the first time, because now we could remember him without it interrupting the occupation of a town or the clearance of the enemy from a hill. Also remembered were Paul and Carl, and guesses were made as to when we would see them again. But no one remembered The Chief, except me.

The talk was small, but it was what belonged to us, and it died down only when we became tired again and lay down by the haystack or in our holes to sleep, and when we went out on the forward side of the hill after dark. Out there we didn't talk, but two in a hole, slept and watched one at a time. And if we were both awake the time was passed one watching and the other digging the hole a little deeper, so that after four nights it was a very good and deep hole, and very safe.

But another thing we did at night was think. We didn't want to, but it was that we had to, and we arranged the events just passed, put them in order, one after the other as best we could, reasoned with some, and digested them. Putting them in sequence, we found they were the taking of a number of hills, and a mountain then, and the crossing of a valley at dawn. Beyond that it was a series of hills again, our town with the wine and potatoes, then more hills until we were now below the river and wondering when we would cross it and start up the hills on the far side, where already we could see our shells landing and the fires they left burning at night. These were the major things, then, the names and numbers that would go into the histories and be charted as advances of the campaign. And through them were interwoven, sometimes tangled, the death of Louis, Paul hung by his crotch in the tree, Carl screaming on the ground, the Indian by the roadside, the other bodies on the paths we took, the thirst and the hunger and the fear. But these things would not go into the histories, nor can they be charted.

It was on the fifth night that Mike left the hole and walked away. There were fires burning in three sections of the enemy ground, making rings of light on the far hills, and the moon was up, and it was not a night made for fighting. Except for the occasional rumble of artillery in the hills, and now and then a shot along the river, there was only the sound of men digging deeper into the ground, a little at a time, for the night is long and it passes slowly. I was asleep when Mike left our hole, and only when another man woke me to ask where Mike was did I know he was gone. But I remembered that he had often spoken quietly of how close we were to the enemy, at least how close it seemed at night when we could see the fires, and occasionally the flash of their artillery, and once we heard the rumble of their trucks. And he spoke also of how tired he was, when would it all be over, and must there always be another objective ahead. And so he went out in the night and we saw him no more. The next day, in the afternoon, we were relieved at our positions and the fighting was over for a while, and we began to move out slowly to the rear.

If it was a straw upon a straw upon a straw that crippled the camel, just so numerous little things coming to you in the night, little things returning, will cripple you. No one can say just what moment of what day you begin to wonder more about yourself than about the others, the time that you are not sure of anything. The time that you are about to date a letter Monday and a friend says it is Wednesday and you put down Wednesday, because, though you are not sure it is Wednesday, you are less sure that it is Monday. The crack in the dike widens and through it tumble the little things one after the other until they break loose. And when they begin to overflow, when you can no longer hold them in check, you are apt to get up from your hole and go away and not be seen again. Or suddenly you may scream and remember nothing. And later, when you are rested, they will tell you that you thrashed about so, it was necessary for six men to carry you to the aid station, and you were babbling when they left you there. But you do not remember that it hurt any, for the weariness and the horror and the stagnation of the mind had suddenly turned to unconsciousness.

This will go on, it will follow you and sometimes possess you so at night that you must get up from your bed and walk by yourself, and fight this thing by yourself, and keep the straws from burdening the camel, the flood from crumbling the dike. And because others cannot understand, they wonder about you, and you must go on alone. Because the days of fighting are over, the days of man killing man, the days of hunting—because those days are over, the extraordinary love of friends has passed also and you are alone. Because the days of staring at the dead faces, of waiting in the wet holes of the earth, the days of thirst and hunger, the days of fear—because those days are ended, they would expect that it is all ended.

But it cannot end for you, nor can you make it clear to them why it cannot end, and the burden is yours alone, and you must only hope that it does not grow too great. That the men walking out into the night do not call to you, that the man writhing on the ground does not stare with mad eyes, that the bodies beneath the blankets do not entrust themselves to you, that the days do not once again lose themselves, and falling, stumbling, wearing away into nothingness, carry you with them into insanity, or, withering slowly yet absolutely, lead you over the brink, into the deep abyss of escape, into the final flight from torture that is death.

THE VALIANT WOMAN

by J. F. Powers

From *Accent*

———◆◆———

THEY HAD COME to the dessert in a dinner that was a shambles. "Well, John," Father Nulty said, turning away from Mrs. Stoner and to Father Firman, long gone silent at his own table. "You've got the bishop coming for confirmations next week."

"Yes," Mrs. Stoner cut in, "and for dinner. And if he don't eat any more than he did last year——"

Father Firman, in a rare moment, faced it. "Mrs. Stoner, the bishop is not well. You know that."

"And after I fixed that fine dinner and all." Mrs. Stoner pouted in Father Nulty's direction.

"I wouldn't feel bad about it, Mrs. Stoner," Father Nulty said. "He never eats much anywhere."

"It's funny. And that new Mrs. Allers said he ate just fine when he was there," Mrs. Stoner argued, and then spit out, "but she's a damned liar!"

Father Nulty, unsettled but trying not to show it, said, "Who's Mrs. Allers?"

"She's at Holy Cross," Mrs. Stoner said.

"She's the housekeeper," Father Firman added, thinking Mrs. Stoner made it sound as though Mrs. Allers were the pastor there.

"I swear I don't know what to do about the dinner this year," Mrs. Stoner said.

Father Firman moaned. "Just do as you've always done, Mrs. Stoner."

"Huh! And have it all to throw out! Is that any way to do?"

"Is there any dessert?" Father Firman asked coldly.

Mrs. Stoner leaped up from the table and bolted into the kitchen, mumbling. She came back with a birthday cake. She plunged it in the center of the table. She found a big wooden match in her apron pocket and thrust it at Father Firman.

"I don't like this bishop," she said. "I never did. And the way he went and cut poor Ellen Kennedy out of Father Doolin's will!"

She went back into the kitchen.

"Didn't they talk a lot of filth about Doolin and the housekeeper?" Father Nulty asked.

"I should think they did," Father Firman said. "All because he took her to the movies on Sunday night. After he died and the bishop cut her out of the will, though I hear he gives her a pension privately, they talked about the bishop."

"I don't like this bishop at all," Mrs. Stoner said, appearing with a cake knife. "Bishop Doran—there was the man!"

"We know," Father Firman said. "All man and all priest."

"He did know real estate," Father Nulty said.

Father Firman struck the match.

"Not on the chair!" Mrs. Stoner cried, too late.

Father Firman set the candle burning—it was suspiciously large and yellow, like a blessed one, but he could not be sure. They watched the fluttering flame.

"I'm forgetting the lights!" Mrs. Stoner said, and got up to turn them off. She went into the kitchen again.

The priests had a moment of silence in the candlelight.

"Happy birthday, John," Father Nulty said softly. "Is it fifty-nine you are?"

"As if you didn't know, Frank," Father Firman said, "and you the same but one."

Father Nulty smiled, the old gold of his incisors shining in the flickering light, his collar whiter in the dark, and raised his glass of water, which would have been wine or better in the bygone days, and toasted Father Firman.

"Many of 'em, John."

"Blow it out," Mrs. Stoner said, returning to the room. She waited by the light switch for Father Firman to blow out the candle.

Mrs. Stoner, who ate no desserts, began to clear the dishes into the kitchen, and the priests, finishing their cake and coffee in a hurry, went to sit in the study.

Father Nulty offered a cigar.

"John?"

"My ulcers, Frank."

"Ah, well, you're better off." Father Nulty lit the cigar and crossed his long black legs. "Fish Frawley has got him a Filipino, John. Did you hear?"

Father Firman leaned forward, interested. "He got rid of the woman he had?"

"He did. It seems she snooped."

"Snooped, eh?"

"She did. And gossiped. Fish introduced two town boys to her, said, 'Would you think these boys were my nephews?' That's all, and the next week the paper had it that his two nephews were visiting him from Erie. After that, he let her believe he was going East to see his parents, though both are dead. The paper carried the story. Fish returned and made a sermon out of it. Then he got the Filipino."

Father Firman squirmed with pleasure in his chair. "That's like Fish, Frank. He can do that." He stared at the tips of his fingers bleakly. "You could never get a Filipino to come to a place like this."

"Probably not," Father Nulty said. "Fish is pretty close to Minneapolis. Ah, say, do you remember the trick he played on us all in Marmion Hall!"

"That I'll not forget!" Father Firman's eyes remembered. "Getting up New Year's morning and finding the toilet seats all painted!"

"*Happy Circumcision!* Hah!" Father Nulty had a coughing fit.

When he had got himself together again, a mosquito came and sat on his wrist. He watched it a moment before bringing his heavy hand down. He raised his hand slowly, viewed the dead mosquito, and sent it spinning with a plunk of his middle finger.

"Only the female bites," he said.

"I didn't know that," Father Firman said.

"Ah, yes . . ."

Mrs. Stoner entered the study and sat down with some sewing—Father Firman's black socks.

She smiled pleasantly at Father Nulty. "And what do you think of the atom bomb, Father?"

"Not much," Father Nulty said.

Mrs. Stoner had stopped smiling. Father Firman yawned.

Mrs. Stoner served up another: "Did you read about this communist convert, Father?"

"He's been in the Church before," Father Nulty said, "and so it's not a conversion, Mrs. Stoner."

"No? Well, I already got him down on my list of Monsignor's converts."

"It's better than a conversion, Mrs. Stoner, for there is more rejoicing in heaven over the return of ... uh, he that was lost, Mrs. Stoner, is found."

"And that congresswoman, Father?"

"Yes. A convert—she."

"And Henry Ford's grandson, Father. I got him down."

"Yes, to be sure."

Father Firman yawned, this time audibly, and held his jaw.

"But he's one only by marriage, Father," Mrs. Stoner said. "I always say you got to watch those kind."

"Indeed you do, but a convert nonetheless, Mrs. Stoner. Remember, Cardinal Newman himself was one."

Mrs. Stoner was unimpressed. "I see where Henry Ford's making steering wheels out of soybeans, Father."

"I didn't see that."

"I read it in the *Reader's Digest* or some place."

"Yes, well ..." Father Nulty rose and held his hand out to Father Firman. "John," he said. "It's been good."

"I heard Hirohito's next," Mrs. Stoner said, returning to converts.

"Let's wait and see, Mrs. Stoner," Father Nulty said.

The priests walked to the door.

"You know where I live, John."

"Yes. Come again, Frank. Good night."

Father Firman watched Father Nulty go down the walk to his car at the curb. He hooked the screen door and turned off the porch light. He hesitated at the foot of the stairs, suddenly moved to go to bed. But he went back into the study.

"Phew!" Mrs. Stoner said. "I thought he'd never go. Here it is after eight o'clock."

Father Firman sat down in his rocking chair. "I don't see him often," he said.

"I give up!" Mrs. Stoner exclaimed, flinging the holy socks upon the horsehair sofa. "I'd swear you had a nail in your shoe."

"I told you I looked."

"Well, you ought to look again. And cut your toenails, why don't you? Haven't I got enough to do?"

Father Firman scratched in his coat pocket for a pill, found one, swallowed it. He let his head sink back against the chair and closed his eyes. He could hear her moving about the room, making the preparations; and how he knew them—the fumbling in the drawer for a pencil with a point, the rip of page from his daily calendar, and finally the leg of the card table sliding up against his leg.

He opened his eyes. She yanked the floor lamp alongside the table, setting the bead fringe tinkling on the shade, and pulled up her chair on the other side. She sat down and smiled at him for the first time that day. Now she was happy.

She swept up the cards and began to shuffle with the abandoned virtuosity of an old river-boat gambler, standing them on end, fanning them out, whirling them through her fingers, dancing them halfway up her arms, cracking the whip over them. At last they lay before him tamed into a neat deck.

"Cut?"

"Go ahead," he said. She liked to go first.

She gave him her faint, avenging smile and drew a card, cast it aside for another which he thought must be an ace from the way she clutched it face down.

She was getting all the cards, as usual, and would have been invincible if she had possessed his restraint and if her cunning had been of a higher order. He knew a few things about leading and lying back that she would never learn. Her strategy was attack, forever attack, with one baffling departure: she might sacrifice certain tricks as expendable if only she could have the last ones, the heartbreaking ones, if she could slap them down one after another, shatteringly.

She played for blood, no bones about it, but for her there was no other way; it was her nature, as it was the lion's, and for this reason he found her ferocity pardonable, more a defect of the flesh, venial, while his own trouble was all in the will, mortal. He did not sweat

and pray over each card as she must, but he did keep an eye out for
reneging and demanded a cut now and then just to aggravate her,
and he was always secretly hoping for aces.

With one card left in her hand, the telltale trick coming next, she
delayed playing it, showing him first the smile, the preview of defeat.
She laid it on the table—so! She held one more trump than he had
reasoned possible. Had she palmed it from somewhere? No, she
would not go that far; that would not be fair, was worse than reneging, which so easily and often happened accidentally, and she believed in being fair. Besides he had been watching her.

God smote the vines with hail, the sycamore trees with frost, and
offered up the flocks to the lightning—but Mrs. Stoner! What a cross
Father Firman had from God in Mrs. Stoner! There were other
housekeepers as bad, no doubt, walking the rectories of the world,
yes, but . . . yes. He could name one and maybe two priests who were
worse off. One, maybe two. Cronin. His scraggly blonde of sixty—
take her, with her everlasting banging on the grand piano, the gift
of the pastor; her proud talk about the goiter operation at the Mayo
Brothers', also a gift; her honking the parish Buick at passing strange
priests because they were all in the game together. She was worse.
She was something to keep the home fires burning. Yes sir. And
Cronin said she was not a bad person really, but what was he? He
was quite a freak himself.

For that matter, could anyone say that Mrs. Stoner was a bad person? No. He could not say it himself, and he was no freak. She had
her points, Mrs. Stoner. She was clean. And though she cooked poorly,
could not play the organ, would not take up the collection in an emergency, and went to card parties, and told all—even so, she was clean.
She washed everything. Sometimes her underwear hung down beneath her dress like a paratrooper's pants, but it and everything she
touched was clean. She washed constantly. She was clean.

She had her other points, to be sure—her faults, you might say.
She snooped—no mistake about it—but it was not snooping for
snooping's sake; she had a reason. She did other things, always with
a reason. She overcharged on rosaries and prayer books, but that was
for the sake of the poor. She censored the pamphlet rack, but that
was to prevent scandal. She pried into the baptismal and matrimon-
ial records, but there was no other way if Father was out, and in this

way she had once uncovered a bastard and flushed him out of the rectory, but that was the perverted decency of the times. She held her nose over bad marriages in the presence of the victims, but that was her sorrow and came from having her husband buried in a mine. And he had caught her telling a bewildered young couple that there was only one good reason for their wanting to enter into a mixed marriage—the child had to have a name, and that—that was what?

She hid his books, kept him from smoking, picked his friends (usually the pastors of her colleagues), bawled out people for calling after dark, had no humor, except at cards, and then it was grim, very grim, and she sat hatchet-faced every morning at Mass. But she went to Mass, which was all that kept the church from being empty some mornings. She did annoying things all day long. She said annoying things into the night. She said she had given him the best years of her life. Had she? Perhaps—for the miner had her only a year. It was too bad, sinfully bad, when he thought of it like that. But all talk of best years and life was nonsense. He had to consider the heart of the matter, the essence. The essence was that housekeepers were hard to get, harder to get than ushers, than willing workers, than organists, than secretaries—yes, harder to get than assistants or vocations.

And she was a *saver*—saved money, saved electricity, saved string, bags, sugar, saved—him. That's what she did. That's what she said she did, and she was right, in a way. In a way, she was usually right. In fact, she was always right—in a way. And you could never get a Filipino to come way out here and live. Not a young one anyway, and he had never seen an old one. Not a Filipino. They liked to dress up and live.

Should he let it drop about Fish having one, just to throw a scare into her, let her know he was doing some thinking? No. It would be a perfect cue for the one about a man needing a woman to look after him. He was not up to that again, not tonight.

Now she was doing what she liked most of all. She was making a grand slam, playing it out card for card, though it was in the bag, prolonging what would have been cut short out of mercy in gentle company. Father Firman knew the agony of losing.

She slashed down the last card, a miserable deuce trump, and did in the hapless king of hearts he had been saving.

"Skunked you!"

She was awful in victory. Here was the bitter end of their long day together, the final murderous hour in which all they wanted to say —all he wouldn't and all she couldn't—came out in the cards. Whoever won at honeymoon won the day, slept on the other's scalp, and God alone had to help the loser.

"We've been at it long enough, Mrs. Stoner," he said, seeing her assembling the cards for another round.

"Had enough, huh!"

Father Firman grumbled something.

"No?"

"Yes."

She pulled the table away and left it against the wall for the next time. She went out of the study carrying the socks, content and clucking. He closed his eyes after her and began to get under way in the rocking chair, the nightly trip to nowhere. He could hear her brewing a cup of tea in the kitchen and conversing with the cat. She made her way up the stairs, carrying the tea, followed by the cat, purring.

He waited, rocking out to sea, until she would be sure to be through in the bathroom. Then he got up and locked the front door (she looked after the back door) and loosened his collar going upstairs.

In the bathroom he mixed a glass of antiseptic, always afraid of pyorrhea, and gargled to ward off pharyngitis.

When he turned on the light in his room, the moths and beetles began to batter against the screens, the lighter insects humming. . . .

Yes, and she had the guest room. How did she come to get that? Why wasn't she in the back room, in her proper place? He knew, if he cared to remember. The screen in the back room—it let in mosquitoes, and if it didn't do that she'd love to sleep back there, Father, looking out at the steeple and the blessed cross on top, Father, if it just weren't for the screen, Father. Very well, Mrs. Stoner, I'll get it fixed or fix it myself. Oh, could you now, Father? I could, Mrs. Stoner, and I will. In the meantime you take the guest room. Yes, Father, and thank you, Father, the house ringing with amenities then. Years ago, all that. She was a pie-faced girl then, not really a girl perhaps, but not too old to marry again. But she never had. In fact, he could not remember that she had even tried for a husband since coming to the rectory, but, of course, he could be wrong, not knowing how they went about it. God! God save us! Had she got her wires crossed and mistaken him all these years for *that? That!* Him! Suffering God! No. That was going too far. That was getting morbid. No. He must not think of that again, ever. No.

But just the same she had got the guest room and she had it yet. Well, did it matter? Nobody ever came to see him any more, nobody to stay overnight anyway, nobody to stay very long . . . not any more. He knew how they laughed at him. He had heard Frank humming all right—before he saw how serious and sad the situation was and took pity—humming, "Wedding Bells Are Breaking Up That Old Gang of Mine." But then they'd always laughed at him for something—for not being an athlete, for wearing glasses, for having kidney trouble . . . and mail coming addressed to Rev. and Mrs. Stoner.

Removing his shirt, he bent over the table to read the volume left open from last night. He read, translating easily, "Eisdem licet cum illis . . . Clerics are allowed to reside only with women about whom there can be no suspicion, either because of a natural bond (as mother, sister, aunt) or of advanced age, combined in both cases with good repute."

Last night he had read it, and many nights before, each time as though this time to find what was missing, to find what obviously was not in the paragraph, his problem considered, a way out. She was not mother, not sister, not aunt, and *advanced age* was a relative term (why, she was younger than he was) and so, eureka, she did not meet the letter of the law—but, alas, how she fulfilled the spirit! And besides it would be a slimy way of handling it after all her years of service. He could not afford to pension her off, either.

He slammed the book shut. He slapped himself fiercely on the back, missing the wily mosquito, and whirled to find it. He took a magazine and folded it into a swatter. Then he saw it—oh, the preternatural cunning of it!—poised in the beard of St. Joseph on the bookcase. He could not hit it there. He teased it away, wanting it to light on the wall, but it knew his thoughts and flew high away. He swung wildly, hoping to stun it, missed, swung back, catching St. Joseph across the neck. The statue fell to the floor and broke.

Mrs. Stoner was panting in the hall outside his door.

"What is it!"

"Mosquitoes!"

"What is it, Father? Are you hurt?"

"Mosquitoes—damn it! And only the female bites!"

Mrs. Stoner, after a moment, said, "Shame on you, Father. She needs the blood for her eggs."

He dropped the magazine and lunged at the mosquito with his bare hand.

She went back to her room, saying, "Pshaw, I thought it was burglars murdering you in your bed."

He lunged again.

WHAT WE DON'T KNOW HURTS US

by Mark Schorer

From *Harper's Bazaar*

———◆———

THE MIDAFTERNOON WINTER SUN burned through the high California haze. Charles Dudley, working with a mattock in a thicket of overgrowth, felt as steamy and as moldy as the black adobe earth in which his feet kept slipping. Rain had fallen for five days with no glimmer of sunshine, and now it seemed as if the earth, with fetid animation, like heavy breath, were giving all that moisture back to the air. The soil, or the broom which he was struggling to uproot, had a disgusting, acrid odor, as if he were tussling with some obscene animal instead of with a lot of neglected vegetation, and suddenly an overload of irritations—the smell, the stinging sweat in his eyes, his itching skin, his blistering palms—made him throw the mattock down and come diving out of the thicket into the clearing he had already achieved.

"Is it hard?"

He looked up and saw Josephine, his wife, sitting on the railing of the balcony onto which the french doors of their bedroom opened. She was holding a dust mop, and a tea towel was wrapped around her head, and her face seemed pallid and without character, as it always did to Charles when she neglected to wear lipstick.

He snorted instead of replying, and wiped his muddy hands on the seat of his stiff new levis. Then he walked over to the short flight of steps that led up to the balcony from the garden, and lit a cigarette.

"It looks as though the ground levels out up there where you're working," Josephine said.

"Yes, it does. Somebody once had a terrace up there. It's full of overgrown geraniums that are more like snakes, and a lot of damned rose vines."

"You've got the pepper tree almost free. It's going to be very nice, isn't it?"

He looked up at the pepper tree, with its delicate, drooping branches and the long gray tendrils that hung down from the branches to the ground. He had chopped out the broom as far up the incline as the tree, and now he could see that a big branch of the eucalyptus at the very edge of the property had forced the top of the pepper tree to grow out almost horizontally from the main portion of its trunk. "Look at the damned thing!" he said.

"It's charming, like a Japanese print."

"I'm going to hate this house long before it's livable," he said.

"Oh, Charles!"

"I didn't want to buy a house. I never wanted to own any house. I certainly never wanted to own a miserable, half-ruined imitation of a Swiss chalet built on an incline that was meant for goats." Vehemently he flipped his cigarette up into the pile of brush he had accumulated.

Josephine stood up and shook out the dust mop. "Let's not go into all that again. There was no choice. It's no pleasure for me, either, living the way we are, nor is it for the children." She paused, and then she added a cold supplement. "I sometimes think that your disinclination to own anything is a form of irresponsibility." She turned swiftly and went into the house.

He stood staring after her, frowning a little, for it seemed momentarily that with studied intent she had cracked the bland habit of her amiability. But in a minute she reappeared in the doorway and said matter-of-factly, "I heard on the radio that Boston has had eighteen inches of snow." Then she went back inside.

"Are you trying to make me homesick?" he asked of no one as he started back up the incline, and he remembered the frozen river, snow blowing over the Esplanade, and city lights faint in a blizzard.

He began again to chop at the roots of the broom. All right, he told himself, so he was being unpleasant. He did not like the idea of being pinned down by a mortgage to a place his firm had picked for him. He did not even like the idea of being pinned down by a mortgage. To own something was, to that extent, to be owned, and he did not like the feeling. His idea of a good way to live was in a duplex apartment owned by someone else, in Charles River Square, or, better than that but always less likely, in a duplex apartment owned by someone else, on the East River. He connected happiness with a certain luxury, and, probably, sexuality with elegance and freedom. These were not noble associations, he was aware, and he knew that it was foolish to let impossibilities, as they faded, become forms of minor torture. This knowledge made him chop more angrily than ever at the broom.

It was vegetation with which Charles felt that he had a peculiar intimacy, perhaps the only thing in California which, in the several weeks they had lived there, he had really come to know. And he loathed it with a violence which he recognized as quite undue, and which, now, made him feel childish and curiously guilty. Yet he could not laugh away his loathing. The stuff was ubiquitous, and sprang up anywhere at all the minute the ground was neglected. If it grew up in a patch, it began a foolish competition with itself, and the thin, naked stalks shot ten and twelve and fourteen feet into the air, all stretching up to the sun for the sake of a plume of paltry foliage at the top. Then the foliage tangled together in a thatch, and when you had managed to chop out the shallow roots of the tree, you still had to extricate its trivial but tenacious branches from those of all its neighbors to get it out of the clump. Once it was out, the wood was good for nothing, but dried up into a kind of bamboo stalk so insubstantial that it did not make even decent kindling. As a tree it was a total fraud, and in spite of the nuisance of its numbers, and of its feminine air of lofty self-importance, it was, with its shallow roots in this loose soil, very vulnerable to attack. Charles beat away at it in an angry frenzy, as if he were overwhelming, after a long struggle, some bitter foe.

He did not hear his son come up the incline behind him, and the boy stood quietly watching until his father turned to toss a stalk up on the pile in the clearing. Then the boy said, "Hi." He said it tentatively, almost shyly, as though his father's responses were unpredictable.

"Hi, Gordon."

"What're you doing?"

"Can't you see? How was school?"

"It stinks," he answered doggedly, his dark eyes half-averted and sorrowful.

Charles felt a twinge of pain for him. "Cheer up. Give it time. You'll get to like it after a while."

"I'll never like it," Gordon said stubbornly.

Charles took up his mattock again. "Sure you will," he said as he began to swing it.

"Nobody likes me."

Charles let the mattock come to rest and, turning once more to the boy, he spoke with an impatient excess of patience. "You say that every day. I've told you it isn't true. You're a new boy in the school, and you came in the middle of the term, and there's never yet been a new boy who entered a school late and made friends right away. You're nearly nine, and you can understand that. Anyway, I'm tired of explaining it to you."

"When can I get a paper route?"

Charles laughed without humor. "My God, boy! Give us a chance to get settled."

"I need money."

"You get an allowance."

"I need more money," the boy insisted. "I want a paper route. How do kids get them?"

"You can work for me. You can get in there with a hedge shears and cut out all those vines."

The boy looked at his father despairingly and shook his head. "No, I need a lot of money."

"You can earn a lot of money working for me," Charles said, swinging his mattock.

"I need a dollar," Gordon said faintly.

His father did not hear him, and he did not turn from his work again until presently he heard his daughter calling him shrilly from the foot of the hill on which the house stood.

"What is it?" he called back. She was climbing the path, and he saw that she had a white envelope in her hand.

Then Gordon broke into rapid, desperate speech. "I need a dollar. I'll pay it back out of my allowance. Remember yesterday I told you about that dollar I found? I have to pay it back."

Charles stared at him. "What dollar?"

Gordon glanced wildly over his shoulder. His sister, holding the menacing white envelope in one hand and her workman's tin lunch box in the other, was halfway up the hill, coming along the side of the house. Pleadingly, Gordon looked back at his father. "The dollar. Remember? I told you I found it. You wanted to know what I did with it."

"What dollar?"

He sighed. "You didn't listen! You never listen!"

Charles patted his shoulder. "Now take it easy. Don't get excited. Tell me again. I don't think you told me anything about a dollar yesterday."

"The dollar I found. You asked me what I did with it, and I told you I gave it to Crow, and you said I should have brought it home to you."

"That Crow! I thought you were joking."

Penelope, the six-year-old, was behind him now, and Gordon's shoulders sagged in despair. "I wasn't joking," he said almost wearily as Penelope handed his father the letter. "You never really listen."

Charles read the precise handwriting on the envelope. "Mr. or Mrs. Dudley," it said, and in the lower left-hand corner, "Courtesy of Penelope." He opened the envelope and read the message:

DEAR MR. AND MRS. DUDLEY,

Gordon became involved in some difficulty about a dollar today, and I wish you would help me. The dollar was lunch money belonging to a girl who says she left it deep in her coat pocket, in the cloakroom, yesterday. When I brought it up with Gordon, he immediately said that he did not steal it. He says that he found it on the floor, and he also says that he told his father about it yesterday and that his father said he should have brought it home to him, and now he is fixed in his confusions. He gave it to an older boy named Will Crow, who spent it, and I have told Gordon that he will have to return a dollar to the girl tomorrow. Gordon is a very worth-while little personality, but I do not think he has been entirely happy here at the Crestview School, and therefore, if you can help me straighten this out to his own best interest, I will be ever so grateful.

Sincerely yours,
GERTRUDE GRANDJENT,
Principal.

Charles groaned in exasperation. "My God, why did you have to drag me into it? What will that woman think?"

Gordon's lips were trembling. "You remember? I did tell you, didn't I?"

"Yes, I remember now. I remember very clearly that you told me you found it on the way to school, and when I asked you what you did with it, and you said you gave it to Crow, naturally I said you should have brought it home. *Listen,* Gordon——" The very simplicity of the boy's strategy infuriated Charles, and it was with an effort that he controlled his temper. He said, "Penny, you go in now and tell your mother you're home."

Penny was staring at her brother. "What did Gordon do?"

"Run along, Penny, as I told you."

She went down the incline reluctantly, staring back over her shoulder, and when she had gone into the house, Charles turned to Gordon again and said, "Sit down."

They sat down side by side on the damp slope. Gordon said, "Will you lend me a dollar and keep my allowance until it's made up? I have to take it back tomorrow."

"We'll talk about that later." Charles tapped the letter with his muddy hand. "Why did you tell me you found it in the street?"

Gordon looked away but answered promptly. "I knew if I told you I found it in school, you'd have said I should have taken it to the office."

"So you lied to me instead. That was better?"

Gordon did not answer.

"Answer me."

"Yes."

"Yes, what?"

"I lied."

That was that. Charles started over. "Why did you tell Miss Grandjent that you did not steal it when she hadn't even said that you had?"

"I knew that's what she thought."

"How did you know?"

"I just knew."

Charles hesitated. When he spoke again, his voice was warmer, friendly, almost confidential. "What's the little girl's name, Gordon?"

"She's not little. She's in high fourth."

"What's her name?"

"I don't know. Joan, I guess."

"What color is her coat?"

Gordon glanced at his father sharply. "I don't know. I never noticed it."

Charles bit his lip in exasperation and stood up. "Let's go inside." He led the way in.

Josephine was standing on a chair in the middle of the living room. She was dusting the hideous chandelier of dark metal and colored glass which hung from the center of the ceiling. It was only one of many distasteful features in the house which the Dudleys hoped to rid it of, but it was hard to find men to do all the necessary work, and none would promise to do it quickly. An electrician had torn away a good deal of plaster and lathing, and a carpenter had ripped out some bookshelves and ugly mantels and taken down most of a wall between the dining room and a useless hallway, but neither had returned, and painters, plasterers, paper hangers had not yet come at all. The Dudleys had decided to leave most of their belongings in storage until the work was done, and to bring nothing out of storage that they cared about. The result was that the house was almost fantastically disordered and bleak and squalid, and while Josephine managed to keep an even temper under these conditions, Charles, who found them very trying, did not.

He stood in the doorway of the living room now and said to her, "Why do you bother?"

"The light was so dim," she said, and then, seeing his expression, asked quickly, "What's wrong?"

"Another problem." He came heavily into the living room and gave her the letter. She read it standing on the chair, her face expressionless. Then she stepped down and went out into the hall where Gordon was lurking and said, "Come in, dear."

There was one old sofa in the room, and Josephine sat down there with Gordon. Charles sat facing them on the single straight chair. Josephine took Gordon's hands and said, "Now tell me everything, Gordon, just the way it happened."

The boy's face was composed in a kind of stolid determination, but when he raised his moody eyes from the bare floor to his father, his chin began to tremble, his eyelids fluttered, and suddenly the dogged expression broke in despair, his body sagged, his head fell back against the sofa, and he burst into harsh sobs. Josephine put her arm around his shoulders and held him close while he cried, and she shook her head sharply at Charles as he jumped up impatiently. He sat down again. Finally Gordon stopped crying, almost as abruptly as he had begun.

"How did it happen, Gordon?" his mother asked.

He straightened up and stared at the floor again. "Nothing happened. I just came in the cloakroom and saw it on the floor. I took it and put it in my pocket, and at recess I gave it to Crow."

"Didn't anyone see you pick it up?"

"There wasn't anyone else there."

"In the cloakroom? Before school? Why not?"

"I was late."

"Late? But why? You left here in plenty of time."

"I stopped on the way and played with a cat."

Josephine frowned. "So there was no one else there at all to see you?" she asked meaningfully.

"No."

Josephine glanced at Charles. He drew his lips apart and, with a heavy satiric edge, said, "Well, Gordon, that's too bad! If there'd been someone else there, you could prove that you hadn't——"

Josephine broke in. "Tell me just where the dollar was, Gordon," she said softly, and her voice had no relation to the look in her eyes as she glared at Charles.

"On the floor."

"But exactly where? Was it near the little girl's coat?"

"She isn't little."

"Was it near her coat?"

"I don't know which coat is hers."

"Was it near any coat?"

"It was on the floor, near all of them. They hang on a rack, and it was on the floor near them."

Josephine paused, and Gordon wriggled his shoulders out from under her arm and slumped in the corner of the sofa, away from her. "When can I get out of here?" he asked.

"When you start answering our questions," his father said sharply. "You insist that you didn't steal it?"

Gordon raised his lids slowly, as if they were very heavy, and stared out at his father from under his brows. "I found it on the floor."

Josephine spoke brightly. "Very well. We have settled that. But, Gordon, surely you don't think that because you found it on the floor, it belonged to you? Don't you see that it was just as much stealing it as if you had really taken it from the pocket of the person it belonged to?"

"Not as much," Gordon said.

"But it wasn't *yours!* You knew that."

The boy nodded.

"Well, then——"

"Someone else would have found it!"

"But would someone else have kept it?"

"I didn't keep it."

Charles leaped up from his chair. "That's the point! Why in God's name did you give it to that Crow rat?"

"He's my friend," Gordon said with simple defiance, and then he slid off the sofa and lay on the floor.

"Your friend! A fine friend!" Charles shouted in disgust, standing over him. "Get up!"

Gordon did not make any effort to move, and Josephine grasped Charles's arm. "Let me," she said quietly. "Sit down."

"Nonsense!" he cried angrily at her, and pulled his arm free of her touch. "I'll take over now." He seized the boy by the shoulders and pulled him up on the sofa. The jerk which he gave his body made the boy's head bob back and forward like a doll's, and he slumped against the sofa back almost as if he had been injured, dull eyes staring out of his pale face. "Now listen to me, Gordon. I don't know if you took that money out of someone's pocket or not, but it looks, from the way you're behaving, as if you did. Anyway, you took it. It didn't belong to you, you knew that, and yet you took it. Do you see that there is no difference between the floor and the pocket as long as you kept it?"

"I didn't keep it," Gordon repeated, but almost listlessly.

"Oh, my God!" Charles ran his hand through his hair, and the rumpled hair gave him a sudden wild look. "Listen," he said as quietly as he could, "we are all having a very hard time here. We are trying to live in a house that isn't fit to live in. I am trying to get used to a new office. Your mother——"

Josephine said, "Don't bother about me."

"I will bother! We are all having a tough time, and Gordon can't think of anything better to do than to get into this mess at school. Of all the friends you could pick, you pick that nasty Crow brat, who is too old for you by three years and is a snide little——"

"Charles!"

Gordon lay back on the sofa. He looked ill and defeated.

"Will you admit that you stole that dollar? That taking it from the floor was just as much stealing it as if you had taken it from the pocket?"

"Yes," he answered faintly.

"Speak up!"

"Yes, I *do!*" Gordon cried, and turned his face away.

Then the room was very still. Josephine stood stiffly beside the couch, her eyes fixed on Charles with dismay. Charles sagged a little, as if he, too, were defeated. And Gordon might have been asleep or dreaming, so remote had he suddenly become. Then they all heard a sly noise at the door, and Charles and Josephine swung toward it. Penelope stood there, embarrassed to have been caught. She giggled and said, "Why did Gordon steal money?"

"Go away," Charles said.

"Go to your room, dear," Josephine said, "or go outside."

"But why did Gordon steal money?"

Charles walked to the girl, gave her a little push, and closed the door on her face. Then he came back to the sofa. He sat down next to Gordon, and when he spoke, his voice was nearly lifeless. "You want to earn that dollar. All right, you can, Gordon. First go to your room and write your five sentences. Do them quickly for a change, and then go out into that patch of broom with the hedge shears and cut down all the vines you can find in it. You have an hour left before it gets dark."

Gordon's eyes dreamed over his father's face, and then he slowly got up and left the room. His parents watched him go, and when he had closed the door softly behind him, Charles broke out. "What is it, what stubbornness, that makes that boy so impenetrable? Did he steal that money or not? I haven't the slightest idea. All I could do was force him to admit that there was no difference between the two things."

Josephine was looking at him with studied appraisal.

"Well?" he challenged her.

"You forced his admission. Did that gain anything? And what did it lose? How much did it hurt him? Is it of very great importance whether he stole it or not?"

"I don't know what's more important."

"No, I really think you don't."

"Well?"

"What's more important is why he took it, and what he did with it, and why he did that. What's more important is that he's a miserable little boy, and that you haven't made the slightest effort to understand *that*. All you've done is played the heavy parent, shown him that you don't trust him or believe him, and left him with a nice new layer of solidified guilt, and what is he supposed to do with *that?*"

"Let's skip the psychology for a change," Charles said. "There is an old-fashioned principle of honesty and dishonesty."

"There's a more old-fashioned one of simple perception!" Josephine's face was red with anger. She stood in the middle of the bare room and looked rapidly around her, as if she felt a sudden desperate need, a hunger, for objects. But there was only the sofa, the chair, and Charles. Her eyes came back to him.

"Have you thought of his difficulties at all? Just the simple matter of his writing, for example? He came from a school where the children printed, and he printed as well as anyone. He comes here where the children do cursive writing, and of course he's made to feel like a fool, and he has to practice at home to learn it when other boys are playing. Or have you once helped him with that? Have you even suggested a sentence he might write? No. All you've done is to give him the extremely comforting bit of information that new boys, especially if they enter school late, have a hard time making friends! The one friend he has made you deride. No, don't interrupt. I know he's a horrid boy. I don't want Gordon playing with him either. But you haven't the sense to see that what has brought them together is that they are both pariahs. I think Gordon's giving that dollar to that dreadful boy is one of the most touching things I've ever heard of!"

"If what you've told me about Crow is true," Charles said quietly, "I won't have Gordon playing with him, and that's that."

"Because Crow taught him some nasty words and told him some nasty, mistaken things about sex! You're perfectly right. But you can't just stand there and say no to him! If you were half a father, you would have told him yourself. *You* should be his friend! You're the one who should be giving him a decent attitude toward those things. You *are* his father, after all."

"Oh, listen—— He's not even nine!"

"All right. But he's getting it, isn't he? And all wrong?" And then, without warning, she sat down heavily on the single chair and began to sob, her reddened face lifted, her mouth twisted in sorrow, tears streaming down over her cheeks. "All *wrong!*" she wailed.

Charles went to her quickly and, half standing, half kneeling beside the chair, awkwardly put his arms around her. "Josephine, listen——"

"Oh, I know!" she sobbed. "We all get in your way. We're all a nuisance that you're saddled with! We all just *bother* you! I know! It just isn't your idea of the way to live. You really hate it, don't you?"

His arms tightened. "Darling," he said, "don't be a damned fool. Listen, I love you, I love the kids. Why, little Penny, I ——"

"Oh, yes. Penny, sure! She's tractable! She doesn't raise any problems. That's different!"

"You're crazy. Gordon, too. You. Maybe I'm not much good with him, but that doesn't mean . . . And listen . . . I'll try. I'll go out there now."

She dug in her pocket for a piece of Kleenex. She blew her nose and wiped her eyes. She pulled the tea towel off her head and shook out her hair. Then she blew her nose again. "I'm all right now," she said, getting up. She picked up the dustcloth which she had flung over the back of the chair, and she said, "It's probably just this awful house, the way we have to camp. I'm going to get cleaned up and dress, and I'm going to find a tablecloth, and we'll have dinner at a table tonight, instead of sitting on the floor with plates in our laps."

He said, "Good girl! I'll go and fix it up with Gordon."

Charles went into Gordon's room. It was empty. He glanced at the table where Gordon worked and saw that there was a sheet of writing there. Then he looked out of the window and saw the boy on his hands and knees in among the remaining broom. He crossed the hall to the bedroom where Josephine was dressing. "I may not be very subtle with him, but I seem to get results," he said. She merely glanced up at him, and as he went out on the balcony, down the steps, and up the slippery incline, he felt no satisfaction whatever in his remark.

"How's it going?" he asked the boy.

Gordon glanced over his shoulder. "All right," he said, and turned at once to his job. The hedge shears made a busy, innocent sound.

Charles found his mattock where he had dropped it, and began to chop at the edge of the overgrowth again. Immediately his nostrils filled with the poisonous smell he had noticed before, his hands began to chafe, and even though the heat of the sun had gone in the late afternoon, sweat broke out with a prickling sensation all over his face and body. Once more he was tense with irritation, and he said, "That awful smell! What is it?"

"I don't know," Gordon replied without looking up.

"Like something decaying."

The boy did not answer, and Charles chopped angrily away at a root. When it came free, he shook the earth off and tossed the slim tree down the slope. "This crazy, piddling stuff!" he shouted, and then reminded himself that it was only a kind of exaggerated weed, a thing that grew everywhere, so futile that it could not even send down a decent root and was hardly designed as a personal affront to him. Or was it? He laughed and started to chop at the next root, but stopped at once. "I'm quitting for today," he said. "Come on, let's go in."

Gordon said, "No, I'll work a while. I want to earn the money."

"Oh, let it go. We'll fix that up."

Gordon stared at him. "I want to earn it," he said, and went on clipping at the rose vines.

"All right," Charles said, "but come in soon. You'll have to wash up thoroughly to get that muck off."

He went back into the house by way of the bedroom, but Josephine was no longer there. He went into Gordon's room, but she
was not there, either. On the table lay the white sheet of ruled paper
covered with the boy's writing, his five sentences in their hasty, uncertain, and very large cursive characters. Charles picked it up. The
first sentence was, "I am going to cut vins." The second was, "I am
going to ern mony." The third was, "The sun is shining." The fourth
was, "When it rains here it rains hard." The last, which seemed to
have been written with greater care, with a kind of precision and
flourish which his writing had never shown before, was, "You hate
me and I hate you."

Charles took a sharp breath and held it, then sagged. After a moment he walked to the window and put his forehead against the
cool glass. He stared out into the desolate garden, at the bare earth
and the darkening tangle, and tried to think. When he heard Josephine moving on high heels somewhere in the rugless house, he
began to fold the sheet of paper, and he folded it again and again,
until it was a small hard square. This he stuffed deep into his pocket.

He came into the hall and saw Josephine standing in the center
of the barren living room. She looked tall in an old but still handsome black housecoat, a straight, severe garment which hung from
the tightly belted waist in heavy folds, and was without ornament
or color anywhere. Her hair was pulled tautly away from her face,
and her face was smooth and white, and her mouth was painted dark
red.

She was detached from the room, from the house, and utterly from
him—remote and beautiful, cold in resolution. Never in the ten years
he had known her had she appeared so wonderfully in possession
of herself. And, helplessly, Charles turned away.

He went into the boy's room again, and looked out to see the
boy. But twilight had obscured the garden now, shadows hung about
it like veils, and Charles could hardly see into the trees. Then he
thought that he saw Gordon's shape, hunched on the ground among
the slim trunks, and he went out quickly to find him. Perhaps, even
now, after everything, it was the boy who, somehow, could help.

THE GREAT FIRE OF 1945

by Margaret Shedd

From *Harper's Bazaar*

———————◄•●•►———————

STANDING on the high ground behind the house, she saw that one small flame had separated itself from the matrix of fire within the house and was gliding up the wall. It licked the shingles nimbly and delicately, and, still only a golden tongue, found the window of her room. She herself had left that window open and had leaned out of it helplessly calling help before she ran from the room down the hot stairs out of the house to the earth never more friendly than then.

Up to now the house had still looked quite natural. From the little hill where she stood, too dumfounded by the totality of this event to speak or call out any more, it had seemed to be alight for some grand secret festival: The main downstairs, the study wing, servants' rooms, the kitchen, the bedrooms, and even the attic—the whole dignified, clannish hulk unchallenged except for the radiance through the windows, rising and falling, luminous, tantalizing. Now that busybody flame which had darted out of a cellar window or a rathole or who knows what tiny aperture and had run swift as a lizard up to the second story had found its kind; and with the flourish of grand finale the vaporous curtain of smoke puffs was transfigured into billows of flame-shot black and then into the pure roaring triumph of fire, fire. From down the valley she heard the engines, but they had a long way to come.

The house, which she could see was going to be burned to its bones before any help could reach it, was the summing up of her life, the figure below the addition line of a long list of digits entered through the years, and added up correctly. Logically included in the slant of its roof, its closet spaces, its lonely distance from the village, was everything that had ever happened to the woman, and included as well were all the other houses she had lived in.

Her first house had been a shack in the mining camp to which she and her husband had gone after their marriage. That, too, had been a lonely house because it had consisted mostly of thin walls and defensive partitions instead of wonder and surprise and love; but there her only child had been born. The second house was a cottage in the dirty steel-mill hills of McKeesport, Pennsylvania, and she seldom remembered it except for the bright red amaryllis which that spring had stuck their blunt heads up through the cindery back yard, unleaved, untended, and unwanted.

But the Christmas before the spring when the thirsty amaryllis tried to bloom, her husband had given her the baby bracelet which had belonged to father and grandfather before them, a gold bracelet made like a tiny, pliant snake to fit around the baby's arm. And the snake had blue eyes.

She had placed a little Christmas tree on the inlaid kidney desk, the only decent piece of furniture they owned at that time, and Donny, the baby, was in his high chair near the tree. Don, the father, was late as usual, and she had had to trim the tree alone. But she had managed to hang tinsel, too, on the jutting nerve ends of their mutual and growing discontent; so that time, when he walked into the stuffy little house, she saw him with tenderness. He had stood just inside the front door with one hand on the newel post and one held out to her, something clutched in his fist. "It's for you."

The room had been half dark, lighted by the Christmas candles and the glow of an airtight stove. His tall, young, and stooping figure had been only an outline; now she found herself trying to remember the expression on his face. She had not seen his face. He had still had his hat on, much too small for him. But just then he had not seemed ridiculous. With his hat still on he had stood beside her while she turned on a lamp to see the bracelet, and the baby Don had laughed, enchanted as she had been with the blue-eyed snake, holding his fat arm up to show it to them. There was no blight on that scene, transpiring or remembered, except that now, when it came up to her as precise as a cameo carving, she wanted to dispense with it once and for all exactly as she had just dispensed with the snake.

Because when, shortly before, the housekeeper had come pounding on her door, screaming, beating on the wood, "Wake up, wake up quick, Mrs. James! The furnace has burst, the house is afire, get up quick!" and she had finally pulled herself out of that sedative-given stupor, which like a sample dose of death she now allowed herself nightly, she had had time to get the bracelet and bring it out. She had, half consciously, gone to the window and called for help. Then she had wrapped herself in a heavy gray dressing gown and had looked around the room deciding whether to take out her fur coats and some letters. In her mind's eye she had seen the bracelet lying in a jewel box in the top drawer of her green French Provençal dressing table along with the other trinkets they had found in young Don's pockets and sent her from Tarawa. She had had time to think, No, I won't take it; it was his good-luck charm for nineteen years but it didn't stand him in good enough stead; leave it where it is. So, remembering now the bracelet's earlier associations, which for many years she had forgotten, she was more glad than ever that it was gone. She was honest enough to admit that life had failed her. And as between apathy and pain she had made her choice.

As if to test that decision, the fire peeled off one wall of the house, and the room she had just left opened up before her. There was no distortion; the fire illumined and had not begun to destroy the room which she suddenly realized was dear to her. There was the Provençal dressing table, bought for a white-plastered bedroom they had had in a house in the Berkeley hills. There was the fireplace, now superfluous, and on the mantel the white Dresden clock and the one of a pair of vases that matched it. The year Donny was five, he and a new dog running through the house had broken the other. The twinning of each curve was the root of their charm, so she had been terribly angry the day one broke.

Now she saw the fire whirl up in a rotating gesture to snatch the clock and the one vase with its white flowers, and, as if that were the signal for holocaust, the room was blotted out in a dance of up-prancing, laughing, clapping flames and the dressing table writhed in their grip. I never even saw the bed, she thought, nor the curtains, that fabric I loved. Now they were gone and, again to her surprise, she was grieved; she had thought she was immune to simple emotions like nostalgia or the faint sadness of having old friends depart who forget to say good-by. Surely by now everything was drained out of her to make room for loneliness; and watching the resplendent flames in that space that used to be her room, she knew why they burned so well: They were feeding on the charged and venomous loneliness that filled that room, and filled the house.

She got up and walked back and forth. She had hardly noticed that up to then she had been crouching like a wild animal in from the woods to observe man's antics. Her hands were clenched each within itself and she had no inclination to unclench them; she told herself that this way she was holding on, standing on a hill in a spring night to see the climax of the "dumb show" in which she was a mime, but at which for the first time in her life she was also an observer.

Someone was walking that way, hailing her. "They've got here at last, Mrs. James. They may be able to save some of the things downstairs."

"It's all right." She did not try to compete with fire and hose roar and the bells of rescuers arriving.

"What?" the voice shouted to her. "What did you say?"

"Never mind."

"They've already got out some of the papers from Mr. James' study, and they've started on the furniture. That brocade settee." The shouting voice was triumphant, an achievement boasted. It was an achievement, men risking their lives to extract furniture from a burning house. She tried to remember if they had ever used that settee. Yes, there had been a time, and she was forgetting it on purpose—not so long ago and not long after Donny's death. Their friends had said that his death would certainly bring them together. The servants thought so too. So they had had to do their quarreling in remote parts of the house, not to disturb the illusion. She had gone into his study, which was a separate wing, and he had looked up from the aureole of fluorescent light around his desk.

They were both lonely, he in the light and she in the shadows at the doorway; this drew them together. But they could not meet, and reiterative failure sharpened their claws and teeth. She could only see the dreary hunch of his shoulders and his fingers tapping on the paper from which he had just raised his eyes, a poor tense gesture trying to be withdrawn and arrogant and looking only peevish. And the wooden hopelessness which by now was one of her major emotions, far better articulated than love or hate, came to harden the muscles of her body. Once they must have been strangers; now they were something much less and much more than that. They had got to a condition as precise as cancer or leukemia—frustration, loneliness which reached its peak in the presence of the other and expressed itself in violence.

Whatever the ritual of that particular quarrel, like moving from locked cell to cell, it had at least ended with finality. He had gone and had not come back. The last she had seen of him, she was sitting on the brocade settee and he was standing in front of her saying one phrase over and over, flogging a dead horse, she had thought at the time, and all the dull, thwarted obscenity of that phrase was suggested by his toneless words, "You dirty, frustrated bitch, you dirty, frustrated bitch, you . . ."—negation become virulent, blankness sick with its own dead weight.

And he was right; she saw this for the first time and saw it as an inescapable conclusion. Of course she had always known it couldn't go on forever, two righteous people tightening the screws on each other. But now she saw that frustration has its own climax. The corruption of a mutually exclusive loneliness may start with one little spot in the heart, but the certain end is the atom bomb. And looking at the splendid fire that consumed her house, she thought, This is my private atom bomb, come to me in the pure justice which any intelligent person knows he will ultimately receive. Look at it, she called to herself, striking her thigh with her clenched hand to insure her own attention to the phenomenon of a life brought around full circle.

The fire had blown to statuesque grandeur and for a plume into the sky it had taken hold of the house trees, which dignified this man-made, wooden contrivance in their midst and now were dying for their pains. The three tall sentinel firs made their pyre apart, but the others, among them the maple outside her window, were meeting common death with the house they shaded. This was a great fire, the biggest in these parts for twenty years. The watchers drew back to safer distances. The rescued settee, which had not been carried out far enough, began to smolder, and no one would brave the heat to rescue it again.

The fire chief, village druggist disguised in a helmet, came up to comfort her and apologize, "It's a pity, Mrs. James, we couldn't save anything to speak of. The way the draft carried the flames you'd have thought that house was built to be burned. Excuse me, ma'am, I guess you're feeling bad enough."

She had no idea what words he expected from her, so she pointed toward the fire by nodding her head upward, as much as to say, What is there to say? But he thought she was indicating the settee, now smoking like a Christmas pudding, and he felt guilty about it.

"I know," he said humbly. "I thought we sure had it out far enough."

"Throw it back into the fire." She heard her own harsh, unkempt voice and she hadn't meant to offend the druggist-fireman, who backed off hurriedly, disconcerted by her ferocity; it was just that she could not help voicing—and in the face of the fire's unrestraint, without inhibition—exactly what was in her mind . . . because she had decided to throw into the fiery furnace every shred of her life that she could lay hands on.

There was very little more to be done to this house. Already gone, in the crumble of dead walls and sparks that chased the stars away, was the house's showy assumption that it could give security. Only the carpenters who installed them knew how many locked windows and doors had sealed security inside. Gone, too, were possessions in the plain sense of the word; the settee was seared testimony to this. Even the inventory of the furnishings, put away in the inlaid kidney desk, was burned up; so she would never know exactly what had been destroyed, except the necessity to possess things like bridge tables and bookcases.

And if that was all, it was easy. Pyromania is not an unpleasant disease when restricted to objects, even one's own. The rub comes, she was thinking, when you start tossing idleness in with the bridge tables and the inertia of vicarious living in with the books in the case. But in her heart she knew she was trying to put something off with this kind of grand talk: "Pyromania is not an unpleasant disease." If only there were a way to burn up the words themselves, *I love you—— I hate you—— I can't bear this another moment——*

You're a fool. So often the words were really inaudible, the tired face muscles rubbering, soundless. Or else they were distorted beyond their function—their meanings had long since vanished and what remained was a club in the hand, gummed up with blood and brains.

But what words were they that dinned in her ears? Not soundless these. It was her own voice again, now reverted to the maledictory, puritan twang of her ancestors. *"You're exactly like your father, Donny, selfish, selfish. You even have his same little neck and big head. Please get out and leave me alone."* Of course he had come back again and again, because he needed so badly what she had never given him. But that had been the winter of the first and, she could see now, unalterable betrayal. Glassed front porch where he always left muddy tracks; he was nine: *"Don't you ever think of how I have to clean up after you? Don't you . . . ever . . . think . . ."* *"Mother, I want to tell you something."* *"Oh, all right, but go first and turn off the basement light, you always leave it on, or do you want me to tramp up and down?"*

Now to throw that house into the fire, long upstairs hall with the fleur-de-lis damask paper and the supercilious sheen of hardwood veneer; consumed, consumed all echoes of whining spiritual penury. What had she ever given him? What could that house, their first step toward comfort, have meant to him except the place and the time when he learned that the soft underbody of childhood has to be hardened against assault, most predatory of all, from his mother? In a sense he had never learned that, had always remained vulnerable. Months after he was dead, she had got a letter, delayed in route, which had said, clumsily—because she had never allowed him much practice in real communication and his other letters had been in that set, inarticulate form which a million lonely kids had separately evolved in Italy and the Pacific but which had become as uniform as if the War Department itself had composed and serialized it for them—which had said in effect that when he came back he was going to get acquainted with her, that it must be his fault that he never got to know his mother, that things would be different; maybe in the nice new house things would be different.

The immature flourishy lines on Red Cross paper were gone now, a minor puff of smoke, a pale incandescence lost in the rumbling core of total fire. She had failed him, and the fire was erasing failure, all tracks and traces, along with his letters and the clothes he had worn the day he was inducted and the bed he had slept in since he was five years old, just as it was also destroying the less poignant and uglier traces of her failure, day in and out, with the other Don. She had failed them both; one was dead and one had fled, and nothing remained—except guilt.

But that burned brightly enough, as fine a fire as hell.

It was hell, nor more nor less. Guilt was hell-fire. It tore at her eyeballs, and looking at it was more than looking because it had already begun to devour her. *Give my body to be burned. . . . And give my body . . .* What was it, a text pricked out on a childish embroidery card, needle holes ready for the yarn? But now the text was pricked in fire: *Body to be burned.*

The clawing flame fingers began to encircle her heart. What did they want? Could they release the dream that had been walled up in there? A dream as soft-feathered and surely molded as a thrush, but lifeless now, head battered and wings shredded from beating against the walls of defeat. That dream of life, giving and taking and of loving—poor love—was dead. She had failed; and failure had hardened into guilt; and the heart was a tomb and the flame fingers could probe and claw to no purpose—forever. That was it. She had forgotten. Hell was a flame forever; that was the whole point. Eternal fire.

She was sure that if she could raise her eyes from the fire she would certainly see looming overhead, exactly as in the aerial photographs of Nagasaki: the great white mushroom of smoke, that set piece, the bloom of frustration, the flower of hell. Almost absently (aware, though, that even if she herself was alight in the eternal fire, she had nevertheless hit on a truth) she thought that Nagasaki was no mere distillation of logarithms and uranium; it was the same hell that man had compounded of brimstone long ago and left raging in the bowels of time and space, but had hauled up now in 1945 and hurled, visible, onto earth's surface. All this because man had got no satisfaction from his brimstone hell. She laughed.

But as for me, she said, this is my fire; I won't have to wait. This is my atom bomb, conceived in me, this weltering, shuddering, percussing violence nurtured within me in silence and in the secret crevices of denial, and now grown to its unchecked prime. So now certainly I can embrace it and go down to destruction and forget eternity and guilt and the voice of a man and a child calling, calling, and I did not answer. Her clenched hands beat on each other, but the matter was settled: She was going to walk into the pyramid of fire before her, which had already melted the sinews of a lifetime and could do as much for the frailer structure of a body. This was decisive, a compulsion finally requited.

And she sighed. For the first time she took her eyes away from the fire. That was all that happened. It was a momentary stay of sentence, like a lapse in the continuous roar of breakers, when by some unrecordable complicity in tides and wind and water stresses there is silence and no breakers' roar. She paused and looked around.

She saw that oddly enough the woods behind the house had had nothing to do with the fire. Under her feet there were buds of bleeding heart and violets. In the valley, beyond the banshee shrieking of guilt and fire engines, a living thrush twittered. Could it be that the sky was reddening not with blood but with dawn? That embroidered text pricked up in her mind again, but this time all of it, the beginning and the end—*if I give my body to be burned and have not love . . . and have not love.*

Spring dawn became something faintly more than the shadow smell of ground flowers under the leaves; and when she breathed she had to unclench her hands, because it was impossible to inhale the violet-tinged, dogwood-tipped air without also moving her neck and shoulders to relax them, then relaxing her arms, and at last her hands, which she held upward waist high and opened into palms.

In one of them, of course, lay the golden, blue-eyed snake. She had saved it without knowing it, and exactly when she thought she had made up her mind not to save it; and she had taken it because it was all she had worth saving.

FIGHTER
by John Caswell Smith, Jr.

From *The Atlantic*

POKE'S BED groaned and squeaked as he twisted spasmodically to avoid the big, faceless man in his dream who leveled a pistol at him. He shrank back, frightened and defenseless. But when the bullet hit him, he laughed to himself with the realization that it does not hurt to get shot. Just a heavy thud like a fist hitting you. Poke felt a detachment from the fight that had started it all. The whole thing seemed ended and far away, now that the great noise of the gun had ended all the lesser noises. He could feel that his right leg was soaking wet, and that the sticky, warm blood was filling his shoe.

As he began to sag and drop weakly where he stood, there came the banging at the door, and the noise of feet stamping about in the hallway. A muffle of voices was trying to penetrate down through his sleep to his tired mind, calling his name; and as he heard the back window raised, he heard frightened voices saying, "They're breaking that door in! Hurry up and jump! Never mind the dog. He's tied up."

The hammering at the door kept on and it seemed to Poke that it was an especial torment designed only for him, to keep him from dozing off into a peaceful sleep. It grew louder and more insistent until at last, in revengeful anger, he gave one final surge and raised his head to shout. It was only then that he heard his name called, clearly this time, and he sat up straight, gasping for breath and clutching through the bedcovers at his leg. He looked around the room and saw that it was daytime, when again there came that heavy thumping of a fist against the door.

"Poke!" The voice called him. "Poke! Wake up, man!"

Poke grinned to himself. "Wait a minute," he called, and drew his big frame out of bed. He stopped cautiously before putting his hand on the latch. "That you, Country Boy?" he asked.

"Yeah, man. Open up. Damn!"

As Country strode into the room, Poke was already back in bed, as though trying to recover some of the heat his body had lost during the moment he had been standing at the door in his underwear. Country was a rustic-looking, flabby youth whose clothes hung loosely on his body. "You jus' a sleepin' po' boy, ain't yuh," he said to the hunched-up shape in the bed. Poke grunted and drew the covers tighter.

Country walked over to the window and raised the shade. The afternoon sun streamed through the window. He tapped lightly on the pane at a shapely brown girl who was passing at the moment. She turned. "Hello, Country!" she yelled. He raised his hat in mock grandeur and bowed. The girl hurried on with a gesture of feigned impatience. He returned his hat to his head and reached into both pockets of his long, shapeless overcoat. From one pocket he drew out several partially smoked cigarettes, from the other a match. Without turning from the window, he lighted a cigarette and returned the others to his pocket. "That Hattie sho' kin truck, you know that, Poke?" he said.

Poke turned over to squint at the figure standing by the window. "Hunh?" he groaned, still half asleep. He shaded his eyes from the winter sunlight that found its way past the window.

"I say that Hattie sho' kin walk fine."

"Yeah." He saw the blue clouds of smoke floating in the sunshine. "Gimme a smoke."

"Ain't got nothin' but stumps."

"Well, gimme a stump, then! Damn, I wanna smoke. Not a lotta yo' mouth."

Country turned and sauntered over to the bed, groping in his pockets. He lighted the cigarette butt he placed between Poke's lips, blew out the match, and seated himself on a chair near by. Poke reached from the bed and flicked the first ash of his cigarette into an ash tray on a small table beside him.

"I ain't never noticed that table before." Country sat forward to place his hand appraisingly on the shining top of the table.

"Jessie bought that. She tryin' to fix this place up a little."

Country pushed his hat back on his head and looked around the small room. "Sho' looks nice," he said quietly. "Jessie comin' in tonight?" He leaned forward to crush out the half inch of cigarette.

"Yeah. S'posed to, anyhow."

"You'n her goin' tuh th' dance?"

"What dance?"

"What dance! You mean you ain't heard about th' stomp's gonna be at the Blue Moon t'night?" Country's face was a study in disbelief.

"Aw, *that* ole dance. Yeah, I 'most fuhgot about it." Poke looked gravely at his own cigarette stub before mashing it out on the ash tray. "Naw, man. I ain't goin' to no dance tonight."

"How come yuh ain't goin'? You broke?"

"Naw, I ain't broke. I jus' ain' goin', thass all." Poke was becoming belligerent. Country stood up slowly and stretched himself without feeling any real need for it. "Le's get outta here," he said softly, and walked back over to the window to look aimlessly at the people walking by. He felt not a little satisfaction with himself, for now he knew at least that he didn't have to worry about Poke going to that dance. It wouldn't help Poke's parole record any if he should tie up with any of those tough hombres from across town. House parties, where you knew everybody, were easier; but public dances were something else again, because nobody was in his own neighborhood, and there were always cops at public dances.

All Poke had to do was just be *seen* where there was a fight and back he'd go to the reformatory to do some more time. Well, he wasn't going to the dance, and that was one worry off Country's mind. He could tell that to Jessie when she came in off her job tonight, and she could take over from there. He often wondered to himself why he bothered about Poke, but he always told himself he just liked the guy.

Besides that, Jessie was his cousin and if he could look out for Poke during the week, it sort of helped; gave him a tie to somebody. When she put her hand on his arm each week and said, "Country, look out fo' Poke and see he don't get in no more trouble," he always laughed softly at her, but he knew he was going to keep on helping. Standing at the window, he smiled again to himself and turned around to look at his responsibility.

Poke was nearly dressed and had removed from his head the section of stocking, knotted at one end, that kept his hair from getting mussed while he slept. He walked to the foot of the bed and slid a necktie from the white iron rail of the bed and began knotting it around his neck. The two were silent, both thinking of the fact that it would not be very long now before they would meet Jessie at the subway station. It had become a sort of ritual on Thursdays, and from this point on there was not much need of conversation. Some lunch and a game of "61" at the poolroom would take care of their thoughts until late afternoon.

Jessie pushed through the crowd that surged through the turnstiles and hurried up the stairs. She did hope Poke hadn't got himself in any trouble; but of course he hadn't—otherwise Country would have called her. Yet she couldn't keep the nagging little worry out of her mind.

Poke wasn't really bad. He didn't even carry a knife; hadn't ever carried one. If he could only get a good job. But he always had such bad luck, and besides, nobody wanted to hire a fellow with a prison record. Trouble always seemed to follow him around so. The cops kept such a close watch on him. He couldn't even take a quick ride over to Jersey without asking permission to leave the state. If only she didn't have to be away from him so much.

She reached the top of the stairs and looked anxiously at the crowd of people standing in front of the cigar store. There they were: faithful, slow-talking Country and her tall, broad-shouldered Poke. Poke saw her and walked over to meet her in the middle of the sidewalk, while Country lagged behind with a show of indifference. Poke kissed her roughly and took the small handbag she was carrying. "Hello, Baby," he said, and made a soft, punching motion at her with his free hand.

"How're you, Poke? Hello, Country—whatcha know good?" Relief and positive happiness flowed into her voice.

"Ev'vything's good. 'At's why I knock awn wood." Country snapped his fingers and pushed his hat forward over his eyes. Jessie laughed and took him by the arm as she walked between the two men.

Music blared at them from radio shops as they walked leisurely along, and there was loud, friendly talk all about them. Jessie liked it. Country's easygoing languidness reassured her, too, and she could know that Poke had not been in any fights.

For his part, Poke seemed unaware of everything around him. He was frequently like this, wordless and presenting a stolid, enigmatic exterior. He never talked much under any circumstances. Silence and muscular expression were his way of life. It seemed useless to him to try to explain about the things that went on inside his head. He knew people would laugh, so he laughed it away himself and put a hard-boiled front in its place.

Sometimes, all the things he felt inside would well up into his arms and hands and they would grow taut, feeling the need to strike out at something visible—something that could be solved or conquered in terms of his limited powers. Tangible energy was what he understood; and whenever he had hit a man and felt him deaden and drop, it gave him a strange sense of triumph and release. Violence offered a crazy kind of peace because he was familiar with it without understanding it.

As they approached a tenement entrance, the door suddenly flew open, and a short, heavy man hurtled through it, leaning dangerously forward. He lost his balance and fell face downward on the sidewalk, but scrambled to his feet cursing and started back furiously toward the building. He was met at the door by a slender, wiry black man who lifted a knee to his stomach and ripped an uppercut into his face. The stout man fell backward with a groan and rolled over into a pile of dirty paper.

Jessie screamed involuntarily and held tighter to Poke's arm, which she felt stiffening like a steel coil. Country looked quickly up and down the street and stepped over to take hold of Poke's other arm. "Shut up, Jessie," he said, and pulled persistently on Poke's arm. "Just keep awn walkin'. Goddammit, Poke, keep walkin', willya! 'F a cop shows up now, he'll swear t' Christ *you* hit 'em." Poke felt as though they were holding open the jaws of a trap, permitting him to escape. Jessie was clinging to his arm, her eyes wide and frightened. Halfway down the block they looked back. A crowd had gathered, and they couldn't see what was going on.

At the corner, the trio turned into a side street, and halfway down the block they entered a place called "Pearly's Bar-B-Que." There was a bar along one side, and a long row of booths on the other. A music box near the door was sending out blues from a deep-throated contralto voice. There was a low hum of voices coming from the booths, occasionally broken into by high-pitched laughter. Somewhere, in the back of the room, a young girl was singing with the music, and at the far end of the bar a small knot of men stood talking in desultory tones.

Up near the door, the bartender brightened as the three people entered. He was a slender, yellow-skinned man with sandy-colored, woolly hair. "Whatcha know, Country?" he said. "Are you in the groove, Smooth?"

Country grinned. "Yeah, man. Groovie as a ten-cent movie." He walked over and leaned on the bar. Poke and Jessie kept on into the room and slid into one of the booths at the far end.

The bartender's face sobered for a moment and he leaned forward. "Ain't that Poke Benson?" he whispered.

"Yeah—why?" Country kept his voice down and glanced at the booth where his two friends were seated. Jessie was facing him and talking earnestly to Poke, who sat across from her.

"Nothin', oney I don' want no trouble in here. The pay-off's tough enough as it is." The bartender looked anxiously at Country.

"You ain' goin' tuh have no trouble. 'At boy's awright."

The bartender wiped a section of the bar with a damp cloth. "He may be awright to you, but I heard about that ghee—plenty. You git 'im the hell outta here. I'm doin' awright wit this little hustle I got, and don' wanna git it all broke up."

"Aw, man, fuhgit it. 'At boy ain' go' hurt nobody. I bin knowin' Poke fuh long time. You jus'g'wan an' sell yo' li'l bit a whisky, an' ev'vything's gonna be groovy." Country began a rhythmic jerk of his shoulders from side to side to keep time with the music. He waved at Jessie, who had looked up at him when he had begun swaying his shoulders and snapping his fingers. She smiled and waved back at him. Country stepped closer to the bar. "Trouble is," he said, "all you cats go bristlin' up when Poke comes round. He ain' go' start nothin' lessen somebody else starts gittin' bad. 'At boy ain' never bin in no trouble he made hisself."

A fat waitress in a maroon-colored uniform stepped up to the bar, near the small group of men. "Draw two!" she shouted. The bartender turned half toward her but lingered a moment where he stood.

"Well, you jus' stick aroun' an' keep your boy straight. I do' wanna take no chances. 'At baby's poison." He turned away then, and sauntered over to the beer taps. Country walked slowly to the booth where Jessie and Poke were sitting. The fat waitress stepped across in front of him, placed two glasses of beer on the table, and looked expectantly up at Country. Ignoring her, he slid into the seat beside Poke.

"Whatchawl gonna do?" he asked, and drummed lightly on the table with his fingers. The waitress walked away and resumed her seat at the end of the room.

Jessie looked nervously at Country and tried to smile. "I dunno, Country," she said. "Me an' Poke ain't decided yet." Country looked at Poke and decided not to say anything. He went on drumming on the table and whistling a tune that he made up as he went along.

"Well, I guess I'll mosey along," he said presently, and stood up. "I got me a little run tuh make, an' I'll pick y'awl up later awn." He nudged Poke gently. "Take it easy, Greasy," he said, and started toward the door. He could tell that Poke needed woman's talk now. There wasn't any place in particular for him to go, but he knew he could find them later on if he wanted to. He waved at the bartender on the way out, and winked reassuringly at him.

Jessie sipped at her beer and looked at Poke, who kept looking at a spot on the table. "Then what did the man say, Honey?" she asked.

"Said he didn' need no help."

"Did he say why?"

"Nope. Jus' said he didn' need no help."

"Did yuh show 'im that card the man gave yuh?"

"Yeah, but he didn' even read it." Poke made a helpless motion with his big right hand, coiled it into a fist, and brought it softly down on the table.

Jessie was trying to be cheerful, but her voice was tight and tense. "Well, maybe you c'n get somethin' nex' week, huh?"

Poke didn't answer. It was always like this whenever he tried to talk. There was too much to talk about and there were no words for some of the things he felt. Besides, there was the dull pounding in him that never seemed to stop. He knew, in some vague, intuitive way, that it was all made from old childhood hurts; from the times when he first felt like crying whenever anyone spoke harshly to him. He knew it was made from the beatings his father gave him that made him run away from home, and from being chased and beaten in white boys' neighborhoods the times he had crossed the ghetto boundaries.

Mixed with the bitter memories were all his futile yearnings; it was all stirred up in him now, each part indistinguishable, flavored with shame and fear and anger and the crushing endlessness of walking up and down in a prison cell. The power and the impotence were a distorting combination, resolving themselves into an uncertain and aimless strength.

"Poke. Ain't you goin' t' speak tuh me?" She could feel his distance, and touched his hand as though to bring him back to consciousness. "Poke," she said again, "did I say somethin' yuh didn' like?" He looked up at her and smiled.

"Pay it no mind, Baby," he said. "I jus' don' feel like talkin' now, thass all. Le's go do somethin'."

"I gotta go get muh hair done, Poke." It relieved her some to see him smile. This was more like him, and she wanted to hurry to the hairdresser's so that they could go to supper. She reached into her pocketbook and took out a couple of one-dollar bills. "Pay for the beer and le's go. Miss Sally's gonna be lookin' fuh me at six o'clock, an' it'll *be* six in a little bit."

Poke picked up the money carelessly. "You g'wan over there, an' I'll drop by that way in about a hour," he said.

Jessie looked uncertainly at him for an instant. "O.K.," she said, and hurried out.

Poke took a cigarette from the package that lay in front of him. As he lighted it, the waitress came to his table to remove the two empty glasses. "Gimme another one," Poke said. She walked away without saying anything. As she strode over to the bar, the front door opened and three men walked in.

They were all dressed alike, and were of about equal stature. Each wore an almost white, wide-brimmed hat, a long, double-breasted dark blue overcoat, and in each outside breast pocket there gleamed the carefully folded points of a white silk handkerchief. All three wore bright yellow kid gloves and all had white scarves neatly folded around their necks. They stepped up to the bar and pretended to be oblivious to the stir their entrance caused in the room. The bartender looked uneasily out of the window, and with a half-smile walked to a spot directly opposite them.

"Whatchawl gonna have?" he asked quietly.

The waitress arrived at the bar and drawled, "Draw one." The white hat in the middle, at the sound of her voice, looked around. "Hello, Jelly-Belly," he said. White Hat Number One, on his left, looked at the woman and smirked. The waitress ignored them. White Hat Number Three kept looking straight at the bartender, who dropped his glance and drew a glass of beer from the tap in front of him. The other two snickered and broke finally into a guffaw as the woman walked away from them toward Poke's table.

"Y'ole lady ain' payin' you no min' t'night," said Number One. Number Three kept looking steadily at the bartender.

Several people got up to put their wraps on in preparation for leaving. The knot of men at the bar had become tense and silent. The bartender spoke politely again to the three. "Y'awl gonna have something?" he asked. Number Two looked astonished and turned to Number Three.

"Yalla Boy wants tuh know do we wants somethin'," he said. "Whyn't yuh tell the man we don' drinks nothin'?" Number One snickered, but Number Three continued to hold the bartender with his impudent stare.

The bartender shifted his feet and prepared to walk away from the position he had taken in front of the three. "Gimme a glassa whisky," said Number One suddenly, and leaned farther forward.

The harassed man selected a bottle and poured a drink from it into a small glass. He poured some ginger ale into a larger glass and placed it alongside the whisky. Number One picked up the small glass and was about to drink when Number Two reached over and knocked the glass out of his hand. It went clattering over the bar with a loud noise, breaking other glasses in the process.

Everyone in the room came to a sudden and watchful silence. Poke turned carelessly to follow the anxious glances he saw on every face around him. The white hats were all laughing and taking in the attention of the rapt audience they had created, noting that everyone seemed not a little uneasy. Poke turned back to his glass of beer.

The middle white hat began apologizing, with feigned seriousness, to his companion. The bartender was wiping up the moisture and tossing pieces of broken glass into a trash can at his feet. Someone had started the music box going again and the shrill, high sound of a clarinet screeched into the smoky air of the room.

"Give muh frien' another glassa whisky, Yalla Boy," said the offending white hat.

The bartender turned an injured look upon him. "Who's goin' tuh pay for th' first drink?" he asked.

Number Two, a malicious grin on his face, said, "Yalla Boy, you git him another drink, an' don' be so busy with yo' mouth." He flashed his right hand toward the white handkerchief in his breast pocket, and there suddenly appeared in his gloved hand a long, slender knife, with an open gleaming blade. He kept grinning and looking at the bartender while he fondled the weapon, as though it had nothing to do with his conversation.

"Now listen, fellas, you-all treat me right, an' ev'vything's gonna be awright," said the bartender in a placating tone.

"Ev'vything's gonna be awright anyhow, Yalla Boy," said Number Two. "Git muh buddy anothuh drink." He closed the knife and slipped it back into his pocket as the bartender turned and reached for the bottle again. At that moment, Country appeared at the doorway. He peered in, opened the door, and started for the booth where he had left Poke and Jessie. Just at that moment, the nearest white hat stepped backward to brush off his coat, and the two collided gently.

" 'Scuse me, pal," said Country, and started forward again, but found himself facing the other two, who had stepped over to block his path. Country was surprised for a moment, and somewhat bewildered as he found himself surrounded by the three men. He smiled and tried to walk past the two in front of him, but one of them pushed him back.

Country was trying to think of an easier way of dealing with this situation when suddenly he saw the big form of Poke walking purposefully toward him. The bartender, stung to action, was moving swiftly around the bar in an attempt to intercept Poke. One of the two men facing Country wheeled to follow this movement and found himself face to face with Poke, who stopped just short of the group.

"Now where in hell you think you're goin'!" the white hat facing Poke challenged. Poke paid no attention to him. Instead, he looked over his head and said easily, "Whatsa matter, Country?" The bartender had reached a spot just behind Poke and was attempting to keep peace.

"Take it easy, Poke. Ev'vything's gonna be awright," he said, and tried to take Poke by the arm. But he was a minor character in the play by now, and Poke flung him off. Country was terrified as he saw the situation gaining more and more momentum.

"You betta keep the hell outta this, Big Boy," said the white hat, but Poke kept his attention on Country. The devils in him were turning the screws now, tightening the drumhead, and slowly they began to beat out an impelling cadence. He swept the three with a disdainful glance.

"You goddamn punks betta let 'at boy alone," he said, and looked back at his friend. "C'mere, Country. Walk awn over heah."

"Aw, Poke, these ole boys ain' go' hurt nobody. Dey jus' playin' aroun', man." There was no conviction in Country's voice. The bartender was still trying weakly to avoid trouble.

"C'mon, you guys," he said anxiously, "lay offa this stuff. You-all gonna git me in trouble. Look—whyn't you-all take a drink awn th' house, an' fuhgit this mess."

Nobody even looked at him. Poke was standing silently, watching the whole array in front of him; and as the pounding inside him reached a crashing crescendo, the taut spring in him snapped and he sent his hard, angry fist smashing into the leering, confident face in front of him. The man's eyes went back, showing only whites, and as his body sped backward it crashed into the bar, upsetting glasses and a cardboard cigarette advertisement. Country turned to attack the man behind him, but was met by a vicious kick in the groin that doubled him over in excruciating pain.

The man who now faced Poke reached toward his white handkerchief, but Poke grabbed the hand, and as he twisted the fist in his viselike grip, the unopened knife it held rattled to the floor. Having lost his weapon, the white hat lifted his knee to kick at this devil of a man, but as he did so, Poke side-stepped adroitly, grasped the up-lifted leg, and lifted the cursing man off the floor to send him crash-ing down beside his unconscious companion.

He had only time to throw up his hand to ward off the blow he saw coming at him, out of the corner of his eye, as he turned toward the man who had kicked Country. The bottle glanced off his up-thrown elbow and crashed to the floor as he lunged forward and grasped the man by the collar of his coat with one hand. With his free hand he drove a hammerlike blow into the terrified face, and as he reversed the direction of his fist he crooked his arm and hit the bloody mouth a hard blow with his elbow and again with his fist as it followed the elbow outward and down in a piston action that rained blows all over the broken face he held before him.

And as he pounded, the release came suddenly in him and he felt free and satisfied. He let the man fall from his grip and for the first time became aware that Country and the bartender were pulling at his arms, attempting to stop him.

By this time the room was full of excited people, and fear came suddenly on the heels of the great peace he had begun to feel. Coun-try was pleading with him, almost crying. "Poke," he was saying, "Poke, c'mon an' le's git outta here. Damn, man, the law gonna be all ovuh this place." He turned dazedly to look at Country, whose face had been kicked in the fracas. Blood was streaking the corner of his mouth, and there were deep lines of pain around his eyes.

The bartender was cursing and groaning over the damage. Out-side, a police whistle sounded, and as though it were a special signal, the crowd ran out into the street to disperse. Instantly, Poke too was alert and ready for flight, and at last gave himself over to Country's urging.

They were running toward the back of the room even as the police car's siren lowered to a growl at the front door. They heard the ham-mering on the locked door of the lavatory as they slid over the win-dow sill and dropped to the ground. Somewhere a dog was barking, and as Poke ran through the alley he had a vague feeling that he had done all this before, in precisely the same way. A pistol shot should come next, he thought, and as he and Country separated at the end of the alley, he heard a shot and the bullet pinged off the bricks overhead. He reached down to his thigh and was surprised to find he had not been hit. In daylight the police might not have missed.

When he reached the avenue, Poke slowed to a steady, panther-like gait. He crossed the street against the lights and carefully moved toward the next avenue. He tried to formulate a plan as he walked along, but flight was too strong in him still for his imagination to call up anything but the most familiar of faces and feelings.

He reached up to pull his hat further down. Something in the gesture made him halt, burning him with the impossibility and futility of hiding. He turned and looked up and down the dark street and then moved again, aimlessly now and with less purposefulness in his stride, certain that the police would be alert and hunting for him everywhere. The heat and drive of the fight had dwindled now and gone out of him; and the old fears and confusions were flooding back into his consciousness, taking the place that the opiates of anger had so briefly filled.

He began to hear the arrogant voice of the judge droning blamefully through the courtroom, Jessie's repressed weeping, and the clumsy, mumbled words of Country's indignation and sympathy. Already he could feel the terrifying loneliness of the womanless prison cell. He kept walking, and the dead click of his heels was accompaniment to his old, cruel sorrow; and as he huddled away from the chilly night air, he shrank deeply into himself, feeling small like a child, and hurt, and wanting somehow to find a way to let himself cry.

THE HOPE CHEST

by Jean Stafford

From *Harper's*

———————◆◆◆———————

MISS BELLAMY was old and cold and she lay quaking under an eiderdown which her mother had given her when she was a girl of seventeen. It had been for her hope chest. Though damask tablecloths and Irish-linen tea napkins, Florentine bureau runners and China-silk blanket covers, point-lace doilies and hemstitched hand towels had gone into that long carved cherry chest (her father had brought it all the way from Sicily and, presenting it to her, had said, "Nothing is too good for my Rhoda girl"), she had never married. The chest now stood at the foot of her bed, and the maid put the tea napkins on her breakfast tray.

It was just before Belle knocked on her door in the gray dawn of winter with the tray that Miss Bellamy quaked so much, as if nothing on earth could ever warm her up again. This unkind light made her remember how old she was and how, in a few minutes when Belle came in, she would be cantankerous; no matter how hard she tried, she could never be pleasant to a servant, black or white, a failing for which her father had once rebuked her, declaring that she behaved like a parvenu. He had scolded her thus when he finally had to admit to himself the fact that she would never marry. There had not, in the history of Richmond society, been a greater fiasco than Rhoda Bellamy's debut. It had, indeed, been a miscarriage so sensational that she had forced her parents to move westward, like pioneers, into Tennessee where her mother soon had died and where she and her father dwelt together in their angry disappointment. *Well, Papa, the laugh's on you. Here I am, thirty-five years old, and in the eighteen years since I came out, I have had no beau but my dear Papa. No, I will not go to the opera. No, I do not want to join you in a glass of claret. I shall return to my bedroom and read Mrs. Gaskell, thanking you every time I turn a page for giving me so expensive a copy of* Cranford.

This was the Christmas morning of her eighty-second year and she steadfastly held her eyes closed, resisting the daylight. She had been like that as a child, she had loved sleep better than eating or playing. She was not sure whether she had had a dream just now or whether there was something she had meant to remember or to think about that was troubling her aged mind like a rat in a wall. At last, vexed and murmuring, she opened her eyes and what did she see hanging upon the wall (very probably staining the hand-blocked French paper with a design of pastoral sweethearts) but a scraggly Christmas wreath to which had been wired three pine cones, one gilded, one silvered, one painted scarlet. At first she was half out of her mind with exasperation and she reached out her liver-spotted hand for her stick to rap tyrannically for Belle. How *dared* she desecrate this, of all rooms, which, as any fool should know, was not to be changed in any way! But memory stayed her hand: it all came back.

Yesterday, when she was sitting on the lounge in the drawing room, making spills out of last year's Christmas wrappings and sipping hot milk, she heard a timid knocking at the door. She had no intention of answering it, although Belle had gone out to shop and the colored girl had gone home. But she said to herself, "Who is it? Who are they that they can't knock out loud like a Christian? If they want something, why don't they try the doorknob? They'll find it locked, but if they had any gumption, they'd try." She slowly made a spill.

It went on, this gentle, disheartened knocking. Was it a squirrel, she wondered, playing with a nut somewhere? *If there is a destructive squirrel in my house, I shall give Belle her walking papers at once.* She did not find the creatures cunning as some people did: they were as wicked as any other rodent and the tail, so greatly admired in some quarters, was by no means a disguise that could not be seen through: essentially they were rats. Perhaps it was not a squirrel but was a loose branch blowing in the wind: *I shall speak severely to Homer. If he calls himself my yard-man, he can attend to these details.* Perhaps it was a dog of the neighborhood, foolishly thumping his tail against the door. *People should keep their dogs at home, tied up if necessary. If they are not kept at home, they come rummaging in my refuse containers and defiling my lawn and littering the garden with things I do not like to know exist.* Aloud in the long drawing room she said, knowing that she smiled cleverly in her lean lips and in her small eyes, "If you want to come in, knock loud enough so that I shall hear you. Call out your name, confound you. Do you think I receive just anyone?"

She slopped her milk and it made a row of buttons down the front of her challis guimpe. Outraged, she threw the spill she was making into the fire and then she hobbled to the door, saying under her breath, "Whoever you are, I will frighten the living daylights out of you. If you are an animal, I will beat you with my stick; if you are a human being, I will scare you out of ten years' growth. I will say the worst thing you have ever had said to you in your life."

In the winter she had a green baize door and a storm door sand-wiching the regular door to keep out any possible draft. She pulled open the green baize one and unlocked the wooden one with a long iron key and she opened it the merest bit, pushing it with the silver ferrule of her blackthorn stick. Through the glass of the storm door she saw a child standing there in the snow, holding a spruce wreath in his hands. He had come across the lawn, making his own path, deliberately to spoil the looks of the clean, unmarked snow when he could *much more easily* have walked in Belle's footprints.

He opened the storm door without asking leave and he said, "Will you buy this?"

She prided herself on never having been tricked by anyone. She investigated first and bought afterward. She, Rhoda Bellamy, would be the last to be taken in by a child, and she did not, of course, answer his question. She pushed the door open a little farther and said, "Who are you? What is your name?"

His teeth, she saw, were short and crooked and a nasty yellow color. She supposed he came from one of those indigent families who clustered together, squalidly and odoriferously, on the banks of the Cumberland. He was not decently shy and he spoke up immediately: "My name is Ernest Leonard McCammon. Will you buy this wreath?"

The spinster said, "Well, Ernest Leonard, you may wipe your feet on my *Welcome* mat and step into the entry, but I am not promising to buy your wreath. We'll see about that later on."

(The sycamores before Miss Bellamy's windows creaked in the cold: *Where is my breakfast? Where is Belle? Why did I invite Ernest Leonard McCammon to cross my threshold in his snowy galoshes, puddling the Tabriz Father bought half price in Belgrade?* She creaked, too, like a tree, and a feather from the eiderdown walked on her ear like a summer fly.)

The child stood before her, small and ambitious, bundled to his ears in a blue plaid mackintosh which was patched with leather at the elbows. He wore blue jeans, and in his mittenless hands he carried now, besides the wreath, the purple stocking cap he had taken off before he came through the door. He bore a faint, unpleasant smell of mud. *I will eat you, little boy, because once upon a time I, too, had pink cheeks and a fair skin and clear eyes. And don't you deny it.*

Ernest Leonard McCammon looked at the Adam hall chair, looked at the portrait of Mr. Bellamy, looked at the priceless Florentine coffer, looked at the luster pitchers in which stood cattails ten years old; she had had a man come out from Nashville one year to oil the books and at the same time had had him shellac the cattails, although he protested a little, declaring that this was not in his line. No workman ever got anywhere protesting with her. She had simply said, "I don't know what you're talking about, sir. My father picked these cattails by the Jordan." This did not happen to be true as her father had been dead for twenty years and she had gathered them herself in her own meadow beside the local river.

The rag-tag-and-bobtail boy looked at her father's treasures as if he had seen such things every day of his life. *Do you know who I am, you smelly scrap? Does the name Bellamy mean anything to you, you wool-bound baggage? Did you ever hear of the Bellamy tobacco fortune?*

(How the wind was blowing! Where was Belle? Where was her breakfast? Where was her stick? Where was her wrapper? Why did no one come to wish her a merry Christmas?)

He said, "Miss Bellamy, will you buy my wreath?"

"What do you want for it, McCammon?"

"A quarter."

"A quarter! Twenty-five cents for a bit of evergreen you more than likely stole off one of my trees!"

His pink cheeks paled under her shrewd gaze and his blue eyes clouded. "I never stole 'um off your tree, Miss Bellamy. I went to the woods, I did, and I got 'um there off nobody's tree."

She said, not giving in, "Perhaps so, perhaps not. All the same, a quarter is too much."

"But I painted the pine cones, Miss Bellamy! I had to buy the gold and the silver. Daddy gave me the red."

"And who is this Daddy?"

"The chimney cleaner. We are the ones with the mule. Maybe you have seen our house with the mule in the yard? My daddy's name is Robert John McCammon."

I will blow your brains out with the bellows Father brought from Dresden. I will lay your slender little body on Cousin Anne's andirons that came from the Trianon, and burn you up like a paper spill.

"Come, come, Ernest Leonard," she said, "I don't care what your daddy's middle name is and I have certainly not seen your mule. I will give you fifteen cents for your wreath."

"No, ma'am," he said. "If you don't buy it, some other lady will."

"Some *other* lady? What do you mean, McCammon?"

"Well, Mrs. Wagner would buy it or Mrs. Saunders or Mrs. Hugh Morris, I reckon. Anyways, somebody."

"I will give you fifteen cents for the wreath alone. You can take off the pine cones."

"No, ma'am. That would spoil it."

She fixed him with a severe aristocratic eye, determined now to resolve this impasse to her own liking and not to his. She said slowly, "If I decided to buy your wreath and paid you the absurd king's ransom of twenty-five cents, would you do a favor for me?"

"Yes, Miss Bellamy."

(Belle! Belle! Where is my breakfast? Come before I die of loneliness. Come before the sycamores break at the top and crush the roof over my head!)

"Do you promise, Ernest Leonard?"

"I promise, Miss Bellamy," he said and moved a step away from her.

She took a twenty-five-cent piece out of the purse she carried strapped to her belt and, bending down, took the wreath which she placed on the coffer. Now Ernest Leonard clutched the stocking cap in both hands. His aplomb had left him; she could tell that he wanted to run away.

"You must give me a kiss, Master McCammon," she said and, leaning heavily upon her stick, stooped toward that small face with pursed lips, coral-colored. They touched her bone-dry cheek and then the boy was gone, and through the door he had left open in his headlong flight there came a blast of cold December. But for a moment she did not move and stared at a clot of snow upon the rug. *I told you, Ernest Leonard, to wipe your feet carefully on my Welcome mat.*

Belle's big country feet were on the stairs. Miss Bellamy trembled for her knock. *Wait a minute, Belle, I have not yet thought out what I am going to say to you.* Had she left any stray spruce needles on the coffer? Had any fallen as she climbed the stairs, breathless with recollection? Belle was at the door. She knocked and entered with the tray.

"Explain that monstrosity," said Miss Bellamy, pointing to the Christmas wreath she had hung last night at the stroke of midnight. *Merry Christmas, Papa dear. Oh, how cunning of you to hang up mistletoe! What girl in the world would want more than a beau like you? Can I have my presents now? It's one past midnight, Papa! Oh, Papa, darling, you have given me a brass fender for my fireplace! Oh, Papa, a medallioned sewing drum! An emerald ring! A purple velvet peignoir! I wish you a very merry Christmas, Papa.*

"Don't pretend you know nothing about it, my good woman. Why did you do it, Belle? Have you no respect for other people's property? Do you think I can have my bedroom repapered every week or so merely for the sake of your vulgar whims?"

Kind, stupid Belle shook out the napkin and she said, as she sprinkled a little salt on the lightly boiled egg, "I'm sorry, Miss Rhoda, that I never seem to do what's right. I thought you'd like the wreath."

The old lady cackled hideously and screamed, "You goose! You namby-pamby! I hung it there myself!"

The maid, unruffled, smiled and said, "Merry Christmas, Miss Rhoda." When she had gone, the spinster closed her eyes against Ernest Leonard's painted pine cones, but she nursed her hurt like a baby at a milkless breast, with tearless eyes.

OLD BOY—NEW BOY

by Benedict Thielen

From *Town and Country*

As THEY DROVE DOWN the main street of the village he saw that everything was just as he had remembered it. Twelve years had made no difference. As they passed the simple New England houses, the slender white spire of the church, and the old trees shading the green he felt their quiet permanence in a world of disorder and change.

He turned to the boy sitting beside him.

"We'll be there in just a few minutes," he said. "You'll like it, Don. It's a great old school."

The boy nodded his head gravely, and as he glanced at his son Paul Carroll had a curious feeling, a kind of sinking of the heart, as if he himself were sitting there about to be registered for school next autumn, and as if the person who was talking was not he but his father.

"You'll have a lot of fun," he said. "It's a great old place"; and he realized he was repeating himself and felt embarrassed.

They came to the road that led to the school. Among the trees he caught a glimpse of the sun on the warm red brick of one of the buildings. Beyond was the valley, with spring flowing up all the hillsides.

He turned in the driveway and drove up to the main building. From the ball field near by, as they got out, came the flat crack of a bat followed by a shout, high-pitched and quickly rising in the clear air.

"They're playing baseball," he said, smiling down at his son, and in a flash of memory he saw his own father, smiling down at him as he walked to the shore with a pair of oars over his shoulder and saying, "Well, Paul, going for a little row?"

He cleared his throat and said, "We'll go see Dr. Prentice first. Then later we'll stroll around and sort of look things over."

A group of boys, older than his son, walked past and stared at him. Paul started to take Don's hand, then stopped and said, "Come on, let's go."

They waited for only a minute after the secretary had taken in their names, then the door opened and Dr. Prentice stood there. The sun glistened on the pink marble baldness of his fine head and his face was ruddy with health. Some of the athlete look—he had been a famous tackle in his day—had left his shoulders to settle in the region of his waist, but otherwise he was little changed. His blue eyes were as bright as ever, and looking at him now as they shook hands, Paul Carroll remembered their two expressions, the one of twinkling humor, the other of cold keen incision, which could be turned on or off like two different kinds of lights.

Dr. Prentice led the way into his office, his loud hearty voice rolling back to them over his shoulder.

"Yes, indeed, as soon as Miss Crane brought in your name . . . always a pleasure . . . any of our Old Boys, always welcome . . ."

Dr. Prentice waved them to two chairs and sat down at his desk. On the wall behind him were photographs of the school teams and a framed copy with illuminated capitals of Kipling's *If*. He picked up his pipe and for a few seconds turned on the full humorous light of his blue eyes. Then the humor switched to sharpness, but a sharpness still tinged with humor, not coldly penetrating as it could be when used to pry out the truth from a boy's shifting glance.

"Paul Carroll . . . let's see . . . as I remember . . ." He pursed his lips and raised his eyes to the ceiling in a look of exaggerated innocence. "As I remember . . . and I've been told my memory is not infallible . . . but as I remember there was once a Paul Carroll who was involved in a little affair of changing some signposts on the outskirts of our village so that they all pointed in the wrong direction, and for a time there was considerable confusion as a result. Correct me if I'm mistaken."

"No, sir," Paul Carroll said, laughing. "You're not mistaken. But I don't see how you remember things like that. Why, I hadn't thought of it in years."

He glanced down at his son, who looked up at him with a surprised and rather pleased expression.

Dr. Prentice turned to the boy and said, "Your dad thought he could change things around to suit himself, Donald, and get everyone confused while he sat back and laughed at them. But it didn't work. It never does work." He turned to Paul. "And as I remember, it was hardly worth it, was it? I seem to recollect the suspension of certain privileges, the curtailment of . . ."

"Of practically everything," Paul Carroll said.

Dr. Prentice nodded his head. "So you see, Donald, your daddy had to be taught too. All of us do." He brought his hand down on his desk and turned on the full force of his smile. "And that's what we'll do with you. That's our job. That's what we're here for. We'll make the kind of man out of you that your daddy is and that you yourself will want to be. We'll show you how to play up and play the game, the greatest game of all: the game of life." He smiled at Paul. "You've found it so, Paul, haven't you? Life, I mean?"

"Why, yes. Yes, it certainly is." He felt he should say something more but nothing seemed to occur to him at the moment. Instead, he smiled too.

Dr. Prentice turned again to Don.

"At first maybe there'll be some things that you won't understand and that you'll think are just silly and the notions of old fogies like us. But in the end you'll see that everything we do has a purpose and you'll understand why we insist on their being done." He lighted his pipe, then pointed it at Paul. "Rather like the Army, I sometimes think. All that drill seems so unnecessary at first, but the day comes when you realize that as a result you're doing things automatically, that you don't have to think: you simply react. You don't have to think because you *know*. Isn't that so?"

"Yes, that's certainly true," Paul said.

"And after all," Dr. Prentice said, "it's not just to teach boys to conjugate Latin verbs that we're here. That's important, of course, but our real job . . ." He brought his hand down again on the smooth surface of his desk. "Our real job is character building. And no amount of mere book-larnin' alone will do that. It's playing the game and keeping a stiff upper lip and fearing God and . . . As a matter of fact . . ." He leaned forward, smiling a little guiltily. "I don't suppose

I should admit it, but sometimes I've wondered whether learning Latin was more valuable to me in the long run than having played on our varsity football team."

He looked down at Don, who looked up at his father, then back at Dr. Prentice uncertainly, then smiled and lowered his eyes.

"So you see, Don," Dr. Prentice said, leaning back again in his chair, "life won't be all work here. There'll be plenty of good healthy play as well."

He laughed and Paul laughed too. For a few seconds both of them sat there laughing, while Don looked from one to the other, then straight beyond them out of the window, as though his eyes were held by something out there, following a narrow path of their own between the high walls of their laughter.

As Paul Carroll looked down at him, sitting there between their laughter, he seemed terribly young and defenseless. A wave of love for him came over him and a desire to put his arm around him and protect him. At the same instant he had a sudden very clear memory of himself when he was about his son's age coming into a room where his mother and father were talking. Both of them had stopped abruptly, looking down at him then and laughing. In this present laughter he seemed to hear the echo of theirs, and to feel again the heavy sense of something important being kept from him, the inescapable suggestion of a betrayal.

"You'll like it here, Don," he said. "You'll have a fine time." But his words sounded hollow to him.

Later, as they got up to go, Dr. Prentice said, "I expect you'll want to show Donald around a bit. Oh, by the way, you haven't seen our new Memorial Hall, have you?" He glanced out the window, hesitated, then pushed back his chair and said, "I shouldn't, but I'll just stroll over with you. It's such a splendid day."

They walked across the sunny campus. Dr. Prentice raised his face to the sky, breathed deeply, and quoted Browning. As they came to Memorial Hall and he pushed open the great oak door he said, "I think you'll be particularly interested in this, Paul."

They walked slowly down the aisle under the carved and vaulted Gothic ceiling, in the diffused glow of colored light from the stained-glass windows. Ahead of them on a raised platform draped with flags was a large bronze plaque on which were columns of names in shining raised letters. The plaque was divided into sections headed, THE WAR BETWEEN THE STATES, SPANISH-AMERICAN WAR, WORLD WAR I, and WORLD WAR II. Each section was filled with names except the last one, which was only partially filled. A space beyond it had been left blank, for the sake of symmetry.

As Paul stood there he suddenly saw his own name. It rose from the others, unexpectedly, like a name being lighted in an electric sign. It startled him and at the same time made him want to turn away. He saw Dr. Prentice looking at him expectantly and felt that he ought to say something. He stared up at the dark high rafters of the hall and said, "This is certainly a fine place."

Dr. Prentice smiled slightly. "Yes, we're proud of it." He motioned toward the plaque. "We're especially proud of what it contains, however."

Paul glanced back at the plaque and then up at one of the windows through which the sun streamed in dusty shafts of blue and scarlet and gold. He looked down at his son, standing in the flood of colored light, his eyes fixed on the shining letters of the plaque. Dr. Prentice put his arm on the boy's shoulder.

"This is what Suffolk stands for, Don," he said. "These men. There's your dad's name and there . . ." He pointed at another column. "There's your granddad's name too."

Paul turned his head quickly and saw his father's name under the column headed WORLD WAR I. He looked at it for some moments, then turned away again. Dr. Prentice took his hand off the boy's shoulder and said, "Whenever I come in here—and I come often—I get a true feeling of peace. Those men . . ." He gestured toward the plaque, then shook his head. "Well, you understand without my putting it into words. Tradition and continuity . . . You feel that, Paul, don't you? The Civil War, the War with Spain, World War I, and now . . ."

Dr. Prentice looked at him expectantly and Paul felt he should say something but could think of nothing to say. His name seemed to be raised in higher, more shining letters than the others and he felt embarrassed and ill at ease.

He cleared his throat and said, "Well, Don, I imagine we'd better be getting along. It . . ."

Dr. Prentice looked at him sympathetically and murmured, "You don't like to talk about it, do you?"

"What? Oh, I don't care. I mean . . ."

"No." Dr. Prentice shook his head. "I know how you feel. And that's a part of our tradition too, of course. Modesty. Doing our duty without . . . You didn't have to go, did you? I mean there was your son and . . . But you went anyway. That's the sort of thing our boys do—as a matter of course. Quietly. Modestly."

"It's a beautiful building," Paul said, raising his voice more than he had intended. "Who . . . I mean, did someone give it or . . ."

"Yes." Dr. Prentice nodded his head gravely. "Mr. Snyder. Luther P. Snyder provided the funds that enabled us . . ."

"The soap man?" Paul asked.

"Yes. As a memorial to his son."

As they moved toward the door Dr. Prentice said, "There was some discussion at first as to how the names should be listed. A number of the trustees thought that each man's rank should appear on the plaque, but some of the others contended that it would be more democratic simply to put the name and branch of service without any indication of rank. Mr. Snyder agreed with that, even though his son was a lieutenant. A very democratic man . . . Of course, practically all our boys were officers, but we felt . . ."

"Yes, that's true, of course," Paul said, and taking Don's hand, walked a little more rapidly toward the door.

"Oh, Paul," Dr. Prentice called, "I thought we might show the boy the refectory. We can go right in through this door."

In the refectory Paul looked down the long hall with the polished oak tables and the enormous moosehead on the wall at the opposite end. He saw that it was draped in black.

"When we've been beaten in football by Norfolk," he said to Don, "they drape that old moose in black for the rest of the year. I didn't know we'd lost," he said.

"You didn't?" Dr. Prentice looked surprised, then shook his head. "In the last quarter. A fumble on the thirty-five-yard line and . . ." His face became flushed and he brought his fist down hard in the palm of his other hand. "It should never have happened. Up to then we had outplayed them completely."

For a few moments they stood there without saying anything. The black-draped moose stared morosely down the length of the hall. Dr. Prentice sighed and they turned and walked out and back into the sunshine.

After Dr. Prentice had left them they strolled slowly across the campus. On a stone terrace at one end where the ground fell off abruptly to the valley they stopped and leaned on the parapet, looking out. A warm breeze, moist with the earth of spring, came up from the valley. The air was filled with sunlight and bird song. As he stood there Paul Carroll felt the profound sense of peace which rose from everything around them, until it filled the day like music gradually filling a great hall. But even now the fact of peace still seemed strange and somehow unreal. It was strange to think that there were no gun emplacements sheltered in the hills, that the land was not strewn with broken machines and bodies. It was strange to look out on a nearby field and see a man behind a plow and the dark furrows cresting over like waves in its wake. It was strange to look out at the kind of innocence of this young and healthy land, as it lay there ready for sowing, fresh and full of hope.

He looked down at Don and said, "Well, Don, what do you think of it? Do you ..."

Just then there was a shout from two boys who were walking past, their adolescent voices starting low, then rising high and breaking, shouting, "Oh, Goo-oo-key!"

Don looked from them to him and Paul laughed and said, "Just wait a second. You'll see."

Two smaller boys came breathlessly running. The older boys said something and pointed and the two little boys rushed off.

"That's one of the old customs here," Paul said. "If a senior wants something all he has to do is stand and yell, 'Oh, Gookey,' and the nearest new boy has to come running and do what he tells him. They've probably sent them down to the store to get ice-cream cones or something."

Don turned and looked at the two boys standing there waiting, looking unconcerned and important.

"It's an old custom," Paul said.

"But why do they do it?" Don said. "I mean why do they run up like that?"

"Why . . ." Paul hesitated. "Why, because it's an old custom, that's all. Everyone always does it. It's part of . . ."

"What does it mean?" Don said, still looking at the two boys standing there. "Gookey."

"Mean? Why, I don't know. Nothing in particular, I imagine. It's just . . . That's just what they call out when they want something and then . . ."

"Well, it must mean something," Don said.

"It doesn't have to mean anything, Don." A shade of impatience came into his voice. "It's just an old custom. Everybody's always done it. It's part of the Suffolk tradition. That's what Dr. Prentice meant. I did it. My father did it before me. You'll do it. It's just . . ."

"Well, what if they just didn't pay any attention? The new boys."

"Why . . ." He looked down at Don and frowned. "Well, it wouldn't be sporting, Don, that's all. When you come to a place like this that has its own traditions and everything, why, you have to become a part of them and . . ." He looked out again over the valley. The sun was still high but shadows were already beginning to form among the lower hills. He glanced at his watch. "Well, you'll get into the spirit of it when the time comes. You'll like it here. Some of the things may seem sort of funny at first, but after a while, why . . . why, you'll understand."

He looked at his watch again, although he had looked at it only a few seconds before, and said, "We'd better get along. It's getting late."

As they walked toward the main building, where the car was parked, his words echoed in his mind. The sound of them irritated him and a kind of rawness seemed to fray the soft edges of this perfect spring day. He felt suddenly tired and like being alone.

He made himself smile and said, "I have no idea who Gookey was. Or maybe it wasn't anybody at all. I don't know. I guess I never really particularly thought about it."

When they got to their car he heard his name called and saw Dr. Prentice beckoning to him from the window of his office.

"You get in, Don," he said. "I'll just run over and see what Dr. Prentice wants."

In his office Dr. Prentice looked at him for a few seconds with a slight smile. He picked up his pipe from the desk and knocked the bowl reflectively against the palm of his hand a few times. Then he said, "Paul, I've been thinking. Your boy. He's rather shy, isn't he?"

"Why, I don't know," Paul said slowly. "I hadn't especially thought so. No."

Dr. Prentice nodded his head.

"Well, it's my impression. Possibly I'm wrong. But I think before he comes here it would be good if you saw that he got out with the rest of the fellows as much as possible. Play baseball. Go to a boy's camp. That sort of thing. He seems to me like a boy who's been a lot alone. Only child, isn't he?"

"Yes. But I don't think . . ."

"Oh, he's a fine boy. Don't misunderstand me. But he's a type." He smiled a little to himself. "I've had some experience in . . . It's always a good thing if a boy like that doesn't have to make too . . . too abrupt a transition, when he leaves home. When he's been used to more or less having his own way and then finds he can't have it. Well, it's always best to be prepared for some hard knocks and . . ."

"I see what you mean," Paul said. "I'll keep it in mind."

"And then, of course," Dr. Prentice said as they shook hands, "you have to remember that during all that time you were away, overseas, he was without a father's influence. Women sometimes tend to be a little soft. . . . Be real pals with him. But at the same time be firm. It's for the boy's own good."

After he had gotten in the car and they had driven off neither of them said anything for a time. Then Don laughed and, looking up at him, said, "That was funny about those signs. Where were they?"

Paul laughed too and said, "I don't remember exactly. It was sort of funny, though."

Their eyes met in a kind of complete understanding which filled Paul with a warm inner feeling of pleasure. For a moment they seemed very close together. Then he thought of Dr. Prentice.

"But it was a silly thing to do," he said. "It might have caused a lot of trouble."

The boy looked at him and the smile gradually faded from his face. He turned and looked out at the road ahead.

Paul said, "It wasn't worth it, really. It . . ." He hesitated.

Presently he said, "Well, what do you think of it? Do you think you'll like it?"

They were approaching a traffic circle and he kept his eyes on the road. When they had gone around it he glanced at the boy sitting at his side. Don's eyes were fixed straight ahead of him and his lower lip was thrust foward. As Paul looked he saw it tremble and a tear roll down each cheek. Paul laughed and, reaching over with one hand, touched him on the knee.

"Why, Don, what's the matter, son?"

The boy shook his head and presently, his voice sounding thin and strained, said, "I don't want to go."

"Why, it's a fine place," Paul said. "I went there and Grandpa went there and . . . Why, you'll have a fine time."

The boy shook his head again. "I don't like him. That . . . that man."

"Dr. Prentice? Why, he's a splendid man. Everybody likes Dr. Prentice, Don. He's a . . . why, he's a fine man."

"I don't want . . . I don't want to run like that when they . . . they yell 'Gookey.' "

Paul laughed and said, "Why, that's just an old custom. It's fun. Everybody . . ." He stopped. He saw himself standing in Dr. Prentice's office and heard Dr. Prentice speaking, his keen blue eyes fixed sharply on his own.

He frowned. He cleared his throat and waited while he forced something within him, something in his heart that had been soft and yielding, to harden. Finally the words came out.

"That's all nonsense," he said, and for a second felt surprised at the changed quality of his voice. "And anyway that's not for you to say. You'll do as you're told. You're going."

He glanced at his son from the corner of his eye. Don was no longer crying. He raised his eyes and looked into his father's, deeply, for a few seconds. Then he turned away and looked straight ahead.

"Don?" Paul said, but the boy did not turn to him.

Then he heard himself speaking, but again with a kind of surprise, as if it were not really his voice coming from him but someone else's, as if the words he was saying were not his own but words that had all been prepared for him by another person. It seemed to him, as he spoke, that he was reciting some lesson learned by heart, or something written in a foreign tongue and of whose meaning he was only dimly aware.

"You can't always have your own way in life . . . one of the things we've all got to learn . . . playing the game . . . discipline . . . a stiff upper lip . . . and the tradition of a fine old school . . . someday you'll realize . . . and co-operation with the other fellows . . . and the happiest years of your life."

He listened helplessly as he heard his words flow out, each one piling on top of the other like bricks being added to a wall.

THE WHOLE WORLD KNOWS

by Eudora Welty

From *Harper's Bazaar*

———————◆◆◆———————

*Mother said, Where have you been, son?—Nowhere, mother.—I wish
you wouldn't look so unhappy, son. You could come back to me,
now.—I can't do that, mother. I have to stay in Sabina.*

When I locked the door of the Sabina Bank I rolled down my
sleeves and stood for some time looking out at a cotton field across
the way until the whiteness nearly put me to sleep and then woke
me up like a light turned on in my face. Dugan had been gone a few
minutes or so. I got in my car and drove it up the street, turned it
around in the foot of Jinny's driveway (there went Dugan), and
drove down again. I backed in a cotton field at the other end of the
pavement, turned, and made the same trip. You know—the thing
everybody does every day.

There was Maideen Summers on the corner waving a little colored
handkerchief. She was at first the only stranger—then finally not
much of one. When I didn't remember to stop I saw the handkerchief slowly fall still. I turned again, and picked her up.

"Dragging Main?" she said. She was eighteen years old. She
promptly told you all those things. "Look! Grown-up and citified,"
she said, and held both hands toward me. She had brand-new
white cotton gloves on—they shone. Maideen would ride beside me
and talk about things I didn't mind hearing about—the ice plant,
where she kept the books, Fred Killigrew her boss, the way working
in Sabina seemed after the country and junior college. Her first
job—her mother could hardly believe it, she said. It was so easy,
too, out in the world, and nice, with getting her ride home with

me sometimes like this and not on the dusty bus—except Mr. Killigrew sometimes wanted her to do something at the last minute—guess what today—and so on.

She said, "This sure is nice. I didn't think you saw me, Ran, not at first."

I told her my eyes had gone bad. She looked sorry. I drove, idling along, up and down Main Street a few times more. Each time the same people, Miss Callie Hudson and all, the people standing in the store doors or riding in the other cars, waved at my car, and to them all, Maideen waved back—her little blue handkerchief was busy. Their avidity would be far beyond her. She waved at them as she did at me.

"Are you tired out like you were yesterday? Today's just as hot."

She knew what anybody in Sabina told her; and for four or five afternoons I had picked her up and taken her up and down the street a few turns, bought her a Coca-Cola and driven her home out by the Old Murray Forks somewhere, and she had never said a word except a kind one, like this. She was kind; her company was the next thing to being alone.

I drove her home and then drove back to the room I had at Mrs. Judge O'Leary's—usually, but on this day, there at the end of the pavement, I turned up the cut to the Stark place. I couldn't stand it any longer.

Maideen didn't say anything until we reached the top of the drive and stopped, and I got out and opened her door.

"Do you want to take me in yonder?" she said. "Please, I'd just as soon you wouldn't."

All at once her voice came all over me. It had a kind of humility.

"Sure. Let's go in and see Jinny. Why not?" I couldn't stand it any longer, that was why. "I'm going and taking you."

It wasn't as if Colonel Waters didn't say to me every afternoon. Come on home with me, boy—argue, while he forced that big Panama down on his head—no sense in your not sleeping cool, with one of our fans turned on you, Mabel says so, Mabel has something to say to you—and he waited a minute in the door before he left, and held his cane (the one Dugan and I had gone in together to buy him because he was president), up in the air as if he threatened me with comfort, until I answered him No Sir.

With Maideen, I walked around the baked yard to the porch, under the heavy heads, the too-bright blooms that hang down like fruits from the trees—crape myrtles. Jinny's mama, I saw, put her face to her bedroom window first thing, to show she'd marched right upstairs at the sight of Randall MacLain coming to her door, bringing who-on-earth with him too. After daring to leave her daughter and right on Easter Sunday before church. Now right back to her door, big as you please. And her daughter Jinny, Virginia, who once Shared His Bed, sent straight into the arms of Trash by what he did. One thing—it was Jinny's family home, after all, her mother still kept alive to run it, *grand* old Mrs. Stark, and this outrage right under her nose. The curtain fell back, as on a triumph.

"I've never been invited to the Stark home," Maideen said, and I began to smile. I felt curiously lighthearted. Lilies must have been in bloom somewhere near, and I took a full breath of their watery smell, as determinedly as if then consciousness might go, or might not.

Out in the front hall, Jinny stood with her legs apart, cutting off locks of her hair at the mirror. The locks fell at her feet. She had on boy's shorts. She looked up at me and said "How do you like it?" She grinned, as if she had been preparing for me, and then she looked past my shoulder. She would know, with her quickness like foreknowledge, that I would come back when this summer got too much for me, and that I would just as soon bring a stranger if I could find one, somebody who didn't know a thing, into the house with me when I came.

I remember Maideen looked down at her gloves, and seemed to decide to keep them on. Jinny hollered at Tellie to bring in some cokes. A spell of remoteness, a feeling of lightness, had hold of me still, and as we all stood on that thin light matting in the Stark hall that seems to billow a little if you take a step, and with Jinny's hair lying on it, I saw us all in the mirror. And I could almost hear it being told right across me—our story, the fragment of what happened, Jinny's and my story, as if it were being told—told in the clear voice of Maideen, rushing, unquestioning—the town words. Oh, this is what Maideen Summers was—telling what she looked

at, repeating what she listened to—she was like an outlandish little
bird, being taught, some each day, to sing a song *people* made. . . .
He walked out on her and moved three blocks away down the street.
Now everybody's wondering when he'll try to go back. They say
Jinny MacLain's got her sweetheart there. Under her mama's nose.
Good thing her father's dead and she has no brothers. Sure, it's
Lonnie Dugan, the other one at the bank, and you knew from the
start, if it wasn't Ran, who else in Sabina would there be for Jinny
Stark? They don't say how it happened, does anybody know? At
the circle, at the table, at Mrs. Judge's, at Sunday School, they say,
they say she will marry the sweetheart if he'll marry her, but Ran
will kill someone if she does. And there's Ran's papa died of drink,
remember, remember? They say Ran will do something bad. He
won't divorce her but he will do something bad. Maybe kill them
all. They say Jinny's not scared. And oh you know, they say, they
run into each other every day of the world, all three. Poor things!
But it's no surprise. There'll be no surprises. How could they help
it if they wanted to help it, how could you get away from anything
here? You can't get away in Sabina. Away from anything.

Maideen held the tinkling glass in her white glove and said to
Jinny, "I look too tacky and mussed when I work all day to be
coming in anybody's strange house."

She looked like *Jinny*—she was an awkward version of Jinny.
Jinny's first full gaze at me suddenly revealed it. (Oh, her gaze
always revealed contamination. I knew it after the fact, so to speak
—and was just a bit pleased with myself.) I don't mean there was
anything of mockery in Maideen's little face—no—but something
of Jinny that went back early—to whatever original and young my
Jinny would never be now. The breeze from that slow ceiling fan
lifted their hair from their temples like the same hand—Maideen's
brown hair long and Jinny's brown hair short, ruined—she ruined
it herself, as she liked doing.

Maideen was so still, so polite, but she glowed with something
she didn't know about, there in the room with Jinny. She took on
a great deal of unsuspected value. It was like a kind of maturity all
at once. They sat down in wicker chairs and talked to each other.
With them side by side and talking back and forth, it seemed to
reward my soul for Maideen to protest her fitness to be in the house.

I would not have minded how bedraggled she would ever get herself. I relaxed, leaned back in my chair and smoked cigarettes. But I had to contain my sudden interest; it seemed almost too funny to be true, their resemblance. I was delighted with myself, most of all, to have been the one to make it evident. I looked from Jinny to Maideen (of course *she* didn't guess) and back to Jinny and almost expected praise—praise from somewhere—for my true vision.

There were knocking sounds from outside—croquet again. Jinny was guiding us to the open door (we walked on her hair) where they were slowly moving across the shade of the backyard—Doc Short, Vera and Red Lassiter, and the two same schoolteachers—with Lonnie Dugan striking a ball through the wicket. I watched through the doorway and the crowd seemed to have dwindled a little. I could not think who was out. It was myself.

Mother said, Son, you're walking around in a dream.

Bella, Mrs. Judge O'Leary's little dog, panted sorrowfully all the time—she was sick. I always went out in the yard and spoke to her. Poor Bella, how do you do, lady? Is it hot, do they leave you alone?

Mother said, Where have you been, son?—Not anywhere, mother. —I wish you wouldn't look so peaked. And you keep things from me, son.—I haven't been anywhere, where would I go?—If you came back with me, everything would be just like it was before. I know you won't eat at Mrs. Judge's table, not her biscuit.

When the bank opened, Miss Callie Hudson came up to my window and hollered, Randall, when are you going back to your precious wife? You forgive her, now, you hear? That's no way to do, bear grudges. Your mother never bore your father a grudge in her life, and he made her life right hard, I tell you, how do you suppose he made her life? She didn't bear him a grudge. We're all human on earth. Where's little old Lonnie, now, has he stepped out, or you done something to him? I still think of him as a boy in knee breeches and Buster Brown bob, riding the ice wagon, stealing ice —your lifelong playmate, Jinny's lifelong playmate—a little common but so smart. Ah, I'm a woman that's been clear around the world in my rocking chair, and I tell you we all get surprises now and then. But you march on back to your wife, Ran MacLain. You hear? It's a thing of the flesh, not the spirit, it'll pass. Jinny'll get over this in three, four months maybe. You hear me? And you go back *nice*. No striking about now and doing anything we'll all be shamed to hear about. I know you won't. I knew your father, was crazy about your father, just as long as he could recognize me, love your mother. Sweetest people in the world, most happily mated people in the world. Go home and tell your mother I said so. And you march back to that precious wife. March back and have you some chirren. How long has it been? How long? What day was it you tore the house down, Christmas or Easter? I said Easter, Mr. Hudson said Christmas—who was right? My Circle declares she'll get a divorce and marry Lonnie but I say not. Thing of the flesh, I told Mr. Hudson. Won't last. And they've known each other a hundred years! The Missionary Circle said you'd kill him and I said, You all, who are you talking about? If it's Ran MacLain that I knew in his buggy, I said he's the last person I know to take on to that extent. I laughed. And little Jinny. I had to laugh at her. Says—I couldn't help it. I says, How did it happen, Jinny, tell old Miss Callie, you monkey, and she says, Oh Miss Callie, I don't know—it just happened, she says, sort of across the bridge table. I says across the bridge table my foot. Jinny told me yesterday on the street, Oh, she says, I just saw Ran. I hope Ran won't cherish it against me, Jinny says. I have to write my checks on the Sabina Bank, and Lonnie Dugan works in it, right next to Ran. And we're all grown up, not little children any more. And I says I know, how could you get away from each other if you tried, you could not. It's an endless circle. That's what a thing of the flesh is. And you won't get away from that in Sabina or hope to. Even our little town. Jinny was never scared of the Devil himself as a growing girl, and shouldn't be now. And Lonnie Dugan won't ever quit at the bank, will he? Can't quit. But as I said to Mr. Hudson—they're in separate *cages*. All right, I said to Mr. Hudson, look. Jinny was unfaithful to Ran —that's what it *was*. There you have what it's all *about*. That's the brunt of it. Face it, I told Mr. Hudson. You're a train man—just a station agent, you're out of things. I *don't* know how many *times*.

But I'd go back to my lawful spouse! Miss Callie hollers at me through the bars. You or I or the man in the moon got no business living in that little hot upstairs room with a western exposure at Mrs. Judge O'Leary's for all the pride on earth, not in August.

After work I was always staying to cut the grass in Mrs. Judge's backyard, so it would be cooler for Bella. It kept the fleas away from her a little. None of it did much good. The heat held on. After I went back to the Starks, the men were playing, still playing croquet with a few little girls, and the women had taken off to themselves, stretched out on the screen porch. They called Maideen, I sent her in to them. It was the long Mississippi evening, the waiting till it was cool enough to eat. The voice of Jinny's mama carried—I heard it— her reminiscent one—but the evening was quiet, very hot and still.

Somebody called, You're dead on Lonnie. It was just a little Williams girl in pigtails.

I may have answered with a joke. I felt lightheaded, almost not serious at all, really addressing a child, as I lifted my mallet—the one with the red band that had always been mine. I brought Dugan to earth with it. He went down and shook the ground, fanning the air as he went. He toppled and sighed. Then I beat his whole length and his head with that soft girl's hair and all the schemes, beat him without stopping my mallet till every bone and little bone, all the way down to the little bones in the hand, flew to pieces. I beat Lonnie Dugan till there was nothing to know there. And I proved the male body—it has a too certain, too special shape to it not to be hurt—could be finished and done away with—with one good loud blow after another—Jinny could be taught that. I looked at Dugan down there. And his blue eyes remained unharmed. Just as sometimes bubbles a child blows seem the most impervious things, and grass blades will go through them and they still reflect the world, give it back unbroken. Dugan I declare was dead.

"Now watch."

Dugan said that. He spoke with no pain. Of course he never felt pain, never had time to. But that absurd, boyish tone of *competition* was in his voice. It had always been a mystery, now it was a deceit. Dugan—born nothing. Dugan—the other boy at the dance, the other man in the bank, the other sweetheart in Sabina, Jinny's other man—it was together he and I made up the choice. Even then it was hard to believe—we were the choice in everything. But if that was over, settled—how could it open again, the destroyed mouth of Dugan? And I heard him say "Now watch." He was dead on the ruined grass. But he had risen up. Just then he gave one of the fat little Williams girls a spank. I could see it and not hear it, the most familiar sound in the world.

There was that breathless stillness, and the sky changing the way a hand would pass over it. And I should have called it out *then*— All is disgrace! Human beings' cries would swell in the last of evening like this and cross the grass in the yard before the light changes, if only they cried. Our grass in August is like the floor under the sea, and we walk on it slowly playing, and the sky turns green before dark. We don't say anything the others remember.

But at our feet the shadows faded out light into the pale twilight and the locusts sang in long waves, O-E, O-E. Sweat ran down my back, arms, and legs, branching like some upside-down tree.

Then, "You all come in!" They were calling from the porch—the well-known yellow lamps suddenly all went on. They called us in their shrill women's voices, Jinny and all and her mama. "Fools, you're playing in the dark! Come to supper!"

Somebody bumped into me in the sudden blindness of the yard. We laughed at their voracious voices. Across the dark the porch of women waited. It was like a long boat to me, or a box lighted up from within. But I was hungry.

I'd go down to Mrs. Judge O'Leary's to sleep in my little western room—that's the house where Mrs. Judge and the three other Sabina schoolteachers sit on the porch. Each evening to avoid them I ran through porch and hall both, like a man through the pouring rain. In the big dark backyard, full of pecan trees, moonlit, Bella opened her eyes and looked at me. They showed the moon. If she drank water, she vomited it up—yet she went with effort to her pan and drank again. I held her. Poor Bella. I thought she suffered from a tumor, and stayed with her most of the night.

Mother said, Son, I noticed that old pistol of your father's in your nice coat pocket, what do you want with that old thing, your father never cared for it. Not any robbers coming to the bank that I know of. Son, if you'd just saved your money you could take yourself a little trip to the coast. I'd go with you. They always have a breeze at Gulfport, nearly always.

When you get to Jinny's, there are yuccas and bare ground—it looks like some old playground, with the house back out of sight.

Just the sharp, overgrown yuccas with up and down them rays of spiderwebs glinting in the light—as if they wore dresses. And back up in the shade is a little stone statue, all pockmarked now, of a dancing girl with a finger to her chin. Jinny stole that, from a Vicksburg park once, and her mama let her keep it.

Maideen said, "Are you taking me in yonder? I wish you wouldn't."

I looked down and saw my hand on the gate, and said, "Wait. I've lost a button." I showed my loose sleeve to Maideen. I felt all at once solemn—fateful—ready to shed tears.

"Why, I'll sew you one on, if you stop by my house," Maideen said. She touched my sleeve for an instant. A chameleon ran up a leaf, and held there panting. "Then Mama can see you. She'd be so glad to have you stay to supper."

I opened the little old gate. I caught a whiff of the sour pears on the ground, the smell of August. I had not told Maideen I was ever coming to supper at any time, or seeing her mama.

"Oh, Jinny can sew it on now," I said.

"Oh, I can?" Jinny said. She had of course been listening to me all the time from the half-hidden path. She looked out from under her shade-hat. She has the face, she has the threatening stare of a prankster—about to curtsey to you. Don't you think it's the look of a woman that loves dogs and horses best, and long trips away she never takes? "Come in before I forget, then," Jinny said.

We went ahead of Maideen. There in the flower beds walked the same robins, where the sprinkler had been. Once again, we went in the house by the back door. We took hands. We stepped on Tellie's patch of mint—the yellow cat went around the corner—the back door knob was as hot as the hand to the touch, and on the step, impeding the feet of two people going in together, the fruit jars with the laborious cuttings rooting in water—"Watch out for Mama's——!" That had happened a thousand times, the way we went in. As a thousand bees droned and burrowed in the pears that lay on the ground.

As Mama Stark almost ran over me. She shrank with a cry, and started abruptly up the stairs—bosom lifted—her shadow trotted up beside her like a nosy bear. But she could never get to the top without turning. She came down again and held up a finger at me.

Her voice . . . Randall. Let me tell you about a hand I held yesterday. My partner was Amanda Mackey and you know she always plays her own hand with no more regard for her partner than you have. Well, she opened with a spade and Fanny doubled. I held: a singleton spade five clubs to the king queen five hearts to the king and two little diamonds. I said two clubs, Gert Gish two diamonds, Amanda two spades, all passed. And when I laid down my hand Amanda said, *O partner!* Why didn't you bid your hearts! I said Hardly. At the level of three with the opponents doubling for a takeout. It developed of course she was two-suited—six spades to the ace jack and four hearts to the ace jack ten, also my ace of clubs. Now Randall. It would have been just as easy for Amanda when she opened her mouth a second time to bid three hearts. But no! She could see only her own hand and so she took us down two, and we could have made five hearts. Now do *you* think I should have bid three hearts?—I said, You were justified not to, Mama Stark, and she gave me a nod. Then she glared as if I slapped her. How well she could turn up her discontent to outrage again, and go on upstairs.

We turned, Jinny leading me, into the little back study, "Mama's office," with the landscape wallpaper and the desk full-up with its immediacy of Daughters of the Confederacy correspondence. Tellie sashayed in with the workbasket and then just waited, eyeing and placing us and eyeing and placing herself between us.

"Put it down, Tellie. Now you go on. Pull your mouth in, you hear me?" Jinny took the fancy little basket and flicked it open and fished in it. She found a button that belonged to me, and glanced up at Tellie.

"I hear you's a mess." Tellie went out.

Jinny looked at me. She pulled my hand up and I shot. I fired point-blank at Jinny—more than once. It was close range—between us suddenly there was barely room for the pistol to come up. And she only stood threading the needle, her hand not deviating, not even shaken at the noise. The little heart-shaped gold and china clock on the mantel was striking—the pistol's noise had not drowned that. I looked at Jinny and I saw her childish breasts, little pouting excuses for breasts, all sprung with bright holes where my bullets had gone. But Jinny did not feel it, the noise had veered off at the silly clock, and she threaded the needle. She made her little face of success. Her thread always went in its tiny hole.

"Hold still," Jinny muttered softly between fixed lips. She far from acknowledged her pain—anything but sorrow and pain. Just as when she was angry, she sang some faraway song. For domestic talk her voice would lower to a pitch of utter disparagement. Disparagement that had all my life elated me. The little cheat. I waited unable to move again while she sewed dartingly at my sleeve; the sleeve to my helpless hand. As if I counted my breaths now I slowly exhaled fury and inhaled simple dismay that she was not dead on earth. She bit the thread. I was unsteady when her mouth withdrew. The cheat.

I could not, dared not say good-by to Jinny any more, and "Go get in the croquet," she told me. She walked to the mirror in the hall, and began cutting at her hair.

I know Vera Lassiter darted in the room and her face lighted. "Mercy me," she said, and in her mischief came up and fingered Jinny's hair, the short soft curls. "Who're you being now? Somebody's little brother?"

But Jinny stood there at her mirrored face half smiling, so touchingly desirable, so sweet, so tender, vulnerable, touching to me I could again hardly bear it, again I could not.

Old Tellie spat into the stove and clanged down an iron lid as I went out through the kitchen. She had spent so much time, twenty-seven years, saying she had brought Jinny into this world: "Born in dis hand."

"No use for you atall you don't whup her. Been de matter wid you? Where you *been?*"

I found Maideen waiting out in the swing, and took her arm and led her down to the croquet where we all played Jinny's game.

Dear God wipe it clean. Wipe it clean, wipe it out. Don't let it be.

At last Mrs. Judge O'Leary caught hold of me in the hall. Do me a favor. Ran, do me a favor and put Bella out of her misery. None of these schoolteachers any better at it than I would be. And Judge too tenderhearted. You do it. Just do it and don't tell us, hear?

Where have you been, son?—Nowhere, mother, nowhere.—If you were back under my roof I would have things just the way they were. Son, I wish you would just speak to me, and promise——

And I was getting tired, oh so tired, of Mr. Killigrew. I felt cornered when Maideen spoke, kindly as ever, about the workings of the icehouse. Now I knew her mother's maiden name. God help me, the name Parsons was laid on my head like the top teetering crown of a pile of things to remember. Not to forget, not to forget the name of Parsons.

I remember your wedding, Old Lady Hartford said at my window, poking her finger through the bars. Never knew it would turn out like this, the prettiest wedding in my memory. If you had all *this* money, you could leave town.

Maideen believed so openly—I believe she told Miss Callie—that I wanted to take her somewhere sometime by herself and have a nice time—like other people—but that I put it off till I was free. Still, she had eyes to see, we would run into Jinny every time, Jinny and Lonnie Dugan and the crowd. Of course I couldn't help that, not in Sabina. And then always having to take the little Williams girl home at night. She was the bridge player; that was a game Maideen had never learned to play. Maideen—I never kissed her.

But the Sunday came when I took her over to Vicksburg.

Already on the road I began to miss my bridge. We could get our old game now, Jinny, Dugan, myself and often the little Williams child, who was really a remarkable player, for a Williams. Mama Stark of course would insist on walking out in stately displeasure, we were all very forward children indeed if we thought she would be our fourth, holding no brief for what a single one of us had done. So the game was actually a better one.

Maideen never interrupted our silence with a word. She turned the pages of a magazine. Now and then she lifted her eyes to me, but I could not let her see that I saw her wondering. I would win every night and take their money. Then at home I would be sick, going outdoors so the teachers would not wonder. "Now you really must get little Maideen home. Her mother will be thinking something awful's happened to her. Won't she, Maideen?"—Jinny's voice. "I'll ride with you"—the little Williams. Maideen would not have begun to cry in Jinny's house for anything. I could trust her. Did she want to? She wasn't *dumb*.

She would get stupefied for sleep. She would lean farther and farther over in her chair. She would never have a rum and coke with us, but she would be simply dead for sleep. She slept sitting up in the car going home, where her mama, now large-eyed, maiden name Parsons, sat up listening. I would wake her up to say I had got her home at last. The little Williams girl would be chatting away in the back seat, there and back wide awake as an owl.

Vicksburg: nineteen miles over the gravel and the thirteen little swamp bridges and the Big Black. Suddenly all sensation returned. Sabina I had looked at till I saw nothing. Till the street was a pencil mark on the sky, a little stick. Maybe outside my eyes a real roofline clamped down still, Main Street was there the same, four red-brick scallops, branchy trees, one little cross, but if I saw it, it was not with love, it was a pencil mark on the sky. Sabina wasn't there to me. If some indelible red false-fronts joined one to the other like a little toy train went by—I did not think of my childhood any more. Sabina had held in my soul to constriction. It was never to be its little street again.

I stopped my car at the foot of Vicksburg, under the wall, by the canal. There was a dazzling light, a water-marked light. I woke Maideen and asked her if she were thirsty. She smoothed her dress and lifted her head at the sounds of a city, the traffic on cobblestones just behind the wall. I watched the water-taxi come, chopping over the canal strip at us, absurd as a rocking horse.

"Duck your head," I said to Maideen.

"In here?"

. Very near across the water the island rose glittering against the sunset—a waste of willow trees, yellow and green strands that seemed to weave loosely one upon the other, like a basket that let the light spill out uncontrollably. We shaded our eyes to ride across the water. We all stood up bending our heads under the low top. The Negro who ran the put-put never spoke once, "Get in" or "Get out." "Where are we going?" Maideen said. In two minutes we were touching the barge. Old ramshackle floating saloon fifty years old, with its twin joined to it, for colored.

Nobody was inside but the one man—a silent, relegated place like a barn. I let him bring some rum cokes out to the only table, the card table out on the back where the two cane chairs were. The sun was going down on the island side, and making Vicksburg alight on the other. East and West were in our eyes.

"Don't make me drink it. I don't want to drink it," Maideen said.

"Go on and drink it."

"You drink it if you like it. Don't make me drink it."

"You drink it too."

I looked at her take some of it, and sit shading her eyes. There were wasps dipping from the ledge over the old screen door and skimming her hair. There was a smell of fish and of the floating roots fringing the island. The card table smelled warmly of its oil-cloth top and of endless deals. A load of Negroes came over on the water-taxi and stepped out with tin buckets. They were sulphur yellow all over, thickly coated with cottonseed meal, and disappeared in the colored barge at the other end, in single file, as if they were sentenced to it.

"Sure enough, I don't want to drink it."

"You drink it. It doesn't taste bad."

Inside, in the dim saloon, two men with black spurred cocks under their arms had appeared. Without noise they each set a muddy boot on the rail and drank, the cocks hypnotically still. They got off the barge on the island side, where they disappeared in the hot blur of willow branches. They might never be seen again.

The heat trembled on the water and on the other side wavered the edges of the old white buildings and concrete slabbed bluffs. From the barge, Vicksburg looked like an image of itself in a tarnished mirror—like its portrait at a sad time of life.

A short cowboy in boots and his girl came in, walking alike. They dropped a nickel in the nickelodeon, and came together.

The canal had no visible waves, yet trembled slightly beneath us; I was aware of it like the sound of a winter fire in the room.

"You don't ever dance, do you?" Maideen said.

It was a long time before we left. All kinds of people had come out to the barge, and the white side and the nigger side filled up. When we left it was good-dark.

The lights twinkled sparsely on the shore—old sheds and warehouses, long dark walls. High up on the ramparts of town some old iron bells were ringing.

"Are you a Catholic?" I asked her suddenly, and I bent my head to hear her answer.

"No."

I looked at her—I made it plain she had disappointed some hope of mine—for she had; I could not tell you now what hope.

"We're all Baptists. Why, are you a Catholic?" Oh, nobody was a Catholic in Sabina.

"No."

Without touching her except momently with my knee I walked her ahead of me up the steep uneven way, to where my car was parked listing sharply downhill. Inside, she could not shut her door. I stood outside and looked, it hung heavily and she had drunk three or four drinks, all I had made her take. Now she could not shut her door. "I'll fall out, I'll fall in your arms. I'll fall, catch me."

"No you won't. Shut it hard. Shut it. All your might."

At last. I leaned against her shut door, spent for a moment.

I grated up the steep cobbles, turned and followed the river road high along the bluff, turned again off into a deep rutted dirt way under shaggy banks, dark and circling and down-rushing.

"Don't lean against my arm," I said. "Sit up and get some air."

"I don't want to," she said in her soft voice that I could hardly understand any more.

"You want to lie down?"

"No. I don't want to lie down."

"Get some air."

"Don't make me lie down. I don't want to do anything, anything at all."

"You're drunk."

"I don't want to do a thing from now and on till evermore."

We circled down. The sounds of the river tossing and dizzying and teasing its great trash could be heard through the dark now. It made the noise of a moving wall, and up it fishes and reptiles and uprooted trees and man's throwaways played and climbed all alike in a splashing like innocence. A great wave of smell beat at my face. The track had come down deep as a tunnel. We were on the floor of the world. The trees met and matted overhead, the cedars came together, and through them the stars of Vicksburg looked sifted and fine as seed, so high and so far. There was the sound of a shot, somewhere, somewhere.

"Yonder's the river," she said. "I see it—the Mississippi River."

"You don't see it. We're not that close."

"I see it, I see it."

"Haven't you ever seen it before? You baby."

"Before? No, I never have seen the Mississippi River before. I thought we were on it on the boat."

"Look, the road has ended."

"Why does it come this far and stop?"

"How should I know? What do they come down here for?"

"Why do they?"

"There are all kinds of people in the world." Far away somebody was burning something.

"Do you mean bad people and niggers and all? Ones that hide? Moonshiners?"

"Oh, fishermen. River men. Cock fighters. You're waked up."

"I think we're lost," she said.

Mother said, if I thought you'd ever go back to that Jinny Stark, I couldn't hold up my head.—No, mother, I'll never go back.—The whole world knows what she did to you.

"You dreamed we're lost. We'll go somewhere where you can lie down a little."

"You can't get lost in Sabina."

"After you lie down a little you'll be all right again, you can get up. We'll go somewhere where you can lie down."

"I don't want to lie down."

"Did you know a car would back up a hill as steep as this?"

"You'll be killed."

"I bet nobody ever saw such a crazy thing. Do you think anybody ever saw such a crazy thing?"

We were almost straight up and down, hanging on the bluff and the tail end bumping and lifting us and swaying from side to side. At last we were up. If I had not drunk that last drink maybe I would not have made such startling maneuvers and would not have bragged so loud. The car had leaned straight over that glimpse of the river, over the brink as sweetly as you ever saw a hummingbird over a flower.

We drove a long way. All among the statues in the dark park, the repeating stances, the stone rifles again and again on lost hills, the spiral-staired and condemned towers.

I looked for the moon, which would be in the last quarter. There she was. The air was not darkness but faint light, and floating sound —the breath of all the people in the world who were breathing out into the night looking at the moon, knowing her quarter.

We rode in wildernesses under the lifting moon, Maideen keeping very still, sighing faintly as if she longed for something herself, for sleep—for going the other way. A coon, white as a ghost, crossed the road, pressed low, like an enemy. And we passed a gypsy camp— all sleeping.

Off the road, under the hanging moss, a light burned in a white-washed tree. It showed a circle of whitewashed cabins, dark, and all around and keeping the trees back, a fence of white palings. Sunset Oaks. A little nigger boy leaned on the gate this late at night, wearing an engineer's cap.

Yet it did not seem far. I pulled in, and paid.

"One step up," I told her at the door.

I sat on the bed, the old iron bed with rods. I think I said, "Get your dress off."

She had her head turned away. The naked light hung far down in the room—a long cord that looked as if something had stretched it. She turned, then, with tender shoulders bent toward the chair, as if in confidence toward that, the old wreck of a thing that tonight held her little white dress.

I turned out the light that hung down, and the room filled with the pale night like a bucket let down a well. It was never dark enough, the enormous sky flashing with its August light rushing into the emptiest rooms, the loneliest windows. The month of falling stars. I hate the time of year this is.

If we lay together any on the bed, almost immediately I was propped up against the hard rods with my back pressing them, and sighing—deep sigh after deep sigh. I heard myself.

"Get up," I said. "I want the whole bed. You don't need to be here." And I showed I had the pistol. I lay back holding it toward me and trying to frown her away, the way I used to lie still cherishing a dream in the morning and Jinny would pull me out of it.

Maideen had been pulling or caressing my arm, but she had no strength in her hands at all. She rose up and stood in the space before my eyes, so plain there in the lighted night. She was disarrayed. There was blood on her, blood and disgrace. Or perhaps there wasn't. I did not remember anything about it. For a moment I saw her double.

"Get away from me," I said.

While she was speaking to me I could hear only the noises of the place we were in—of frogs and nightbirds, a booted step in the heavy tangle all around, and the little idiot nigger running up and down the fence, up and down, as far as it went and back, sounding the palings with his stick.

"This is my grandfather's dueling pistol—one of a pair. Very valuable."

"Don't, Ran. Don't do that, Ran. Don't do it. Please don't do it."

I knew I had spoken to her again in order to lie. It was my father's pistol he'd never cared for. When she spoke, I didn't hear what she said; I was reading her lips, the way people being told good-by do conscientiously through train windows. I had the pistol pointing toward my face and did not swerve it. Outside, it sounded as though the little nigger at the gate was keeping that up forever —running a stick along the fence, up and down, to the end and back again.

Poor Bella, it was so hot for her. She lay that day with shut eyes, her narrow little forehead creased. Her nose was dry as a thrown-away rind. The weather was only making her suffer more. She never had a long thick coat, was the one good thing. She was just any kind of a dog. The kind I liked best.

I tried to think. What had happened? No—what had not happened? Something had not happened. The world was not going on. Or, you understand, it went on but somewhere it had stopped being real, and I had walked on, like a tightrope walker without any rope. How far? Where should I have fallen? Hate. Discovery and hate. Then, right after . . . Destruction was not real, disgrace

not real, nor death. They all got up again, Jinny and Dugan got
up . . .

Up and down, the little idiot nigger. He was having a good
time at that. I wondered, when would that stop? Then that stopped.

I put the pistol's mouth in my own. It tasted, the taste of the
whole machinery of it. And then instead it was my own mouth put
to the pistol's, quick as a little baby's maybe, whose hunger goes
on every minute—who can't be reassured or gratified, ever, quite in
time enough. There was Maideen still, white in her petticoat.

"Don't do it, Ran. Please don't do it."

Urgently I made it—made the awful sound.

And immediately she said, "Now, you see. It didn't work. Now
you see. Hand that old thing to me, I'll keep that."

She took it from me. She took it over to the chair, as if she went
possessed of some long-tried way to deal with it, and disposed of
it in the fold of her clothes. She came back and sat down on the
edge of the bed. In a minute she put her hand out again, differently
—and touched my shoulder. Then I met it, hard, with my face, the
small, bony, freckled (I knew) hand that I hated (I knew), and
kissed it and bit it until my lips and tongue tasted salt tears and
salt blood—that the hand was not Jinny's. Then I lay back in the
bed a long time, up against the rods.

"You're so stuck up," she said.

I lay there and after a while my eyes began to close and I saw
her again. She lay there plain as the day by the side of me, quietly
weeping for herself. The kind of soft, restful, meditative sobs a
child will venture long after punishment.

So I slept.

How was I to know she would hurt herself like this?

Now—where is Jinny?

HORACE CHOONEY, M.D.

by Jessamyn West

From *Mademoiselle*

———◄◆►———

ALTHOUGH Dr. Chooney had lived in the country for six months he was still unaccustomed to the sudden country alternations of sound and silence. He had never, as he remembered it, heard from his city apartment anything as startling as the abrupt scream and accompanying loud machinelike drilling which now filled the air just outside his bedroom window. Dr. Chooney, at once wide awake, he thought, sat up in his bed; still, before the sight of the big live-oak tree and its resplendent hard-working woodpecker had accounted for the sounds, two other possibilities had immediately come to his mind. The minute he had seen where he was, he had of course dismissed these and watched with pleasure as the industrious, systematic bird uncovered its bountiful and surprised breakfast.

At this hour of the morning Dr. Chooney missed his wife Harriet, who since their removal to the country had found it more convenient to occupy another sleeping room. Upon awakening, his mind often teemed with analogues and whimseys, and it was a real loss to have no one with whom he could share them. He always made an effort to recall them for her, but as is often the case with such imaginative sparkles, they were not quite so good when rewarmed.

The height at which the sun came through the tangle of oak and madrone trees on the slope above the house told Dr. Chooney that he had overslept. Though there was no longer any need for early rising, the old habits still held, and he stepped at once from his bed and touched the push button which rang in the kitchen below and told Harriet that he was now up and would be ready in thirty minutes for his breakfast.

From his bedroom window Dr. Chooney regarded with pleasure the remoteness and solitude of his new home. There had been nothing in a large city practice to prepare him for it, and since he had left the city without premeditation he had no opportunity before his arrival for even an imaginative sampling of country delights. Standing now looking out over his own wooded acreage, he was able to see its birds, trees, and occasional small animals in all their uniqueness; to focus upon them the same absorbed attention which he would have given in the past to some unusual lesion or malformation.

While the long-legged old-fashioned tub was slowly filling (the water pressure in the second story was bad), Dr. Chooney got out of his pajamas and walked about in his room enjoying the touch of the brisk morning air upon his unclothed body. As he passed and repassed the mirror in the combination washstand and dressing table he noted with satisfaction the unsagging firmness of his well-larded frame and its healthy mushroom color. Before he went into the bathroom Dr. Chooney, in case Harriet when first he rang had been outside feeding her chickens or perhaps milking the goat, once more touched the bell; then, unflinching, he stepped into his cold tub.

Dr. Chooney used for his bath a bar of yellow soap and a coarse cloth, both intended for dishwashing. Dr. Chooney was in many ways a connoisseur of sensations, and he made a real effort to slight none, not even the smallest. For bathing, an experience cleanly, of course, but neutral, he had little regard: warm water, soft cloth, mild soap. These things did not interest him. Every experience, he believed, should be made positive through either pleasure or pain. If the pleasure itself had become an old story, all of its reality worn down into an undifferentiated smoothness, Dr. Chooney elected a flick or two of pain to teach his nerves a continued responsiveness. He relished now every stroke of the somewhat abrasive cloth; he delighted in the sensation as of a mild burn which the yellow soap left across his chest and forearms.

There had been whole weeks recently when Dr. Chooney had not seemed very real to himself: days when his personality, capable on occasion as he so well knew of the most amazing richness and intensification, became thin and diffused; long periods when he had felt almost completely bereft of that constellation of interests which makes a man so uniquely himself.

Red-striped now as any flagellant, Dr. Chooney stepped from his bath and gently dried himself. Psychically, he supposed he had been suffering somewhat as so precise an organization as a tiger might, had it found itself forced to exist for months on end as a mollusk of some variety—impotent, but never forgetful beneath the layers of jelly of its former subtlety and power.

Dr. Chooney finished his drying before the open window of his own room. There the zestful aromatic scents of laurel and madrone leaves, dampened earlier in the morning by fog and now heated by the sun, flowed up to him, and Dr. Chooney, inhaling, made them a part of himself. Dr. Chooney was a careful and methodical dresser. He had proceeded from the top drawer which held his underwear to the third from the bottom which held his white shirts when his wife entered.

He spoke to her a little shortly, which he certainly had not intended, but he had an aversion to unannounced entrances.

"I didn't ring, Harriet," he said without straightening.

"I know, Henning, but . . ."

Dr. Chooney closed the drawer, lifted himself, and looked down at his wife.

"Horace," she amended.

"Yes?" said Dr. Chooney. He put on and buttoned his shirt, very precise buttoning, calculated to prevent the appearance of any half-filled buttonholes later in the day.

Dr. Chooney would have preferred to have been more aware of his wife. She was a small, dark cloudy woman with a tender mouth. He berated himself for his faded responsiveness. In their former life in the city, where they had been somewhat gregarious, Dr. Chooney had heard it said occasionally that he stirred up Harriet as one might a placid, quiet animal simply to see it come to life. This was not so. He had never been interested in Harriet's impetuosity or lack of it. If he stirred her up sometimes, it was only as a means of becoming aware of himself. He smiled a little now at the naïveté of his friends' conclusions. Was frost interested in the boulder it split? Or wind in the height of the wave it piled up? No, no. His friends had not studied, as he had, natural forces and did not understand, as he did, that natural forces were interested in effects only as a means of knowing and testing themselves.

Still smiling as he thought of the incorrectness of his friends' suppositions, Dr. Chooney handed his wife a small white card. "Why wasn't this burned with the others?" he asked.

His wife read the card, then turned it over as if hoping to find something upon the underside to negate what she had just seen. "Where did you find this, Horace?" she asked.

"Under the paper in my white-shirt drawer. How did you happen to miss it?"

"I don't know," Harriet Chooney answered. "I can't imagine. I've tried to be very careful. I was sure everything had been burned."

"Perhaps you left it on purpose," Dr. Chooney suggested.

His wife's small brown hand was trembling. "Horace, you know I never, never——"

Dr. Chooney cut his wife's protesting short. "Very well, then. Let's drop it. Let's speak of it no more. It was simply a mistake and doesn't call for so impassioned a defense. It would be better though if it did not happen again and if this were burned."

Dr. Chooney's wife first bent the card double, then folded it so that the bit of pasteboard was lost in the palm of her hand.

"You have a patient waiting," she said.

"At this time of the morning?"

"It's not really early, Horace. It's past ten."

"Who is it?" asked Dr. Chooney.

"No one we know," his wife said. "A Miss Chester from the place over the hill called Oakknoll. I think you ought to see her. You should build up a practice once again."

"You think so?" Dr. Chooney asked.

"Yes, Horace, I do."

"I'll have my breakfast now," he said.

"Horace, this girl is timid and nervous. She's waited thirty minutes already. If you don't see her now, she won't be back again," Mrs. Chooney urged.

"How old is she?"

"Perhaps twenty-five," Mrs. Chooney said.

"Show her into my office," said Dr. Chooney, "and bring us two cups of coffee."

Dr. Chooney felt very large in his small office, but efficient and commanding too. His thighs still burned pleasantly from the irritation of the harsh soap, and he could smell from the kitchen the fragrance of coffee beginning to boil. The office was filled with sunlight; his well-polished desk glittered, the madrone blossoms in the bowl on top of the case which held his medical books were translucent in the strong light. With an increasing sense of integration and well-being, Dr. Chooney seated himself and faced his patient.

"Yes?" he asked pleasantly.

Miss Chester, who herself sat stiff and unrelaxed before him, was not, he saw at once, twenty-five. Twenty-two or -three at the most. Miss Chester was one of those young women who have considerable breadth but no thickness. Her shoulders were wide, her waist narrow, and beneath her light summer dress her breasts, which did not seem organically related to her broad, flat chest, were very noticeable. She was his own color with some of the murk leached out. Her hair, by which women chiefly show their awareness of themselves and their times, was in a soft and dowdy pile.

Miss Chester's dress was of a kind Dr. Chooney could not remember having seen since childhood: soft, peach-colored, it did not expose the body but was a continuation of it. It appeared to have been made at home, someone saying, "A little more fullness here," or, "Does it bind now under the arms?" Miss Chester's dress gave Dr. Chooney as much pleasure as a disease. He could not have been more lingering in a diagnosis. At the neck the dress had small peach-colored frills which touched the skin and seemed almost as if they might be an extension of the flesh.

Unclothed, Dr. Chooney speculated, Miss Chester would look somewhat like a Botticelli Venus, formed not in a warm southern sea but in some cool northern pond.

"Yes," Dr. Chooney said again, agreeably.

"I am Flora Chester," the girl told him.

"Yes, Miss Chester," said Dr. Chooney.

"I haven't been well," the girl said, "or at least I've thought I wasn't well."

Dr. Chooney understood the doubt which comes over patients in doctors' offices. Unaccustomed to speaking of their ailments, they hear their own words, "I am not well," and begin to wonder if their disease is not a hallucination which has made it possible for them first to imagine, then to credit their symptoms.

"Just what did you think was the trouble?" Dr. Chooney asked.

"Perhaps I imagine it all," the girl told him, with a somewhat breathless, confessional rush. "Perhaps it is just something I dream up"—she looked up at Dr. Chooney as if she had used a daring piece of slang—"to fill my days."

"Are your days empty?" asked Dr. Chooney.

"Not empty . . . but not important."

"Just what," Dr. Chooney persisted, "are your symptoms?"

"Oh, they're really nothing." The girl paused as if asking Dr. Chooney permission to continue.

"Go on," Dr. Chooney said.

"Everything tastes like pasteboard," said Miss Chester. "I can't sleep, yet I seem to be always dreaming so that when I do sleep I wake up tired. Toward evening I feel less tired, but by then my head begins to ache."

Having told her symptoms, Miss Chester at once politely disclaimed them as a woman brushes aside a compliment. "It's probably just my imagination," she insisted.

"Why do you keep repeating that?" Dr. Chooney asked. "What kind of mechanism do you think the body is? Do you suppose it sends out false reports as to its lesions and aberrations? Why should you imagine what is painful and distressing to you?"

"My father and mother imagine things," said Miss Chester.

"You live with your father and mother?"

The girl nodded.

"An only child?"

The girl smiled excitedly, as if Dr. Chooney had said something very personal to her. "Yes. Yes, I am."

"How old are your parents?"

"Sixty and seventy-two."

"What does your father do?"

"Nothing. Nothing, that is, except his hobby," said Miss Chester. "Father's a retired dentist. One day he just walked out of his office— with a man in the chair and his mouth propped open. He came home and said—this was before I was born, but I've heard my mother tell it—he came and said, 'I will never put my hand inside the mouth of another human being.' " She looked up at him as if she had just reported a revolutionary act.

"That doesn't strike me as being particularly imaginative."

"But now he really does imagine things," said Miss Chester. "For one thing, he's not really interested in anything but teeth. He listens to the radio just in order to be able to tell about the plates or bridges people are wearing. He thinks he can tell by the way they speak or sing. He writes them letters saying, 'You have never had your six-year molars removed,' and has them sign the letter if he is right and return it."

"Is he right sometimes?" Dr. Chooney asked.

"Oh yes, he is," said Miss Chester. "Almost always."

"Then he's really not imagining things, is he, Miss Chester?"

"My mother——"

"Look, Miss Chester. Let us first consider you. Your troubles, whatever you may think of your parents, are not mental nor imaginary. No little quirk is responsible for them. Turn this way, please."

"I've never been in a doctor's office before," Miss Chester said, turning toward Dr. Chooney with stiff self-consciousness.

"You should have been," Dr. Chooney told her gravely.

Miss Chester smiled as if she had been praised.

Dr. Chooney leaned forward and with his cool, heavy-tipped fingers explored Miss Chester's slender throat: first, at the jawline, then lower where the throat widened above the fragile collarbones.

"It is just as I thought," he told her.

Dr. Chooney was not surprised at the brilliant, quivering look his patient gave him—as if she were hearing a declaration of love.

"You mean there really is something wrong?" she asked.

"Decidedly wrong."

Dr. Chooney's fingers continued their skilled probing. This girl had probably never before been the object of so concentrated an interest, certainly never the object of so concentrated a male interest. Her parents old, lost in their own worlds, she without friends, this was doubtless the first time anyone had so leaned toward her or expressed concern for her well-being; the first time she had been so touched —with hands professional, of course, but conveying to her inexperienced nature feelings not wholly clinical.

"Feel just here," Dr. Chooney told her. He guided the long-fingered, soft hand to a spot beneath the jaw.

"The little lumps?" Miss Chester asked.

"Nodules," Dr. Chooney corrected her. "Indications of a serious glandular affection."

Dr. Chooney saw that his patient was both pleased and frightened.

"I don't really feel so very sick," she said.

"Pardon me, Miss Chester," Dr. Chooney said, "but you actually have no idea how you feel. You have had this disorder for so long that you no longer know what it is like to feel well. You have forgotten what health is."

Miss Chester put a hand to her face. "Don't I look well?" she asked.

"No," Dr. Chooney said, "to a doctor you do not look well. Lovely, charming," Dr. Chooney said, smiling charmingly himself, "but certainly not well."

The girl flushed. "Is this glandular . . . affection . . . serious?" she asked.

"Very," said Dr. Chooney gravely. He leaned back, fingertips delicately touching, and rocked gently in his swivel chair.

"Serious enough," Miss Chester asked in a low voice, "to be fatal?"

Dr. Chooney laughed, from deep in his chest. "My dear girl," he said.

Miss Chester smiled and once more leaned back against the dark chair, but Dr. Chooney was immediately grave again. "As a matter of fact," he said, "that depends entirely upon you. You can go on, as you have been doing, from bad to worse. Or, you can put yourself into the hands of a competent physician and become the girl nature intended you to be."

"It isn't too late then?" Miss Chester asked.

"Certainly not," Dr. Chooney assured her heartily. "Not if you care, not if you try. Look at this," Dr. Chooney said.

He opened a drawer of his desk and took out an envelope. "At one time I was something of an amateur photographer. I made it a practice to take pictures of my patients. They were not only helped by being shown graphic evidence of their improvement, but others with similar disorders were encouraged when they saw what had been done in the way of arresting their disease. Would you like to see some of the pictures?" he asked.

"Oh yes," said Miss Chester eagerly.

Dr. Chooney handed her a photograph. "This girl," he said, "had your affliction, though in a somewhat more advanced form."

Miss Chester gasped. "She looks dead," she whispered.

Dr. Chooney nodded in agreement. "Yes, doesn't she," he said. "Though that is largely a result of the bad lighting and her closed eyes. And as I've already told you, she was a considerably more advanced case than you.

"Now," said Dr. Chooney genially, "have a look at this." Before handing over the second picture, however, Dr. Chooney himself regarded it for some time: a really lovely study of Anne. Frail, eyes considerably sunken, but laughing. He remembered just her posture that afternoon on the lawn chair and the way she had flung up her arm as he snapped the shutter and what she had said afterward.

"Oh," said Miss Chester, "she's better, isn't she? Much better. She's lovely here."

"A very charming girl," Dr. Chooney agreed. "This," he said, "is the third. Plump, brown, playing tennis. You could scarcely ask for a healthier-looking girl than that, could you, Miss Chester?"

"Oh no," Miss Chester said. "Here she looks"—Miss Chester paused, apparently searching for a word which would describe the change that had taken place—"quite normal. As if there were nothing in the world wrong with her."

"When that picture was taken," Dr. Chooney said, "there was nothing wrong with her. Well," he asked playfully, taking back the pictures, "is seeing believing?"

"Oh, yes indeed," said Miss Chester. "I'm so glad you showed them to me. I can't thank you enough. I don't want to lose a minute getting started. What am I to do first?"

"First," said Dr. Chooney, "a prescription." He scrawled one swiftly. "Have this filled, Miss Chester, and follow the directions exactly."

"Shall I come back tomorrow?" Miss Chester asked.

Dr. Chooney looked through his engagement book. "No," he said, "not tomorrow. Could you come on Thursday at three?"

"Oh yes, Dr. Chooney, I'll be here. I won't let anything interfere."

Miss Chester turned back from the door. "I feel better already," she said shyly. "I thank you so much."

Dr. Chooney, who had risen and was standing now beside his desk, said, "Hope is a great restorative, Miss Chester."

Dr. Chooney was still standing when Harriet came in with the tardy coffee.

"You're a little late," Dr. Chooney told her.

"I didn't bring it sooner on purpose," she said. "I didn't think it seemed professional—serving coffee to a patient you had never seen before—and I do so want," she explained, "everything to get started properly."

Dr. Chooney sat at his desk and his wife paused, waiting for him to clear a space upon which she could place the tray she held. As she looked down, waiting, the tray sagged, then slanted, as if all strength had left her wrists, until coffee and cream together poured downward upon the three pictures Dr. Chooney had just been showing his patient. Dr. Chooney imperturbably shook the drops of scalding coffee from his hands and himself regarded the pictures, now so ranged upon his desk that the eye moved from the girl—what had Miss Chester called her?—from the normal girl to the frail one and from the frail one to that girl who, lights or no lights, had the appearance of death.

"Let me have that tray," said Dr. Chooney. He took it from his wife and put it firmly down. "Now get a dish mop of some kind and clear away this mess."

After his wife left, Dr. Chooney first took out his handkerchief and dried his hands, touching meditatively the small yellow blisters which were already beginning to form. Then he cleaned, but did not change the order of, the three pictures. Looking at them, the well-being he had begun to feel while bathing became more pronounced. He could feel quite clearly, along channels too delicate for reason to follow, forewarnings of a delicious reintegration. The tiger's outline had begun once more to assume—from his well-stored mind Dr. Chooney chose the poet's phrase—its fearful symmetry.

BIOGRAPHICAL NOTES

JOHN BELL CLAYTON

was born forty years ago on a farm in the mountainous section of Virginia west of the Blue Ridge. He spent three years at the University of Virginia, leaving to marry and to start work as a reporter on a small daily newspaper. With the exception of a few intervals of publicity work and a job with the Federal Communications Commission during the war, he has spent the rest of his working years as a newspaperman. He lives at present in San Francisco, of which he writes: "It is the only city of any size I have even liked a little bit." Of his work he says: "A man trying to tell stories can only say about himself that he has some stories he wants to tell, some short ones and some long ones, and then sit down and—come hell, high water, or rejection slips—try his level best to tell them honestly and well." Previous to "The White Circle" Mr. Clayton had published one story in Esquire.

EUGENE L. BURDICK

was born in 1918 in Iowa, but writes that "like all good Iowans, I moved to California at the first opportunity." After finishing high school he worked first as a clerk, ditchdigger, and truck driver until he saved $150, with which he entered Stanford University, where he worked his way through, finishing in 1941. Shortly after graduation he was married, taken into the Navy, and sent to Guadalcanal, all in three months. He spent twenty-six months in the Pacific as a gunnery officer aboard various types of vessels and wrote "Rest Camp on Maui" aboard a ship off Okinawa in the closing days of the war.

Since the war he has been working on a Ph.D. in political science at Stanford and has taken several courses in writing with

Wallace Stegner. He has been a fellow at the Bread Loaf Writers'
Conference, which he says "was one of the happier experiences of
my life." He is at present working on his first novel.

ELIZABETH PARSONS

was born in Hartford, Connecticut, in 1909, and received her edu-
cation in private schools, afterward traveling widely in this coun-
try as well as in England, Ireland, Switzerland, and the West
Indies. Her stories have appeared in The New Yorker, Harper's
Bazaar, *and elsewhere, and were collected in a volume entitled*
An Afternoon, *published last year by the Viking Press. This year*
she received a grant from the American Academy of Arts and
Letters. Her official residence is Vinalhaven, Maine, where she
lives with a son aged eleven and a daughter seven.

ROBERT LEWIS

was graduated from St. John's College, Annapolis, in 1937, studied
for a year at the University of Bologna, and in 1938 began his
work at Johns Hopkins for a Ph.D. in English literature. Between
1939 and 1942 he worked at various jobs and did free-lance writ-
ing "from which," he says, "I have enough rejection slips to paper
a room, and no acceptances." His jobs ranged from welfare work
to working in a distillery as head of the export department. He
was drafted in 1943 and "after training me as an ordnance clerk,
after cramming me full of German language and Russian history
at New York University," he was sent to Naples as court inter-
preter. He then went into training as an infantry replacement
and was sent to Algiers as a French translator attached to the
Seventh Army. He made the invasion of southern France with
this army, became a court interpreter, and picked up the material
for "Little Victor," went to Germany as a translator, and came
home with "81 points, four Hershey bars, a bronze arrowhead,
five battle stars, and a French Croix-de-Guerre." He refuses to dis-
close the deed for which he received the last-mentioned decora-
tion. He has now returned to Johns Hopkins to pursue his doc-
torate, this time in the field of romance languages.

Mr. Lewis's hobby is fencing, at which he is three-weapon
champion of Maryland. At Heidelberg he beat the three-weapon
champion of Baden. He is now collaborating on a book of fencing
with Clovis Deladrier, Swordmaster of the United States Naval

Academy, which, he writes, "will be published soon, and will be a honey."

PAUL BOWLES

was born in 1911 in New York City and had his early education in the public schools there. He went to the University of Virginia because Poe had been a student at Charlottesville, but fled during the first year, 1928, direct to Rue St. Guillaume, Paris, while police and parents searched for him. He began writing imaginative prose at the age of four and switched to poetry at fifteen, publishing in transition *and* This Quarter *at sixteen. A meeting with Gertrude Stein in 1931 was followed by a loss of interest in writing and by periods of living in Morocco in semi-primitive surroundings, during which Mr. Bowles turned to French as his medium of expression. He lived in various countries of Latin America during the late thirties and early forties.*

He was briefly music critic of the New York Herald Tribune *and did incidental scores for many Broadway shows, including* My Heart's in the Highlands, The Glass Menagerie, Watch on the Rhine, *and* Cyrano de Bergerac. *He translated Jean Paul Sartre's* Huit Clos *with the title* No Exit *for Broadway production and has also done Jean Giradoux's* Folle de Chaillot *for next season. In 1941 he received a Guggenheim Fellowship to write an opera on text by Federico Garcia Lorca. His short stories have appeared in* View, Partisan Review, *and* Harper's Bazaar. *His literary interests he lists as anthropology, folklore, Sartre, Kafka, Borges, "and not much else."*

Mr. Bowles lives in New York City and is married to Jane Bowles, who has published a novel, Two Serious Ladies, *written a number of short plays, and has recently completed her first fulllength drama,* In the Summer House.

RAY BRADBURY

was born in Waukegan, Illinois, in 1920. His stories have appeared in Harper's Magazine, The American Mercury, Mademoiselle, Charm, Collier's, *and* The Californian. *A novelette of his has appeared in the Marshall Field magazine, U.S.A., and his first book of short stories,* Dark Carnival, *was published in the spring of 1947. For the past year he has been traveling in Mexico and completing work on his first novel,* The Wind of Time. *He has written for the World Security Workshop on the A.B.C. Network and has had one play each on the N.B.C. and C.B.S. networks.*

BESSIE BREUER

was born in Cleveland, Ohio, and after some time on the staff of a New York newspaper went abroad. While in Europe her first short stories appeared in various magazines, and she has published two novels, Memory of Love *and* The Daughter. *She won second prize in the 1944 O. Henry volume with "Home Is a Place" from* Harper's Bazaar *and was represented in the 1943 collection with "Pigeons en Casserole" from* The New Yorker, *and again in the 1945 collection with "Bury Your Own Dead," also from the* Bazaar. *A collection of her stories,* The Bracelet and Other Stories, *is appearing this autumn. She is living in Florida at present and writing more Air Force stories.*

JANE COBB

was born in 1924 in New York City and has lived there or in Weston, Connecticut, nearly all her life. She went to the Dalton School in New York and then to Wellesley. Her first job was with the New York Times, *checking on the amount of cereals, cold cream, or other articles of merchandise shopkeepers were selling, and she went from this to writing feature stories and a column for the Sunday paper. Her first story was sold to* The Atlantic *when she was only nineteen, and since then her work has appeared in* The American Magazine, Charm, *and* McCall's. *She is married to Robert Elton Perry, a writer and editor, and they have two children, Margaret and Ben. Miss Cobb's former hobbies, Persian cats, tea roses, and "cooking with herbs and wine and sour cream," have momentarily vanished, she writes, before the utilitarian activities connected with rearing her children, aged four and two, respectively.*

MARY DEASY

was born in Cincinnati and is a musician as well as a writer. She was educated at the University of Cincinnati and took a Bachelor of Music degree in piano at the Cincinnati Conservatory of Music. She has lived in Ohio and California and is at present residing in Philadelphia. Her short stories have appeared in Prairie Schooner, Mademoiselle, The American Mercury, The Virginia Quarterly

Review, *and* The Yale Review. *She was represented in the 1945 O. Henry collection with "Long Shadow on the Lawn" from* The Virginia Quarterly. *Concerning the pronunciation of her name, she has written: "For the record, my surname rhymes with the equally Irish but pronounceable name of Casey."*

WALTER ELDER

was born in Clark County, Ohio, in 1921. He attended the public schools there and in Springfield, completing his undergraduate studies at Kenyon College in 1942. He served three years in the Army Air Forces, six months of the time in France as a bombardier-navigator with a combat group of the Ninth Air Force. After his discharge he spent a year at Kenyon College teaching and working in administrative positions. He entered the Graduate School of Arts and Sciences at Harvard in the autumn of 1946 as a student of philosophy and expects to complete his studies in two years. He is married and has one daughter.

HELEN EUSTIS

was born in Cincinnati in 1916. She was educated there in private schools and received her A.B. from Smith College in 1938. Her stories have appeared in Accent, Story, New Directions, Chimera, The New Yorker, Harper's Bazaar, Mademoiselle, Tomorrow, *and elsewhere. In 1946 her novel,* The Horizontal Man, *received the Edgar Allan Poe award from the Mystery Writers of America as the best first mystery of 1946. She was married to Alfred Young Fisher, professor of English in Smith College, in 1939, and they were divorced in 1944, their one child, a son, Adam Eustis Fisher, having been born in 1940. In 1945 she married Martin Harris, a magazine photographer. She lives in New City, New York, and is at work on her second novel.*

CHRISTINE NOBLE GOVAN

was born in New York City in 1898. She arrived in Tennessee at the age of four years and has lived there ever since. She has written eight juveniles, three mystery stories, and two novels, one of the latter, The Shadow and the Web, *appearing under the pseudonym of Mary Allerton, an ancestor. She is married to Gilbert Govan, editor of the book page of the Chattanooga* Times, *editorial writer, and lecturer. They live in a twenty-room house with numerous children and grandchildren. Mrs. Govan's most recent novel was called* Jennifer's House *and was a story of changing standards in the South. "Miss Winters and the Wind" is her first short story, and its reception, she says, tempts her to write more of the plight of the helpless elderly in present-day society. Gardening is one of Mrs. Govan's principal hobbies, although she insists that she has a brown thumb instead of a green one.*

DAVID CORNEL DEJONG

was born on June 9, 1905, in Blija, Friesland, the Netherlands, and was brought to this country by his parents at the age of thirteen. They settled in Grand Rapids, Michigan, where he learned English in the grammar school and where he finished high school in two years, working his way through. He studied at the universities of Michigan and Wisconsin and received his A.B. from Calvin College in Grand Rapids. He took his M.A. at Duke University and spent a year at Brown working on his Ph.D., both periods on fellowships.

Mr. deJong's first novel, Belly Fulla Straw, *was published in 1934, and his next,* Old Haven, *which he wrote on a Houghton, Mifflin fellowship, appeared in 1938. He also published* Light Sons and Dark, Day of the Trumpet, Benefit Stories, *and* Somewhat Angels, *novels; and a collection of short stories,* Snow-on-the-Mountain. *His stories have appeared in* Harper's Bazaar, Esquire, Redbook, Virginia Quarterly Review, Yankee, New Mexico Quarterly Review, *and other magazines. His first appearance in the O. Henry collection was in 1937, with "The Chicory Neighbors." In 1939 his "Calves" won third prize; in 1941 he was represented with "Seven Boys Take a Hill," and in 1942 with "Snow-on-the-Mountain."*

SUSAN KUEHN

was born February 19, 1926, in Minneapolis, where she attended high school and took courses in creative writing. She is a 1947 graduate of Wellesley and majored in English composition. In her high-school days, like most young writers, her work was mostly concerned with faraway places, but she has now turned to her native Minnesota for her subject matter, as in "The Rosebush." At Wellesley she enjoyed writing book reviews for the college newspaper and doing scripts for the college radio station.

She has spent two summers in editorial work on the staff of
Mademoiselle. *At an early age she became a coin collector, but
says that this hobby was quickly abandoned when the coins were
all spent, and has never been replaced.*

JOHN A. LYNCH

*was born in Detroit July 24, 1922, and began his education there,
taking his B.A. at Notre Dame in the spring of 1943, although he
had enlisted in the Enlisted Reserve Corps of the Army in August
1942 and was called to active duty immediately after leaving
school. While in college, he worked at a variety of occupations,
including acting as student secretary to Richard Sullivan, who, he
says, "through his fine judgment and encouragement, proved one
of the greatest helps in my writing." He served as a member of
a machine-gun squad of the 88th Infantry Division in Italy, and
later, as a litter bearer, was wounded so severely that he spent
fifteen months in hospitals abroad and at home. Upon his discharge last year, he studied writing for a time at the University
of Oklahoma and at Columbia, hitchhiked back and forth across
the continent, and worked at various jobs. His present plans are
to settle in California and to follow his writing career, which
began in high school, where he was editor of the school paper
his senior year.*

J. F. POWERS

*was born in Jacksonville, Illinois, in 1917, and in recent years has
lived in Chicago, where he has worked for several bookstores.
His short stories have appeared in* Accent, The Rocky Mountain
Review (*now* The Western Review), The New Mexico Quarterly
Review, The Catholic Worker, The Commonweal, Opportunity,
*and elsewhere. He made his first appearance in the O. Henry
collection three years ago with "Lions, Harts, Leaping Does,"
which appeared in* The Commonweal, *and was represented in the
1945 volume with "The Trial." His first book, a volume of short
stories called* Prince of Darkness and Other Stories, *was published this year and contains "The Valiant Woman" in addition
to the other two stories which have appeared in the O. Henry.
Several reviewers of the volume singled out "Lions, Harts, Leaping Does" as one of the best examples of Mr. Powers's unusual
gifts in dealing with material relating to the Catholic clergy.*

"Prince of Darkness," which was first published in Accent, *is in length between a long short story and a short novelette.*

MARK SCHORER

was born in 1908 in Sauk City, Wisconsin, where he began his education, and was graduated from the University of Wisconsin in 1929. There he was encouraged to write by Zona Gale, who awarded him one of the scholarships she maintained at the time for students of artistic promise. Mr. Schorer's first stories began to appear in the "little" magazines while he was a part-time instructor at the University of Wisconsin, and he also collaborated there with August Derleth, a friend from childhood, in writing for the "pulps." As a graduate student at Harvard, he wrote under the supervision of Robert Hillyer. He taught at Dartmouth after receiving his Ph.D. at Harvard and is at present a professor of English at the University of California in Berkeley. He is married and has two children.

His stories have appeared in Harper's, Story, Esquire, The New Yorker, The Atlantic, The New Republic, The Yale Review, The Virginia Quarterly Review, The Kenyon Review, *and* Mademoiselle, *and he made his first appearance in the* O. Henry *collection with "Blockbuster" in 1944. He has published two novels,* A House Too Old *and* Hermit Place, *and is working on a third,* Face to Face. *Most of his short stories were republished in a collection called* The State of Mind: Thirty-Two Stories. *His largest work,* William Blake: The Politics of Vision, *for which he was twice awarded Guggenheim Fellowships, was published in 1946 and met a highly favorable critical reception.*

MARGARET SHEDD

was born in Urumia, Persia, where her father was a missionary. His father was also a missionary. She went to a boarding school in Auvernier, Switzerland, and attended the Manual Arts High School in Los Angeles and then Stanford University. At the time she was much more interested in becoming an actress than in writing. She is married to Oliver Michael Kisich, and they have three children, William, Timothy, and Deirdre. The Kisich family has lived in Mexico, British Honduras, Guatemala, and the British West Indies, and Miss Shedd says that isolation and idleness in the tropics led her to start writing. Her first novel, Hurricane

Caye, *was published in 1942 and was followed by* Inherit the Earth *in 1944. Her articles and stories have appeared in* Theatre Arts Magazine, Harper's Bazaar, Harper's Magazine, Collier's, *and elsewhere. She is a niece of Charles G. Dawes and is at present living in Westchester County. Her first appearance in the O. Henry collection was in 1946, when her story "The Innocent Bystander," from* Harper's Magazine, *won second prize.*

JOHN CASWELL SMITH, JR.

was born in Montclair, New Jersey, March 14, 1907. He began his education in the public schools of Northampton, Massachusetts, and was graduated from Springfield College (Mass.) in 1930, later studying at the New York School for Social Work, 1937–38, with a fellowship of the National Urban League. He has held positions with the Y.M.C.A. in Northampton, with the Wharton Settlement in Philadelphia, and as dean of men at Virginia State College. He left the post of executive secretary of the Urban League of Greater Boston to spend three years in London during the war with the American Red Cross and has now returned to his former position in Boston. He has been a writer for several years and has published in Opportunity, PM, Common Ground, *and* The Journal of Social Case Work. *He is at present working on a novel. He is married and has one son, Nikki.*

JEAN STAFFORD

was born in Covina, California, in 1915, and was reared and educated in Colorado. She spent a year in Germany after college, then taught in Missouri for a year. Since then she has lived in Massachusetts, Louisiana (where she worked on The Southern Review*), Tennessee, Maine, and New York City. Her first novel,* Boston Adventure, *was published in 1944. Her second novel,* The Mountain Lion, *also published by Harcourt, Brace and Company, appeared in March 1947. Both were warmly received by the critics.*

Miss Stafford's short stories have appeared in Harper's Magazine, The Atlantic Monthly, The Kenyon Review, Harper's Bazaar, The Sewanee Review, The Partisan Review, *and* Mademoiselle. *Her story "Home Front" won a* Partisan Review *prize; another story, "The Reunion," first published by* The Partisan Review, *has been included in an anthology published by the* Swallow Press. *Miss Stafford won a Guggenheim Fellowship in*